"I BELIEVE IN EVIL," SAID THE PRIEST, "NOT IN THE DEVIL..."

". . . not in mumbo jumbo, abracadabra, and seances! Come on, Father!"

"I have no other answer," Conant said.

"I thought you were an intelligent man."

"I *was*." Conant's tone was resigned.

"I'm getting it from all directions," Liscomb said. "About the Devil being there. I hear you even tried to exorcise it."

The priest nodded slightly and refilled the glasses.

"You're trying to tell me that Satan is responsible for the severed finger, the severed hand, for everything that happened at that seance? You're trying to tell me that the Devil is loose in Holland County?"

Effigies

by
William K. Wells

A DELL BOOK

For Jane

With a very special thanks to Knox and Kitty
And gramercy to Linda Grey

Published by
Dell Publishing Co., Inc.
1 Dag Hammarskjold Plaza
New York, New York 10017

ISBN: 0-440-12245-7

Printed in the United States of America
First printing—November 1980

From his brimstone bed, at break
of day,
A-walking the Devil is gone,
To look at his little snug farm of the
World,
And see how his stock went on.

Robert Southey

PART ONE

PROLOGUE

On a bright, clear afternoon in July, a Seville bearing Wisconsin plates detached itself from the southbound traffic of the interstate and swept into the cloverleaf at King's Landing. Proceeding eastward along Route 14, it bypassed King's Landing, drove through East Landing, Arrow, and Leydenburg and finally turned into the driveway of a small fishing camp just west of the village of Broadmoor.

Its sole occupant, a tall, heavyset, red-faced man in his late fifties, emerged from the cool interior and walked to the camp office. He wore a broad, wreathlike smile, and as he conducted the business of his reservation, his voice rumbled, full of warmth and good humor. His clothes were stylishly expensive. He might have been a successful salesman, perhaps an executive.

The only flaw in an otherwise impeccable appearance was his left ear.

It was a tangle of pulpy, shapeless flesh that resembled a purple fungus growing in a dark cavern of some primeval forest. It was the ear of an ex-prizefighter and perhaps, many, many years in the past, the man had been so employed.

As he unpacked his things in the cabin, the man whistled a haunting if not happy tune, a sing-song, eerily shaped melody that ran up and down the scale in a pointless succession of tones, one note never quite fitting to the next. It was, like his left ear, twisted.

Like his clothes, his fishing gear bore the mark of quality, with rods, reels, lines, leaders, and lures of the most expensive variety. His fishing vest was of safari cloth and his waders of superior make.

He carried a camera, a Nikon with a complement of lenses that would make even Avedon look twice.

It was the camera that occupied his time for the first two days of his stay, and he went at it with the zeal of a born naturalist on the prowl, snapping pictures of the surrounding countryside: high shots and low shots, angles and straight-on, mountains, dells, trees and water, crags and meadows, high ground and swampland.

On the third day, camera hanging from his neck, lens case slung to his side, he ventured into Broadmoor.

On the streets he nodded, he smiled, but he spoke little and made no friends, neither in the stores nor in the bars.

His subjects now changed from natural history to human history. People became his quarry, and he snapped them feverishly, preserving them on film with the same determination he had shown in the woods.

But he photographed them surreptitiously, with a 100–200mm zoom lens, from across a street, from his car, or from the darkness of a hidden doorway.

Children seemed to be his favorites, small boys and girls, none older than twelve, all in close-up with the long lens.

The film he used was not color, but black and white, and he did not send it to the local drugstore or to Eastman Kodak, but developed and printed it in his cabin, in the dead of night with portable equipment.

On the whole, he seemed satisfied with his endeavors, and one night, drinking bourbon, he spread the prints out before him on the cabin bed and stared at them, peering, scrutinizing, picking them up one after another, until, as if in a trance, he closed his eyes and thought for long minutes, his fingers kneading his brow in a steady rhythm.

In the end, he chose one picture from more than a hundred and proceeded to burn the rest in the small standing fireplace that heated the cabin on cool nights. As he watched them burn, he knelt as though in prayer, but his face was set in lines of hatred.

The next morning he placed the remaining picture in an envelope, sealed it, addressed it, and posted it in a letterbox in Broadmoor across the street from John's Bakery.

Then he went fishing on The Reach, the stream that ran in front of his cabin, riffling, turbulent, and full of the promise of huge speckled trout.

But the fish seemed to elude him, as though they sensed his presence even before his waders broke the water; and the birds in the overhanging trees scattered before his hulking walk. Even the trees seemed to lean away from his passage.

That evening, as the man sat in a chair overlooking the stream, sipping from a tall glass of bourbon and water, a squirrel, accustomed to feeding in the area, took one brief look at him and scurried off into the woods.

But a snake, a water snake, gliding easily through the evening, raised its head from the waters and regarded the man with dispassionate, beady eyes.

The man with the withered ear stared back.

They seemed to understand each other.

CHAPTER
1

It was an ordinary day. An everyday kind of day.

In the kitchen, two electronic female images were arguing about whose wash was whiter. Upstairs, a vacuum cleaner droned; outside, the delightful shrieks of children.

Nicole looked at her watch: 11:30. Mail time. Lifting her fingers from the typewriter, she flipped the switch, rose, and started downstairs.

She swung the screen door, stepped out onto the walk, glanced in the direction of the pool, at the children, her daughter Leslie, and little Charlene Reilly, and at twenty-year-old Susan Dixon, who was "pool sitting."

It was a good day, coolish for August. A soft breeze nudged the pines. The gravel walk crunched beneath her sandals. She breathed greenness and water, and in the distance she could hear the rush of the falls over the dam.

It was a usual day at the mailbox, too. Bills: telephone, Saks, insurance company, the usual junk mail. No royalty checks.

But a package. Plain brown wrapper and Scotch tape. About five inches long, slender.

She turned it in her hand. It was addressed to her: Nicole Bannister. No return address. She frowned. Not from her aunt. Her boxes were always large and bulky, and what they contained, always small. This was too neat. A cocaine spoon? She laughed to herself, walked back to the house.

In her study, she opened the Saks bill first. Jonathan's eyebrows would arch, and she'd have to explain.

She sorted the other bills and arranged them in a neat pile. Time for that later. She wanted to get back to work.

Picking up the package, she mused, frowning. Delores? Of course, Delores who was in Sri Lanka and was forever sending incredibly small gifts from unimaginable parts of the world. A cocaine spoon it well might be.

She looked at the postmark. Broadmoor. Definitely and distinctly Broadmoor. Who, in her own village, would be sending her a package? Stores had a return address. Friends didn't send gifts, they arrived with them. Something she'd lost and the sender wanted to remain anonymous? A practical joke? An insult?

She opened the package quickly, curious. The small box beneath the brown wrapping paper was black. Inside were layers of white tissue. She parted them.

She didn't scream. She retched. Her stomach turned, and turned again, and she clutched at it as she stumbled toward the door. Terrible wracking grunts came from her throat, and when she reached the top of the stairs, everything she'd eaten for breakfast gushed from her mouth, and she plunged downward.

She was found unconscious at the foot of the stairs by Pearl DeWitt, the maid. The ambulance was fifteen minutes in coming. The State Troopers were there in five, and the township police in seven. At 12:35, Nicole Bannister was in the emergency room

of Good Samaritan Hospital in King's Landing, the
county seat.

Half an hour later, the medical examiner stood in
Nicole's study in Broadmoor, pondering the contents
of the box.

"How old is it, Doc?" Frank Liscomb, Chief of
Police of Holland Township, rolled a long panatella
in thin fingers.

"Six, I'd say. Maybe seven. That's a guess." Dr.
Thomas Blauvelt dropped his two-hundred-thirty-five
pounds into a chrome and leather director's chair,
grunting.

"Male or female?"

"That's hard to tell," Blauvelt said. "At that age,
kids' fingers look pretty much alike. Lot of fatty
tissue."

Liscomb turned to Trooper Leon Harris. "You get
any reports on missing children?"

"Nothing when I came on duty, Frank." Harris's
usually robust air was subdued, his complexion sal-
low. "I'll check if you want."

"I'd appreciate it."

As Harris went out to the patrol car, Blauvelt
nodded toward the small box on Nicole's desk.

"We should freeze it soon. For the autopsy."

"Yeah." Chief Liscomb looked uncomfortable. "It's
so small," he blurted and then stopped, as though
puzzled by his own words. "What the hell! Who'd
do a thing like that? Who'd do it!"

"I don't know, Frank." Blauvelt stared into the
cold fireplace.

There was a silence, then Liscomb said, "We'll get
a print on it first."

"Print? It came from a child. A print won't be on
file."

Liscomb shrugged. "I thought that I heard some hospitals were doing it at birth."

"Footprints, not fingerprints. At least in this state. It's not 1984 yet, Frank."

"Maybe it is. There's enough insanity around." He cleared his throat, raised his voice, called almost harshly: "Volner!"

When Volner appeared, his chief asked, "What about the husband?"

"Maid says he's in the city. At a meeting. Supposed to be home around four."

"What about Griffen?"

"On the way, Chief."

Liscomb chewed on the cigar. He looked over at the small box almost reluctantly. "I want him to take a print. And dust the box and wrapping paper, although I doubt anything'll show but the woman's prints." He relit the cigar, staring over it toward the medical examiner. "Take a walk with me, Tom."

As they rose, the State Trooper entered the room. "The only Missing Persons Report we've got," he said, "is a male, aged thirty-five white. Lives in Perrytown. That's two hundred miles from here."

"Thanks, Leon," Liscomb said. "But I think we should keep at it. There's a child missing *someplace.* I'll check with Washington."

"Why does the kid have to be dead?" Volner asked suddenly. "I mean . . ."—he looked at the desk—"I mean what if the kid isn't . . ." He stopped.

Liscomb glared at him. "You're crazy." Then he walked out of the room, followed by Blauvelt.

At the swimming pool, Liscomb sat on a redwood bench. Blauvelt dumped himself into a canvas African chair, his huge buttocks almost bursting it. His soft, doglike eyes took in the surroundings. "Pretty spot, isn't it?" he said.

The pool was a widened stretch of Willow Creek, flowing down from the mountains to the east and north, dammed and deepened, and surrounded by natural rock and trees. The sun filtered through the heavy overhang of tall pine and spreading birch, dappling the water with bright sprinkles of dancing light, lending tone and texture to the gray-brown rock, illuminating the soft pastel shades of the poolside furniture, diving board, and flagstone terrace.

"Pretty indeed," Liscomb said. Then: "You know the family?"

"We've exchanged invites. They're new, you know. About a year. I've been to a few of their parties."

Liscomb grunted.

"He's a commercial artist. Earns pretty good money. But his serious stuff is very good too. Maybe you noticed."

"That thing behind the desk upstairs?"

"Yes. That's one of his."

"What is it?"

"An abstract. Nonobjective."

"I know. But what is it supposed to be?"

Blauvelt shrugged. "An abstract. It doesn't have to *be* anything. An arrangement of color, shape, form. A feeling."

Liscomb grunted, drew on the unlit cigar. Across the pool, a bluejay shrieked shrill defiance. "You can get a blood type?"

"There wasn't very much blood. Very little in fact. We'll try. Electron-microscopy might tell us whether the kid was male or female."

"That would help," Liscomb said. "What would you think at this point? An axe? A cleaver?"

"Possibly. Or a surgical tool of some sort. It was clean. Very clean."

Liscomb spat. "Who'd do a thing like this? And then send it to somebody. And why? I ask you, *why?*"

Blauvelt shifted in his chair. "I don't know the why. But the who? A psychotic."

"We've got our share of nuts in the county," Liscomb said. "But in all my years here—and I was born ten miles away—I never thought anybody was *that* crazy."

At the crunch of feet on gravel, Liscomb turned his head. Volner stepped up from the path onto the flagstones. "Griffen's here. I told him what you said." He squatted near the edge of the pool, picked up a small stone and threw it. He turned, looking at Liscomb vacantly, then at Blauvelt. "What the fuck," he said.

"Go on back to the car," Liscomb said. "See if there's anything for us."

Volner's thick soles crunched away.

"Are they rich?" Liscomb asked. He was gesturing to the house, the pool.

"I wouldn't say 'rich,'" Blauvelt answered. "Well-to-do. Between the two of them, they must pull in eighty-five, ninety a year."

"That's not rich?" Liscomb was thinking of his own meager income.

"Taxes are high in those brackets," Blauvelt said.

"What does she do? The wife?"

"She writes books. Illustrates her own work. She's well known, widely read."

"What kind of books?"

"Children's books," Blauvelt said and found himself staring back into Liscomb's suddenly bright eyes.

CHAPTER 2

Leslie Bannister's small fingers, sticky and oozing raspberry, curled around the remains of the ice-cream cone. "Can I have another?"

"Sure," her sitter said. "Why not?"

Susan Dixon bought the child a second cone and ordered a vanilla for herself. Back in the car, she licked the ice cream absently, staring through the windshield.

"When're we going to get there?" the child asked.

"Where?"

"Where we're going to."

"Soon," Susan said. She turned the ignition, backed out of the small roadside lot, turned west.

On the road toward North Lake, she was pensive, answering the seven-year-old only when necessary. Keep her out, Chief Liscomb had said. Take her little friend home and keep this one out until we've finished up here. How long would that take, Susan wondered.

Since dropping the Reilly girl off, she'd been driving aimlessly. Marijane Reilly hadn't offered to take Leslie. In fact, she had looked annoyed at the return of her own child.

"I want to swim some more," Leslie said.

"We will. At North Lake."

"I don't like North Lake."

"It's pretty there," Susan said.

"The bottom's all sticky," Leslie said.

"So are your fingers," Susan said—and shuddered. When the maid had called her from the screen door, she'd skirted Nicole's unconscious form and run up the stairs to the study phone rather than step over her into the kitchen. It was after calling for help that she'd noticed the small box on Nicole's desk. And peered inside.

She shuddered again.

"What's the matter, Suzy?" Leslie asked.

"Nothing," Susan said.

"I don't want to go to North Lake."

"All right, we won't, Bratty."

"My name isn't Bratty," Leslie said and giggled. This was a familiar game.

"Oh, yes it is," Susan said.

"Oh, no it isn't."

"Oh, yes it is." A sudden thought came to her. "How about the West Branch?"

"Oh, goody-goody-goody!" Leslie cried. "I can go under the waterfall."

Susan slowed down, readying for the turn-off to Rut Road. *Rut Road,* she thought. *Aptly named.* Maybe Ken would have some grass. Or a drink. She could use a drink.

* * *

As he paid the bridge toll and eased onto the interstate, Jonathan Bannister laid on the accelerator and brought the Volvo to a pure and even sixty-five.

"Jesus, I'm glad to get out of that stinking city," he said.

"It's a hellhole, isn't it," Henry Dixon said.

"It's evil."

"Evil?" Dixon glanced over at him with a malicious

lift to his eyebrow. "That's a pretty strong word."

"Murder, rape, mayhem. Soot, shit, noise, and no room. Mix it all up, and what've you got? That." He was nodding at the tall apartment buildings across the river. "One trip a week to that sinkhole is enough. I'm glad we don't have to commute."

"But it's where the money is," Dixon said.

"Unfortunately."

Dixon leaned into his open attaché case and pulled up a quart of Boodles. "Since you're driving," he said, then gulped thickly from the neck. He lowered the bottle to his lap. "What'd the MacCready place set you back?"

Jonathan frowned. Hank Dixon had two annoying habits: he drank too much, and he had no sense of propriety. However, he was a good artist. When he stayed sober. "A lot," Jonathan said. "But it's worth it. Worth it to know that in about two hours, at approximately four P.M., I can breathe fresh air, smell pine, loll by the pool or cast a fly on The Reach, start a charcoal fire a little later on, hear some birds, maybe spot a few deer. And finally, to top off the evening, fuck my wife to the cheerful chirping of happy crickets."

"You coulda got it for a hundred-fifty thousand," Dixon said. He took another long swallow of gin.

"What makes you think I paid more?" Jonathan was feeling uneasy.

"You did. You paid a hundred sixty-seven five."

"Who told you that?" Jonathan snapped.

"A bird. A small yellow bird. Word gets around."

"It sure as hell does!"

"And you coulda got it for a hundred-fifty. Maybe less."

"Oh?"

"Sure. It's haunted."

Jonathan laughed. "That's called inflation, Hank. Ghosts drive the price up. Who's the spirit supposed to be, anyway?"

"Two of them," Dixon said. "MacCready killed his last two wives there."

"I heard one died of a brain hemorrhage, and the other of respiratory disease."

"MacCready was a doctor. He fixed it." Dixon said it as though it were fact.

"Is that the word around the county?"

"That's the word." Dixon swilled from the bottle. His speech was thick now, and his eyes had that dark brooding look that Jonathan knew always heralded the onset of bitter anger. The closer Hank Dixon came to home, Jonathan knew, the more angry he became. And the more drunk. He often wondered why he offered rides to and from the city to Dixon. Talented as he might be, the man was sometimes unbearable under alcohol.

"You've lived in Holland County a long time, haven't you, Hank?"

"Too long." Dixon had recapped the bottle, and his head was drooping toward his chest. "Twenty-five years."

"That's a long time."

"Too long. It's evil."

"What's evil?"

"The county. It's evil. Just as evil as the city." Dixon's words were slurred but incisive.

Jonathan shifted uneasily behind the wheel. He checked his speed, the gas gauge, oil pressure. "You're drunk, Hank," he said, and glanced over at the man on his right.

But Dixon was beyond hearing. His eyes were

closed. A slight snore came from his lips. Jonathan noticed he needed a shave.

The Volvo sped northward, the odometer peeled its numbers, and Jonathan tried to recapture the carefree mood that Dixon had blunted just north of the bridge.

That was the trouble with Dixon. He was a bitter failure, and bitter failures were poor company. They punched good fortune in the face and kicked happiness in the groin. Failure had taught them not to expect, and, expecting nothing, they sought refuge in anger and self-inflicted frustration. Henry Dixon was a first-rate artist, but instead of working, he drank.

He pushed thoughts of Dixon aside and turned his mind to his day in the city. The contract with IBM for six centerfold spreads in national magazines would make many things possible for him and Nicole now. That couple of months in Europe they'd been talking about for six years. Some salmon fishing on the Dee. London for a week or two. Then Paris, Rome. Rome—Jesus, how he'd like to see Rome again. He could devote more time to his own work, too. Maybe another show in the city. Neiman, watch out. LeRoy, move over.

The advance check was fat in his pocket, and Jonathan began to hum under his breath. They could do some more work on the MacCready place. Enlarge his studio, fix up the attic. MacCready place, hell! It was the *Bannister* place now.

The car came at him as he took the graded curve near Leydenburg. He acted instinctively. The Buick with the wobbling flat was directly in the center lane, straight ahead. He sensed traffic to his rear right and left. Brakes. The Volvo shuddered. Dixon's head went forward. The Boodles fell to the floor. The car ahead loomed. A horn blasted to his left and a shape darted by. He slipped behind it, narrowly escaping the limping Buick in the center lane, his own front wheels grazing the median. Then the rear wheels hit and the Volvo bounced into the center lane again. His foot fed gas. He struggled with the steering yoke, pulling out of the skid slowly. Then he let out his breath. His hands were trembling. There was a dryness in his throat, and he could feel the pulse in his neck throbbing heavily. He slowed to fifty, his hands tight on the wheel, his breathing deep.

Dixon was massaging the back of his neck.

"You okay?" Jonathan asked.

"I hope you're well covered, chum. In case I got whiplash." There was a sneer in his voice. "You shouldn't drive so fast."

"I was doing sixty-five."

"The limit's fifty-five."

"The guy ahead of me must have been doing a big ten when I came around that bend."

Dixon ducked under the dash to retrieve the Boodles. He uncapped it and held the bottle aloft. "Here's to the future," he said, and drank. "You can't ever tell, can you?"

Susan bounced along Rut Road, keeping her wheels in the well-worn grooves, braking before holes, easing up out of deep depressions. Overhanging branches scraped the top, and jutting limbs parted before the hood.

"When're we going to get there?" Leslie whined.

"Soon," Susan said.

After another mile she came upon the faded sign in psychedelic script that proclaimed "Welcome All

Good People," and further on another that said
"Love is Peace." At the rusty gate that led into the
camp, a more recent sign, in bold black paint, shouted
"Private Property! No Trespassing Allowed!" and on
the right, a smaller one warned "Pigs Keep Out!"

Times had changed at Job's Camp since the coming
of Freddie Loftus. Goodwill had given way to anger,
and good works to orgies. But Ken Brady was a hold-
over from the original group of settlers, and Susan
liked him. Too much, she sometimes thought. And
far too carnally.

Up ahead, a thin, long-haired figure with a girl
attached to its arm was crossing the road between
two of the more broken-down shacks. Noticing the
car, it stopped dead in its tracks, defiant. It was
Freddie Loftus.

When Susan stopped, Freddie detached himself
from the girl and came around the car, leaning into
the driver's window. "Mornin', Miss Suzy," he said in
a broad country and western drawl. "My, you lookin'
purty this day!"

Before she could answer, his hand was in the car,
grasping hard on Susan's left breast. She felt her
nipple harden. She hated this black-bearded, black-
eyed man, and yet her body was responding. She let
the hand squeeze for a moment, then covered it with
hers and dug her fingernails in as hard as she could.

Freddie Loftus jumped back. His thin, gaunt face
was contorted with hatred and his eyes blazed. "You
cunt! I'll get back at you for this," he said, wiping
his hand on dirty denims. "I'll fix your little wagon,
bitch!" The country drawl was gone. In its place
were the flat tones of educated Midwest.

"Get lost, Freddie," Susan said.

Freddie turned and the girl he was with put an

arm around his shoulder, glaring back at Susan. She was a thin little rag with long, dirty, unkempt hair, drug-hardened and worn out at the age of twenty-five. She wore soiled denims and torn sneakers. Her face was pinched and drawn, the skin clinging to the skull like stretched canvas. They called her Dimples. "Nobody hurts Freddie," she said. "Nobody hurts Freddie and lives to tell the tale." Then she turned her back.

Susan pedaled the gas, moving onward. *And lives to tell the tale? Where did she pick that one up? From a 1930s horror movie on television?*

"I don't like Freddie," Leslie Bannister said after a pause.

"Most people don't," Susan said. "But a lot of others do." She wondered again about the feeling of his hand on her breast, then the peculiar excitement it had stirred between her thighs.

Ken Brady's cabin was on the outskirts of the camp on a tributary of Willow Creek known as the West Branch. Amorphous psychedelic shapes and patterns in red, purple, green, blue, magenta, and yellow adorned its sides, roof, doors and windows, fading reminders of the past, of happier days when the commune had been formed. A haphazard clutter of weeds and flowers crept around the porch, and a small vegetable garden was a tangle of stunted corn, shriveled radishes, overripe cucumbers, and mottled tomatoes.

As she approached the porch, Susan could hear the deep booming of Ken's electric guitar and the fainter quaver of his slight but unusual voice. A sign over the door notified all that "Thru These Portals Pass the Most Beautiful Chicks in the Universe."

He stopped strumming when he saw her. He said nothing, but rose and, coming forward, took her in his arms and kissed her. Then he picked up Leslie and kissed her too. He was smiling.

"I want to go under the waterfall," Leslie said.

"I'll take you down," Ken said.

"You have a drink?" Susan asked.

"I've got some Acapulco Gold."

"No, I want a drink."

"Look in the cabinet. I'll be right back." He slipped through the door with Leslie on his shoulders.

The cabinet was an old ice box, circa 1932, that Ken had hauled down all the way from Job's Ruins. In the top compartment was a half gallon of Almaden Mountain Red Burgundy and a fifth of Great Western Chablis. In the bottom, behind cereal boxes and a jar of honey, she found part of a pint of Red Label Scotch. She washed a tumbler because nothing was clean. As she poured two fingers, she noticed her hand was shaking. She drank and looked around. He lives like a pig, she thought, and smirked, remembering the hand-lettered sign about "pigs" that Freddie Loftus had put up.

He didn't own much, but what he did was scattered all over the place: a jarring jumble of books, records, stereo equipment, newspapers, magazines, pieces of driftwood, rocks, pebbles, old-time movie posters, a television set with a broken screen, a disassembled radio, half of an old coffee grinder, nails, screws, rusty tools, a tattered American flag.

The kitchen consisted of a small sink, a four-burner bottled gas stove, one overflowing garbage bag, and a drop-leaf table covered with a checked tablecloth full of charred holes from marijuana droppings. In the living room, the fireplace was a heap of ashes crowned by beer cans and one old sock. His sleeping bag lay on the bedroom floor, open, soiled, brittle. There was a bookcase, but it contained only three books. The remaining space was stuffed with soiled shirts and underwear.

When he returned, he crept up behind her silently and slipped his hands under her armpits, cupping her breasts, kissing the nape of her neck lightly. "I'm glad you came, Sue."

"Is she all right down there?"

"She's fine. Ted and Agnes are with her. She won't get hurt."

"Get me another drink, Ken," Susan said. "The Red Label."

When he handed it to her, he said, "What's the matter?"

She told him about Nicole Bannister. About the ambulance. About the package on the desk.

When she finished, he said, "That's really weird," and stared out the window. "Who'd do a weird thing like that?"

Freddie Loftus, she thought.

"What?"

"I didn't say anything," she said. Then she laughed. "Sometimes I think you're psychic."

"Why? What were you thinking about?"

"Freddie Loftus." And she told him about their meeting.

"So he squeezed your tit," he said. "What's so heavy about that?"

"Nothing. Except that I can't abide the bastard."

He laughed. "You've got an old-fashioned vocabulary."

"I'm an old-fashioned girl. Listen. Really. He got

mad and forgot his hick accent. Why does he go around with that drawl, anyway?"

"He's a rock star."

"Rock star, my ass," Susan said.

"He made a record."

"Who ever heard of it?"

Ken shrugged. "When you sing rock these days, you got to have a country and western twang. Look at Randy Newman."

Susan poured another drink.

"You're regressing," Ken said, watching her lift the glass.

"It's *in*," she said. "Grass is out and booze is in. Don't you read the papers?"

"What do your parents say?"

"They don't approve. My daddy's an out and out alcoholic and my stepmother's a sneak tippler. But they don't approve."

Ken frowned. "What's wrong with parents?"

"They don't approve of their children," Susan said. "One wonders why they ever have them if they don't approve of them."

"Let's go into the bedroom," Ken said.

Susan rose. "Will she be all right?"

"She'll be fine."

Bedroom, Susan thought. *That's a laugh riot.*

On the third floor of Good Samaritan Hospital in King's Landing, Father Daniel Conant walked with his head down. He had just administered last rites to an automobile accident victim.

He took the stairwell to the second floor and turned toward room 212. Inside, the shadows were gray and deep under the drawn blinds, and the air conditioner whispered smoothly. A nurse sat, knitting.

"Is she awake?" Father Conant asked.

"She was for a few minutes, Father," the nurse said. "She's sleeping now."

The Father looked at Nicole Bannister. *What a lovely face,* he thought. Like a Botticelli face, pure and well angled, full of a distant wisdom. "Will she be all right?" he asked.

"Just a slight concussion, Father," the nurse said. "She'll be fine. She should be awake in about an hour, if you want to come back."

"Maybe I will." Father Conant made a small gesture of blessing in the air, then turned and left silently.

The nurse purled one, dropped two. *When did they start making priests like that,* she wondered. That soft but chiseled face. The dark, brooding eyes. The quiet, yet deep voice. The aura.

The aura. That was it. The aura.

Aura, hell. It was stark naked sexuality.

I'm fifty-six and no Popist, she thought. *But sweet Jesus Christ I'd* convert *for a piece of that.*

She sighed, and purled two and dropped one.

In the West Branch of Willow Creek, under the waterfall, Leslie Bannister splashed, screamed and shrieked, laughed, choked and gurgled.

In the cabin above, Susan Dixon and Ken Brady groaned and grunted, writhed and rolled, panted and gasped.

When it was over, they lay trembling.

Later, sipping her drink, Susan asked, "What do you know about Freddie Loftus?"

"Freddie's all right. Deep down, I mean. He's got his hangups. Shit, who hasn't? But underneath he's a good person."

"Why does he go around with that phony country accent?"

"I told you. He's into rock, you know? We all do it. Freddie's really smart. A little weird but smart. He's got a divinity degree, you know."

"No, I didn't."

"He's really into religion. He's writing a book about it. About good and evil."

"He should know!"

Ken was tracing patterns on her breasts with the tip of a finger. "Why don't you come to the Rites next time?"

"What do you do at the Rites?"

"You know what we do."

She paused. She saw Freddie's face for a moment, felt his hand on her breast. "And suppose I made it with Freddie at the Rites? Wouldn't you mind?"

"Why should I?"

"You're really laid back, aren't you?"

"People get too involved. That's the trouble with this world. Involvement." He inhaled deeply on the thin cigarette, held it for long seconds, then let out the heavy sweetness. "Involvement leads to wars. Just look around you. This big ball we live on is headed for zero minus one anyway. All we got left is to get laid. Mass love instead of mass murder."

There was a scream from the direction of the stream. Ken was on his feet and out of the door like a bolt, naked, flying. Susan pulled on her jeans, slipped into the blouse. On the porch, she looked down toward the creek.

Ken was climbing the steep path from the West Branch, a sobbing Leslie on his shoulder. Blood dripped on his chest.

"She scraped her foot on a rock," he said. "It's not serious."

"I want to go home," Leslie whimpered. "I want to go home."

Susan was shivering.

CHAPTER 3

The Volvo crossed the county line near Pikeville, ten miles south of King's Landing, and an odd feeling of peace, almost solace descended upon Jonathan.

Somehow, he always felt that way as he entered Holland County, and he often wondered whether it was purely a physical thing. Certainly there were subtle differences between Holland County and the county that lay behind him. The air seemed fresher, cooler, possibly because of the sudden looming of the mountains to the north and east, or the dip in the interstate that led into a long, broad valley. Everything here seemed greener, more lush, full of a wild, untamed beauty. It seemed to Jonathan like a small bit of frontier that had gone unnoticed, unseen, unspoiled.

The streams and rivers of Holland County ran deep and strong, often turbulent, and native trout could still be taken. The mountains rose slowly at first, then gathered themselves into a mighty crescendo, thrusting upward, sharp and craggy over the valley. The forests were thick, uncleared for the most part, and the tall stands of pine were dark and mysterious. Deer were common, and there were still bear back in the hills. Some said a bobcat had been seen the year before.

The towns and villages were sparse, untouched by developers, shopping malls and light industry. True, there were two centers in King's Landing, but that was the main town. A supermarket had come to Broadmoor, but it more resembled a braggart general store. Many of the villages, including Broadmoor, looked as they had at the turn of the century, a mixture of white clapboard and gray fieldstone on twisting streets. The surrounding roads were narrow, winding through the rich flat farmland of the valley.

Slipping neatly into the cloverleaf at Interchange 42, feeling a new rush of sweet air as the concrete dipped and melded into Broadmoor Road, Jonathan felt both at peace and at home. A child of the city, he had become, at forty, a successful rustic.

"I think I'll have me a large brookie before sundown," he said aloud.

Dixon glanced at him from under untrimmed eyebrows. "Stop and have a drink at my place," he said. "I'll show you a picture of a brook trout I landed about six years ago. Over five pounds."

"No, thanks, Hank," Jonathan said. "I'll take a raincheck."

"Suit yourself," Dixon said. Jonathan felt the guilt creep up out of his collar like a sudden red blush. He had been curt, condescending, full of the overbearing disdain that the rich reserve for the poor, the successful for the unsuccessful, the teetotaler for the alcoholic. Maybe he should have the drink with him. To apologize. The poor bastard didn't want to part company, to find himself alone with his wife.

And then Jonathan thought of Estelle Dixon and decided against the drink.

The Dixons had been married for fifteen years.

Fifteen years with that spook? Jonathan could hardly blame the man for drinking. As they approached Broadmoor, he said, "How about one at my place? I've got a new spinning reel I want to show you."

Dixon looked at him, again with the very slight lift of a lip, a raised bushy eyebrow. "You got Boodles?"

"I got oodles of Boodles."

In Broadmoor, he made an excuse to stop at John's Bakery, bought some rolls, then slipped into the liquor store for a quart of gin.

When Dixon saw the package, he said, "You didn't have to get it. We could have picked it up at my place."

"Forget it," Jonathan said. "I'll get you later in the week when I decide to get smashed."

Out of Broadmoor, he crossed the covered bridge over The Reach into Willow Creek Road, and two miles further on, turned right into his own driveway, stopping dead behind the police car.

As he shoved the door open and stumbled out on the gravel, his eyes caught the figure of a young policeman approaching from the swimming pool. Then Tom Blauvelt's big face was waving in front of him, the lips moving, making no sense. He started toward the house, but the medical examiner's hand caught his arm, squeezing.

"It's all right, Jonathan," Blauvelt was saying evenly. "It's all right. Nicole and Leslie are fine. Nothing wrong."

His eyes began to focus, but his neck and head kept throbbing. Not Nicole. Not Leslie. The housekeeper? "Something happen to Pearl?"

"I'm Patrolman Volner, Mr. Bannister. Why don't you sit down over here for a minute?"

Jonathan sank into the African chair. He looked from Volner to Blauvelt, from Blauvelt to Volner, waiting for someone to speak. Dixon stood, half in, half out of the small group.

"Tell me!" Jonathan said. "For God's sake!"

After they told him, Hank Dixon disappeared behind the corner of the house and threw up.

Chrissake, he kept repeating to himself. *For Chrissake.*

Father Conant rose as Jonathan entered the hospital room. "I was just saying a little hello to Mrs. Bannister," he said to Jonathan. "I hope you don't mind."

"Of course not, Father. I'm glad you had the time."

"Good night, Mrs. Bannister," the priest said.

"Good night, Father."

Jonathan watched him go. Then he pulled a chair up to the bedside and took Nicole's hand. His head gestured backward. "What did he want?"

"Just a talk," she said.

"Priests make me uncomfortable."

"Me too." She paused. "He's a nice man."

"I know. But he still makes me uncomfortable."

She laughed very weakly. "He's suggesting I come back to the Church."

"At a time like this?"

"He says times like this are the best times."

He smiled. "Well, if you go, I guess I'll have to follow."

"I'm not going back," she said and squeezed his hand.

"Here's a silly question," Jonathan said. "How are you?"

"Lousy. Absolutely lousy. Who's with Leslie?"

"Pearl. She's staying over. Everything's fine."

"I feel so ridiculous," Nicole said.

His eyes questioned her.

"Reacting that way." She went on. "Fainting."

"You didn't faint. You tripped on the stairs and hit your head."

"Did I?" She thought about that for a moment. "What does it mean, Jonathan?"

"I don't know," he said. "Chief Liscomb seems to think there's a nut loose someplace. Maybe out of the happy house over in Clarendon. By the way, he'll want to talk to you. He says he'll wait till tomorrow. You'll be home by tomorrow."

"I should have been stronger," she said.

"You should have been what?"

"I shouldn't have fainted."

He pressed her hand and she returned the pressure. Then she looked at him and said, "The child. Do they know who the child is?"

"No. Nothing about that yet."

They were silent, held only by the pressure of their hands. After a time, Jonathan said, "Hank Dixon's outside. Can you bear it?"

"Is he sober?"

"Of course not."

"Then bring him in," she laughed. "You know I like him better when he's drunk."

When Jonathan called him, Hank Dixon straightened his spine and walked as well as he could into the room.

As the door silently eased to its rubber stop behind

Dixon, Frank Liscomb draped his long thin arm around Father Conant's shoulders. They stood just outside the room.

"Take a walk with me, Father," Liscomb said, steering the priest toward the solarium at the end of the east corridor.

They settled into broad, comfortable Naugahyde cushions supported by wicker frames. Liscomb found two panatellas in his breast pocket, and the priest accepted.

They smoked for a moment, and then Liscomb began, eyeing the priest carefully as he spoke, sizing him up, taking his measure, qualifying, quantifying. About forty, forty-two, he thought. Handsome for a priest. Intense. Sexual. Probably Italian. Maybe Greek.

"There's a nut loose, Father," Liscomb said. "A madman. A psychotic. A sick person. Anything you call it, any way you add it up, it amounts to evil. I get a little sick and tired of labels, don't you? Good is good and evil is evil, am I right?"

Daniel Conant had his legs crossed, his fingertips touching as though in prayer. There was a gentle smile on his lips. "Are you a Catholic, Chief Liscomb? I haven't seen you at mass."

"I'm a Lutheran," Liscomb said, "just like most of the other townies around here. But that doesn't make me un-Christian."

"Of course not," Conant said and winced. What was this dry-voiced stick of a man getting at?

"Now, I'm no criminologist," Liscomb was saying. "I'm just a small-town cop. But I do read. I do keep up. I do have experience and learn from it." He leaned forward on the plastic cushion. "You understand what I mean?"

"Of course," Father Conant said and wondered

again what Liscomb was leading up to. He nodded. "Of course."

"They say that criminals always return to the scene of the crime, Father," Liscomb continued. "That's crap, if you'll pardon the expression. I've had enough experience and done enough reading to know that."

Conant began to feel himself liking the man. He puffed on the cigar and nodded for more.

"The best criminals are the ones who don't get caught," Liscomb said, "who do it again and again and never get caught." He paused. "And there are a helluva lot of them, Father. A helluva lot."

"What," Father Conant interrupted, "has all this to do with Mrs. Bannister? Or me?"

Liscomb leaned back in his chair, pointing his cigar. "It has this to do, Father: this one's a psychotic. And psychotics can't stand to be left alone, to remain unknown, to be anonymous. They have an urge to confess, Father, and whether it's for atonement or because of ego doesn't concern me in the least."

A sudden tension gripped the priest and, for the first time, he leaned forward. There was a small, slightly cruel smile on his lips. "Montgomery Clift?" he asked.

Liscomb stared, uncomprehending.

"I remind you of Montgomery Clift, right?"

"Well," Liscomb said hesitantly, "maybe a little."

"I've forgotten the story," the priest said, "how it ended. But that was it, wasn't it? That's it *now*, you think, isn't it? A murderer confesses his sins to a priest and the priest agonizes over civil justice versus mortal sin."

"I just thought . . ." Liscomb began.

"You just thought that if the killer confesses to me, that I might just tell you."

Liscomb straightened. "It's a child, for Christ's sake, Father! A little child!"

"And it would be privileged information," the priest said, "which you would ask me to divulge."

"Privileged, shit!" Liscomb shouted. "Privileged to whom? To the Church? To you? To the killer? To Mrs. Bannister or the kid? Bullshit!"

Suddenly Liscomb felt ashamed. "I'm sorry, Father," he said. "This thing's got me upset, that's all. I never came up against anything like this."

"I understand." Conant's eyes softened and he twisted his hands. "How do you know it's a Catholic in the first place?"

"I don't. But if he is, and he were to confess to you . . ."

"*He?*" Conant smiled grimly. "And do we know it is a *he* in the first place?"

"No we don't," Liscomb said. "We don't, do we?"

"He or she. You'd expect me to divulge the information?"

Liscomb paused. "No. No, I guess not."

Father Conant rose. "I wish I could help. For the sake of Mrs. Bannister, for the sake of the child. But I can't, Chief Liscomb. I can only tell you this. It's not the Church's job to seek out and to punish. That's your job. The Church can only listen and in some small way offer absolution. Then it's Our Lord's job to punish. Or to forgive."

Liscomb watched the priest's graceful figure recede down the corridor.

Smart bastard, he thought. *Probably a Jesuit.*

* * *

Gossip, rumor, and conjecture were as necessary to the people of Holland County as bread and butter, staples of their lives, and that evening, as the sun arched downward across the river from King's Landing, the story spread from Broadmoor west to Clarendon, south to Pikeville, and to Leyden's Ferry in the north. The local radio station led off with the item, and no town, village or crossroads went naked for want of news. Party lines hummed until well after dinnertime. In King's Landing, people exchanged views on street corners, in front of movie theatres, in restaurants, across bars. Heads nodded, lips pursed, eyes rolled.

"*Imagine opening a box and finding that. Ughh!*"

"*Little girl's finger, it was. 'Bout ten years old, I hear.*"

"*It had a gold ring on it. A gold ring . . . . It's them hippies up to Job's Camp, I tell ya.*"

"*Darling, please! We're having dinner! Waiter, let me see the wine list.*"

"*Bloody, it was. Blood all over the place, they say.*"

"*I ain't seen the little Hickenson boy lately, have you?*"

"*Wonder where the body is?*"

"*We oughta form a search party. Search the woods. Milt, you game?*"

"*It's weird, y'know? A really heavy scene, man.*"

"*I feel so sorry for Nicole.*"

"*How have they been getting along? She and Jonathan, I mean?*"

"*Frank Liscomb'll get 'im. You watch.*"

"*Frank Liscomb ain't had no more to do than give out traffic tickets these past ten years.*"

"*They're new, you know. Only been in the old MacCready place a little more than a year.*"

"And he didn't tell them it was haunted? Hah!"

"If they're smart, they'll move back to the city."

"I wish they'd all move back. Holland County's gettin' too crowded."

"Pretty soon, them city people'll own all the land. Tell ya one thing—I ain't sellin'. Never!"

"I hear there's a coven up near Job's Ruins."

"Witches? What witches?"

"It was a little boy's hand."

"It had the mark of the devil on it, it had."

That night, Nicole Bannister slept a deep Seconal sleep. If she dreamed, she did not remember.

Leslie Bannister lay awake for a very long time, blanket binding clutched closely, eyes fixed on the amber nightlight, a dull, inexplicable fear gnawing at her mind.

She could not understand why her Mommy had gone, why they had taken her away in that funny car with the red lights.

It wasn't that she was working. Sometimes when Mommy worked, Leslie was lonely, but Mommy always worked in her study. Not in a car.

"Elsie?" Leslie spoke aloud. "Elsie, why did they take Mommy in that funny car?"

No sound filled the room, but a voice was heard in Leslie Bannister's mind. "I don't know," it said.

"Do you think she'll come back, Elsie?"

"Of course she'll come back," Elsie said rather petulantly. "Mommies always come back. They have to make breakfast, don't they?"

Whenever Leslie Bannister was lonely or afraid or angry, she invented Elsie, her playmate, her alter ego, her reassurance against threat and unhappiness. Elsie had been her best friend from the time she was five.

"She always tells me when she goes out," Leslie said.

"Oh, you know mommies," Elsie said. "Sometimes they forget."

They talked long and eagerly, and solved many of the world's problems between them, until Leslie Bannister's eyelids closed and slumber came.

To the north of the living room of their home, originally constructed in 1769, added to in 1837, Jonathan Bannister sat in his studio, a wing extended in 1929 by Horace MacCready the elder. He sipped scotch slowly. His mind, tired and confused, would not focus. Too much had happened. He finished the drink, made his way upstairs to Leslie's room. He lay down beside her. He took the child in his arms. He slept.

At about that same time, Thomas Blauvelt was examining his fingers, turning his hands over and over before his face, as though they were something apart from him. So much could be gleaned from a patient's hands and fingers. The nodules of gout, the swollen joints of rheumatoid arthritis; the purplish hue of the palm that hinted at cirrhosis of the liver. The clawed fingers of ulnar paralysis. The clubby shapes of chronic heart and lung disease, the spoon-shaped nails of anemia. But most often, nothing could be diagnosed. As with the specimen earlier in the day. So small, so pure, so soft, so young.

Dr. Blauvelt peered closely at a small mark on the back of his own hand near the wrist. He winced. A liver spot? At fifty-two?

At Job's Camp, Ken Brady was tripping out on a pipeful of hash and a Moog rendition of Johann Sebastian Bach. He was far away, watching himself on a stage, guitar slung, hips weaving, lips moving, words and notes pouring forth to a heavy, resounding beat. The audience moved with him. They screamed. They shrieked. They applauded. They stomped. He began to dance, lightly, airily. He was Gene Kelly, Fred Astaire, Nureyev, Baryshnikov.

On the stone altar below Job's Ruins, Freddie Loftus was making love to Dimples, plunging her, plumbing her, banging her, beating her, shafting her. His thin stick of a body loomed like a dark mantis, and her hips rose to meet his bony groin in lustful leaps. "You're divine, you're divine, you're divine," she screamed, and in his head Freddie heard *divine, divine, divine, divinity, divinity, divinity student, divinity student, oh, my God whip me, punish me, scald me, burn me, kill me, murder me, make me yours!* And he came, and choked, and was still.

Susan Dixon dreamed that night. She dreamed of an assembly line spitting out hundreds of small, black boxes. They all looked like finger-length black coffins, and each contained a tiny figure of Freddie Loftus, arms folded, staring upward from a bed of bloody tissue paper. But she didn't remember when she awoke.

Hank Dixon drank bourbon that night, being out of gin. He observed his wife with the detached air of an intellectual drunk, stiff but still limber of mind, smashed but still inwardly together. Estelle was doing the Ouija board thing, sitting at the coffee table in the living room, eyes closed, slender fingers outstretched on the planchette. She had started with tarot cards, but one was missing, and she had cursed and jammed them back into the box and reached for the Ouija. There was a spirit at large, she said, an evil spirit, and the Ouija would name it for them. Dixon tipped his glass and, as the liquor ran into his throat, his eyes scanned the collection of junk in the walnut bookcase. Six books on astrology, four on palmistry, a dozen or more dealing with witches, devils, demons, and exorcism. Tomes about fortune-telling, UFO's, seances and mediums. Uri Geller. Von Daniken. The I Ching. *Christ,* he thought, *she'll be buying a crystal ball next.*

Frank Liscomb was drinking beer. It was his habit, before bedtime, to finish three or four bottles of Heineken. It helped him sleep. He sat at the kitchen table, a lined, yellow, legal-size pad on the table before him, three pages of it scrawled with notes. He had made a new heading, *Motive Number II,* and wrote: *Just as important to figure out why murd. sent finger as why he killed in first place.* Under this he indented:

a. A warning? About what?

b. Ransom? Note to follow? The kid may still be alive. Is Volner right?

c. Is child related to Mrs. Bannister? (add to Victim, identity of)

d. For shock effect? Why? Why Mrs. Bannister? Was she just chosen at random? She writes children's books!

e. Is it ego? Boasting?

f. A confession of sorts?

g. Pure madness?

Liscomb belched. Too much beer. He felt sleepiness creeping upward in him. He scanned the pages of notes, clipped them neatly and placed them in a file folder. He yawned and finished the Heineken.

In the rectory of the Church of St. Ignatius of Loyola, Father Daniel Conant sipped wine and pondered the quality of evil. Chief Liscomb had equated it with psychosis, an idea, Conant thought, not without value, since most of the world was crazy and most of its works evil. Whether it put modern psychology back two or three hundred years was no matter. Perhaps it was time to begin anew, for Freud had solved nothing. In the early days, the insane were thought to be possessed by the Devil. If Satan were behind it all, it became a simple and clear contest. Or did it? In Hebrew, Satan meant "enemy," and in Christian theology, the great "enemy" of man. And who was man's greatest enemy but himself? Back again to psychosis. Was there a mass psychosis, stemming from Original Sin itself? Psychosis or Satan, did it matter? You fight psychosis with reserpine, lithium, electroshock. But how would you fight Satan, Chief Liscomb? Or even find him?

The atmosphere was heavy over Holland County that night. A southeasterly wind had sprung up, and the cool air had retreated before it, replaced by a warm dankness, heavy, oppressive, and fetid.

And above Broadmoor, evil hovered like an ancient black falcon, flapping its broad wings, extending scaly talons, its hooked beak already bloody with first kill.

It would feed more, and nourish its nesting young.

CHAPTER 4

From the Journal of a Satanist:

Why do I feel impelled to write about this rotten thing, this despicable deed, to put it down in cold black and white and have it stare me in the face and remind me that I am dirt, turd, shit!?

What drives me? Who drives me?

He?

And why was I driven to send the horrible evidence of my failure through the mail, almost as if I wanted to flaunt my evil before the world, hold it up to their faces and boast and brag and gloat. Is it some kind of punishment for my crime?

I cannot write anymore.

I am sick. I want to vomit.

On a map, Holland County is an isoceles triangle with its base fronting on the North River, and its apex fifty-five miles to the east at Indian Falls, the outlet of Indian Head Reservoir. From Indian Falls, The Reach flows its twisting course from east to west, sometimes strong and silent, sometimes shallow and turbulent, riffling over boulders and fallen trees that hide German brown and eastern brook trout. Near King's Landing, The Reach widens, deepens, becomes brackish and forms a broad tidal pool emptying into the river and leaving King's Landing to the south.

Traffic is considerable on the river, a succession of tankers, barges and small freighters plying to and from the city 135 miles to the south. On a good day, the colorful jibs and mainsails of the King's Landing Yacht Club trace erratic patterns on the broad water, tacking, reaching, jibbing, racing or just plain cruising, but with every skipper alert for the first signs of the renowned and infamous North River squall.

It was in such a squall, in the year 1732, that a young trader by the name of Horatio King looked a watery grave in the eye, prayed quickly, and was delivered by Providence and a floating spar to the eastern shore. King never set sail on the river again, but settled in with the Indians, established a trading post, and lived to the ripe and wrinkled age of ninety-two. King's Landing had been unofficially founded.

Between The Landing, as it is locally called, and Indian Head Reservoir, which serves both the county and the city to the south, Route 14 traces its path along the south bank of The Reach, following almost every curve and crook. Along this blacktop county road, eastward from The Landing to Indian Head Reservoir, lie many of the towns and villages that form the backbone of the new Holland County and provide peace, comfort, and rusticity for the new settlers from the city, the artists, writers, musicians, and generally independent souls who "discovered" the county in the mid-fifties; bought old homes or built, and settled into lives of quiet work and oftentimes loud play: East Landing, Arrow, Leydenburg, Broadmoor, Shokan Forks, East Indian, Tyrone, Buttonville, and Indian Falls.

With a population of 819, Broadmoor leads the rest in size and was the original focus of settlement by the artists and writers. Its situation on The Reach, the backdrop of looming mountains to the north and east, its mixed bag of English and Dutch Colonial houses and churches appealed to their aesthetic taste. Beyond that, land and living were cheap.

Not so today. Acreage has almost quadrupled since the sixties, and property and homes north of The Reach are still zooming.

Transportation to and from the city is a question of car or bus along the interstate that loops around King's Landing like a giant concrete ribbon, the railroad no longer carrying passengers, but only occasional freight.

"Across the tracks" in Holland County means across The Reach, the haves living north of the stream along Willow Creek, Indian Falls Road, and the many small, twisting routes that lead toward the hills, the not-so-haves residing south of The Reach along Route 14 and the roads branching off.

The forests of Holland County are still deep and wild, stretching from the wet, marshy country near Devil's Pond in the south upward to the Great Ledges in the northeast, then eastward in a curving arc to North Leydenburg on the river. Much of this land is State Game Preserve, untouched and virgin. Hunters have been lost in these woods, some found, some never seen again.

There is much water in Holland County. The Reach itself, its myriad feeder streams, North Lake, Indian Pond and Black Pond in the north, and Devil's Pond in the south surrounded by treacherous marshland. Giant pickerel cruise the waters of Devil's Pond, and at least four known fishermen have given their lives in the quest.

And to the east, Indian Head Reservoir, lying just

outside the county line, but still considered part of it. Thirty miles long, ten wide, deep, secretive, mysterious.

Somewhere, Frank Liscomb thought, staring at the map, somewhere within this confusion of grids, contour tracks, elevation marks, dots, stars, crosses and twisting lines denoting roads, rivers and creeks, lies the body of a child.

And most probably close to Broadmoor.

The search was on.

On North Lake, two deputies from the village of Arrow sat in an outboard-powered rowboat, dragging bottom.

In the woods west of Willow Creek Road, between the West Branch and North Lake Road, Milt Framer and a party of nine spread out in a long flank, stepping steadily forward, beating the bushes, peering into ravines, overturning brush and fallen trees.

"It's up there, I'll bet ya," Framer said, standing erect, his eyes hard in the direction of Job's Ruins. "Up there in Hippieville. That's where we'll find it."

At the Broadmoor post office, patrolman Eddie Volner was questioning Zack Timmons. "Don't remember stamping a package like that," Zack was saying. "Was probably left in the box outside. I cancelled it sure, but I didn't sell no stamps for it."

At the Broadmoor garbage dump, Trooper Leon Harris waded in waist-deep with Carl Leyden, custodian of the dump and honorary chief of the Broadmoor "Department of Sanitation," emptying bags, overturning boxes, kicking aside tin cans, dead soldiers of Johnnie Walker, Booth's, Gordon's, Haig & Haig, Four Roses, and Hennessy.

"You sure got a high alcoholic rate in this town," Harris said.

"It's them writers and artists," Carl Leyden said. "I never seen people drink so much."

Harris got a sniff of Carl's breath and decided he went with the territory.

Nicole Bannister was released from Good Samaritan Hospital at 10:00 A.M. At 11:30, she and Jonathan sat with Frank Liscomb on the back lawn.

"You're asking me questions I can't answer, Mr. Liscomb," Nicole said. "How could I know who the child might be? It's not mine. It's none of my friends'. Nobody's missing. No child that I know of."

Liscomb's eyes were fastened on the small waterfall that dropped into Willow Creek, burbling over the stones and flowing out of sight around the corner of the house to the swimming pool. He cleared his throat uncomfortably, looking at Jonathan.

"What about you, Mr. Bannister?' he asked. "You been married before?"

"Yes, but like Nicole, no children. Why?" he asked. "What're you getting at?"

Liscomb shifted in his seat. "I don't know. It just occurred to me that . . . well, forget it." He rose, his eyes hooked to Jonathan's.

Jonathan got out of his chair. "I'll be back in a minute," he said to Nicole.

Alone, she sat quite still. There was a fear in her, a dark, primitive, welling horror. Why, after all these years, had it risen again? Had it something to do with that package? She shuddered.

The face of the priest came before her. She remembered his voice, soft, deep, reassuring. She would go to him. She would confess again.

How many times did she have to confess?

* * *

That afternoon, Liscomb called the FBI Field Office in Harringburg, forty miles to the north.

"I could use some help," he said. "I'd like everything you can get on two people: Jonathan Bannister, white, male, aged forty. Artist. Originally from New York City. Manhattan. His wife, Nicole Bannister, née Savidge. Age thirty-five. Born Topeka, Kansas." As many facts as Liscomb had gleaned, he gave; birthdates, parents' names, work, background. "Thanks very much," he said and depressed the button for a moment before dialing Tom Blauvelt.

"Tom? Frank Liscomb. What've you got?"

"We're working on it," Blauvelt said.

"Is it male or female?"

"That's difficult. We have blowups of electron-microscopy cells, but its not an exact science."

"I thought you said yesterday it was."

"If I did, I was wrong. We're looking for chromosomes, for chrissake. You know how big those are, Frank?"

Liscomb clucked. "Nothing seems to be exact with you people when you get right down to it. What about the age?"

"I'd say seven or eight, give or take six months."

"Very exact. Thanks, Tom."

"My pleasure."

Phones were cradled.

Liscomb picked up Griffen's report:

> The small print is, of course, from the exhibit. Wrapping paper revealed only smudges, probably from Zack Timmons and whoever delivered the package, plus Mrs. Bannister. Box itself gives excellent clear prints of Mrs. Bannister, plus thumb and forefinger of unknown. Unknown

prints match other prints found on desk, phone, and chair arm.

There followed a good deal of technical gobbledegook. Liscomb skimmed this and flipped through the pages of prints. Mrs. Bannister's were clear and well defined; those from the exhibit very small and soft and quite perfect. He was wondering about the "unknown."

In 1946, Colonel Josephus Hart had come from South Carolina to King's Landing with a bagful of money, an unquenchable thirst for bourbon, an unbridled ambition, and a total disdain for danger.

The money had come from the Army of the United States, where, as an officer in Special Services, Hart had engaged in any number of nefarious deals involving cigarettes, nylon stockings, blankets, clothing, meat, potatoes, dried eggs, and assorted provisions and supplies.

His thirst for bourbon was inherited, and his ambition was to build the finest resort in the state, a place of remoteness, good fishing, hunting, and hard drinking.

He began with a rough but comfortable camp on the slopes of Pinnacle Peak. Since the rivers ran with trout and the woods welled with deer, the camp prospered; so well, in fact, that Josephus Hart began a hotel, higher up the mountain, on no road but an uphill path, but with a view for a hundred miles south and west, naming it the New Columbia, in honor of the city in which he had been born.

The New Columbia opened in 1952. Six months later, due to the negligence of a guest who fell asleep smoking a cigarette, it was a charred ruin.

By now going broke, Josephus Hart retired down-hill to the original camp, New Charleston, which cred-itors found impossible to touch because it was a separate corporation. Here he lived until 1958, happy, robust, healthy, spinning yarns of his army days with friends and guests, until that night in November, dur-ing the deer season, when two of his old army buddies got into a drunken shootout over the screaming body of an attractive female. All might have gone well if the husband had not walked in.

After the dead and wounded had been removed, the New Charleston closed, never to re-open. The camp was sold to a disinterested party in New York City and Colonel Hart retired to the King's Landing Inn on the river. Here he sat, night after night, sip-ping bourbon, telling tall tales, conjuring up visions of the past from Salerno to the Bulge.

"There's old Job," they'd say, watching from the bar of the King's Landing Inn. "Lookit 'im guzzle. Shit, that man's got a hollow leg."

Unlike the Job of the Old Testament, Josephus never complained. He went along with a smile, a glint, full of new ideas and new hopes. He was going to build a new hotel, a new camp.

"Up to the top of the Great Ledges, they say. How's he goin' to make a road up to that?"

One night in the fall of 1962, Josephus Hart ap-appeared in the dining room of the King's Landing Inn dressed in khaki tunic and suntan pants, his colonel's chickens dazzling on his shoulders, his breast aflare with campaign ribbons. He had a drink and left, never to return.

They found him, six weeks later, in his uniform, face smashed almost beyond recognition, at the foot of the Great Ledges, towering four hundred feet above. Some said he jumped. Others said he was pushed. Some said he was just plain drunk.

No matter. The spot where he was found became known as Job's Jump.

Job's Jump. Job's Camp. Job's Ruins.

Freddie Loftus, picking blueberries, caught sight of Milt Framer and his group from a rise between the Camp and the Ruins. He left the pail of berries on the hill, went into his cabin and emerged with a loaded .30-caliber Winchester.

"What's going on?" Ken Brady asked.

"We got us some trespassers."

"Is that thing loaded?"

"Fuckin' A-right, it's loaded," Freddie said.

Ken dropped in beside Freddie as he headed toward the gate. "Take it easy, man. You don't want to kill somebody."

"They're on our property," Freddie said, rushing down the hill.

"Let me check this out alone, Freddie."

But Freddie plunged ahead, gripping the rifle tightly.

When Milt Framer saw the two figures approaching on Rut Road, he stood upright. "Here come the Jesus freaks," he said.

Slowing to a walk, Freddie came to a standstill on his side of a fieldstone wall. "You want something, man?"

Milt Framer spat. "We're a search party," he said.

"You're on private property," Freddie said.

"No we ain't." Framer took a step forward.

"This wall's the boundary," Freddie said, "and you got your foot on it."

"I got my foot on *my* side of it," Milt Framer said.

"Well, fuck you, man. Get it off."

Ken Brady took Freddie's shoulder. "Come on, Freddie. They're not on our property."

Freddie wrenched away. "Keep your cotton pickin' hands off me, man."

Ken looked at Framer. "What do you guys want up here?" he asked.

"This here's state land, this side of the wall," Framer said.

"I know that. But what're you looking for?"

"You ain't heard about what happened yesterday?"

"We heard."

"We're looking for the body," one of the men said.

"You won't find it up here," Freddie said. "Now get your asses movin'."

"Don't talk to me like that, you fuckin' degenerate," Milt Framer said.

The sound of the rifle split the forest air. High overheard, the bullet tore through the overhanging branches, loosening a pine cone that fell to the ground with a soft plop.

Freddie fed another cartridge into the breech, lowered the muzzle, pointing it straight at Framer.

"Move your ass," he said.

Ken waited, measuring the distance from the end of the rifle out of the corner of his eye.

Framer's mouth was dry, and there was a thickness in his throat.

"Come on, Milt," one of the men said. "We ain't got no cause up here."

Milt Framer spat once and then turned. The brush crackled as the men moved off.

* * *

Liscomb sighed. "What do you mean, he took a shot at you? You just told me he shot in the air."

"He didn't have no right!" Milt Framer said. "No fuckin' Jesus freak has a right to go blasting away with a rifle around me. I want him arrested, Chief."

"On what grounds?"

Milt Framer fumbled for words. "Well, what the hell," he finally said, "you figure out the grounds!"

"Look, Milt," Liscomb said, "what were you doing on his property in the first place?"

"I wasn't *on* his fuckin' property! I told ya! I was on state land. We all was! Ain't that right, Jerry?"

"That's right, Chief," Jerry Kraft said. "We was standing south of the old fieldstone wall. That's state land."

"Doing what?" Liscomb asked. "What were you all doing up there?"

Jerry Kraft looked at the floor. "Lookin' for the child, Chief."

"And what right have you got to do that? Are you guys some kind of self-appointed posse or something? Is that it?"

There was silence.

"I'll let you all in on a little secret," Liscomb said. "If the authorities want any help on this thing, we'll ask for it. You got that?" He paused. "All right, I'll have a talk with Freddie Loftus about his target shooting. Now, get the hell out of here. I got work to do."

The men rose and shuffled to the door. Milt Framer lingered for a moment, looking back.

"Well, Milt?" Liscomb said.

"I'm tellin' ya, Chief," Milt Framer said, "the body's up there. Up there with that Loftus and his freaks. They're degenerates. All of 'em."

CHAPTER 5

On the drive over to Oliver Marquith's office, Liscomb reflected on the recent history of Job's Camp.

In 1968, the hippies had descended on Holland County in droves to attend a two-week rock concert in Indian Falls. It was the county's first experience with "the beards," as they became known, and it was a bad marriage from the start. There were over ten thousand of them, and their sneakered, sandaled, and most often bare feet made soft patterns on the streets and roads from King's Landing to Broadmoor to Indian Falls, the site of the concert. Pot fumes and raucous laughter filled the restaurants and bars, and the heavy reverberations of electronic guitars boomed like thunderclaps in the hills and across the flatlands. There were a few pot busts, but in view of the huge numbers of users, the small number of available cells, and the ambiguous laws, the town fathers decided that a waiting game might be wiser. So the populace shrugged, pursed its lips, peered through curtained windows at the dirty jeans and long skirts, and prayed for the day of exodus.

When it was over, the concert site at Indian Falls was a wasteland of twisted beer cans, broken wine bottles, melon rinds, egg shells, crusts of bread and crushed roaches of marijuana. The champions of environmental protection had come and gone, and for all the damage, a huge sigh of relief swept through Holland County. The beards were gone. But not for long.

Six weeks later a psychedelic van filled with a dozen hirsute young men, eight long-haired, long-skirted girls, and three naked children moved through Broadmoor, crossed The Reach, turned left on Indian Falls Road, right toward North Lake, and right again on Rut Road to disappear in the direction of Job's Camp.

The following week, in response to a complaint about "squatters" at the Camp, Frank Liscomb found a commune of fifty-three adults and children in full operation. A deed to the land, held cooperatively by the "squatters" themselves, only confirmed to Liscomb and the village of Broadmoor that Hippieville had been legally founded, sold by a man in New York City, one of whose children turned out to be chief sachem of the commune.

Once again, the doors and shutters of Broadmoor were barred, and the "beards" found little acceptance or warmth. But progress, like natural erosion, is a slow and steady process, and within two years the hippies had carved their niche. They opened The Sensuous Herb, a coffeehouse, and The Tripping Out Inn, a beer, wine, and rock establishment, within the confines of Broadmoor itself.

Again, the booming beat of rock and the sweet smell of pot filled the air, and the population of Broadmoor, townie and city settler alike, rose in protest. After a few busts and a greater number of warnings, the decibel level at The Tripping Out Inn dropped, and the kids retreated to the commune to plan the next attack.

"I'm no arbiter of morals," Frank Liscomb was heard to say. "What people do in the privacy of their own homes or on their own land is their business. This pot thing is being blown way out of proportion anyway. Prohibition didn't work with alcohol, and it won't work with pot. What the hell, I used to take my own kind of trips on Four Roses when I was sixteen. But heroin," he added, "now that's something different."

The kids had been lucky in their choice of Broadmoor for a commune and lucky in having Frank Liscomb as Chief of Police. In Indian County, next door, they might have been crucified.

They were lucky too in their backgrounds. The progeny of educated, well-to-do parents, they came to Broadmoor with their own credentials—good schools, college years, a few full-fledged degrees—and with a seriousness of purpose that at once awed and fascinated the people of Broadmoor. Though bearded, bedenimed and somewhat careless of dress, they were also clean and polite. They took baths. They were softspoken. They smiled. They were friendly.

At the Camp, their vegetable gardens were neat and well planned, and the extra produce, health foods, and herbal teas they hawked at The Sensuous Herb did not go begging.

Twice a year, they brought their acrylic paintings, beadwork, and macramé into Broadmoor, and once they held an Old-Timer's Festival at The Tripping Out Inn, an unforgettable experience, since the strains of "Peg O' My Heart" to a rock beat becomes a study in confusion.

But below the surface the chasm yawned, the gap stretched wide and unfathomable. Though the townies, the settlers, and the hippies exchanged smiles, nods, words, and greetings, there was, in a word re-coined by the young, no real "dialog." The kids remained aloof, any inquiry into the real nature of their philosophy, way of life, or aspirations meeting with blank stares or mumbled words about "karma" or "energy flow." They did not seem to know, in the opinion of many among the intellectual set, who they were or where they were going. Ideals were enough. Ambition was "establishment." They were part of the "movement," yet they did not seem to move.

After 1968 and the death of Robert Kennedy, the movement itself seemed to become vapid and sluggish, began to dry up, crust and flake away. A new silence drifted down on the campuses, and slowly, gradually, the communes began to disband.

By the end of 1979, only a nucleus of the original cell at Job's Camp remained. The Sensuous Herb closed and The Tripping Out Inn became a German-American restaurant.

Bearded transients drifted in and out of the Camp, but it never again regained its original shape, size, or quality.

Then, in November of that year, a rattling truck bearing California plates lumbered into Rut Road. It held Freddie Loftus, Dimples, and a dozen others.

A strange amalgam of hippie and cult had been formed.

As he turned onto Main Street in King's Landing, Frank Liscomb was wondering just what sort of cult he was dealing with.

Judge Oliver Marquith swiveled slowly in the high-backed leather chair, twirling a silver pen end to end between his fingers. His thick, carefully marcelled hair was like a silver halo in the sunlight that streamed through the blinds.

"I guess I can issue a warrant, Frank," he said. "But why? What've you got to go on besides Milt Framer's grudge against the kids?"

"He made a complaint."

"Which is pretty thin any way you look at it. You yourself admit the warning shot was provoked by Milt."

Liscomb shifted uncomfortably. "I'd still like to search the place."

"All right," Marquith said, "I'll get you a warrant. But go easy, Frank. Some of those kids have powerful family connections downstate. Let's not upset the status quo."

"Freddie Loftus isn't connected," Liscomb said.

"Where does he hail from, anyway?"

"Somewhere in the west. He came from California. There's talk he was part of the Manson Family at one time."

"You sure?"

"No, I'm not, Ollie. It's just talk."

Marquith swiveled until he was gazing out through the blinds. "You ever hear of The Church of Higher Awareness, Frank?"

"Higher Awareness? What's that?"

"A group in England. They're supposed to be Satan worshipers."

"So?" Liscomb was puzzled.

"Very similar to the Manson group," Marquith went on. "Drug oriented, antisocial, way out, if you know what I mean. They hold sexual orgies, things like that." He swiveled back to stare at Liscomb. "As a matter of fact, the two groups are supposed to be connected in some way. The Manson Family and this Awareness Church."

"That's all very interesting, Ollie," Liscomb said. "But where does it fit?"

"This new bunch up at the Camp. They hold some kind of "Rites" every month, I hear. Sex orgies?"

"Maybe." Liscomb struck a match and brought it to the tip of his cigar. "But so what? You want to open up the books on the fornication law? Hell, we'd never get finished. And probably end up with everybody in the county behind bars."

Marquith laughed softly. "I wasn't thinking along those lines, Frank."

"What lines were you thinking along?"

"Well." Marquith paused. "Look at it this way. Sex orgies, drug-crazed people. It could lead to something more serious, couldn't it? Ritual murder? Human sacrifice? Don't forget Guyana."

"You'd sure like to run those kids out of Job's Camp, wouldn't you, Ollie?"

Marquith shrugged. "They certainly haven't improved the property value. And that's a mighty valuable piece of land."

"And no doubt you have a buyer in your pocket right now. Am I right?"

Marquith bristled. "You're the one who wants a search warrant."

"I just make it a habit to follow every lead. That's what I'm paid for." He rose. "Thanks, Ollie. If we find anything, you'll be the first to know." He started toward the door.

"Frank?"

Liscomb turned.

Judge Marquith was smiling. "You should never have been a cop."

"Oh? Why not?"

"You're too tolerant."

"I have an appointment with Dr. Hammond," Tom Blauvelt said to the receptionist.

"Yes, Dr. Blauvelt," the receptionist said, picking up the phone. "Will you have a seat, please?"

Blauvelt sat, sinking deep into the expensive leather couch, surveying first the receptionist, then his surroundings. Both met with his utmost approval, the girl being young, pretty, sexual, and most pleasant. Blauvelt felt a vague tightening in his groin. *If only I could take off a few pounds,* he thought, then checked himself, and examined the reception area. It was spacious and cheerful. Three walls were of glass and the fourth, pure white, formed a backdrop upon which large and obviously expensive abstracts hung in exploding blasts of bright color. The wall-to-wall carpet was a pastel blue, and the furnishings of chrome, glass and marble provided a pleasing balance of simple line and solid mass. Tom Blauvelt wondered what it would be like to work here, and whether or not the high salary would salve his conscience.

Set back deep in the woods between Broadmoor and Shokan Forks, Webster Laboratories was an anomaly in Holland County. A subdivision of one of the largest pharmaceutical concerns in the country, WebLabs, as it was known locally, provided jobs in an area otherwise on the brink of industrial poverty. Except for a traprock company near North Leyden and a cable extrusion plant near Pikeville, Holland County had been a depressed area for years, its local revenue coming from restaurants catering to tourist and transient trade, a few resort hotels and motels, three fishing camps, and a succession of antique shops along Route 14 south of The Reach.

In appearance more like a country club than a division of giant industry, WebLabs offered a small but reasonable amount of work to the local citizenry as laboratory assistants, clerks, typists, janitors, and kitchen help.

The elite of WebLabs—the doctors, scientists, Ph.D.'s, managers, and vice-presidents—came from the outside, in fact from many nations around the world. These were the intelligentsia, the people who studied cell structure, genes, chromosomes, hormones, enzymes. Many of them owned the best houses in the county, and none of them seemed to work terribly hard.

At least that's what Tom Blauvelt was thinking when the receptionist said, "Dr. Hammond will see you now, Dr. Blauvelt. He's in Room Two-North-One-twenty-four in the lab building."

"I know the way, thanks," Blauvelt said and waddled out of the reception room.

In Hammond's large corner office, overlooking the lawn, Blauvelt plumped himself into an uncomfortable narrow wooden chair. Except for Hammond's own Eames behind the desk, the office was Spartan.

"Good to see you, Tom," Hammond said. His words were short, clipped, as was his whole demeanor. A sharp, chiseled little man, he resembled a jumping bean with a bald head. "Jesus, Tom," he said, passing the palm of his hand to where hair had once sprung. "Jesus, I'm only thirty-seven and look at this! Why doesn't WebLabs work on that problem, huh?"

Blauvelt smiled. "You were born to be an egghead, Marion."

"There's an answer, you know that, don't you?"

Hammond said. "It's a simple matter of hormone balance."

"If it's that simple, count me in," Blauvelt said. "We'll make a fortune. What'll we call the product?"

"*Hair*," Hammond said. "Simple, concise, and to the point. *Hair*."

"That's not bad," Blauvelt said. "I'd never have thought of it."

"It's a girl, Tom," Hammond said at last. "At least I think it's a girl."

"You sure?"

"I said I *think*. C'mere." He rose and moved quickly into an adjoining room that served as a laboratory. White vinyl tables were spread with notebooks, graphs, plastic overlays, columns of figures. Tacked to a bulletin board were blowups of electron photo-microscopy.

Hammond took a pencil and tapped. "There's the double-X chromosome. Faint. But it's there."

Blauvelt leaned closer. "Very faint. Can we be sure?"

Hammond paused. "I think so."

"You seem hesitant."

"This is the fourth series of photographs, Tom. For chrissake, it's not an XY."

"But it's faint, as you said. Could it be the photography?"

"We checked it against a control group. It's not the photography."

"Then you'll bet it's a girl? The finger came from a female?"

Hammond turned his palms upward and smiled. "I bet."

"Okay," Blauvelt said. "If you say so, I say so.

You're the expert." He turned to leave. "I'll let the police know."

"One thing, Tom," Hammond said.

Blauvelt turned.

"There's no Golgi apparatus." He was looking at the photographs.

Rusty wheels cranked in Blauvelt's brain. Golgi apparatus? It was all very dim. "All right, I'm getting old," he said. "Golgi apparatus?"

Hammond was tapping the pencil against the enlargement of the cell. "You remember, Tom. In every human cell"—the pencil tip moved with his words—"we see these things: nucleus, nucleolus." The pencil moved upward. "Lysosome."

"Centriole," Blauvelt said as the pencil moved down to the left.

"Right. And mitochondria." He indicated two wormlike blotches near the plasma membrane. "But," Hammond said, and began to draw four elongated, rod-shaped forms within the cell, downward and to the right of the nucleus, "no Golgi apparatus. I have to draw them in."

"Golgi *bodies*," Blauvelt murmured. "I knew them as Golgi *bodies*. But damned if I remember what they're supposed to do, what function they serve."

"They're a kind of storage area," Hammond said. "A warehouse for proteins manufactured by the cell." He dropped the pencil and turned to Blauvelt. "They're supposed to be there. And they're not." He turned his palms upward again, and his eyebrows arched. "I've never seen anything like this before, Tom. Have you?"

When Blauvelt did not answer, Hammond started back into his office. "C'mon," he said. "I've got a bottle in the bottom drawer. We'll celebrate an earth-shattering discovery. The hell with *Hair*."

* * *

"How old are you, Susan?" Liscomb asked.

"Twenty," she said.

"I thought you were headed for college."

"I did a year at UCLA," Susan said.

"You didn't like it?"

Silence.

Liscomb grunted. "How's Ken Brady?"

"Ken's all right."

"He's a nice boy."

Susan did not answer.

Liscomb put a flame to his cigar. "You two figure on getting married?"

Susan flared. "Now look, old Chief," she said, "I came in here when you asked me to. I gave you my fingerprints. I admitted I picked up that weird box. Now what else do you expect? You sound like a shrink!"

"I've known you since you were three years old, Sue. Doesn't that make any difference?"

"Not one bit," Susan said. She rose.

Liscomb clamped down hard on his cigar and got up, accompanying her to the door and then out to the parking lot.

"How's your father?" he asked as they crossed the gravel toward her car.

"He's all right." Her tone was flat, noncommittal.

"Mother okay?"

"My stepmother?" Susan shrugged. "Ask her."

Susan was in the car, turning the ignition, when Liscomb said, "How's Freddie Loftus behaving himself?"

Susan's look was sharp. "How should I know?"

"You go up to the Camp now and then, don't you?"

The engine coughed into life as Susan said, "Not to see Freddie Loftus." The car inched ahead.

Liscomb watched it exit the lot and turn on Main Street. *Kids,* he thought. *Kids!*

Estelle Dixon's eyes were slits. There were deep frown lines between them. Her lips were tight, compressed, her concentration intense.

Under the light touch of her fingers, the planchette moved slowly, erratically over the Ouija board.

"You're pushing!" she said.

"I'm not pushing," Hank Dixon said.

"Yes, you are! I can tell when you're pushing!"

"I'm telling you, I'm not pushing, goddammit!"

"Make your fingers light. Very light. Concentrate."

"On what?"

"On nothing," Estelle said. "Concentrate on nothing. That's what you're supposed to do."

"How can I concentrate on nothing?"

"You can! Now try it! Do what I tell you!"

Dixon sighed. *Jesus,* he thought. *What a way to spend an afternoon. Jesus.*

The planchette described an awkward arc toward the center of the Ouija board. It stopped.

"*O,*" Dixon called out.

"Don't take your fingers off!" Estelle's voice was tight. "It's going to move again. I can feel it!"

But the planchette remained inert, still, unyielding.

Dixon rose. "I got work to do," he said.

"You're spoiling it!" Estelle cried.

"Horseshit. The thing's tired. Can't you see that?" He drifted off to the staircase.

"Don't you *drink* anything!" she called after him.

"I wouldn't think of it," he said, mounting the stairs.

Taking a pad, Estelle jotted down the seven letters at which the planchette had paused. She frowned. They made no sense. Then she thought, *It's an anagram. That's what it is, an anagram!*

Her pencil moved quickly, arranging, rearranging, blocking, circling.

Finally, she rose from the chair and went to the foot of the stairs.

"Henry!" she screamed.

"What?"

"Fuck you, too!"

Father Conant slid the confessional panel gently to the open position. On the opposite side of the screen, he heard the slight rustle of clothing, the hesitant breathing.

"Yes, my child," he said softly.

"Oh, my Father I have sinned," the voice said.

"In what way have you sinned, my child?"

There was silence, broken only by the soft whisper of breath.

Father Conant coughed lightly. "In what way have you sinned, my child?"

"It wasn't my fault, Father."

"What wasn't your fault?"

"I have killed, Father."

Father Conant's hands tightened on his knees. His throat felt constricted. He was conscious of a strong pulse in his neck.

"Go on, my child."

The voice began again, then was lost in a choking rasp, then found itself and said, "I have killed a child, Father."

Conant was sweating. He inhaled deeply and when

he spoke, his voice was still soft. "Tell me," he said. "Don't be afraid."

The voice went on, hesitant, anguished, torn. Father Conant listened, his fingers tight on his knees, his neck stiff, his throat dry.

When it was over, when the figure had risen unseen and silent, had brushed through the curtains, when the steps had echoed down the aisle toward the altar, he sat very still in the confessional, not moving.

CHAPTER 6

Freddie Loftus was sleeping when the three police cars rolled into Job's Camp. Dimples roused him.

"It's the man!" she shouted.

"What?" Freddie's eyes were open but unfocused. He was still half out on LSD.

"It's the fucking law," Dimples said. "They're all over the place!"

"Lemme alone," Freddie said, and dropped back on the mattress.

Dimples clawed at him, pulling his shirt. "Get up, Freddie! Get up for chrissake!"

Freddie screamed, brushing at the girl's hands, his eyes wide and frenzied. "My heart!" he shouted. "I'm having a heart attack! Don't let 'em stop my heart! Please!"

Then his eyes closed, and his head slammed back against the pillow.

"Jesus!" Dimples said. "What a time to pick!"

Outside, on a path near the West Branch, Ken Brady approached Frank Liscomb.

"Hi, Chief," he said. There was a broad smile on his face, but his eyes were wary, flicking here and there as the uniformed police, looking sullen and hostile, began to disperse through the Camp.

"Hello, Ken," Liscomb said. "Got a light?"

Ken flicked a Zippo and held it to Liscomb's cigar. "What's this, a bust?"

"Not exactly," Liscomb said.

"What're you looking for?" Ken was glancing sidewise. Some of the cops were peering into garbage cans. Others were looking into gullies and piles of scrap. One was kicking at a compost heap.

"Take a walk with me, Ken," Liscomb said.

They followed a path along the stream under heavy branches of pine. Liscomb puffed on his cigar. Ken chewed on a blade of grass.

"Where'd you go when you left here a few years ago?" Liscomb asked.

Ken shrugged. "Everywhere."

"Mostly on the communes?"

"I did the commune scene, yeah," Ken said. "Oregon. Washington. California. I crashed in San Francisco for a while."

Liscomb picked out a flat rock and sat on it. "You ever come across the Manson Family?"

Ken stared at him, brows raised. "Are you kiddin', man?"

"I just wondered."

"What would I want with that?"

"Nothing, I'm sure. Only I hear Freddie Loftus might have been part of them at one time."

"That's ludicrous," Ken laughed.

"Is it?"

"Of course."

"What do you know about Freddie?"

"Nothing. Just that he was here when I got back a few months ago."

"You get along with him?"

"He minds his business, I mind mine. He bought into the place, he's entitled to his share." Ken paused. "Anything else, Chief?"

"No, I guess not." Liscomb rose, pointing himself back to the Camp. "You kids sure stick together, don't you?"

"Don't you and your kind?"

"We're not that different, Ken," Liscomb said. "I was young once. And someday, you'll be old. Don't forget that."

Further on, Liscomb stopped and searched his pockets for matches. Ken gave him his lighter. "Ever hear of The Church of Higher Awareness?" Liscomb asked, straining his words through the blunt end of the panatella.

"The what?"

"The Church of Higher Awareness, something like that. Satan worshipers."

"Nope. Never heard of them," Ken said.

Liscomb grunted. "Okay, Ken," he said and walked on.

In Freddie's cabin, Liscomb asked, "What's wrong with him? He drunk?"

Freddie Loftus was out cold. Nothing would wake him.

"Not exactly," Ken said.

"He's tripping," Dimples said. "Didn't you ever trip?"

"I'll trip you right on your ass!" Volner said.

"Shut up, Volner," Liscomb said.

Dimples pulled out a battered cigarette case, took a joint from it, lit up, and blew thick pot fumes into Liscomb's face.

"That's grass," she said. "G-R-A-S-S, grass. Like ass but with a G. You want a drag, fuzzy-wuzzy?"

"No," Liscomb said.

"You want to arrest me, fuzzy-wuzzy? Go ahead. Arrest me. You got all the evidence."

"No," Liscomb said. "But I'll tell you what, miss. If I do arrest you, there's a judge over in King's Landing who'd just love to get his hands on you and all the rest of your friends here. And you know what? You and Freddie and everybody else would be out of Holland County on your asses sooner than you could say marijuana. And if you ever came back, you'd find the land wasn't yours anymore. So blow any more of that shit in my face and we'll test it out, okay?"

Dimples inhaled deeply, held it, then exhaled toward the floor.

"Get off my property," she said. "Your feet are dirtying up my floor."

In the car, Volner could not contain himself. "Why didn't you arrest that fucking little slut!"

"Because," Liscomb said, "that's exactly what she wanted me to do."

Volner was silent for a moment, then said, "You sure called it quits early, Chief. That wasn't much of a search."

"I didn't expect to find anything," Liscomb said. "If it's up there, it's well hidden. If not destroyed by now."

"Then why go up in the first place?"

"I wanted to get the feel of it," Liscomb said. "And meet Freddie Loftus." He paused. "Unfortunately, he wasn't very meetable today."

Six o'clock. Things come alive then, Jonathan thought. Warblers practice their scales and flit from tree to tree. The kingfisher cocks his head and swoops in low to the water, shrieking. Early insects begin to hum in the woods. There is the tail-slap of a feeding fish.

He stood at the poolside, flipping a small golden spinner to within a foot of the opposite shore, retrieving slowly, flipping again, retrieving. Fishing without heart, without interest. A reflex action.

The lure was near the surface of the water when the fish hit with a hard thump. Jonathan's wrist snapped back. The rod bowed, throbbed. The water swirled. He played it slowly, carefully.

It was a small trout, less than eight inches. Squatting, he carefully opened the mouth, delicately removed the single small hook. Holding the tiny fish gently, he dropped his hand into the pool, opening his fingers. The fish darted into the darkness.

At the gravelly step behind him, Jonathan twisted quickly, his fists clenched.

"Any luck?" Hank Dixon asked.

"I wasn't really trying," Jonathan said. He rose.

"This is what I call life-style," Dixon said. "Man wants to go fishing, all he has to do is walk to his swimming pool."

"They stock the stream above and below," Jonathan said. "You can fish your section."

"I don't have a pool like this," Dixon said. "Just an iddy biddy poo. A hole." A bottle of Boodles appeared like magic from behind his back. "Have one on me for a change."

Jonathan went for ice and glasses, and they sat on the back lawn under a small stand of birch.

"How's Nicole?"

"All right," Jonathan said. "A little shocked. Who wouldn't be shocked? But she's taking it all right." *No, she's not*, he thought. *She's warping. She's turning into herself again, like she did during that last break-down.*

"Susan took a look at that thing," Dixon said. "She almost puked."

Doesn't the man have any tact, Jonathan wondered.

Dixon seemed to read his mind. He shuffled uneasily. "I'm sorry," he said. "Didn't mean it to come out that way."

Jonathan gave a slight shrug. "It's got us all upset, I guess."

"I don't understand it."

"Who does?" Jonathan had been staring up at Nicole's study window. The light was still on, but the clatter of the typewriter had ceased. She was drawing now. He pictured her, huddled over the drawing board, her fingers moving in quick, deft strokes, creating the mischievous eyes, the sly smiles of children, their small, pudgy bodies running, rolling, cavorting. And the animals, the wise bears and gentle deer, the proud birds, the comical insects.

"Christ!" he said aloud. "Why the hell would anybody want to do that to a person like Nikki?"

"I know what you mean," Dixon said.

"There's things a man can understand," Jonathan said. "Or try to understand. Like robbery, mugging. Rape, even. But shit, Hank! A child! And to send— to send part of it like that to her? Why?"

Dixon was uneasy. He'd come to gossip, not to face reality. "Evil," he said. "There's evil in the world. The world stinks of it."

"Evil! This is worse than evil!"

They sat there, uncertain in their fears, afraid of the future, powerless in the face of the inexplicable. They drank.

Dixon looked at his watch. "I'd better be going,"
he said. "Estelle's serving roast leg of pizza for dinner." He rose, looking down at Jonathan, feeling
embarrassed by his attempt at humor. "I guess the
party's off," he said.

"Uh?" Jonathan looked up, vacant, his mind elsewhere.

"Nicole's birthday party. I guess you're going to
postpone."

Jonathan poured another round. "Sit down a minute," he said. "This is your booze. Let me get a whack
at it." He rolled the ice around in his glass, staring
upward over Dixon's seated shoulder toward the light
in Nicole's window. "I don't know. It might do her
good, Hank. Having people in."

"You know her best."

"She likes a good bash. Maybe this is the time to
have one. It'll make her come out of herself. What
do you think?"

Dixon shrugged. "Can't hurt. Think she'll want
to?"

"I can ask. It was supposed to be a surprise party,
but I think I'd better talk it over with her."

"It's next week, isn't it?" Dixon asked.

"Next Friday."

"You can count on us." Dixon said.

"Now you swim it back to me," Leslie said.

It was a plastic duck, a rather expensive plastic
duck that Nicole had bought at F.A.O. Schwarz. It
jerked lazily down the tub, reeling, bouncing, describ-
ing awkward circles as Leslie's hands roiled the water
behind it.

"Now you come on, Elsie," Leslie said when the

duck arrived at the other end of the bathtub. "You swim it back."

The duck rolled and bobbed and flashed its large amber eyes, but never moved.

"Oh, damn you, Elsie! You never want to play! Now you push the ducky back! Do as I say!"

"Who you damning, girl?" Pearl DeWitt's broad hulk stood framed in the bathroom door.

"Elsie never does what I tell her to," Leslie said.

"Elsie don't exist, that's why she don't do what you tell her."

"She *does* exist!"

"Well, if she do exist," Pearl said, looking toward the tub, "she sure as thin as the air. Now you get to washing your back and stop talking to that no existing child."

"Damn you, Elsie! Push ducky back, I said!"

"And you watch your mouth!" Pearl said. "Elsie don't use such mean language. Do you Elsie?" She found herself staring at an empty space in the tub. *Lord have mercy!* she thought. *I getting as bad as that child!*

"You scrub your back good," Pearl said and departed, shaking her head.

"Pearl will never understand, will she, Elsie?" Leslie asked of the end of the tub. "She doesn't see so good, either!"

Elsie was silent.

"Let's sing, Elsie," Leslie said.

"Goody, goody, goody!" Elsie said.

And Leslie in a piping tremolo, began:

> Up went the spider,
> Up the water spout,

Down came the water,
And washed the spider out. . . .

The child, a little girl, was holding an insect, a rather haughty ladybug, in the palm of her hand. But the child's fingers were missing. Instead, there were only smears and squiggles of india ink.

Nicole flicked a cigarette lighter, holding it with both hands. They shook alarmingly.

She inhaled deeply, blew the smoke, and leaned back in the high director's chair. Why couldn't she get it out of her mind? Why did it persist? Must she relive that moment over and over again?

How vivid it was, and all that led up to it. The sunlight bright on the mailbox. The letters and bills inside. The sound of her heels on the gravel. Upstairs. Looking at the package. The unwrapping. The slender black box. The lifting of the lid.

The nausea suddenly gripped her again, wrenching at her stomach. Her breath became short.

She rose and went quickly to the cabinet below the bookcase where she kept a bottle of cognac. As she poured, the bottle neck clinked against the glass. The liquid swirled, almost slopped over the brim.

She dropped into the couch facing the fireplace and sipped slowly, letting the brandy ooze downward, feeling its swift magic warm and soothe her.

She'd been overdoing this lately, she knew that. But she couldn't let Jonathan see her shake. She couldn't. He'd worry. He'd think she was going into another nosedive, another breakdown. No. She'd be all right. It would pass. It was the shock. After all, it was only a few days ago. She had to give it time.

She glanced down at her drink, measuring. She'd poured quite a bit. Over two fingers.

Fingers! Oh, my God!

She held the tears back, fighting them, clenching her muscles, almost biting on her tongue. She drank. The warmth drifted outward into her limbs, inward into her being. She began to feel lightly afloat, but the images remained—softer now, but there.

It's a punishment, she thought. All her life she had expected this punishment, and now it was here. Somebody knew. Somebody knew her sin.

Somebody was trying to get back at her for that sin, confront her with her own guilt. That was the reason, the only reason, she decided, that the package had been sent. To torture her, to make her suffer the unbearable agony of remembrance.

But who? Who knew? Who *could* know? She had never told anyone, not even Jonathan.

She was aware of silence. The voices on the lawn had drifted away, then stopped altogether. Then she heard the screen door bang and Jonathan's heavy tread on the stair.

Jonathan lurched slightly as he entered the room, holding an old-fashioned glass of gin.

"Look," he said, perching himself on the drawing board chair, "this was supposed to be a surprise, but since I'm telling you, it's not a surprise."

"That figures," Nicole said. She had regained her composure, thrust the thoughts of terror aside. She attempted a smile.

"What I mean is," Jonathan continued, "next Friday's your birthday."

"That's not a surprise. And I'll be an old bag of thirty-five."

"Bag or no bag, you deserve a party. That's the surprise."

"What?" Nicole was confused.

"I'm throwing you a surprise party."

"Well, that's a surprise."

"No, it's not. I mean it isn't anymore. I mean, if you don't feel up to it, say so."

"Why shouldn't I feel up to it?" Her answer was too quick, but Jonathan seemed not to notice.

"All right, it's a deal," Jonathan said. "I'm throwing you a surprise party."

Nicole laughed. "This *is* a surprise."

"All right, now here's who I'm inviting," Jonathan said. "Anybody you don't want, anybody you think you might not want to see, you just say so, kid."

"Fire away."

"The Dixons, of course. The Hammonds, the Brewsters, Nick and Marijane Reilly. Judge and Mrs. Marquith."

"So far, so good," Nicole said.

"Joe Tremper and that broad who's living with him."

"I don't know about that," Nicole said.

"Why?"

"That 'broad' is twenty-six and built like a brick Taj Mahal. Every lecher at the party—and so far you've named only lechers—will be chasing her through the cattails."

"You're just jealous."

"Of course I am. All right, so invite Joe and his sackmate."

"Tom Blauvelt and Maria."

Maria was a woman of fifty-five who looked thirty. She had olive skin, a slender figure, dark hair, lustful eyes, and spoke with a foreign accent. Her full name was Maria Rivera Braithwaite. She was a widow who dabbled in art, writing, and gossip, and who lived on a fixed income of about two-hundred-thousand a year.

"They don't go together," Nicole said. "Maria and Tom."

"Well, what do you suggest?"

"For Tom? How about Agnes Bittel?"

Jonathan lifted his shoulders. "Nebbish. But why not?"

"It's Maria I worry about. There are so few single men around. Attractive single men."

"How about Les Carter?"

"Invite him, by all means. But not for Maria. She likes the unusual, the offbeat."

"So?"

"So what about that priest?"

"What priest?"

"That nice priest we met at the hospital. Father Conant."

Jonathan's right eyebrow went up. "Are you kidding? A priest at a bash like this? This'll be a meeting of Alcoholics Anonymous!"

"Priests drink," she said. "Every Sunday."

"Not like this! Besides, all that crowd talks about is sex and adultery. And they don't pay much attention to their language when they get sloshed."

"Oh, come on, Jon," Nicole said. "You know we've never thrown a party without inviting somebody offbeat. It adds tang, zest. Anyway, it's not like he's the Pope."

"Now *there* would be a coup," Jonathan said. "All right, let's ask him, although I doubt he'll come. Now, what about Les Carter?"

"I was thinking of Carole Kollars," Nicole said.

They went on, adding to the guest list, planning

the menu, the music, the service. The tension of the previous days eased between them, and soon it was like old times, careless, free, hopeful, funny.

Finally, Nicole asked, "Is this still supposed to be a surprise party?"

"Sure. Why not?"

"Okay. I'll be surprised."

As the days passed, Frank Liscomb became increasingly more irritable, smoking twenty cigars a day instead of his self-rationed twelve, drumming his fingers on desk, dashboard, table, any convenient flat surface.

"I don't understand it," he said to the FBI agent over the phone. "Here we have an obvious child-slaying and no body."

"We're doing our best, Chief," the agent said.

Liscomb grunted. "You mean to tell me you have no reports on missing children?"

"Sure. The usual crop. But none in your area, and none of that age. The youngest we've got, and that's in Iowa, is fourteen."

"I don't understand it," Liscomb said.

"We're doing our best, Chief."

"You said that before."

There was a light growl on the other end of the line. "Can you show us evidence of a kidnapping, Liscomb? That's our bailiwick, you know."

"I can show you a child's severed finger!" Liscomb snapped.

"I've seen the pics and read the reports," the agent said, and his tone softened. "Sorry, Chief, but we have nothing to report at this time. I'll let you know soon as we turn up anything. How's your search going?"

"We've got over fifteen hundred square miles of woods and water in Holland County alone. And who knows whether the crime was even committed here."

"Nothing, huh?"

"Nothing. And I'm only township police."

"Well," the agent fumbled, "we'll keep on it, Chief. By the way, you'll be getting those backgrounds you asked for. On the Bannisters."

"Good," Liscomb said. "And you can add one more. Freddie Loftus."

"Freddie who?"

"Loftus." Liscomb spelled it out. "He might have had something to do with The Church of Higher Awareness."

"I think I've heard of that," the agent said. "Okay, Chief, we'll get back to you."

"Thanks."

Liscomb cradled the phone and sat for long moments, chewing the end of his cigar.

Goddammit, he said to himself. *Goddammit, I don't understand.*

CHAPTER
7

Judge Oliver Marquith finished his second martini and dug into the sauerbraten and potato pancakes. Two drinks before lunch was his rule, never more unless the occasion demanded, and then only one additional. Never any alcohol *with* the food. It spoiled the palate, wrecked the flavor, dizzied the senses.

And Oliver Marquith's senses were acute today, bright, humming, alive with the sugarplums of acquisition and greed.

It was a bright day, a good day. Strong sunlight shafted through the leaded windows of Granger's Bull and Bear Restaurant, dappling the dark oak tables and glancing off the pewter dinnerware. Throughout the dining room, the conversation was a subdued bantering, mostly about money, land, progress, enlargement and development, interspersed with light chuckles or sudden roaring laughter.

People looked in the direction of Judge Marquith's regular table, nodded, crooked a finger, smiled, or waved a hand. Some approached him. Most were swiftly dealt with and rebuffed.

Tuesday was Oliver Marquith's day for dining alone, for savoring his food and his life.

In evaluating, estimating, measuring his life span,

Marquith often compared himself to the men he had grown up with—Milt Framer, Tom Blauvelt, Frank Liscomb, Harold Brewster.

All of them sons of Holland County, as boys they had done and seen the same things: played baseball together, skated on North Lake, hunted up toward the Great Ledges, fished The Reach and its feeders, dated the same girls, seen the same movies, read the same books. Not that Milt Framer ever read much of anything except the funnies.

How long past it seemed, and yet so near in the mind. He had gone to Fordham, Blauvelt to Harvard, and Frank Liscomb straight into the army, slogging his way north up the Boot, until they met, close to V-E Day in Paris where Marquith was attached to the Judge Advocate General's Department.

Milt Framer had come back from the South Pacific vacant-eyed and a nervous wreck, and had spent three years in the mental hospital in Clarendon. Harold Brewster had returned with only one leg and a bitterness he was never to lose.

Marquith had set up a law practice in King's Landing, while Blauvelt had established himself in Broadmoor as an internist. Brewster had nursed his bitterness and earned a living from his father's rock quarry in North Leyden. The fighting infantryman, Liscomb, had been content to become a cop, the bright Harvard medical graduate, a coroner. The young eager lawyer was now a judge.

Not a bad life, Marquith thought. *I've done pretty well.* He sighed. The sauerbraten was sitting badly, and he burped lightly into a napkin. He finished his coffee, vowing never again to have more than one cup with lunch, signed the check, rose, smiled vaguely in all directions, nodded once or twice and then, erect and judgelike, strutted proudly to the door and out into the parking lot.

Traveling westward from Tyrone to King's Landing, Marquith was about to turn left on the bridge at East Indian when his mind clamped like a vise on Job's Camp. Rather than crossing The Reach and taking the smoother Route 14, he continued along Indian Falls Road, the engine of the Continental a soft accompaniment to his thoughts.

Visions of sugarplums again danced in Oliver Marquith's head as he counted eighty acres and multiplied by five thousand. Simple arithmetic. By the time, one or two years hence, when the new IBM think tank and seminar center went up at North Lake and the new spur of the interstate turned east, those eighty acres would fetch at least ten thousand apiece.

Already in Marquith's head the plans were taking shape, the excavations made, the foundations laid. He saw the new glass-fronted Skytop Motel nestling into the shoulder of Pinnacle Peak where Job's Ruins now stood. He looked down upon the campsite itself and saw it suddenly devoid of the broken-down shacks, cluttered instead with the split-level homes and neatly trimmed lawns of junior executives. Along North Lake Road, he spied villa after villa, hidden among the trees, and heard the soft laughter and tinkling glass of executive cocktail parties. And on the lake itself, a new disco, sparkling with chrome, nested with Naugahyde booths, its dance floor aglitter under hidden spots, its stone terrace overlooking the moonlit lake. Shades of 1937, he thought, and chuckled.

He whizzed past the bridge that led into Broadmoor, and seven miles further, took a right into

North Lake Road, his mind turning as fast as the Continental's wheels.

He knew damn well what old Josephus Hart had paid for the land. Twenty-five dollars an acre! A steal! Christ, why hadn't he been that smart? But it was hilly, uncleared land, and no one had wanted it. Except Hart. A visionary. Too early for his time. The time was now.

The kids had picked it up for a song. Marquith knew that, too. One of the young men's fathers had sold it to them, probably just to get his own kid out of the house.

Approaching Rut Road, he made a quick decision, swung the wheel and turned in.

Five hundred yards further along, the left rear wheel of the Continental spun crazily in a mired hole. The rear end of the machine swung to the right and scraped a sharp rock.

Marquith shoved the shift into neutral, got out, mopped his forehead and swore. "Goddamn kids!"

Back in the car, he spun the wheels again.

"Keep doing that and you'll hang your axle up," a voice said.

Marquith looked up the road to the advancing figure, tall, lanky, long-haired, smiling. "Goddamndest road I ever saw," Marquith said.

"You don't want to ride a set of wheels like that in here," Ken Grady said. "You could just as easily total it on the interstate."

"I was looking for the Brewster place," Marquith lied.

"That's up three driveways. Let's see if we can shove this out. Best for you to back out. She in neutral?"

Marquith nodded and stepped in beside Ken, standing before the hood.

"One, two, three!" Ken said, and pushed.

One, two, three occurred six times. The Lincoln stared back at them unmoving, uncooperative, a modern mule of steel, chromium, and glass.

Marquith lifted his arms to allow sweat to trickle down his shirt sleeves. "You got a phone?" he asked.

"Up at the Camp? Yeah, one. But we don't need a garage. I'll get a board." He started away.

"I'll come along," Marquith said. "Mind?"

"I always like company," Ken said. He wondered who his company was. A quick glance at the car's plates, OM-3, had told him this was VIP material. "My name's Ken Brady."

"Oliver Marquith."

They shook, and Ken liked the strong grip of the man.

By the time they reached the Camp, Marquith's shirt was sweat-stained and his collar was a soggy choker around his neck. He was panting from exertion.

But he smiled broadly when he asked, "You happen to have a beer handy, Ken?"

"Sure, down at my place. Come on."

They drank in silence for a while. Then Marquith, who had been making an act of looking about, at the trees, at the sky, at the flowing waters of the West Branch, cleared his throat and said, "Nice piece of property, Ken. You own it?"

"This?"

Marquith didn't understand.

"You mean this? This cabin?"

"This cabin. The others. The land."

"We all do," Ken said.

"We?"

Ken stared at him for a moment and then broke into a high-pitched laugh. "You're on a commune, man."

"You mean a group of you own it."

"Yeah, that's it. A group of us. We bought shares."

"Must have cost you a pretty penny."

Ken shrugged. "Not when you divide it up. I think there were about a dozen of us originally. The whole package was about four thou."

Marquith's head spun. *Jesus! Fifty dollars an acre! Goddamn kids!*

He smiled and rose. "Well, thanks for the beer, Ken. I appreciate it."

"I'll go back with you," Ken said, reaching for the board.

As they walked through the Camp, Marquith's eyes shifted from right to left, back and forth. "How many acres all told, Ken?"

"About eighty, I think."

"Eighty. That's a nice spread. I guess you youngsters could realize a pretty good profit if you ever wanted to sell."

They had reached the car. Ken jammed the plank under the tire, and after two tries, Marquith was free of the ditch.

"If any of us want out," Ken said, "we have to sell to the others. It's in the agreement."

Sitting at the wheel, Marquith fumbled for his wallet and took out a card.

"Well, who knows," he said, handing the card to Ken, "one of these days you might all decide to shift gears."

"Maybe," Ken said.

"And if that ever happens, I'd be glad to talk to you. I have a few friends who might be interested in land up this way. 'Course it's on the rough side. Hilly. Uncleared. Lot of stones. But you know, I might be able to make you a rather handsome profit on your investment. Maybe two, two-fifty an acre."

There were several seconds of silence and then Ken began to laugh.

Marquith suddenly knew he had made a mistake in underestimating the boy. Yet he smiled, arching his eyebrows. "You think that's not a fair offer?"

"Man!" Ken said. "We *know* we can get more than that. Eight hundred, maybe even more."

Marquith shrugged. "Maybe so," he said. "I'm not much when it comes to estimating real estate."

"Anyway," Ken said, "we don't want to sell. Right, Freddie?" The last words were called out to the approaching Freddie Loftus.

"Right what?" Freddie said, nearing the car.

"That we don't want to sell any land. This dude here was making an offer."

"I didn't exactly make an offer," Marquith said.

Freddie's head was inside the car window. "And just who *is* this dude?"

"Marquith," Marquith said. "Oliver Marquith."

"How'd you get in here?" Freddie's tone was mean.

"He made a mistake, Freddie," Ken said. "Don't beat up on him."

"What kind of a mistake?" Freddie was glaring.

"I was looking for the Brewster place."

"There ain't no Brewsters here."

"They're up the road from here, Freddie," Ken said. "Don't lean on the man."

"Look, I'm sorry," Marquith began.

"You get your ass outa here!" Freddy said. "Right away, hear? And I don't want to see its crack one more time in my life, or I'll split it in two with buckshot! Understand?"

Marquith was already backing out. On the way, he scraped his left front fender and tore a door handle off on the right side. When he turned onto North Lake Road, he was shaking so badly he drove at ten miles an hour.

Goddamn kids, he kept repeating to himself. *Goddamn kids!*

By the time he had crossed the covered bridge into Broadmoor, he had recovered his composure, and along with it, a grim determination to make life utter hell for the goddamn kids and for Freddie Loftus in particular. It was in this state of mind that he sought out Milt Framer.

Broadmoor Road was the long way into King's Landing, but Milt Framer's house, a white cinder-block rectangle with a dirty green roof, was en route to Marquith's office.

The front yard was a jungle of rusted automobile parts, broken television sets, pipes, wooden sawhorses, assorted tin cans, pots, kettles, discarded toilets, and weeds. Framer dealt in junk, and his surroundings, like his life, were devoid of any beauty. Once Framer had been married, but that had not lasted long, like all other tinges of happiness in Milt's life. His young bride had run off with another man soon after the wedding. That had been years ago, after Framer's release from the hospital in Clarendon, and it left him an angry, hollow man, living alone, interested in little else but collecting and selling his junk, and eating and drinking more than necessary.

Marquith slid from behind the wheel, looked about the yard and sniffed with distaste.

"Hey Judge! What do you know?" Milt Framer was sitting on the ground, his back against the side of the house, swilling from a quart bottle of Utica beer. "What brings you around?"

"Just passing by, Milt." Marquith dusted off a battered kitchen chair. Sitting down, he felt it creak and give, and he shifted his weight carefully.

Framer extended the bottle. "Want a swig?"

Marquith's hand came up in silent admonition, and his head shook quickly. "Had my share today, Milt, thanks." He studied Framer for a moment. "Hear you ran into a little trouble a few days ago."

Framer spat beer and saliva onto the cement strip running the length of the house. "Fucking freaks!"

"Somebody took a shot at you."

"Freddie Loftus."

Marquith hesitated. "The skinny one? With the long beard and sunken eyes?"

"That's him. You know him, Judge?" Framer was the only one of Marquith's childhood acquaintances who called him Judge.

Marquith coughed lightly. "I think I've seen him around town. Mean-looking bastard."

"Fucking Jesus freak! Crazier than a bedbug, that one."

Marquith nodded. "None of that type are very stable, Milt. But," he paused, "I don't know about the Jesus freak part."

"What do you mean?"

Marquith shrugged. "Jesus freaks I can understand, Milt. They can be a pain in the ass, but I can understand. But Satan freaks?" He raised his shoulders again. "I don't know."

"Satan freaks?" Milt Framer's eyes were wide. "You kidding?"

"I heard something about Freddie Loftus," Marquith said. "That he was tied up with some kind of a Satan worshipers group in San Francisco."

"Satan worshipers?"

"Something like that. I don't like it, Milt. I don't like having something like that around here."

"Goddammit!" Milt Framer said, waving the Utica wildly. "Goddammit, I told Frank Liscomb where to look for that kid's body!"

"He's doing his job, Milt. Don't fault Frank."

"Satan freaks! You mean they actually believe in the Devil?"

"Something like that. A kind of modern interpretation of the Black Mass. Sexual orgies. Things like that."

"Gang bangs? Right here in Broadmoor?"

"I didn't say that exactly, Milt."

"You can bet your ass that's what those freaks are doing up there!"

"There's nothing to prove that, Milt. It's just hearsay."

"And more than that, Ollie! More than that, I tell ya! Sacrifices! Chickens, dogs, anything!"

"Now, now, Milt." Marquith raised a cautioning hand.

"You don't believe it? You don't believe them fuckin' degenerates is doing things like that?"

Marquith didn't answer.

"I'm telling you, Judge," Framer said, staring out into the front yard, "that's where that finger came from."

"There's no proof of that," Marquith said. He

sighed. "It's all hearsay, that story about the Satan worshiping. You know how people talk."

"Where there's smoke there's fire," Framer said.

Marquith shook his head sadly. "I'll tell you one thing, Milt," he said. "I'd feel a lot more comfortable with those kids out of Holland County."

"Throw 'em out! That's what I been saying for years! Ever since they come!"

Marquith sighed again. "How? They own the land. They have legal rights."

"You're a judge, Ollie."

"What can I do? My hands are tied."

Milt Framer was silent, which for him was unusual. He wrapped his hands around his bent knees and pondered for a minute. "Well, mine ain't," he finally said. "My hands ain't tied, Ollie."

Marquith leaned forward almost imperceptibly. "What're you thinking, Milt?"

"I'm just thinking, Judge," Milt Framer said. "Let me keep on thinking."

The judge rose. "Well, let me know how it goes."

When Oliver Marquith had left, Milt Framer sat for a long time, brows knitted, mouth drawn, thinking.

Fucking Satan freaks, he thought. *Fucking Satan freaks!*

Oliver Marquith thought too, on the way from Framer's home to his office in King's Landing, about sex orgies and gang bangs. His mind filled with images and his senses became aware and tumescent.

Near six, he called his wife and said, "I'm a spoilsport again, sweetheart."

"Don't be silly, Mar," she said. "I'm an old hand at being a wife."

"You remember Charlie Metcalf?"

"Vaguely," Norma Marquith said. "Isn't he in real estate?"

"He only owns about half the state, Norm. Anyway, he asked me to drive up to his place this evening. To talk over that Indian Falls prospectus. I'm having dinner with him."

"Will you be late or is it a stayover?"

"I can't be sure."

"I won't hold my breath. Have a good dinner, Mar."

Marquith turned not toward Charlie Metcalf's home, but south on the interstate to the city. Three hours later he was lying naked on a king-size bed in a once-fashionable townhouse on the East Side, looking down over his paunch at two girls, one blond, one brunette.

"Suck it good," he kept saying. "Suck it good! Oh, yes, that's the way, kids! That's it! Suck it good!"

Father Daniel Conant was experiencing a sleep-start, a sudden awakening without breath, hands clenched and chest tight, his eyes wide but unable to see, his body unable to move.

Save me, save me, he cried, but no voice came from his throat.

He felt again that he was dead and yet thinking, and fear coursed through his body in harrowing waves. But soon he was fully awake again, in control of his muscles, breathing once more, his forehead and the back of his neck drenched with cold sweat.

Fragments of the dream came back, and he tried to remember, to sort them out in his mind.

He had found himself in Rome, within the Vatican, in the Piazza, down front in a huge moving mass of millions, staring up at the black-robed priest or Pope or Demon who shouted and purred at once: "Sinners of the World unite! Sinners of the World come forward and unite! Sinners of the world and the Underworld, follow me, your leader."

Then, suddenly he was in the confessional of St. Ignatius of Loyola in Broadmoor—or was it Brooklyn, he could not tell—and the confessional was open on all sides, and lifted upon what appeared to be a scaffold with a hanging noose. And he was sitting there naked, his penis huge and engorged, hearing confession from a small child while hundreds of others, townspeople, city people, people from all over the world looked on, and listened and licked their lips, and masturbated.

While the child, the boy, said, over and over, *I killed them all, oh my Father, I killed them all and I wanted to kill them so I killed them all and now come unto you for sufferance.* The humming of the throng increased until it became a roar, deafening, filling the air and the square and the church and reaching to the heavens, a rising, gasping moan of orgasm and ejaculation.

Conant rose, pushing the covers from his body, reaching to the night table for the lamp and the carafe of wine.

As he lifted the glass in trembling fingers, another part of the dream came upon him. He had been serving mass, and lifting the wine to his lips, had found it to be blood, and in drinking the blood had found himself laughing and thinking, *But that's what it really is, His blood, and I must drink His blood. I want His blood and I'll drink all of it I can get!*

Father Conant passed out, and the wine spilled

on his naked chest, sliding downward over his navel and into his crotch.

As he again dropped into unconsciousness, his mind shouted: *Capture the dream! Capture the dream! Remember! Remember the dream!*

But in the morning he remembered nothing, and wondered about the wine stains on the bedsheets.

CHAPTER 8

Among the literati of Holland County—the settlers from the city, the writers, the artists, the musicians, the "tired of it all" refugees from public relations and advertising—the announcement of a party was no special event. Most of them partied all the time.

Cocktail parties, dinner parties, morning-after parties that started with coffee and progressed into Bloody Mary's and then straight vodka, were part of the life-style, and it didn't take much to start a bash. Two people would suffice, meeting in a local pub or along the road, perhaps over a split-rail fence, or on a back lawn. The bottle would be proferred, the elbow bent, a glass raised in salute, and the party was on.

It was strange. They had come for peace and quiet, a place to work in solitude, away from the city with its sirens and garbage trucks, blasting stereos and screams in the night. They had come to establish a new kind of working privacy.

Instead, they seemed to seek one another even more eagerly, to band together even more closely, to drop in, pass by, just say hello in an orgy of gossip, gin, and friendliness.

Perhaps it was the quietness itself, the dearth of siren, scream, and metallic clanking. They had only nature now, that which they had wanted to "get back to," the chirp of birds, the drone of insects, the rustle of wind. Here the nights were dark and, after the hours of the insects, very quiet, almost deafeningly quiet. There was a pervasive fear in this new-found way of life, and they huddled together against it in common defense, living a cave existence on well-kept lawns and around terraced swimming pools, gossiping, laughing, trading spouses every now and then.

The simple reason behind it all was boredom. After all, after a good day's work at the typewriter or easel, you just couldn't pick up and go to a play, the ballet, even a movie. What else was there to do in the country except eat, sleep, make love, drink?

Like northerners in the tropics, they had gone native, a view which, in light of the drinking habits of the locals, was not too far afield. The settlers had no monopoly on boozing, and the townies held their own, living it up in the local saloons.

Holland County boasted one AA chapter. It was located near the mental hospital in Clarendon and had a membership of seven.

If it only takes two to start an AA group, it also only takes two to start a party. And the parties were winning out.

So the invitation to Nicole Bannister's birthday ball came as no surprise to anybody, much less Marion Hammond.

"Jonathan's giving a surprise bash for Nicole on Friday," he said to his wife.

"Oh shit!" she said. "Another one!" Bette Hammond hated Holland County, its quiet, its solitude, its bashes, and its binges. She wanted to move back to the city.

"Shall I tell him we can't make it?" Hammond dreaded to see his wife upset.

"Of course not," Bette said. "After what happened, I guess it's the best thing for her. Of course we'll go. Only I *wish*, I really wish some night we could go into the city and see a *play!*"

"We will, Betts."

"When?"

"I'll call the broker next week."

"You'll call him tomorrow, that's what you'll do!"

"All right, all right. I'll call him tomorrow."

Bette Hammond put the charcoal aside and closed her sketch pad. She was no artist and she knew it, but she liked to dabble. It filled her time, eased her mind, allayed the boredom. "When are we going to move back, Marion?"

Hammond clenched the glass in his hand. "What would I do, Betts?"

"You liked it at the university."

It was the same old subject, and Hammond always tried to find new answers, but they were always the same old ones: "Even if I could get back there, I'd take a fifty percent cut in income. Even more."

"Money. It's always money. For chrissake, Marion, is money that important?"

"You're goddamn right it is! Look at the way we live, Bette!"

"I hate the way we're living!"

"You don't hate it! You don't hate the two cars, the maid, the clothes, the luxuries. You just hate the country."

The sketch pad sailed like a Frisbee across twenty feet of living room, hitting the mantel with a splitting crack and falling to the hearth.

"Now, Betts . . ."

"You're goddamn right I hate the country! I hate the peace, I hate the quiet, I hate the dull look on the dull dumbos in the dull towns!"

"You liked West Eighty-fourth Street better?"

"Yes, I liked it better! It's a short walk to the ballet!"

"With maybe a ripped-off purse and tickets before you get there?"

"Yes!"

They stared at each other.

"I'm sorry, Betts."

"Sometimes, Marion," she said, sitting again, "sometimes I think: wouldn't it be nice to see a group of PR's again, a guy twitching his way along the street, a woman sprawled in a doorway, drunk. Even a mugger."

"You're crazy."

"I guess I am," she said. She stared at the floor. "But what's so normal about Broadmoor? About the whole county? I never found a severed finger in my mailbox on West Eighty-fourth."

Hammond was silent.

"What do you think about that, Marion? You haven't said much."

"I don't know," he said. "I don't know what to think." He was thinking about the Golgi apparatus. He rattled the ice in his glass, rose, and crossed to the bar. "Even the authorities don't know what to think. There's no body. No child missing. Nothing. Maybe," he continued, building them both a highball, "there isn't any body."

Bette looked quickly around. "What do you mean?"

He came toward her, hand outstretched with the drink. "I'm helping out on it, you know. Tom Blauvelt came to me because we have the electron-microscope at the lab. They wanted to know whether it was male or female."

"What was it?"

"Female. At least we're pretty sure."

"That wasn't in the papers."

"They're trying to play it down," Hammond said. "The whole story. Advice of the FBI and all. Anyway, there's something strange about the cell structure."

"What?"

"No Golgi apparatus." He explained, and when he was finished Bette was reflective for a moment.

"You mean it isn't human?" she asked.

"Of course it's human!" He laughed. "I didn't mean that. I only meant, well, that maybe there's no sign of a body because no child was murdered. That it came from an already dead child."

"But who?"

He shrugged.

"And why? Why do that to it. And then send it to Nicole?"

He shrugged again. "I don't know. All I *do* know is that the kid was . . . must have been abnormal. Everybody has a Golgi apparatus."

"Have you told the police?"

"I told Tom Blauvelt. He said he'd pass it along."

"Then the child was—some sort of freak?"

"You could say that."

The conversation lapsed for some time. Bette gazed into the fireplace. Hammond swirled the ice in his drink. Then Bette said, "I've had the most— *uncanny* feeling lately."

His eyes questioned her.

"I don't know how to explain it. As though something were about to happen. Something—horrible."

"Nerves, Betts."

"No, it's not just nerves. It's from the outside. Something pressing in. And *down*. On all of us."

"I don't feel anything," Hammond said. He was lying and he knew it.

"I saw Estelle today. She feels it too."

"Estelle Dixon? She feels uncanny all the time. She *is* uncanny."

"You don't understand her, Marion."

"Don't understand her! Are you kidding? Ouija boards? Tarot cards? Seances?" He laughed. "Betts, come on!"

"I know Estelle is strange, but she's smarter than you think. She's got—I don't know, not an aura, not ESP or anything like that—but she does have—what can I say? Perception? Intuitiveness? Feeling? Insight? I don't know. She's got something the rest of us don't have."

"Tits," Hammond said. "I love Estelle's tits. That's the best pair of knockers in Holland County."

"Oh, Marion!"

"Sorry, Betts."

"You're the most serious bastard in the world when it comes to you or your work. When I get serious, you get hysterics! You're a male chauvinist, Marion!"

"I said I was sorry, Betts. I'll listen. I will."

After a moment, she said, "There was a snake on the lawn today."

"Probably just a garter snake." For a moment Hammond was thrown by the abrupt change in subject. But then he realized it was not a change. Betts was not like that. It had to fit.

"It wasn't a garter snake," she said. "I know a garter snake when I see one."

"What was it?"

"A rattler."

"Couldn't have been a rattlesnake, Betts. Not down here. They're all up toward the Great Ledges, the Devil's Caves."

"It was a rattler."

"Did it rattle?"

"No."

"They always rattle when they're disturbed, Betts."

"I didn't disturb it! For chrissake, Marion!"

"What'd you do?"

"Nothing. What do you think, I went over there to play with it?"

"How long was it there?"

"About an hour. Like it owned the whole goddamn lawn. I was afraid to step outside the door. To breathe."

"What happened?"

"It went away."

"Where?"

"Toward the pump house."

"That's strange," Hammond said. "For a rattlesnake. I'll look for it tomorrow. Kill it."

"I wish you would," Bette said. Then: "We'll have to get something for Nicole. Any ideas?"

"I'm lousy when it comes to ideas for presents," Hammond said. "That's your department."

"I can't even think."

"Well, just suppose it was your birthday. What would you want?"

She turned, looking at him straight in the eye. "More than anything else in the world?"

"Nothing's too good for you, sweetheart. Just tell me."

"Okay. A new lease on the old apartment on West Eighty-fourth."

"Sounds like a gas, Jonny," Joe Tremper said into the phone. "We'll arrive early and stay late. Yeah. See you, buddy."

After cradling the phone, he propped his head on a pillow and gazed down at his nude body. He noticed a single gray hair on his chest and plucked it out. Then he patted his belly, still flat, still hard, but with a slight bulge beginning at the sides. He would have to work out more often, do regular pushups and sit-ups. He lifted his limp penis, turning it, examining it carefully. That was still working well enough.

The shower stopped and Lauren Shane came out of the bathroom, toweling herself. Tremper moved his eyes upward along the long legs, the lush hips, the narrow waist, the full, slightly quivering breasts. Damned if his cock wasn't beginning to tingle again.

He crooked a finger at her. "C'mere, broad," he said.

"No more today, Lochinvar. You'll wear me out." She stood before the mirror, shimmying the towel around her buttocks.

As she reached to get a cigarette from the night table, he grasped her wrist, pulling her down. She gave him one kiss, pulled away, and said, "You've got work to do."

His head dropped back on the pillow. "Fuck work," he said.

"Fuck work and you don't fuck me."

"All right, all right," he said, "I'll work for a while. Two hours. I'll put in two hours and then we'll ball."

"We'll see," Lauren said. She rose and fished in a drawer for underthings.

Work to Joe Tremper was a four-letter word which, freely translated, meant agony. For twenty years he had labored, done his peonage in the musty halls of corporate public relations, playing his roles as the occasion demanded, the nodding yes-man, the non-committal onlooker. His rise had been startling, his salary increases, profit sharing, and stock options fat and fruitful. And with the proceeds of those twenty years, he had flung his last smiling good-byes into the corner offices of the executive floor, packed his possessions and come to Holland County to finally get to work on "that novel."

After a year in Broadmoor, "that novel," the story of his life, was exactly fifty-three-and-a-half pages toward denouement.

"You know," Joe Tremper said, his eyes scanning the ceiling, "I think I'll start another one."

Lauren turned. "Are you kidding?"

"A mystery story. A thriller."

"Did you ever write one before?"

"No. But it shouldn't be that hard."

Lauren shrugged. "Genius knows no bounds, I guess. You have an idea?"

"Ideas are all around. You stumble all over them every day." He propped himself up on an elbow. "You take this thing that happened right here in Broadmoor. Now is that an idea or isn't it?"

"Ugh," Lauren said. "Don't even talk about it. It gives me goose pimples."

"It's an idea, right?"

"Sure it's an idea," Lauren said. She slipped into a pair of jeans. "You have an ending?"

His head plopped back on the pillow. "No."

"I should think you'd have to know what would happen, who did it."

"I'll work that out later."

Lauren put on a light checked shirt, leaving the upper buttons undone. "Who do you think actually did it, Joe?"

Tremper gazed into her cleavage lustfully. "C'mere, broad," he said.

"Answer my question, Lochinvar."

"How the hell should I know who did it? If I knew that, I'd have my book."

"But that wouldn't be fiction."

"No, it wouldn't, would it. C'mere." She propped herself on the edge of the bed. His fingers slipped around to her back. He began to massage it slowly, firmly. His breath was warm in the opening of her shirt. "You're the sexiest broad," he breathed. "The goddamndest sexiest broad."

She tickled him under the armpits and he jumped up with a scream. "Go work," she said. "I want to know who did it."

"All right, all right! Frigid broad!" He pulled on jockey shorts and chinos. "By the way, we're invited to a blast Friday night."

"Where?"

"The Bannisters'."

"You mean it?" A sudden look of concern, almost dread, had crossed Lauren's face.

"Don't you want to go?"

"It's not that."

"Then *what?*"

"I don't know. I just—wouldn't know what to say to the woman."

"You don't say anything. That's the point. The point of the whole party." He slapped her on the buttocks and rose. "I'll try to work for a while. Shit, I hate work."

"Do we have to go, Joe?"

"I said we would. It's a surprise party. Nikki's birthday."

"We'll have to get something."

"No problem. A couple of bottles of booze."

"Booze, broads, and bed. You're depraved, Lochinvar."

"What a wonderful way to die."

"I'll think of something better for her. Now you go work."

"For two hours."

"Ten pages."

"Two hours. Then we ball."

"Then we eat, Lochinvar. One thing at a time."

Maria Rivera Braithwaite finished her prayer, crossed herself, and rose from the altar. She walked lithely and silently down the aisle of St. Ignatius of Loyola, turned, genuflected once more, dipped her slender fingers in the lavabo and slipped from the church into the open air.

"A beautiful day, Mrs. Braithwaite," Father Conant said. He stood on the stone steps, a large crucifix around his neck.

Maria Rivera sniffed. When she spoke, her words were tinged with the slight flavor of cultured Spanish. "Too humid, Father. Much too humid of late. Have you noticed?"

"But the sun shines, Mrs. Braithwaite," Father Conant said. "As long as the sun shines."

A silly man, Maria Braithwaite thought. So full of wretched small talk. Yet so handsome. Unfortunate he had to be a priest. "You are Spanish, Father," she said.

Conant's eyebrows arched.

"Or Italian," she said. "But I would guess Spanish."

Conant smiled. "My father was born in County Tyrone, Mrs. Braithwaite."

"And your mother?"

This time he laughed. "In New York."

"And her mother?"

Conant's eyes twinkled. "Cordoba," he said.

Maria's bright teeth gleamed in a broad smile. "You see, Father, it takes one to know one."

"Indubitably, Mrs. Braithwaite."

They walked down the steps together. "I am myself," Maria Braithwaite said, "from Toledo."

"A beautiful city," Conant said.

"No, Father, a dark city. As dark and foreboding as El Greco painted it."

"The sun shines everywhere," Conant said.

"I shall never forget my childhood, Father," Maria said. "Its poverty and its darkness. That's why I pray. To *thank* God, not to ask of him. To thank Him for my good health, my good life."

Poverty, Conant thought as they approached the sleek, polished Mercedes. *Has she ever really known poverty? Real poverty? Like mine?*

"You are young, Father," Maria was saying, "and you are lucky. Lucky to have been born here and not in Spain."

"Why?" Conant asked, stopping suddenly.

"Because Spain, Father, exists in the past. In darkness and cruelty. It has not much changed since the Inquisition."

"Juan Carlos—"

"Juan Carlos is an idiot. As was Alfonso. As was de Rivera. As was Franco. Do you think any of them wished to see the Spanish people read books?"

They had reached the car. Conant noticed a number of packages in the backseat.

"It's very odd, Father," Maria was saying, "the way I met my husband. He was with the Abraham Lincoln Brigade, of all things. The son of a millionaire with the Lincoln Brigade. I was only a child then. Dirty, unkempt, an orphan of the war. But he took me away to safety when Franco's troops were coming. Years later he came back. Found me."

"He must have been a good man," Father Conant said.

"He was."

"It's funny," Conant said. "You've been attending mass—oh, for eight years or so. Ever since I came to St. Ignatius. This is the first time we've ever talked, isn't it?"

Her dark eyes sparkled. "Yes, Father Conant," she said. "The very first time. But you are a reticent man."

"Am I?"

"And a priest. Too bad."

Conant seemed suddenly ill at ease. He swallowed visibly and his glance drifted away, into the car. "I see you've been shopping, Mrs. Braithwaite."

"Yes. A few things for Nicole Bannister. Her husband is giving a surprise party next Friday."

"Yes, I know," Conant said. "They asked me."

"Oh? You'll be there?"

"I will," he said.

Maria studied him for a moment. "It's a horrible thing that happened to her, Father."

"Yes," he said.

"There is evil in the air, Father."

"There is evil everywhere, Maria."

Her eyes flicked at the use of her given name. "I'll see you then, Father. On Friday."

"Yes," he said. "I look forward to it. We'll talk more. About Spain."

The Mercedes pulled away, and he stood for a moment looking after it. What poverty had she *really* ever known, he wondered again. Could she have fathomed *his*?

As he ascended the church steps, Daniel Conant's forehead was lined with pain from the past. In the rectory, he poured a glass of wine, and settling into a worn armchair draped with yellowed antimacassars, let his mind wander backward over valleys of time, pausing here and there, then rushing on, until, at last, the small Dominican church in Brooklyn, its spire somber in the sun, rose in his vision, its bells tolling in his ears.

Father Conant seldom dwelt upon his boyhood. It was too painful, too full of a dark and twisted turmoil, and he blocked it from his mind with a grim determination.

But something had happened today, a spark, a tinder, perhaps the mention of Cordoba, and now his past was before him in all its naked sordidness.

The church. Small, confining, never enough room, it seemed, to accommodate the mostly Spanish congregation, its incense-laden air made sickly by the odor of Sunday sweat.

His mother beside him, kneeling, rising, kneeling again, hands clutching her beads tightly, muttering the responses with Iberian fervor, her dark, Spanish eyes alive with a strange fiery light.

And later at home, drunk again on Calvados.

"You can be a priest."

"Mom, I can't be a priest!"

"It's the only thing you can be."

And then the laughter. The short, teasing laughter.

Daniel Conant rose, his fingers a vise on the wineglass. He walked to the decanter and poured to the brim.

"Your father wanted to be a priest. A Jesuit. Of all things, a Jesuit. But Jesuit or Dominican, I'm glad he remained a man! He was such a man! Such a man!" Laughter. *"Not like you. You're nothing. Nothing."* And then the sudden flinging of the glass against the wall, the rising scream. *"You embarrass me, you hear that! You embarrass me! You nothing! You nothing!"*

Father Conant drank deeply of the wine and then, putting it aside, lowered his head into his hands and began to cry. He wept long minutes, his shoulders heaving, his torso jerking. When the sobs subsided, he raised his head, and on his lips there was a small but soft smile.

He was seeing his father, the tall ascetic-looking man, the dark Irishman with the soft gray-blue eyes who read Shakespeare and Dickens and Stevenson to him, who had wanted to be a priest but who married and made his career in the Fire Department.

His father had died when Daniel was ten, but the priest remembered him vividly. When his mother raged, they had taken long walks together in Prospect Park, sometimes long subway rides into Manhattan, and once in a while as far as the Bronx where they walked on shady afternoons through the woods of Van Cortlandt Park.

"Pop, when I grow up, I want to be a fireman."

The soft chuckle. *"No, you don't."*

"Yes I do! Really I do!"

"There's so much more, son. So much more." His father had looked away into the distance.

"Like what?"

"Like an engineer, a doctor, a scientist."

"Pop, I can't even add straight!"

His father had stopped and turned, and looked down at him, so tall and towering. *"You can do anything if you put your mind to it."* Softly.

"What did you want to be when you were growing up, Pop?"

The long, faraway look again, and the soft chuckle. *"Me? A priest, son. A priest."* The large, bony hand had come down to grasp the boy's hand, and they had walked on. *"A Jesuit priest. But I didn't put my mind to it."*

So the son had filled the father's place, had realized the unfulfilled dream, and in choosing the Jesuit order over the Dominican, had stood with the beloved father against the hated mother.

His life, his happiness had begun at the seminary. There he had found solitude, privacy and, in a sense, souls like his own, refugees from reality, finding in love and devotion to God a solution to their own problems, their own private sufferings.

And strangely, on becoming a priest he had overcome his innate shyness with women, had, in fact, learned to know them, understand them and, in a way, had come to identify with them, to put himself in their place.

So few of them were like his mother. In the confessional, they became alive and human, revealing, in their recitation of real or imagined sin, a sense of love and devotion that filled him with a strange mixture of awe and respect. Yet behind it all, he felt their plight, their proximity to desolation, envy and guilt, their everlasting struggle with feelings of weakness and girlhood innocence.

Outside the confessional, women liked him because he was quick to recognize their dilemma, see their point of view, seize their thoughts. Many of his friends were women because he understood them, and they knew it. Many men suspected him of being homosexual, which he was not.

Daniel Conant's only regret was that he could not marry and have children. For he loved children, and to be a father, to have a child, was, to his mind, perhaps the closest man could come to heaven before death.

But all denied to him, a priest.

He had, of course, thought about it, fantasized, toyed with the idea. But for him, leaving the Church, marrying, having children, was impossible.

His thoughts turned to Nicole Bannister.

What a beautiful woman! How angelic of feature. And the child Leslie, what a creature of God!

My God, what misery, what suffering the woman must be going through!

And he wondered why she would not talk to him as a friend.

CHAPTER
9

Dr. Thomas Blauvelt was coming out of John's Bakery with four eclairs and two cherry tarts when Jonathan Bannister's blue Volvo darted into a parking space two slots down.

"I was just thinking about you, Tom."

"Oh? Everything all right?" It was a week since Blauvelt had seen Bannister.

"Fine," Jonathan said. "Listen, Nicole's birthday is Friday. I'm giving her a little surprise party. You're free, I hope."

"Sure."

"Anybody you'd like to bring?"

"You know me, Jonathan. Perennial bachelor. Fifth wheel. I'll just roam around. What time?"

"Eight. Eight-thirtyish."

"I'll be there," Blauvelt said. "How is Nicole, by the way?"

"Fine, Tom. Just fine."

Blauvelt hesitated. "Chief Liscomb wants to see us in a couple of days. He tell you yet?"

"Yeah. You going to be there?"

"Yes."

"Well, guess I'll be seeing you before the party."

"Take care, Jonathan."

On his way home, Blauvelt drove with his left hand

and used his right to hold one of the cherry tarts. He had finished half of it by the time he reached the covered bridge, and in a sudden fit of self-disgust, shoved the uneaten portion back into the box. He had begun another diet.

Thomas Blauvelt remained unmarried, unattached, but far from uninterested. Although his libido was as strong as any healthy male's, he had missed the marital boat on any number of occasions, not from poor timing, but because of what he himself referred to as "the two *W*'s." Work and weight.

At six feet and two-hundred-thirty-five pounds, Blauvelt was not unattractive in a Laughtonesque kind of way. His features were carved in soft, sensitive lines, and with his large, rather sad, doglike eyes, sparse red hair and somewhat childlike smile, he resembled a huge, lumbering golden retriever, ready to fetch on command. He had warmth and gentleness and humor, and these traits made him a favorite at parties and a success in his practice.

Women were drawn to Thomas Blauvelt. There had been more than a few who would have married him, had not he himself closed the gate. With all his intelligence, wit, compassion and charm, vanity lurked beneath the rolls of fat, making Blauvelt's life a hell. Each new tenuous affair took its toll in fasting, calorie-counting, gram-weighing, and exercise. But with every passing day of increased passion and mounting sexual appetite, his hunger would expand until all came crashing down in an orgy of fats and carbohydrates, lady fingers, peach ice cream, and pancakes. And looking into the mirror, Blauvelt would wonder what woman in the world would want him. Neurosis, he would conclude. Absolute neurotic eating.

Neurosis was at the bottom of his work ethic too.

Once faced with an unusual problem, a question, a puzzle, the world about him would simply disintegrate, its people, its politics fading away. His ordinarily fluent conversation would become a series of unintelligible mumbles, his stare would become vacant and fixed.

Until he found an answer. And it was an answer he was searching for as he parked his car in the driveway, trundled into the house, and called Marion Hammond.

"Marion, Tom Blauvelt here. Listen. I want to talk to you about those Golgi bodies."

The human brain. Thirteen billion cells. Not static, solid silicon chips, but living cells, breathing, feeding, undulating in fluid like sea grass under water. Thirteen billion human cells packed into a computer the size of a grapefruit and weighing little more than two-and-a-half pounds. Programmed for hundreds of thousands of years, perhaps millions. Within its walls the data, the information, the statistics spanning eons of existence, enigmas of experience from the caves to cathedrals. Science and superstition, art and violence, music and pollution, philosophy and stupidity, literature and loneliness. Life and death, living and dying. The scent of hope and the stench of war.

Something like that, Jonathan thought. He was in his studio, staring at a canvas that existed only in space, in the inner space of his mind.

Something like that. The first computer. The *original* computer. Start with that. Everything proceeds from the human mind. The jet plane, the automobile. The telephone, radio, television. The UN building, the cathedral at Chartres. The Mona Lisa.

The Pietà, the David. Dali, Rembrandt, Botticelli, Mondrian, Picasso, Wyeth.

Human computers. He laughed. The computer that built the computer. He was walking the room now, hands in pockets, head bent. That would be the theme. Man's vision. Quest for knowledge. Truth. Science, Medicine. Literature. Poetry. Computers.

He kicked at a scatter rug. He turned abruptly and paced back along the path he had come. He sat. He rose. He stared out the window into dark night. He saw explosions of bright color, bold line and contour, texture.

But how? How do you transpose that to canvas? How do you paint the idea of the human mind? The writers have it easy.

He dropped into a chair, suddenly deflated. All this for a few lousy commercial centerfolds? For a computer company? What do they know about the computer that built their own computer? Salesmen, managers, vice presidents. Stuffy, self-important little men with short hair wearing Oxford button-downs. Always smiling. So smug and complacent in their little world of silicon chips, magnetic tapes, charts, graphs, feedbacks, and printouts. Jargon.

He rose again, walked to a small bar and poured a light scotch. Of course, they do write checks. Computers write checks. Give them that.

Maybe, Jonathan thought, *maybe after this one, I can get back to my own work. Christ, I hope so.*

Drink in hand, he left the studio and started back to the main house. Passing Leslie's door, he stopped, listened. She was talking to Elsie again.

Jonathan opened the door. "Hi, sweetheart."

"Hi," Leslie said.

He walked over to the bed, sat down, leaned to kiss her lightly on the cheek.

"What's up?"

"Elsie and me were having a conversation."

"Elsie and *I*. What about?"

"Elsie wants to swim in the pool tomorrow, and I want to go to the West Branch."

"The pool's nice."

"But the West Branch is so cold, Daddy. So nice and cold. It makes me shiver!"

"I'll bet. Anyway, we'll see what Mommy says."

"Oh, Mommy'll say the pool. I know *her!*"

"Well—maybe I'll take you up to West Branch."

"Oh, good, Daddy! Goody, goody, goody!" She smiled up at him, and then she frowned. "Daddy?"

"Hmm?"

"Mommy says Elsie don't exist."

"*Doesn't* exist."

"Pearl says 'don't.'"

Jonathan sighed.

"Daddy, you believe in Elsie, don't you?"

"Of course I do." He turned his head and spoke to the wall. "Hi, Elsie."

"You're a good daddy," Leslie said, and twined her arms around his neck, pulling him down.

Jonathan kissed her and slapped her buttocks and rose. "Go to sleep," he said. "You and Elsie go to sleep." He smiled and left.

In the living room, he found Nicole reading a book.

"Fuck computers," he said.

She looked up. "Do you want to send the check back?"

"Of course not. Anyway, I've already deposited it."

Her eyes went back to the page, but her attention seemed to be elsewhere. "Is Leslie asleep?" she asked.

"She's talking to Elsie."

Nicole closed the book. "You know, I still worry about that."

"Why? It's a stage."

"It's been going on too long. She shouldn't be lonely. She's got enough friends."

"Not that many. And she's talented. Very talented."

"What's that got to do with it?"

"Just what that shrink said. Children with imagination, talent, kids with that often make up other people in their minds. Hell, it's normal for Leslie. Maybe normal for most of us. I don't remember, but it's possible I did the same thing. Or you. Do you remember?"

"Remember what?" Nicole's voice was strained.

"Making up a playmate when you were little. Talking to it."

"No."

The word was abrupt, sharp. He changed the subject. "Bumped into Tom Blauvelt this morning. He's okay for Friday."

"Good," Nicole said. "I like Tom." She seemed to relax.

Jonathan did not mention the projected meeting with Liscomb. He said nothing about the finger. They had not talked about it for days.

They seemed to be waiting.

Upstairs, awake and restless, Leslie continued her conversation with Elsie.

"Daddy's a nice daddy, isn't he Elsie?"

"He said for us to go to sleep," Elsie said.

"What?"

"I said he said for us t—" And the voice faded, became distant, and was gone.

"What?"

There was silence.

"What'd you say, Elsie?"

But Elsie did not answer.

"Elsie? Elsie, are you there?"

Silence.

Leslie clutched the blanket tightly. Her eyes flicked. She felt suddenly uncomfortable. Elsie was always there when she needed her.

"Elsie? Elsie, where did you go?"

Worry was not a normal part of Leslie Bannister's makeup, but it came now, in a sudden onslaught, filled with panic.

"Elsie, are you sick? I mean, did you die, Elsie?"

When no answer came, Leslie began to weep, heavily but silently, in grief and despair. It was her first confrontation with death.

Then she heard what sounded like childish laughter, thin and hollow, and very far away.

But when she listened again, there was only silence.

The abstruse, often callous efficiency of the FBI both annoyed and disturbed Frank Liscomb. In a nation experiencing an inordinate amount of general violence, street crime, muggings, and rape, with much of its business held in a death grip by the Mafia, it seemed inconceivable to Liscomb that the data banks in Washington should contain so much information on Jonathan and Nicole Bannister.

For the simple reason that Bannister had served in the navy, his fingerprints were on file. For the simple reason that he had once done a freelance job for the Department of Defense, there were five pages of life history on Frank Liscomb's desk. These pages contained his vital statistics, navy record, education, marriages, employment record, passport number, countries visited, political identity as a Democrat, and three minor traffic violations. Nothing of importance, nothing of consequence.

For the simple reason that Nicole Savidge Bannister had attended a peace rally during the Vietnam War, there were ten pages covering similar points of background, including the fact of a nervous breakdown and voluntary confinement in a private sanitarium. She was, as a result, considered "unstable" and thought to possess "possible leftist leanings."

Liscomb grunted and pushed the files aside. He believed in policework, but not *secret* policework. He believed in files on criminals, but not on innocent citizens. And he believed the Bannisters to be innocent.

There was not one word on Freddie Loftus, nor could the Bureau find anything.

Liscomb grunted again.

At 1:30 P.M., they all met, Liscomb, Bannister Blauvelt, and Marion Hammond. Liscomb had not expected Hammond, and although puzzled by his presence, kept his silence.

The discussion began with a description and analysis by Blauvelt of the key evidence, and as the medical jargon inundated the small audience, Liscomb chewed on his cigar and rolled his eyes toward the ceiling. Finally, he interrupted. "Leave out the Latin, Tom. Just tell us what you know."

"Well," Blauvelt said, "it's the finger of a female child—girl—between the ages of seven and ten, thereabouts."

"How do you know it's female?" Jonathan asked.

"Electron-microscopy. Marion here was kind enough to furnish the facilities at WebLabs. Incidentally," he said, looking at Liscomb, "in the course of his analysis, Marion came up with something quite unusual about the specimen." He turned his eyes to Hammond and the others turned with him. "It's yours, Marion."

"There's no Golgi apparatus," Hammond said.

"What's that?" Liscomb grunted.

Hammond's presentation was brief and lucid, and when he had concluded, the others were silent, thoughtful.

Finally, Jonathan said, "In other words, the victim, the little girl, was abnormal."

"Quite abnormal," Hammond said.

"A freak," Liscomb said.

Hammond shrugged. "A kind of freak. A freak of nature, you might say."

"Suppose this—this," Jonathan said, fumbling, "this Golgi thing has something to do with the brain, with intelligence or retardation." He looked at Liscomb. "I was thinking of the mental hospitals, the institutions."

Liscomb nodded wearily. "A good thought, Mr. Bannister. But we've checked them all out. There's no youngster, girl *or* boy, missing." He sighed and reached for another cigar from the box on his desk. "Anybody want a smoke?"

Hammond took one, and when they were lit, Liscomb said, "There are two things I don't understand. One, where is the corpus delicti—if there is a corpus delicti; and two, what was the motive?"

"There's the finger," Blauvelt said.

"That's *part* of a body," Liscomb said. "There's still no evidence of a dead child." He paused. "You know, one of my men, the kid Volner, he suggested early on that maybe there wasn't a corpus delicti. That the kid was still alive and that—well, I told him he was crazy. Now," and he paused again, "I'm beginning to wonder."

Hammond coughed lightly. "That's a horrible thought," he said.

There was silence.

"Well," Liscomb said, resuming, "body or no body, we do have evidence—a severed finger—and a strange and insane modus operandi of some sort, and we're left wondering what the hell the motive is." He looked at Jonathan. "Your wife, Mr. Bannister, has had a nervous breakdown. In fact two."

Jonathan was startled. "What's that got to do with it?"

"I'm just trying to put two and two together and make four, Mr. Bannister. So far, I'm coming up with fives and threes and zeroes."

"Are you saying that Nicole, that she in any way had anything to do with—"

Liscomb cut in sharply. "Of course not. I'm only trying to get down to a question. The question being, when she did go away, when she was hospitalized, when she was a child first, and later on, about five years ago—?"

Jonathan nodded.

"—Could she have met, have made friends with anybody at the hospital who might conceivably have something to do with this?"

There was no response from Jonathan for some time, and when he finally spoke, his voice was soft. "She never told me very much about her stays in the hospital."

"She never talked about her friends there?"

"She kept to herself. She never made any friends there."

Blauvelt cleared his throat and spoke softly. "Did the doctors say anything?"

"About what?" Jonathan snapped. He was suddenly irritated. "Jesus Christ! For some inane, fucking reason, you're all sitting around trying to tie Nicole into this! Pretty soon, you'll be saying she did it herself! That she even sent the goddamned thing in the mail to her own home! Jesus!"

"Now don't get paranoid, Jonathan," Blauvelt sighed. "Nobody said or suggested anything like that. We're only trying to establish a motive."

"There isn't any motive! Can't you see that? There isn't any goddamned motive! And my wife's the victim! Not the murderer!"

"I think," Liscomb said in a very loud voice, "I think, we're getting off the track." He blew smoke toward the ceiling and then let his eyes consult the others. "I wanted to have this meeting so we could all talk reasonably. If we're not going to be reasonable, let's say to hell with it." His gaze settled on Jonathan. "You're right, Mr. Bannister. Mrs. Bannister is the victim, not the accused. I'm satisfied with that. So let's not go off the deep end when I ask a question that might *seem* to suggest a train of thought that it actually doesn't. You know?"

Jonathan nodded. "I'm sorry."

"For example," Liscomb went on, "your wife's a writer and illustrator of children's books. What's that got to do with it? I don't know. But let's conjecture. She pleases kids. She's admired, loved by them. Now let's say there's some crazy who hates children, hates her because of the joy, the pleasure she brings to them. Maybe they met at the hospital. Maybe they didn't meet, but he only observed her there. Maybe they never had contact at all. Maybe, for all we know, he comes from a thousand miles away. The point is, now we're getting to a motive. A crazy motive, yes. But still a motive. That's all I'm trying to get at."

Jonathan seemed perplexed. "Why haven't you asked *her* these questions?"

"It's a rough time for her," Liscomb said. "I thought it might be easier if you could fill us in."

"I wish I could," Jonathan said, "but"—and he seemed flustered—"I don't know very much about her stay in the hospital."

"You talked to the doctors," Blauvelt said.

Jonathan looked up at him.

"She asked me not to," he said.

Blauvelt looked puzzled and Jonathan hurried to explain. "Nicole's a very private person, Tom. I suppose every person of talent is. I respect that privacy when she asks me to. As she respects mine. I suppose you might say her inner realities are none of my business."

"That's pretty Freudian," Blauvelt said.

"Sorry. But that's the way it is. Love is based on trust. Not on prying."

Hammond seemed to have missed the point. "What was the cause of the breakdown, Jonathan?"

"I don't know. Call it a sudden inability to cope, to handle, to face reality. Or the emergence of the unreal to the surface. The dream becomes the everyday world."

"But there's always a cause for that," Hammond persisted.

"Is there? You're looking for a reason. As Chief Liscomb is looking for a reason in the form of a motive. Maybe there is no reason, as we know it, in either case."

Liscomb coughed. "There's a reason for everything."

After the meeting broke up, Blauvelt wondered about that seemingly perfect marriage of Jonathan and Nicole. What kind of people were they? To be married so long, to have a child, and to know so little about each other? To live together but not to confide? Or was he right that trust is worth more than confidences? But wasn't true love, full marriage, the sharing of secrets, even though they be sin?

And he wondered under what great guilt Nicole must be cowering? *God help her*, he thought.

Alone, nursing a tumbler of cheap red wine, Estelle Dixon bitterly surveyed the remnants of a once lush living room, a testament to ten years of slow but sure marital deterioration. Her eyes took in the once cared-for furniture, scratched and scarred now, pockmarked with the dark smudges of long-forgotten cigarettes. The Persian rug stared back at her with mock pity, its intricate designs stained with countless spilled drinks, thrown bottles, and upset food.

She shivered. She took a long swallow of wine. She crushed a cigarette into an overflowing ashtray and lit another.

The years go by. The body ages. Love dies.

Her eyes caught a photograph of Henry to the right of the fireplace. Henry fifteen years ago. Henry in his prime, at the height of his powers. Henry when he was working steadily, doing well, making money.

Henry when he was handsome. Henry the magnificent. Good old well-hung Henry.

She suppressed a sob, swallowed wine, drew long on the cigarette.

What a talent he'd once had. Where had it gone? Where had he spent it? *Goddammit, he had no right to waste it like that! If I had a talent like that . . . I wouldn't just—*

But I have a talent, Estelle suddenly thought, and a small playful smile came to her lips. *I have a talent. I really do. They don't believe I have, but I do. They make fun of me, but that's because they don't understand. They're afraid.*

She rose and walked unsteadily to the bookcase where the Ouija was kept. She was just about to reach for it, when she heard a step on the stair, and turning, saw a tall figure in tight shorts and a halter pass the living room arch on the way to the front door.

"Where are you going, Sue?" she called.

"Out," Susan said without turning.

"Wait a minute." She had expected to hear the door open and slam, but it did not. There was a pause and then Susan, on silent, sandaled feet, was in the living room, standing curvaceously, a defiant tilt to her hips.

"What?" Susan said.

"I just wanted to know where you were going, that's all."

"I told you," Susan said. "Out."

"Out where?"

"Look, Estelle, I'm free, white and twenty."

"What's white got to do with it?" Estelle asked. "You sound like a bigot."

"I'm not a bigot and you know it! And it's none of your business where I go! You're not my *mother!*"

Estelle dropped her head in hurt. "I worry. I do worry about you."

"Balls!"

"Sue, do you *have* to use those words all the time?"

"Shit!"

"And fuck you too!" Estelle screamed. "And that's about as good an Anglo-Saxon conversation as I've had in a long time! Now get out of here!"

"Fuck?" Susan exclaimed, brows arching. "Estelle, you can't fuck anything anymore. That's your trouble. I'll bet you haven't been able to fuck dear old Daddy in years."

The slap exploded in the room like the crack of a bullwhip. Tears of rage came to Susan's eyes, her face flushed, and her lips quivered. Then her hand came up from her hip in a swift, swinging arc, catching Estelle suddenly, sending her sprawling toward the fireplace. The poker clanged and the tongs rattled, and as Estelle's head hit the hearth, there was a sickening thud.

Susan was on her knees, reaching. "Oh, shit, Estelle. I'm sorry! Oh, Christ, I didn't mean—"

But her ministrations were met by an upraised arm, flailing, clawing, and the hoarse wail of a woman in pain.

"Evil! You're evil!"

"Estelle—"

"Evil! That's what you are! Evil! Get out of here. Get out of here! Get out, get out, get out! Evil! Evil!"

In the car, on the way to Job's Camp, Susan shook, and wept, and almost retched. The word reverberated through her mind. *Evil, evil, evil.*

Oh, my God, why? Why did I do that? Why did I say that? Why did I hit her? She's always been nice to me. It's just that she's so—so damned weird!

She's right. I'm evil. I must be evil.

CHAPTER
10

That afternoon, Estelle Dixon descended into the torpor of drunkenness, finally dropping into the unmade bed and sleeping fitfully to a series of random dreams filled with a meaningless, disconnected tableau of terror.

When she awoke, Henry was standing above her, looking down, his body limp in exasperation.

"What happened?"

"Nothing," she said.

"You're going to have one hell of a shiner," he said. "What happened? You fall down again?"

She looked at him for a moment, frowning, searching. "Yes," she said.

Dixon sighed. He lowered himself to the side of the bed and glanced at the half-full tumbler of wine. He pushed it aside to the further end of the night table. He shook his head slightly and then reached out, bringing his hand gently to his wife's face, softly caressing her forehead, then letting his touch travel to the bruise at her left eye, probing it solicitously.

"You know," he said, "sometimes you give me a pain in the ass."

She had to laugh, a small laugh, but a laugh. "I guess I am a pain in the ass," she said.

His fingers were on the back of her neck, kneading, massaging, gently comforting.

"Where were you?" she asked.

"On The Reach. Up by the covered bridge. I did a little sketch. In oil."

"Let me see it," she said, and her eyes were lighting.

"Later," he said, and his hand was on her shoulder now, gently rubbing.

He was looking at her hair, remembering the once soft silkiness of it. Now it was flat and brittle from bleach, a false, cadmium yellow thatch, which at the roots still hinted at a once deep burnt sienna, now fading into gray.

There were lines on her forehead and under her eyes, and her neck was beginning to wrinkle. Her mouth was still full and sensual, but the corners had begun to show traces of jowls.

Her eyes were still the same and would never change. Alive and alert, glistening and sharp, defying all comparisons to a color chart, neither cerulean nor azure nor green nor gray. Just Estelle. There should be a new color. Estelle.

"What are you thinking about?" she asked.

"Nothing," he said.

Then slowly, very slowly, he bent to her, and gently, very gently, he kissed her. Their lips grazed gently and their tongues met and his hands wandered to her breasts.

And slowly, they undressed each other, as if for the first time, marveling in each other as each new sight came into view.

And gently, they made love, until rising passion empowered them to thrust and counterthrust, gaspings and raspings, grunts and groans, and in the end, the mingling of juices, and, surprisingly, a gentle laughter.

Later, sharing a cigarette together, she said, "You know, I didn't think I could fuck anymore."

"You can fuck," he said.

That evening, Henry Dixon treated the Boodles with care and caution, nursing only two martinis before dinner and feeling surprisingly relaxed, even enjoying his food.

He and Estelle charbroiled a steak outside, threw some unhusked corn in the coals, and prepared a romaine salad with tomatoes and an oil and vinegar dressing.

And for the first time in many months they talked without rancor. Their conversation was bright and animated, familiar and personal. They remembered trips they had taken, places they had been, restaurants they had discovered, beds they had shared, and when, after cognac, Estelle hinted at the Ouija board, Dixon offered no objection, but felt himself unaccountably looking forward to it.

Across the table from her, his fingers resting lightly on the planchette, Dixon neither tried to push or pull, nor control it in any way, content only to play the little game, humor her, while his eyes studied her face and his mind wandered across their experience.

She had always needed something, some skill, some special knowledge to set her apart, he knew, to raise herself from the lack of confidence she so strongly felt. Unable to paint, write, act, do anything artistic, her lack of talent in a talented milieu had led her to seek self-expression first in Zen, then in other mystical pastimes, and finally in the occult.

She had gone at it with the single-mindedness and

fanaticism that marked all her strivings, reading voluminously, voraciously, attending parapsychology lectures, visiting fortune tellers and readers/advisors, and taking part in quack seances. In time, she could talk of little else, and became, in a sense, an amateur-expert, laughed at, ridiculed, a favorite subject of cocktail party character assassination.

If only, Henry Dixon thought, studying her face, the half-closed, slightly slanted eyes, the slightly parted full, sensuous lips, *if only I could give her my own talent, what's left of it, if I could give it to her, I would so gladly.*

It was then that the planchette moved.

"It's moving," Estelle said.

"I know it's moving."

"Are you doing that?"

"No, I'm not."

"Don't do that, Hank."

"I'm not doing it, I told you!"

"Quiet. Keep quiet!" she said excitedly. "Keep your fingers on it. Don't move. Just stay there. Tell me. Tell me what it spells."

The planchette moved slowly four times.

"I . . . S . . . H . . . A . . ." Dixon said.

"What?"

"I-S-H-A."

"Remember that."

"A cinch."

A minute passed. Two. Three.

"This is ridiculous," Dixon said.

"Don't take your fingers off," Estelle said. "I feel something."

At five minutes, the planchette moved again.

"Read it," Estelle said. There was a light perspiration on her forehead. The pulse in her neck throbbed visibly, strongly.

"L . . . L . . . ." The planchette paused. Then: "S . . . P . . . E . . ."

Three minutes went by.

"You remember?" Estelle asked.

"L-L-S-P-E," Dixon spelled.

"Before that."

"I-S-H-A."

"Don't forget."

"It doesn't make sense."

"Quiet."

The planchette was moving. Dixon felt his fingers being carried. Estelle's eyes were closed. Her breathing was heavy and harsh. A bead of sweat crept down her nose.

"Estelle, let's cut this out!"

"Quiet, goddammit! Quiet! Read! Read it!"

Two more groups of letters came from the planchette, and after another pause of two minutes, a third. Then it was still.

They waited. Five minutes. Eight. Ten.

Estelle's breathing became regular. Her eyes fluttered open. She lifted her fingers from the planchette.

"Can you remember?" she asked.

"Yes."

"Write it down."

Dixon found pen and paper. He scribbled quickly. "It doesn't make sense," he said.

"Let me see!" Her eyes were bright, manic. She almost tore the paper from his hand. "I know we're experiencing something! I just know this is an experience!" She flattened the paper on the table, bending over it, frowning.

ISHA   LLSPE   AKSO   ONELV   IDA

Dixon pushed his chair back, rose and walked to the bar. He poured a stiff one, neat, no ice. He found his hands were trembling.

"Did you do this, Hank?"

"For chrissake, I told you I didn't! Did you?"

"You know better than that."

"It's gibberish, anyway."

"No, it's not. It's a message."

He walked back to the table, leaned over her shoulder. "It is, huh? I suppose you're a cryptologist, now."

"I don't have to be. It's not in code. Look."

With a pen, she circled the groups of letters.

ISHA   LLSPE   AKSO   ONELV   IDA

"Huh?"

She spoke slowly: "I . . . shall . . . speak . . . soon."

"Oh." He studied the letters. "What's the rest of it? ELV . . . IDA?"

"A name, I guess. Elvida."

Dixon took a long swallow of gin, sighed, and lifted his eyes to the ceiling.

"And just who is Elvida?" he asked.

"I don't know," she said.

"Well, I sure as hell don't," he said, gulping. "Unless it's that stewardess I ended up with on the lawn at Bannister's last party. She had some kind of Scandinavian name."

"Stop trying to make it a joke, Hank."

"Who's trying to make it a joke?" He shrugged and started for the door. "I'm going to bed."

"It's an anagram," Estelle said, and the tone of her

voice, the flat, unintentioned fear in it, stopped him at the arch.

"What's an anagram?"

"The name. Elvida. E-L-V-I-D-A."

"So?"

"A devil. Don't you see it? Elvida . . . a Devil."

Dixon's vision was beginning to blur slightly from the drink, and he was a little unsteady on his feet. Thoughts were escaping him, words would not form. So all he said was, "Bullshit, Estelle! Bullshit!" He started for the stairs.

But that night, lying in bed, he considered two things: He had not controlled the planchette, consciously or unconsciously. Nor had Estelle.

She was incapable of lying.

Somewhere in his travels, Ken Brady had secured a small, fine surgical clamp, so the roach being passed about that night was guaranteed good to the last flake of leaf. Since this was the first joint of the evening, nobody was yet really spaced, though Dimples, who had started earlier, was well on her way.

"I'm in clover," Dimples said. "Rolling in clover. Roll me over in the clover, Freddie. Roll me over in the clover like a good boy."

Freddie Loftus was in no mood for jocularity. "That's crabgrass you're sitting in, smart ass."

"Roll me over in the crabgrass, Freddie."

"Later, cunt."

"You're no fun tonight, Freddie," said Dimples, then lapsed into vacant-eyed silence.

The surgical clamp made its rounds once more, the roach brightening in the darkness with each stop along the way from Dimples to Freddie to Ken Brady to Susan, who drew on it shallowly, not averse to its taste or effect, but preferring the sips of wine from the bottle of Almaden Mountain Red that stood in the circle they formed around the flickering candle.

"There's no difference between good and evil," Freddie was saying, "no difference when you examine it close up. That's gonna be my sermon for the Rites next time."

"No shit, really?" Ken Brady said. "You really going to say that?" There was a slight redness beginning to show in the whites of his eyes, and his mouth was curled in a silly smile.

"It's true," Freddie Loftus said. "All you gotta do is look at it, man. Look around you, you know? Wherever you look, you see evil, man. Evil. If there was all good, there wouldn't be evil, right? And if there was all evil, there wouldn't be good, right?"

"I don't follow that, Freddie," Susan said.

"What don't you follow?"

"What you just said."

"Like good and evil, they exist together, that's what I said."

"Side by side," Ken said.

"Right within each other," Freddie said, "bound up, y'know? Like existence is good and evil together, y'know? You can't have one without the other."

"Like love and marriage," Susan said with a sarcastic edge.

"What?"

"Nothing, Freddie," she said. "Tell us more about your philosophy of good and evil." She sat apart, not physically, but almost spiritually, as though she were an observer, looking through a window at another side of the universe, watching four people—Ken, Dimples, Freddie, and herself—acting out some

strange, meaningless ritual before an audience of no
one.

"You're not impugning the tenets of my faith, are
you?" There was an edge in Freddie's voice now.

"Not at all, Freddie," Susan said. "I'm interested.
Really." She was beginning to understand her attrac-
tion to Freddie Loftus now. It went beyond the
gaunt, skeletal bone structure, the commanding, almost fanatical glint to his eyes. There was something
more to Freddie than the fascination a snake holds
over the fearful. Behind the facade of country twang,
four-letter words and bad grammar, lurked a person
of no mean education, reading, and wit. His ideas
were twisted, but she wondered how much he was
putting the world on.

"Where you see good, you also see evil," Freddie
continued. "Wherever there is one, there is the other."
Oddly, his words had taken on an almost evangelical
chant, his measures the cadence of the pulpit. "Look
into yourselves. Look into yourselves only to see the
warp and woof of good and evil."

Ken laughed. "You're great, Freddie! Really! You
missed your calling, man! You certainly missed your
calling!" He laughed again and reached for the wine
bottle. "Freddie should've been a preacher-man, right,
Sue?"

"You're getting stoned, Ken," Susan said.

"That's the idea, isn't it? Let's all get stoned!" He
waved the bottle, spilling wine on his shirt reaching
for the newly lit joint.

"Then we're all evil," Susan said.

"The experience of evil shall set you free."
Freddie's eyes shone in the candlelight.

"Bullshit," Ken Brady said. "What's that supposed
to mean?"

"What it says," Freddie said.

"Bullshit!"

"That we have to be aware of evil to be aware of good," Susan said.

"You're close." Freddie was looking at her intently, his eyes locked on her halter. "Come to the Rites next time," he said.

"To experience evil? To set myself free?" Her voice was flat. She reached to Ken for the roach.

"Who said sex was evil?" Ken asked, smiling and raising the wine. "Hell! It's good clean fun! Here's to sex!"

"Sex?" Dimples came up from limbo. "Roll me over in the crabgrass, Freddie-boy!" She fell sideways, clutching, but in the wrong direction, ending up sprawled in Ken's lap. "Sex me, lover-boy!"

Kens hand's went to Dimples's rudimentary breasts, kneading, cupping. Then they were stretched out, head to head, lips to lips, groin to groin, hands searching, stroking.

Susan watched, face blank. Her pulses hammered, her nipples came up stiff and tingling against the halter. But it was not the sight of Ken Brady and Dimples turning her on. She could sense Freddie's eyes boring into her. She could hear his quickened breath. Then she felt him beside her.

"Will you come to the Rites?" His voice was uncommonly soft, his hands on her waist gentle.

"I'll think about it," she said. They kissed. His mouth was rough, crushing. His breath was foul, and his hand on her breast twisted and pulled and mashed. She let herself be pushed back on the ground, and she absorbed his long tongue in her mouth. But when his hand went to her crotch, she crossed her legs. Her fingernails dug deeply into the prominent bones of his back, and then she was pushing him away, confused yet excited, revolted yet attracted.

"Freddie . . ."

"What?"

"Do you think I'm evil?"

His eyes had a light of their own in the darkness. "He that is without sin among you," he said, "let him first cast a stone at her."

Thirty feet away, Milt Framer leaned awkwardly against a tall silver birch, his right hand grasping it for support, his left, below, working, kneading, moving, faster, faster! He could see very little, only shapes, vague forms, silhouettes. But he could hear the breathing, the gasps, the small moans. He was trying hard to silence his own breathing, his own passion, his mouth tight, drawn, grim. When it was over, when his trembling had stopped, when his spasms had subsided, he crept silently away, head bowed, shame welling in him like a rising tide.

But the shame did not last for long. By the time he reached the intersection of Rut and North Lake roads, he was muttering to himself, "Pigs! Dirty pigs! Degenerates!"

And by the time he reached his car, parked off the shoulder thirty yards on, vengeance was his. *They'll pay for it! They did it and they'll pay for it! Dirty, evil pigs!*

It rained on the morning of Nicole Bannister's thirty-fifth birthday. By midafternoon the depressing drizzle had stopped, and the sun came through only wanly in a vain effort to burn off a wet, low-lying miasma. But the rest of the day and evening promised only more of the same.

In the kitchen of the Bannister home, Leslie was

helping Pearl with the egg salad. "How much of this stuff do I put in, Pearl?"

"That dry mustard, honey. You don't want to put in too much of that. Here, lemme show you." Pearl DeWitt waddled to the table, measured an amount in her palm, sprinkled it into the bowl and returned the spoon to Leslie. "You go ahead and mix that up real good now. And don't slop it all over the place."

"Oh, I know how to do it!"

"You like Pearl's egg salad?"

"Oh, I guess."

" 'N how about Elsie. She like egg salad?"

"Elsie likes everything I like."

"But you don't know if you like egg salad?"

"Sometimes I like it. Sometimes I don't. Elsie says that, too."

"Elsie says what?" It was Nicole, entering the kitchen from the driveway with a shopping bag of groceries.

"Neither one of them don't know if they like egg salad, Miz Bannister." Pearl's high chuckle lilted through the air.

"Well, if they don't like it, they don't have to eat it," Nicole said and suddenly caught herself. *They?* Had she too given in to the existence of Elsie?

"Everything just about done, Miz Bannister, on the cold side. Potato salad, pickled beets, cole slaw. I fixin' to put the turkey in soon."

"That's fine, Pearl. I'll help you with the ham later. And Leslie, I want you to get ready to—" Turning, she saw the empty chair, the abandoned bowl of egg salad. "Leslie!"

"I think she out by the pool, Miz Bannister. I think that her through the window."

Nicole was out in a streak, slamming the screen door, half slipping on the wet grass as she ran to the small figure at the water's edge.

"I was only looking at the fish." Leslie's voice held a plaintive note, her face beseeching.

"How many times have I told you you're not to go to the pool alone?"

"Why can't I?" Defiance now.

"Because you can't swim, that's why!"

"I'm learning to swim!"

"You haven't learned yet!"

"You're always telling me what to do!" The small face crinkled. "You never let me do what I want!" The mouth dragged down, the eyes became tearful slits. "You think I'm a stupid! You think I'm dumb! You don't love me! You never loved me!" By this time, Leslie's small face was a torrent of tears.

It was a moment for comfort, for outstretched arms, a warm breast, a cuddled head, a firm hug, and to Nicole Bannister such moments came as naturally as the sun rises each morning. She cradled, she rocked, she spoke softly, she smiled gently, and in the end, mother and daughter were one again.

"When will I be able to swim, Mommy?"

"Soon."

"Next week?"

"Maybe. We'll see."

"Daddy says I'm a good swimmer."

"Daddy says you *will* be a good swimmer."

"Elsie's a good swimmer."

"Elsie?" A frown crossed Nicole's brow. She took Leslie by the shoulders, holding her slightly away, looking into her eyes. "Tell me something, Leslie. Do you ever *see* Elsie?"

"See?"

"Yes, see. I know you talk to her. But do you—*see* her?"

"Sometimes."

"What does she look like?"

Leslie pondered, then shrugged slightly. "Oh, I don't know."

"Is her hair blond? Or dark?"

"I don't know."

"Does she have blue eyes?"

"Like mine?"

Nicole nodded.

"Sort of." Leslie had begun to fidget restlessly. Nicole wondered whether it was an evasive action or mere impatience.

"When did you last see Elsie?"

"Oh . . . not for a long time."

"How long?"

There was a pause while Leslie's brow knit in a childish frown. "Maybe Elsie's sick," she said at last.

"Why?"

"Well . . . well, she don't . . . *doesn't* . . . come much anymore."

Something suddenly collapsed inside Nicole Bannister. A huge bridgework of fear suddenly gave way, disintegrated, became weightless. It was like a gigantic inner sigh of relief, a washing of the spirit.

Nicole Bannister realized that her daughter was not hallucinating.

"If Elsie ever comes back," she smiled, "I'd like to meet her."

The distant jangle of the phone wafted to poolside. After a moment, Pearl's head jutted from the screen door.

"Dr. Blauvelt, Miz Bannister. You want him to call back?"

"Have him hold on, Pearl. I'll be right there." Taking Leslie's hand, she started for the phone.

"Upstairs with you," she said, smacking Leslie playfully on the behind. "You know what's required on party nights."

"A bath, a sampoo, and the new nightie."

"And we'll let you stay up late."

"Oh, goody, goody, goody!" Feet pounded on the stairs.

Then the phone: "Tom, don't tell me you're not coming! Oh, great! . . . Fine. . . . No, we've got plenty of everything, Tom. Just bring yourself. . . . Oh, nineish . . . you know the Bannister time syndrome by now. . . ."

Upstairs, in her bedroom, preparing for her bath, Leslie paraded nude before the mirror.

"*Up* late, *up* late, Leslie's gonna stay *up* late!"

Then she heard the voice.

"Leslie?"

She turned. Emptiness. "Who's that?"

"It's me, Leslie." The voice seemed to be coming from the window. "Over here, Leslie."

She walked to the window.

"No. Over here, Leslie." The voice seemed to come from the ceiling.

"Elsie?"

"No. Over here, Leslie." Now it seemed to come from the closet.

"Who is it?" Leslie asked.

"Elvida."

"Who?"

"It's me, Elvida. You remember me," and there came a childish laughter, hollow and thin.

PART
TWO

CHAPTER
11

It was hot. The moist air was tainted with a dank fetidness that arose from the marshes at Devil's Pond and drifted as far north as Job's Ruins. The moon was full, but broke only weakly through the overcast, spilling a pale, sickly light on the landscape.

The peepers had long since ceased their alto raspings, but every now and then a bullfrog croaked his skepticism in a dark basso profundo. Somewhere, an owl hooted dismally, and in the distance a dog lifted his head skyward and let forth a long, mournful wail.

But from the brightly lit home and poolside of Jonathan and Nicole Bannister, the carefree, irresponsible sounds of partying rose into the hovering gloom in a bright, lilting counterpoint: the rapid, nonstop jumble of overlapping voices, punctuated now and again by a shrill giggle, a raucous guffaw, the tinkle of ice in tumblers, the clatter of serving platters, the bass boom of the stereo, the springy thump of the diving board, the flat splash of a body hitting the water broadside. Somewhere a girl shrieked and then laughed provocatively in response to a pinch. A group of four men at the french doors suddenly broke into ribald belly laughs as the punchline of a dirty joke was delivered. In the living room, to the accompaniment of the stereo, a woman began to sing "Love for Sale" in an off-key, whisky soprano.

Conversation ran a scale from the serious to the silly, from small talk to deep talk, from religion to politics to the latest films, fashions, pumpernickel bread, and personalities.

"Did you hear the one about the Polish firing squad?" . . . "If they raise the skirts again, I'm going to grow shorter legs." . . . "Wertmuller? She doesn't compare with Herzog!" . . . "Nikki, dear! What's in this scrumptious dip?" . . . "No, I'm strictly a white-winer now. I've given the hard stuff up." . . . "We never get to the city anymore. I haven't seen a play in three years." . . . "What's this about a new subdivision up in Tyrone, Ollie? You got your greedy fingers in that?" . . . "My place Wednesday afternoon. Jack'll be out of town for three days." . . . "Fornication, anyone?"

"Looks like everybody came," Jonathan said.

Nicole grimaced. "Don't they always?"

"What's that girl's name? The one with Joe Tremper?"

Nicole leered at him. "You too, huh?" She started for the kitchen. "Pearl? Pearl, do we have any more egg salad?"

Marion Hammond approached Tom Blauvelt. "Tom, can we talk for a minute. Private?"

"What's up?"

"That finger."

"Later," Blauvelt said. He had noticed Nicole coming back into the room.

At poolside, Lauren Shane watched Henry Dixon bounce up and down on the diving board. "Who's that?" she asked Joe Tremper.

"Hank Dixon. He's an artist. Why? You got the hots for him?"

"He's not bad."

"Old enough to be your father."

"So are you, Lochinvar. And don't get jealous," she said, squeezing his leg. "You know where my heart is."

"It's your twat I worry about."

In the den, waving her highball glass before her like a weapon, Estelle Dixon had backed Father Daniel Conant up against the fireplace. "Tell me about Satan, Father. You must know a lot about that."

Conant fidgeted. "I don't know whether this is the time or place, Mrs. Dixon. . . ."

"Do you believe in the Devil, Father?"

Conant smiled uneasily. "I believe in God."

"God's been dead since 1966," a voice chimed in. "That's when the Satanic Age started." Harold Brewster lumbered in on his prosthetic leg to form a group of three.

"Who told you that, Mr. Brewster?" Conant asked. "Or have I missed something?"

"He's right," another voice added. Agnes Bittel's pinched face darted into the group like a pecking bird. "How can we have God when we have heroin, pot, LSD, crime in the streets, and sex orgies?"

"Sex orgy? Who wants to have a sex orgy?" Henry Dixon, dripping wet from the pool, empty glass in hand, stared at them drunkenly.

"Get lost, husband," Estelle said.

Dixon lost himself at the bar, looking for the Boodles.

Conant was looking quizzically at Harold Brewster. "Why 1966?" he asked.

"You're behind the times, Father," Brewster said. " 'God is dead.' Don't you remember? And the Sexual Freedom League? The rise of the hippies and the drug-sex culture?"

"You playing the devil's advocate again, Brewse?" Oliver Marquith and Maria Braithwaite had stopped to listen.

Brewster glared. "You just have to look around you, Ollie."

Marquith nodded. "Up toward Job's Camp you mean. But that still doesn't mean God is dead." Marquith welcomed the opening Brewster had provided for his dig at the kids at Job's Camp, but at the same time he realized Brewster was only half serious. He was a staunch Episcopalian, a regular churchgoer, and a generous contributor. But in his cups, Brewster was prone to be bitter, argumentative, and cynical.

"You're all missing the point!" Estelle's voice was raised against a sudden increase in music volume and in response to some inner excitement of her own. "You're generalizing. I'm not talking about social problems, crime in the streets. I'm talking about what's happening here, right here around us in Holland County."

The others stared at her, waiting.

"The other night," Estelle started, "the other night . . . ." She paused.

"The other night what?" somebody on the fringe of the group asked.

Estelle gulped at her drink for fortification. "Hank and I were at the Ouija board. . . ."

Somebody snickered.

"All right, laugh!" Estelle rasped, turning. "Laugh if you want to! To hell with you."

There was an embarrassed silence, then Conant

said, "And what happened, Mrs. Dixon?" His tone was soft, but his eyes glared over her shoulder, apparently staring down the accuser. A couple moved away.

Estelle raised her head. "It spelled a name," she said meekly. "And a message."

"What name?" Father Conant's eyes were warm, sympathetic.

"Elvida."

"And who is Elvida?"

"I don't know," Estelle said. "But I think it's an anagram."

"An anagram of what?" Conant pressed.

"A Devil." Her voice was small. "If you change the letters around. A Devil."

"And the message?"

" 'I shall speak soon.' "

Oliver Marquith coughed lightly, hesitated, and then said, "Excuse me folks. I think I'll freshen my drink."

Marquith moved away, along with a few others, leaving the priest and Estelle with Maria Braithwaite and Agnes Bittel. Joe Tremper, Lauren Shane, and Tom Blauvelt had joined the group a few moments before.

"And what do you think it all means?" Maria Braithwaite asked.

Estelle looked steadily at Maria. They had not met before, but somehow, intuitively, Estelle felt a kindred spirit.

"I think it has something to do with the finger," she said.

"Come on, Estelle." Hank Dixon, new drink in hand, was tugging at his wife's elbow. "This is no place to talk about that stuff!"

"Leave me alone, Hank!"

"Of all places! Don't you know what the party's for?"

"Let her finish, Mr. Dixon," Maria Braithwaite said. "We're alone in the room now."

"I'll look out for Nicole," Agnes Bittel said.

Dixon looked at Blauvelt, who merely nodded slightly. Then he sighed in exasperation, turned, and stumbled out to the pool.

Looking at the circle of faces around her, at the studied concentration, the expectancy, the slight hints of anxiety, Estelle was suddenly aware of a new-found strength, a faint but glowing sense of power and command. Like an actress on a stage, she had the audience in her hand, and like any good performer, she had an innate instinct about people. The priest and the doctor, she knew, were the most important of the group, but when she spoke, she directed her gaze at Maria Braithwaite.

"I think," she said, "that the voice . . . Elvida . . . wants to speak through me. I think we should have a seance."

"A seance!" Father Conant's visage was dark, disapproving. "That's not quite what I thought you were leading up to, Mrs. Dixon."

"Oh, come now, Father," Maria Braithwaite said. "Don't lecture us about the evils of science, parapsychology, and the occult. Remember your history. The whole mass is little more than a seance."

"Conducted by a priest," Conant admonished.

"Then you'll conduct this one for us," Maria said with a taunting smile.

"No, I won't go that far," Conant said, "but if you're all determined to do this, I'll make myself available." When they looked at him in puzzlement, he went on, "I'm not an unsophisticated man, Mrs. Braithwaite. I've done my reading, I've questioned, I've opened my mind. I've delved into spiritualism, what you call parapsychology, I've even attended a seance. And I know," he said, turning his head to Estelle, "what it can do to the medium. Are you aware of these things, Mrs. Dixon? Do you have any idea how debilitating it might be? Even dangerous?"

Estelle nodded slightly, staring into her drink. They waited. Then she raised her head. "I know," she said. "I know all about those things. I remember that man, the medium in Rochester in 1952. He committed suicide."

"Then you come as a sort of protection," Maria Braithwaite said to the priest.

"Something like that," Conant said. He turned to Estelle. "Are you sure, Mrs. Dixon? You want to go through with it?"

She raised her face. Their eyes met. "I'll chance it," she said. "I'll chance it because there's something evil going on around us. I can feel it."

"I'm with you on that," Bette Hammond said. She had come in from the pool, seated herself and crossed bikinied thighs. "There's something rotten in Holland County. Something not dreamt of in our philosophy. Am I invited to your seance?"

"Of course," Estelle said.

In the kitchen, Carole Kollars nibbled daintily at a deviled egg and regarded Harold Brewster over the rims of her wire-frame glasses. "How come you know so much about Satanism, Brewse? I thought your specialty was Holland County."

"I guess I have a little of the devil in me," Brewster

said, and reached out to pinch Carole's left breast.

Carole jumped and egg plopped on Brewster's hand. "Cut it out, Brewse!"

Brewster licked the gop from his hand. "You taste good, Carole."

"You're a horny old bastard, Brewse." She reached for another egg. As much as she ate, Carole Kollars never gained an ounce, and her figure was as trim at forty-five as it had been at twenty. "But no kidding. Were you serious with all that God is dead stuff?"

"Sometimes I think He is." Brewster was pensive for a moment, then snapped his head up. "No, it was all crap, Carole. But then again, the county has had its share of evil. I finished my book, by the way."

"Your history of Holland County? When can I read it?"

"I'll give you a copy this week."

"It's published?"

"Uh-huh."

"Doubleday?"

"No," Brewster said. "Valor Press."

"Oh," she said, "that's great, Brewse." But her tone lacked enthusiasm. She knew Valor to be a vanity house, and she wondered how much money Brewster had spent to publish his own work. As an editor herself, she had read a few chapters of the tome, and had found, that although well-researched and documented, it was turgid, unimportant, and dull. She changed the subject.

"What do you think of Estelle Dixon?" she asked.

Brewster shrugged. "It takes all kinds," he said, "nuts as well as bolts."

"Are you going to her seance?"

He shrugged again. "It's something that might

break the monotony," he said. "Who're you paired with tonight, Carole? The priest?"

"I think it's supposed to be something like that."

"What do you think of him?"

"He's a turn-on, all right."

"But unfortunately, priests don't ball, huh?"

Carole arched her brows. "Really? *All* of them?"

Nick and Marijane Reilly arrived very late after attending four parties in an adjoining county. Nick was finding it difficult to judge the distance from walls, and Marijane was walking in slow motion.

"Where's Nikki?" she asked the mirror.

"I'm right here," Nick said.

"Not you, stupid. Nic . . . ole."

"Nicole's in the euphemism," Bette Hammond said, approaching them.

"The what?" Nick said, crashing into the door jamb.

"The little girl's room," Bette said. "The lavatory, the water closet, the john, the can, the sandbox. The pisspot."

"Oh," Nick said.

"What you two need is a drink," Bette said. "Come along."

"We want to give her her pleasant," Marijane said.

"Her what?"

"Her pleasant," Marijane repeated.

"Her pheasant," Nick corrected.

"Just put it there on the thingamajig with the others," Bette said. "She's going to open them all later."

"Jesus Christ, what's that?" Nick said, pointing to a large box on the foyer table.

"A CARE package," Bette said.

And so it was. Three feet by three by three, wrapped in glistening foil, and screaming the word CARE on six sides.

Outside, away from the pool, on the wooden footbridge that spanned Willow Creek, the flare of a match lit Thomas Blauvelt's face and part of Marion Hammond's. Blauvelt drew deeply on his cigarette and stared down into the rippling water.

"It's hard to believe," he mused.

"Come down and see for yourself tomorrow," Hammond said.

"I will, but I take your word for it, Marion. But why? How could it happen? You were keeping it in formalin."

Hammond shrugged. "It's beyond me, Tom. Far and away beyond me. I've seen decay, putrefaction, but I've never seen anything like this."

"It happened suddenly? Just like that?"

"I tell you yesterday it was absolutely normal. This morning it was old, dry, wrinkled, hard. That goddamn finger mummified overnight!"

"Impossible."

"Sure, it's impossible," Hammond said. "I fully agree it's impossible. But there it is." He paused. "I swear, Tom, if I didn't know better, if I hadn't seen it before, I'd swear that finger was four thousand years old!"

Blauvelt did not reply. Finally, he said, "The older I get, Marion, the less I know. Sometimes I don't think I know anything."

"What are you getting at?"

Blauvelt raised his shoulders and sighed. "Estelle Dixon. I always took her for a pretty heavy neurotic. Now, I wonder."

At poolside, Judge Oliver Marquith, erect and

dignified in blue blazer and white flannels, leaned over to get a better look down Lauren Shane's cleavage and fell, drink in hand, slowly, gently, but most gracefully, into the water.

The burst of laughter from the onlookers swept through the night, reaching the den where Maria Braithwaite, Agnes Bittel, and Daniel Conant sat in studied conversation. They seemed oblivious to the partying around them, and the raucous ribbing from poolside went unheeded.

"Satan is an *idea*, Miss Bittel," Father Conant said, "not a *being*."

"But you say God is a *being*."

Conant smiled. "God is in us. And we are beings."

"An idea of what, Father?" Maria Braithwaite asked. "What is the Devil an idea *of*? And why?"

"Let's say he's supposed to be the omnipresent chthonic snake."

"Chthonic?" Agnes Bittel was puzzled.

"Greek," Conant said. "In the earth. Of the gods and spirits of the underworld. And why?" he asked, turning back to Maria. "Simply because in early man's search for the cause of failure, he invented the Devil."

"Like he invented God," Agnes said.

"No, Miss Bittel," Conant said. "God invented man."

"And *woman*," Agnes said, arching.

"You're ribbing me," Conant said, and they chuckled.

"Then the Devil, Satan," Maria Braithwaite said, "is a projection of man . . . of his evil."

"Yes. The chthonic snake functioning at man's unconscious level, reflecting his animal being. Carnality. Self-indulgence."

Agnes Bittel pounced. "Greed, sloth, gluttony, anger, pride, envy, lust!"

Conant nodded, smiling lightly. "Seven in all, Miss Bittel."

"But if Satan is the projection of man's evil," Maria Braithwaite said, "isn't God the projection of his good?"

"Man is the projection of God," Conant answered.

Maria laughed. "You won't be shaken, Father."

"Have you been shaken, Mrs. Braithwaite?"

"Why a snake?" Agnes Bittel asked. "Why do we see the Devil as a snake?"

"But he isn't seen as that always," Conant said. "Satan has often been pictured in other animal shapes. As a goat or ram—a bull, a stag. Usually always with a horn or horns. Perhaps it's phallic. Many of the old religions were based on the phallus as the symbol of fertility. And in the most popular version, the Devil has pointed ears and a forked tail, of all things, and carries a three pronged spear." He laughed lightly. "To hell with the Devil. Let's talk about something else."

But Maria Braithwaite had been pondering, studying the young priest. "So Satan changes form with the times, Father. Now let's suppose he were to become a *being* rather than an *idea* in today's world. How would you picture him?"

Conant frowned. "I said before that God is *in* us. Maybe Satan is, too. Maybe he is in our anger, our prejudice, our bigotry—in our rancor and bitterness, our envy and our lust. So he doesn't have to come. He's here."

"But he was once here—as an angel," Agnes Bittel said. "Suppose he were to return. What do you think he'd look like?"

Conant paused, looking past her out the window. "God is The Creator, Miss Bittel. Satan cannot create. I would see the Devil as a noncreator, aching to create, and using evil as his tool." He chuckled nervously. "So he might appear as an artist. Like one of our hosts—or Henry Dixon over there."

Upstairs, Leslie Bannister lay in the half world between sleep and consciousness, the binding of the blanket drawn up to her lips.

"I was never there," she was saying. "What's it like?"

"Oh, it's lots of fun. You'd like it."

"I would?" Leslie said. Her half-closed eyelids were directed at the hanging silver mobile in the center of the room, the area from which the voice seemed to emanate.

"There are all kinds of big lizards, and fish, and even snakes," the voice said.

"But I don't know if Mommy would take me."

"I can take you," the voice said.

"But you aren't even here," Leslie said.

"But I will be. I told you before, I will be. And then we can go together, all right?"

"Why do they call it Devil's Pond?" Leslie asked. "Why?" she asked again.

But the voice did not answer, and soon Leslie was sleeping.

At the bar, Henry Dixon had progressed to his Mr. Hyde state of drunkenness, his eyebrows seeming bushier than ever, and curling devilishly upward at the ends, his face contorted in bitterness. His barbs were becoming sharper, his insults broader, and he was lashing out at anyone nearby.

"I hear you published it yourself," he said to Harold Brewster. "I suppose that's the best way when you can't find anyone else to do it. I suppose even I could write a book and go that route."

"If you could write one," Brewster said with a straight face. If Brewster had any feeling, he seldom revealed it, and he was as quick as Dixon with the knifing remark.

"What's it about, anyway?"

"It's a history of Holland County."

"Oh, a dirty book? I'll read it."

Brewster grinned. "I don't write for masturbators, Hank. But if you're interested in a few gory murders, you might get your kicks."

"How many have you committed?"

"None. But I'm thinking of one."

Dixon laughed. He sipped his drink. "How about the MacCready case? You cover that one?"

Brewster frowned.

"Old MacCready knocked off his first two wives. Right here on the premises."

"I've heard the story, but I put no credence in it."

"And the house is haunted. Did you know that?"

Brewster shrugged. "I've heard that one, too."

"So how many murders has Holland County had?"

"Quite a few," Brewster said. "Job Hart, among others."

"He fell off Great Ledges."

"He was pushed."

"Can you prove that?"

"Read my book."

Dixon was weaving slightly, squinting owlishly over the top of his glass. "Who else?"

"That child about thirty-five years ago."

"Yeah? I never heard about that."

"The body of a nine-year-old girl was pulled from Devil's Pond in 1945."

"She could have fallen in," Dixon said.

"She could have," Brewster said, "but she didn't. The body was in a suitcase. All cut up in pieces."

Dixon's face turned color. He looked sick. Brewster turned and started away, laughing, pulling his plastic leg in an awkward shuffle.

In the kitchen, Jonathan came behind his wife, placed his hands on her arms and kissed the back of her neck. "Tired?"

She turned, grinning. "Hell, no. I just got a second wind. Thanks, lover."

"For what?"

"The party. Just what I needed." She finished slicing the rest of the ham, then turned, kissing him. "Leslie asleep?"

"A log. I just looked in."

"Should we wake her when I open the presents?"

"You opened hers. I don't think we have to. Who brought that CARE package?"

She shook her head. "I don't know. How's the booze holding up?"

"Fine. We've got a lot of BYO's."

"Hank Dixon's getting smashed."

"Drunk as a fiddler's bitch. Doesn't know what he's doing. He just made a pass at Agnes Bittel."

Off in a corner, Estelle Dixon and Maria Braithwaite were planning the seance.

"When do you think it should be?" Maria asked.

"Soon," Estelle said. "I don't think this . . . this whatever it is, this Elvida, wants to wait."

"We could have it at my home."

"No," Estelle said quickly. "It all started at my place. We should continue there. The aura's right."

"As you say." Maria peered into Estelle's eyes curiously. "Are you sure you're up to it, Mrs. Dixon? The priest is right, you know. It can be dangerous."

"Call me Estelle, please."

"Of course. You want really to do it, Estelle?"

"I've been to seances before."

"As a medium?"

"No. But I'm sure I can do it."

Maria Braithwaite nodded slowly. "Whatever you say." She seemed to have finished, but then added, "Perhaps I can be of help. I mean, I have been to a number of meetings, and once even conducted one."

"You believe then?"

The Spanish woman smiled mysteriously, her head waved from side to side. "I believe, I do not believe. But perhaps I believe more than I do not believe."

In the kitchen, Oliver Marquith lurched against the table and knocked a new platter of potato salad to the floor. In the living room, Henry Dixon made a grand gesture and swept four drinks and two decanters of whisky from the bar. In the rec room Norma Marquith sat on a plate of cucumber salad. Somebody burned the coffee table with a cigarette, another guest dropped his pipe on the rug, and a late arrival sat down at the piano and promptly broke G sharp over middle C.

The men's voices rose raucously, the women shrilled, and the decibel level peaked into the red.

Agnes Bittel passed out under the piano with her drink resting upright on her chest. Harold Brewster locked himself into an upstairs bathroom and spent twenty minutes shouting for help. Two more guests fell into the pool fully dressed. Carole Kollars lost the cap to a front tooth, and Joe Tremper found it in Henry Dixon's Boodles. Tom Blauvelt dropped into a director's chair and fell through to the floor.

Somehow, mustard got into the stereo turntable. A plate of macaroni upset itself behind the couch. The turkey disappeared. The ham followed.

Altogether, it was a good party.

"Present time!" somebody shouted, and the guests gathered in the living room as Jonathan carried the presents from the foyer, and Nicole sat on a cushion in the center of the floor.

She was flushed, slightly drunk, happy-looking, like an eager child on Christmas morning. She picked up a heavy oblong package, shook it and announced, "I have a sneaky suspicion as to what this is. Bo-o-o-zze!"

And booze it was. Two bottles of Boodles from Henry and Estelle Dixon.

What else, Jonathan thought.

More booze followed. Nicole seemed to have an instinct for liquor packages and opened in turn bottles of Chivas, Red Label, Black Label, Forrester's, Old Grand-dad, Smirnoff, and three cognacs, a Courvoisier and two Hennesseys. As they shed their wrappings, Jonathan took them to the bar, knowing they would be less by morning.

A package containing a thick book followed and Nicole looked over at Harold Brewster with a smile that, though somewhat forced, was as honest as she could make it. "Harold. How nice. I just know it's going to keep me up nights."

A History of Holland County was passed around amid "oohs" and "ahs," and Henry Dixon looked toward the ceiling and swore silently.

"Open the CARE package, Nikki," somebody said.

"Yeah," Nick Reilly said. "I've been wondering about that all night."

"Not yet, not yet!" another voice said. "Save that till last."

"No, I want to know what's in it," somebody said.

"It's *big* enough to hold a midget," someone else said.

Nicole undid the wrapping carefully. "It's so beautiful," she said. "I hate to spoil it."

Inside, there was a great deal of plastic excelsior, and then Nicole found a card. She looked over at Maria Braithwaite. "Maria," she said. "I guessed it was you."

"For Christ's sake, Nicole! What's in it?"

The first item out of the CARE package was a one-pound tin of fresh Beluga in a Styrofoam container packed with ice.

A long drawn-out "Aah!" passed amongst the onlookers.

"Jesus Christ!" Henry Dixon said to Estelle. "That alone must've cost four hundred bucks!"

A large crock of imported foie gras drew a long "ooh" from the crowd. The smoked eel promoted three "aahs" and one "ugh!"

A jar of crimson pickled eggs got a "What the hell's that?"

Smoked trout, pickled tiny corn, dried fruits, nut cake, and assorted goodies received their various levels of approbation, and when Nicole pulled out a second tin of caviar, somebody said, "Let's have another party!"

"I'm game!"

"Break out the egg yolks!"

"I can't stand the stuff!"

"I like mine with just plain buttered toast."

"Just give me a spoon. And a drop of lemon juice."

"What the hell, it's only fish eggs."

"The caviar," Nicole finally announced, "is going into the fridge. Tied down and booby-trapped, by the way. And the day I open it, I shall invite a few, a very select few, to the orgy." She paused. "So everybody better be nice to me from here on in."

There was laughter and Nicole proceeded to open more packages. There were books; large books, small books, thick books, thin books; books for reading, books for the coffee table. And there were records: Handel, Mahler, Purcell, Copeland, a complete Cole Porter, the preludes of Gershwin, and a thing called "Soundtracks from Great Pornographic Films."

The contents of a small package brought a hush to the room, and as Nicole looked at Daniel Conant, she said softly, "It's just beautiful, Father."

The priest smiled gently.

She held the crucifix aloft. "Isn't it beautiful?" It held no figure of Christ. There was not a mark on it. It was a simple cross in silver with a soft finish. Very Danish modern. "You know my taste, don't you, Father?"

"I'm happy you like it," he said.

More books, more records. A set of old-fashioned tumblers. A complicated corkscrew from Hammacher-Schlemmer. A toy typewriter with a coloring book and crayons. A "one-man-band" set containing a kazoo, a Jew's harp, a harmonica, and a whistle. A cocktail shaker from Tiffany's. A leather game chest from Schwarz containing a roulette wheel, a back-gammon board, dice, chessmen, decks of playing cards, and appropriate cloths and boards. Perfume. Scented soap. Incense. A pair of theatre tickets from Bette and Marion Hammond.

"Bette! I've been wanting to see this!"

"You and me both! And there's another pair in my hot little fist for the same night. We'll all go together."

It was news to Marion.

There were three packages left. "What's this?" Nicole said, shaking the smallest.

"Sounds like an overdone cupcake," Hank Dixon said.

"Estelle been baking again?" someone asked.

"It's a petrified ice cube," somebody else said.

"Don't joke. It might be the Hope Diamond."

"This I gotta see."

There was a great deal of tissue, and Nicole searched for a card but found none. When she uncovered the object she looked up and said, "It's a paperweight. I should have known by the sound." She was looking inside the box again. "Made out of some kind of petrified . . ."

Jonathan caught the change in her first. The color drained from her face. Her mouth hung open. Her eyelids fluttered and her hands shook. She got up quickly, letting the box drop to the floor, and stumbled out of the room, choking.

The thing fell out of the box onto the rug, but Jonathan scooped it up quickly, jamming it back in the box as he raced after Nicole.

"What the hell's going on?" somebody asked.

"Jesus!"

"Did you see it?"

"I'd swear it was a . . ."

Tom Blauvelt followed Jonathan up the stairs. He found Nicole in the bathroom, retching, Jonathan holding her head.

"My bag's in the backseat of the car," Blauvelt said. "Go get it. I'll handle her."

Later, when they had her sedated and in bed, Blauvelt walked over to the box on the bureau.

"Jesus Christ!" he said.

It was a hand. Slightly clawed. Very small but appearing to be very old. It was wrinkled. Dry. Hard.

The little finger was missing.

CHAPTER 12

In the morning, in Marion Hammond's laboratory at WebLabs the specimen lay exposed on a clean white cloth, the missing digit beside it.

"You can see that they belong together," Hammond said to Frank Liscomb. "Of course we can dissect and test for perfect articulation, but I don't think we have to. The proportion is perfect. And all the other properties; color, texture, hardness."

Liscomb was staring at the hand in disbelief, a cigar hanging from his lips. "Can you get prints from that thing?"

Hammond raised his shoulders. "We can try. But you've already got a print from the finger."

"Yeah." He turned. "What do you think, Tom?"

"I don't think anything anymore, Frank." Thomas Blauvelt leaned against a wall, arms folded.

"Shit! What the hell is this all about!" Liscomb said. "I never saw anything like this!"

"Nor have I," Hammond added.

"I think we better keep this out of the papers," Liscomb said.

"How are you going to do that, Frank?" Blauvelt said. "People saw it last night."

"Then let the papers get it by hearsay, rumor. If we don't let any pictures out, it'll stay local. I don't want reporters from every city in the country barging into my office."

"You think that's wise?" Hammond asked.

"It'll give us time to think," Liscomb said. "Sure, let's get help—medical authorities, museums, FBI. But let's keep it out of the papers until we know what it's all about."

"If we ever know what it's about," Blauvelt said.

"What do you mean by that?"

Blauvelt shrugged.

"I'll find out what it's about," Liscomb said. "I'll find out for goddamn sure!"

In fact, very little gossip was generated by the incident at the Bannister party because of Jonathan's alacrity in picking up the evidence and charging away with it. A few of the guests had a vague idea about the contents of the box, but because they could hardly believe their own eyes, they were close-mouthed and hesitant, unwilling to discuss something that would make them appear eccentric if not outright crazy.

For her own part, Nicole seemed to have forgotten. She arose the next morning in a cheerful mood, full of chatter and gossip about the guests. She never mentioned the presents.

Jonathan saw through the facade, but decided not to press. If it was a defense, as he was certain, it would either succeed or break down. Only time would tell, and he was content to wait and play along.

"Tomorrow's Sunday," he said. "Suppose we take Leslie over to the Pikeville Fair. It's the last day."

"Sure," she said. "Right after church in the morning."

"After *what*?"

"I think I'd like to go to church in the morning."

"You haven't been to church in years," Jonathan said. "What goes?"

"Nothing goes," she snapped. "I just feel like going to church, that's all."

"Okay. We'll go to church."

"You don't have to go," she said.

Jonathan shrugged. "Whatever you say." He was conscious of a distance opening up, a small but definite chasm. Her facade was not cracking, but there was a fear beginning to work against it, an underlying dread, and he sensed it.

She was arranging glasses in the dishwasher. He walked over and kissed her on the cheek. "I'd like to go."

She smiled. "You won't even know what to do in church."

"Neither will you," he said.

Reclining in a deck chair on the upper terrace overlooking her pool, Maria Braithwaite sipped slowly at the black Brazilian coffee and let her mind wander over the events of the night before.

It had definitely been a hand. She was certain. But the fleeting glimpse had told her little. Its size, its shape, its color escaped her. Just the form. The form remaining in her mind. In the ensuing confusion most of the other guests had seemed perplexed, uncertain in their responses, and there had even been some nervous laughter. The brief instant in which it lay bare and exposed had left little time for recognition.

But the priest had seen it, recognized it for what it was, of that she was sure. Their eyes had met instantly, and in his she had seen horror and fear, a sudden confrontation with evil.

"Well?" she had asked. "Do you still feel that Satan is only an idea?"

He had not answered. In an almost ashamed manner he had dropped his eyes, then turned to stare out the window.

Maria twisted uncomfortably in the chair. The weather was still heavy and humid, the sun struggling to break through the dull overcast.

The phone rang. "Good morning. To whom am I speaking?" she asked in a formal European way.

It was Estelle Dixon. "I'm planning the seance for two weeks from today," she said. "Is that good for you?"

"If I have any engagements I'll break them," Maria said. "How many will be there? Not too many, you know."

"Hank and I, you, Father Conant. Dr. Blauvelt and Agnes Bittel. The Hammonds. Joe Tremper and that new girl of his. And I'm thinking of asking Carole Kollars. Does that sound right?"

"Excellent."

"Maria?" There was a hesitation in Estelle's voice. "Did you see what I saw last night?"

"What did you see?"

"A hand. I could swear it was a hand. All . . . withered and wrinkled."

There was a long silence until Maria said, "I don't think so, Estelle. It must be your imagination."

"But I'm sure of it, Maria. *Almost* sure."

"You have a very vivid imagination, Estelle. All psychics do. You must control it, no? Not to let it get in the way of the seance."

"What did you see, Maria?"

"I? I saw nothing. I was turned away. But we must

talk about the seance, Estelle. We should meet a few times before."

After cradling the phone, Maria Braithwaite sat up and lit a Gitane, inhaling deeply. She did not look forward to the seance and was concerned with her own fears. She knew the dangers to the medium, perhaps even to the others present.

Maria Braithwaite was no stranger to the occult in any of its forms. In the fifties, she and her late husband had attended an exorcism in Madrid and watched a young priest slit his wrists. Later they had taken part in a seance in London, feeling the air about them grow dense and impenetrable while the medium went into shock and bled through the nose. After her husband's death in 1963, she had witnessed a Black Mass in a Paris cellar where a cockerel had been sacrificed.

She sighed and leaned back in the chair. These Americans. How little they know about spiritualism, mystery, the inexplicable, the unforeseen.

They come upon a philosophy or way of thought that is new to them, and they embrace it as if it were their own, moulding it, shaping it, changing it into something it was never meant to be, and in doing so, losing its meaning. Astrology, yoga, Buddhism, meditation, all become fads, something to "do," something "in," something to act out, talk about, brag about, show off like a new possession.

Psychiatry had been twisted, warped, torn asunder and completely reshaped into a meaningless mass of pseudoscience; Dianetics, Scientology, TM, est, all of them do-it-yourself kits for the American dream of happiness, but leading only to further misunderstanding and eventual annihilation of the soul. Where Freud had established a therapy, there was left merely sense-less jargon.

And now the American masses had lately discovered the occult. As though it had never been there in the first place! It was as if they had manufactured it themselves, on a production line, their own toy to do with as they pleased. Satan, Lucifer, Beelzebub were new characters in the American drama. Witches, covens, the Black Mass, Ouija boards and seances cropped up on book racks, on television screens, in films. The occult was the new order of the day, the high point in cocktail party chatter. And soon, if the drift continued, a family that could not boast a wandering spirit would be relegated to the uninvited, and a house that was not haunted would find no real estate agent.

Maria smiled. What will these Americans do with their new fad? The same as always. Never attempt to fully understand it, but reform it, glaze over it, and in the end, cast it aside for some new toy.

No, she did not look forward to the seance. It would be amateur night again. Everybody talking at once, telling one another what to do, everyone an expert in a field no one comprehended.

But she would go. Because of her feelings for Estelle Dixon, her faith in her as a medium. And because of her own fear.

In the car, on the way back from WebLabs to King's Landing, Frank Liscomb was morose. He glanced over to his right at Thomas Blauvelt.

"All right," he said, "you tell me."

Blauvelt shrugged. "I can't tell you anything, Frank. How the hell should I know?"

"Somebody brought the goddamn thing. Who?"

"Frank, there were fifty, maybe sixty people there," Blauvelt said irritably. "Maybe more."

"Somebody left the package on the table in the hall. Who?"

"Of course somebody left it. But you can't find prints except Bannister's and his wife's. So what are you going to do? Charge one of them?"

Liscomb removed the cigar from his mouth and spat a flake of tobacco. "Shit," he said.

Blauvelt watched the passing greenery for a while and then said, "Maybe nobody left it."

"Huh?"

"Nobody at the party, I mean. That door was open all night. And hardly anybody was in the foyer by the presents. We were all at the pool, or in the living room, or the kitchen or rec room. All over the house."

"You mean it might've been somebody from outside."

"Uh-huh. It's more than possible somebody slipped into the house during the party, left that package on the table, and left. Just like that."

"Yeah." Liscomb was silent for some moments. Then he said, "What do you know about The Church of Higher Awareness, Tom? Ever hear of it?"

"Never heard of it. Why?"

"I dunno. It came up in a conversation I had with Ollie Marquith. They're supposed to be Satan worshipers."

Blauvelt turned his head from the window. He did not say anything. He only stared at Liscomb.

Liscomb shifted behind the wheel uncomfortably. "Look, all I know is Ollie's got some idea about this Freddie Loftus character. Loftus may've been involved with the Manson group at one time. Anyway, this church and Freddie Loftus seem to be linked. At least in Ollie's mind."

"Who's Freddie Loftus?"

"That crazy who runs things up at Job's Camp. Looks like he weighs maybe ninety pounds."

"I think I've seen him on the streets."

"Anyway, they hold rites of some kind up at the Camp. Sex orgies, I hear. But who knows? Maybe something more serious."

"Like what?" Blauvelt had become interested.

"I don't know. Ollie suggests even, well, sacrifices."

"Sacrifices? Of what?"

"Ask Ollie. How the hell should I know!" Liscomb paused. "Look, Tom, just between you and me, Ollie's out to control that land up there by hook or by something else. He'll do anything to get his hands on it, including character assassination. You know Ollie."

"Yes, I know Ollie," Blauvelt said. "But at the same time, if all you say may be going on up there, maybe you ought to do a little looking. Rites, sacrifices, that's pretty far out, Frank."

"I'm looking. Don't worry about that, I'm looking."

"The world is strange," Blauvelt said. "It seems to get stranger every day. When I was a kid, when you were, Frank, we didn't have to use drugs. Maybe a little alcohol now and then, okay. But we never needed pot, LSD, speed."

"We did our own bit, Tom."

"Yes, but it was different then, Frank. We didn't need drugs to commune with ourselves and the universe. The universe was there, still is. And we were there. Hell, I knew when my cock was hard and the girl had hot pants! What the hell did I need pot for? It's better without it. And it's always better without alcohol. Right?"

Liscomb nodded. "Right."

"It amazes me," Blauvelt went on, "this quest for self-awareness by the kids. Shit, all you have to do is put your hand behind you and pinch your own ass. You know you're there."

Liscomb's cigar was jauntily high and his eyes were wide as he turned from the road and looked at Blauvelt. "You do that often, Tom?"

"What?"

"Pinch your own ass to prove you exist."

Blauvelt laughed. "As a medical man, I'd say it was as good a diagnosis of life as anything else. Better than drugs."

Liscomb was thoughtful. "Maybe pot should be legalized," he said.

"Why?"

"Alcohol is."

"Frank, we've had legal alcohol for thousands of years. And we still have people dying from cirrhosis, brain damage, accident, and suicide because of it."

Liscomb looked surprised. "You gone AA, Tom?"

Blauvelt sighed. "No. I just like to talk, Frank. Devil's advocate, you might say. I don't practice what I preach. Christ, I had my share last night."

"Then why are you so down on the kids' drugs?"

"I'm not. Just cautious, that's all. The evidence on acid has hardly begun to come in. And I'm not so sure about pot."

"I always try to keep an open mind, Tom."

"So do I. But lately I feel it closing."

"About what? Drugs?"

"A lot of things. Causality, for example."

"You're leaving me behind, Tom," Liscomb said.

"What causes us to act in certain ways, Frank? Drugs? Chemicals? Diet? The right or wrong intake?

Are we only engines that rely on the quality of our fuel? Or is it something else? Something outside ourselves?"

"Like what? God?"

"God. Good. Evil. If there is a God, we believe there is good. But if there is a God, there is a devil."

"Balls!" Liscomb said.

"I thought you believed in evil."

"I believe that evil is made by men, Tom! It doesn't come from something outside," Liscomb said. Then he laughed loudly. "That's what I like about you. You make me argue, think. You keep me on my toes. New thoughts. New ideas. Don't stagnate. Open your mind to every possibility. Hell, I've got this whole thing solved *now*. The Devil is loose in Holland County."

Tom Blauvelt looked ahead at the approaching ribbon of road, at the trees rushing by, at the dull overcast sky. He felt the humidity in his bones, the fetidness of the air in his nostrils.

"Maybe," he said. "Maybe."

On the streets of Broadmoor and in the surrounding countryside the low and eerie whistling of an unhappy tune joined with the winding crank of a camera as the man with the shriveled ear, eye to lens, made his way, snapping picture after picture of people on their daily rounds, always from a distance, always from some secret place.

When passing anyone at close quarters, he always had a friendly nod and a broad smile, sometimes a deep, rolling "good morning," or "good afternoon."

It was such a salutation that he gave to Father Daniel Conant as he strolled, one morning, in front of the Church of St. Ignatius of Loyola.

Conant, standing on the church steps, returned the

greeting, then stood frozen, blood pulsing, the hairs at the nape of his neck prickling in fear. For behind the wide smile and the twinkling eyes, he thought he had momentarily glimpsed an evil such as he had never before imagined. It was as though he had looked down into the depths of Hell.

As the stranger disappeared into the distance, Father Conant felt his knees grow weak and his stomach turn, his senses become dizzy.

Back in the coolness of his church, he stood for long moments staring up at the hanging figure of Christ, blessing himself and muttering a prayer.

For he was convinced he had seen a creature of the Devil—perhaps one of his heralds.

And he thought: *Am I insane? Who would believe me?*

On the following morning, the man with the misshapen ear again carefully chose one of his snapshots, sealed it in an envelope, and posted it in Broadmoor.

But he did not return to the fishing camp. His rods, his reels, his gear, camera, and clothes were neatly arranged in the trunk of the Seville. He turned east on Route 14, his mouth set in a slight, impish smile, whistling softly between clenched teeth, the melody of his little tune rising and falling in melancholy dissonance.

His work was done in Broadmoor. Other places called.

From the Journal of a Satanist:
    He wants two, now. He says He needs two.
      How in God's name did I ever do the first?
      WHY did I do it?

(Christ, why doesn't somebody kill me, burn me, destroy me! I am filth!)

I would take my own life but I am afraid— afraid of what I know must be.

Because I know I shall soon be dead.

And my soul in everlasting Hell.

CHAPTER 13

It was Oliver Marquith's habit to work on Saturday, and he made the habit contagious by insisting that his secretary be with him.

The mercury was hovering just above ninety-one in the midafternoon when the air conditioner in his office decided to give up the ghost. Marquith stood the rising heat for an hour, but when he noticed himself plucking at the armpits of his shirt, he swore, rose from the desk, told his secretary to contact the air conditioner people, ducked out into the parking lot, dove into the Lincoln, let the engine go in a roar, and turned the air conditioner on to full high.

It was close to four o'clock, and the sun, if the sun could be seen, was well over the yardarm. He was headed for the Bull and Bear, but changed his mind and swung the car onto Route 14 toward Jerry's Tavern in Shokan Forks. Milt Framer could usually be found at Jerry's in the late afternoon, and since Marquith had not heard from Milt for some time, he decided to kill two with one; down a martini and put the nudge to Milt.

Passing through Arrow, he honked a greeting at Frank Liscomb's police wagon coming the other way, and caught a glimpse of Tom Blauvelt in the passenger seat. He brooded about this all the way through

West Branch, Leydenburg, and Broadmoor, and by the time he reached Shokan Forks, he had concluded that they knew no more about the previous night than he did. But Liscomb was close-mouthed to begin with and Blauvelt was no prattler.

He had nodded agreement at Liscomb's insistence on keeping things under wraps for the time being, but had been hard put to believe anything about the hand. It was a fake, he had told Liscomb, someone's idea of a grim joke. The thing couldn't have anything to do with the original finger. But Liscomb had merely nodded and said nothing, and now Marquith had begun to have second thoughts.

He shook his head. The whole thing was ridiculous. A mummified hand! A thousand-year-old finger! What did Liscomb take him for? Still, it might be something he could use.

Jerry's Tavern was quiet when Marquith arrived, a handful of customers at the bar, a few at tables. Mostly strangers, new people from the city, but down at the far end, Marquith saw Milt Framer, brooding over his beer.

"Evenin', Ollie," Jerry Gerhardt coughed.

"Happy to see your air conditioner's working, Jerry. It's a boiler out there."

"It's that, all right." Jerry Gerhardt was eighty-five years old, wrinkled, bald, and shrunken, but he still possessed most of his faculties, and he could be found at work every day, ensconced on his accustomed stool behind the bar. He had built the place in the mid-thirties and it had served the county well, offering good steaks and chops at reasonable prices. Now, it provided an atmosphere reeking with nostalgia. The original mahogany bar had never been replaced and it was stained with the rings of a million drinks and myriad memories. The furniture, the fixtures, the lamps, even the crockery and utensils were old, and the walnut-paneled walls gave off a soft sheen through a meticulous polish. A piano, an old parlor grand, was tucked away in a corner, and on weekends locals and settlers gathered there to sing old songs. There was a jukebox too, but it held no rock, and offered Porter and Kern, and Rodgers and Hart, along with vocalists like Sinatra, Clooney, Patti Page, Crosby, and Como. It was a place from yesterday, and its patrons loved it, and feared the day Jerry Gerhardt would die and the Tavern would go the way of all things: to Hell.

Marquith walked along the bar and pulled a stool next to Milt Framer. "It's a scorcher out there, Milt."

"Hot as a June bride in a feather bed," Framer said. "I don't ever remember it like this." Framer's eyes were watery and red, his face was flushed; he had not shaved in three days and his breath stank of beer.

Marquith moved back a bit on his barstool and ordered a martini. "Well, we're not coming into a new Ice Age, Milt," he said.

Framer was staring gloomily into the mirror behind the bar, then his eyes roamed upward and around the walls, fixing on pictures, trophies, framed dollar bills, a stuffed bobcat. "Patti and me used to come in here all the time, Judge."

"Patti?" Marquith groped backward, while Framer eyed him suspiciously. "Oh, Patti. Why, sure, Milt, of course. I remember some good times the three of us had. Over there at the piano." Patti must have been Framer's wife, the doe-eyed slut with the pointed tits. Rumor had it she had laid half the county, and

Marquith winced that he had never had the guts to make a pass.

"You remember Patti's favorite song, Judge?" and Marquith groped again, fearful of another gaffe until Framer filled in for him: "The Ole Piana Roll Blues. That's what she liked. The Ole Piana Roll Blues. She used to sing it all the time. That was her favorite. The Ole Piana Roll Blues." He sat silent for a while and then said: "Bitch!"

Marquith coughed and lifted his martini. "What's new, Milt?"

"Huh?"

"You in your cups, Milt?"

"Shit no! I'm as sober as the day is long."

Marquith looked at his watch. "The day's almost over, Milt." He ordered Framer a Utica and himself a second martini. "You been thinking, Milt?"

Framer looked at him vacantly.

"You remember, Milt. The last time we talked. We decided to do some thinking, you and I. About that crowd up the mountain."

"Sure, I remember, Judge," Framer said. Anger was rising in his eyes. "Fuckin' Satan worshippers."

Marquith sighed. "I've been racking my brains, Milt. But I don't see what we can do. They own the land free and clear. They haven't done anything illegal."

"You don't call murder illegal! Shit, Ollie! That kid's body is buried up there someplace! You can be fuckin' well sure of that!"

"Easy, Milt, easy," Marquith hushed him. "This is all between you and me. You understand? Just between the two of us."

Framer lowered his voice. "You can bet your ass the body is up there."

"We can't prove that yet, Milt. We've been through this. There's nothing we can prove right now."

"We will. If I have my way, we will."

"Anyway, that's Frank Liscomb's job."

"Liscomb don't know his ass from his elbow," Framer said. "He don't act on anything but speeding tickets. He's soft, Judge. Soft on them kids 'specially. You remember that commotion a few years ago about the grass? Liscomb never came down hard like he should've. He coddles them kids. Now if Volner was chief, he wouldn't take any shit. You can bet your ass on that."

"Volner's not chief, Milt." He sighed again, sipped his drink and ordered another beer for Framer. "You hear about last night?"

Framer looked at him quizzically. "No. What?"

Marquith shook his head. "Nothing of import."

"Come on, Judge."

Marquith looked around the bar carefully, surreptitiously, acting out a cameo cabal. He studied Framer's face, then his own fingers, rolling the tips in his palm. "Nicole Bannister had a birthday party last night. Somebody sent her the rest of the hand."

"Jesus Christ!"

"Keep it down, Milt."

"Fuckin' Satan freaks!"

"Nobody can prove it was them."

"What the hell is Liscomb doing about it?"

Marquith shrugged. "There are no fingerprints, evidence. His hands are tied for the time being."

"Well, if he can't prove it, I'll goddamn well prove it myself!"

"How?"

"I'm going to do a little moseying around, Judge. Just moseying around. Matter of fact, I done a little last week." A look of disgust twisted Framer's face. "You were right about the sex orgies."

Marquith felt drawn to ask Framer to fill in details, but checked himself. "Moseying around could prove dangerous, Milt."

"Bullshit."

"Freddie Loftus. He's crazy, you know."

"Don't make me laugh!" And Framer laughed. "I could break him in half with one hand."

Oliver Marquith considered the probabilities. Framer was built like a bull, and Freddie Loftus resembled a swizzle stick. A very thin swizzle stick. The one in Marquith's fingers snapped with a loud crack, and Marquith could not help but think of Freddie Loftus's scarecrow body. On the other hand, if Freddie blew Milt Framer's head off with a twelve-gauge shotgun, things would go helter skelter and the land would be up for sale in no time flat.

When he looked up at Framer, there was the shadow of a smile on his lips. "Be very careful, Milt."

"Don't worry about me, Judge."

Marquith ordered another round and as he sipped, he said, "Tell me about that orgy, Milt."

Shopping together at the Superette in Broadmoor, Bette Hammond and Carole Kollars ran into Lauren Shane in the parking lot.

"I've got a head like a balloon and I need something to shrink it," Carole said. "What to join us?"

"Fine with me."

"Let's go to the Bull and Bear," Bette Hammond said. "Leave your car here, Lauren. We'll take mine."

In the car, they discussed hangovers, whammies, the ich, and various cures and potions. Bette Hammond swore by a raw egg laced with Worcestershire sauce, Carole countered with straight gin, and Lauren Shane held out for fresh air and sun.

"There is no sun," Carole Kollars said. "I think it got lost."

They crossed The Reach at East Indian and continued along Indian Falls Road toward Tyrone, hugging the bank of the stream as it twisted and turned, its waters dark and still and barely moving.

"Does the sun revolve around us, or do we revolve around the sun?" Carole asked.

"Don't ask me," Bette Hammond said. "I don't even live around here. Or wish I didn't."

They did not discuss the party until they were seated in the Bull and Bear and halfway through the first drink.

"Whatever got Nicole so upset last night?" Bette was looking directly at Lauren Shane.

"I have no idea," Lauren said.

Bette's eyes shifted to Carole's and a look passed between them. They were testing the weather.

"Where were you when it happened?" Carole Kollars asked.

"Right there. In the living room. But I didn't see anything to cause it. Why? Is there something I missed?"

"You haven't heard anything?" Bette asked. "Any talk?"

"I haven't been on the grapevine," Lauren said. "I've been home all day nursing Lochinvar's head."

His head? That's a new one, Carole thought. She decided not to pursue the subject of Nicole at the moment. "How's Joe's book coming?" she asked.

"Slowly," Lauren said.

"Joe's a good writer," Carole said. "I've seen some

of his stuff. I'd like to get first peek when he's got a few chapters."

"I'm sure you'll get first shot, Carole."

The waiter passed and Carole drew a large circle in the air with a down-pointed forefinger, indicating another round. "Estelle Dixon called this morning," she said. "She's holding a seance two weeks from to-day."

"You too?" Lauren said.

"And me," Bette Hammond said. "Actually, she asked me last night. Or I asked myself. You going?"

Lauren Shane made a face. "I don't know," she said. "Joe wants to go. He says it might be good material for a book. What about you, Carole?"

"I wouldn't miss it for the world. When life gets dull, a few solid raps on the tabletop might wake it up."

"If you're going for fun and games, Carole, you're not being fair to Estelle," Bette Hammond said.

Carole Kollars looked surprised. "You don't really believe in all this occult crap, do you?"

Bette raised her drink, sipped lightly, and frowned. "Estelle's very serious about this," she said, "and I think we all ought to be the same if we're going to take part."

"That's crud," Carole said. "And you're spoiling an otherwise delightful cocktail hour."

Bette Hammond bristled. "I suppose you think last night was a perfectly delightful birthday party?"

"Nicole was drinking too much, that's all."

"Drinking too much, my eye. Too many people saw it."

"*I* didn't," Carole said.

"Maybe you were the one drinking too much."

"You didn't see it, either, Bette. Now, come on, admit it."

Lauren Shane's head had been turning from one to the other as if she were watching a tennis match. "Saw what?" she asked. "Who didn't see what?"

"The hand," Carole said. "And as far as I know, nobody else saw it."

"What hand?"

A silence came over the table. Bette Hammond crushed a cigarette in the ashtray.

"What hand?" Lauren repeated.

Carole Kollars's light sigh was filled with intolerance and disdain. "The word's being bandied about," she said, "that the box Nicole opened last night contained a hand. The hand that goes with the finger she was sent before." She paused and then added, "Only nobody I've spoken to actually *saw* it. Am I right, Bette?"

"Hank Dixon says he saw it," Bette said.

Carole's eyes turned upward and her lips curled down. "Hank Dixon. Of all people. Hank can't see anything when he's in that state. He even made a pass at Agnes Bittel. What's the matter, Lauren?"

Lauren Shane's complexion had turned, and there was a sickly expression on her face. "Anybody want another drink?"

Carole made the circle in the air again. "You sick?"

"I'm okay. But what's going on? I don't understand what's going on."

"Nothing's going on," Carole Kollars said. "Just the same old Holland County rumor mongering."

Bette Hammond lit another cigarette and inhaled through tight lips. "Snakes anybody?"

"What?"

"Anybody seen any snakes, lately? That's all."

"I saw one yesterday," Lauren Shane said. "Right outside. Very close to the front door."

"What kind?"

Lauren shrugged. "I don't know. I can't tell one from the other."

"Marion killed three rattlers last week," Bette Hammond said, crushing the cigarette. "All on the front lawn."

"Rattlers haven't been down from the Ledges in years," Carole Kollars said.

"Well, they are now," Bette said. "And they're all over the place."

"Have you seen any, Carole?" Lauren Shane asked.

Carole chuckled. "All the time, honey. And sometimes pink elephants, too."

The waiter collected glasses and served new drinks. Lauren raised hers immediately, followed by Carole, but Bette merely stared into hers. "Estelle Dixon is an unusual person."

"You can say that again," Carole Kollars sighed.

"I always felt sorry for Estelle," Bette said, ignoring Carole's dig. "I always thought she was the emptyhead in a community of intellectuals, the untalented in a nest of artists. But I've changed my mind. She has another kind of talent, a subtle prescience that we lack. She's in touch with things we can't imagine."

"Such as?" Carole Kollars asked.

Bette sighed. "I don't really know," she said. "That's what I mean. What we don't know, Estelle somehow does. Or will." She paused. "One thing I do know. There's something wrong lately. Something horribly wrong."

Carole Kollars was about to raise her voice and rip

Bette's words to shreds when there was a commotion at a table near the end of the bar. A woman shrieked, a man grunted hoarsely and stood, overturning the table, sending drinks, ashtrays, and tableware clattering to the floor.

A waiter rushed over with a long-handled mop and began beating at the man's ankles. The woman screamed outright. Another man left the bar and pulled at the first man, hustling him toward the door and finally getting him out, the woman on their heels.

The waiter continued to beat at something on the floor, joined by the manager who wielded a broom. Others at the bar and tables jumped up and bolted through the door as the waiter and manager continued to beat and flail at the thing on the floor.

Outside, an engine roared into life in the parking lot and a car sped away. Others followed.

When the thing on the floor was dead, the manager lifted it, draped over the broom handle, and started for the parking lot.

The silence in the room was deafening. Then somebody coughed. Glasses clinked. Conversation began again, subdued, clandestine. A number of checks were ordered.

As the waiter with the mop passed their table, Carole Kollars signaled him. "What was it?" she asked.

"It's really weird," he said with the amazement of twenty-five years. "A copperhead. There hasn't been a copperhead reported in these parts since I was born." He shook his head.

Carole Kollars looked around the table. "I need a drink," she said. "Everybody in?" When the others did not answer, she made the signal in the air, saying, "Make them doubles."

The waiter left, and silence hung over the table. Carole Kollars lifted the remains of the previous drink in a toast. "See you at the seance," she said.

CHAPTER
14

Head resting on upturned palms, eyes contemplating the ceiling, Susan Dixon lay on her bed and listened to the faintly suggestive lyrics of Leonard Cohen while she pulled lazily on a cigarette. From the rooms below came the voices of her father and Estelle.

The sultry weather was oppressive, and Susan met it with little defense but nudity, reclining on the bed in sheer panties and nothing else. The discussion below ended abruptly, and then she heard the heavy step of her father coming up the stairs. He paused before her door, and for a moment Susan thought he was going to knock, but the steps resumed again and she listened to them fade, then ascend the stairs to the studio.

Susan sighed. When was the last time they had talked, talked about anything besides money, or any of the prosaic things of family living and day-to-day existence? A very long time. When had they last really smiled at each other?

She sighed again and rose to a sitting position. *Maybe I should try harder,* she thought. *Be a little Avis, maybe.*

She pulled on a pair of jeans and a faded blue T-shirt, slipped into a pair of Adidas. She drew a brush through long blond hair that reached to her waist, pocketed her cigarettes, and made her way up to the studio and knocked.

She found her father seated on a battered ice-cream parlor chair, his feet raised to the drawing board, his hands embracing a glass of clear, unadulterated gin.

"Hi, Daddykins," she said. It was an expression dating back to her ninth year, used in these latter days only to placate, cajole, or otherwise undermine his defenses.

Henry Dixon regarded his daughter with ill-disguised suspicion. "What brings you to these parts?" he said.

"Nothing," Susan said. "Just thought I'd say hello, is all."

Dixon grunted. "What do you need? A fin? A sawbuck?"

"Daddy," Susan pouted, "your vocabulary reeks of nostalgia. Hey, this is great!" She was looking at a small oil, the paint still glistening wet.

"It's crap," he said.

"No, it isn't," she said. "It's really neat. It's the old covered bridge over The Reach, isn't it? I like it, really."

"You must want something," Dixon said.

"You're always so suspicious, Daddy. I like it, I really do. You should really paint more."

"For what? Therapy?" Dixon drank deeply. "That stuff don't make the money, honey. This does." He indicated the drawing board.

Susan walked over and looked down. "What is it?"

"A watchband."

"It doesn't look like a watchband."

"It's not supposed to look like a watchband. It's supposed to *sell* watchbands."

"It stinks, Daddy."

"I know it stinks. But it pays the butcher, the baker, the candlestick maker, and the IRS. Want a drink?"

"Have any wine?"

"Not up here."

Susan sighed. "I'll take a raincheck."

"You don't like hard booze, do you?" Dixon asked.

"Not particularly." She lit a cigarette, leaning back against the drawing board, her curves showing.

Dixon squinted. "How much are you using pot?"

"I'm not into it too deeply," she said. "Five, maybe six joints a week."

"LSD?"

"Come on, Daddy, what do you take me for? I wouldn't touch it with a ten-foot pole."

"That boyfriend of yours. He uses it, doesn't he?"

"Ken?" Susan shrugged. "Maybe. I don't know. But what he does is his business."

Dixon was silent for a moment, then said, "I hope you never get into that stuff, baby. It destroys brain cells."

Susan considered for a minute. "So do atomic bombs," she said.

They both laughed, and Susan came behind his chair and placed her hands on his shoulders. She leaned down and placed a soft kiss on the top of his head. "You're a nice daddy, sometimes," she said.

"I try," he said. "And I guess you're not a bad broad for a daughter."

"You should paint more, you know?"

"We should talk more, too," he said.

"That's what I was thinking, Daddy," she said and began to massage his shoulders lightly.

Dixon could feel the soft warmth of her all about him, and when she leaned over to kiss his head again, he was conscious of her breasts on his back. He coughed roughly, sat forward and rose, dragging the bottle of gin to the drawing board and pouring a drink.

"You ought to talk more to Estelle, too," he said.

"Oh, shit!" Susan said. "Here we go again."

"Why are you so down on Estelle, for chrissake?"

"Talk about brain damage, that stuff you're swigging didn't come from the fountain of youth."

"Don't change the subject. You used to get along fine with Estelle. Why not now?"

"I don't want to talk about it."

"You two used to talk about things together, go places together, get along just fine. What's the matter, Sue? What happened?"

"I *said!* I don't want to talk about it!"

"Goddammit, you kids, all you kids give me a pain in the ass! You talk about 'relationships,' 'dialog,' 'communication' . . . but when it comes down to a serious subject, all you say is, 'I don't want to talk about it. Leave me alone, I don't want to talk about it!' Shit!"

"You can say that again. Shit. You don't give a shit what I think anyway!"

"Do you have to use that word?"

"Don't you?"

Silence ensued, broken only by the gurgle of liquor slopping into Dixon's glass. Susan eyed the scene with disgust. "You drink too much," she said.

Dixon swallowed. "I can handle it."

"You want to know something?" Susan asked.

"What?"

"Estelle's made herself the laughingstock of the county."

Dixon was silent.

"You know what I mean," Susan said. "And now she's into seances. Seances! I mean, Daddy, hell, I feel like I've got two heads and a hunchback when people talk to me!"

Dixon was silent.

"Don't you feel it? I mean, don't you feel people laughing behind your back all the time? Estelle Dixon and her weird Ouija. And now seances. Daddy, can't you talk to her?"

Dixon remained silent.

"What am I, talking into space?" Susan demanded.

Henry Dixon raised his head slowly and looked at his daughter with a cool, level stare. "You're very intolerant," he said. "You don't make any effort to understand other people at all. You can't understand anything that's outside your own sensations. If something doesn't suit you, it's weird, or way-out, or bananas, or you have some other unintelligible word to describe it. For a girl who's had a very liberal education, you're very intolerant."

"Shit!" Susan said and jumped for the door, slamming it behind her.

Henry Dixon remained seated, staring into his drink. *The gap,* he thought. *How do you close the fucking gap when they won't listen, refuse to talk about it?* Not that way, he decided, and sipped at the gin.

She's right, though. I drink too much. Well, why not, and what else is new?

He raised the glass and drank again.

There was no relief on Sunday. The skies remained gray and the drizzle continued. Inside the Church of St. Ignatius of Loyola, the air was close and heavy, and Jonathan Bannister periodically wiped perspiration from his forehead and stole sideways glances at his wife. Nicole seemed unnaturally serene and distant, and Jonathan worried. Leslie fidgeted, totally ignorant of the strange incantation and ritual, innocent of what was expected of her. Jonathan, himself one-quarter Catholic with an attendance record of approximately twelve masses before the age of thirteen, felt the strangeness and wished the mass were over.

Later, Father Conant was on the steps outside to greet them. "Good to see you here, Mrs. Bannister," he said. "And you, Mr. Bannister." He laid a hand on Leslie's head and roughed her hair. "You too, little lady."

"We're going to the Pikeville Fair," Leslie said.

"Oh? That sounds like a lot of fun." He lifted his eyes to Nicole and smiled. "I hope the weather's a little better over in Pikeville."

"That was a beautiful mass, Father," Nicole said.

The smile remained on his lips. "We try," he said.

Jonathan coughed uncomfortably, locking his eyes on Nicole. "It's near twelve," he said.

The priest was deferential. "Yes," he said, backing away, "don't let me hold you up. Have a good time, little lady. See you all next week."

"Next week, my ass," Jonathan said as he swung the car onto Broadmoor Road and headed south toward the interstate. "You want to go, okay. Me, I'll stay home and paint. Or go fishing. Frankly, I feel closer to God doing either."

"You're in a foul mood this morning," Nicole said.

"Understatement. Look at this weather."

"When're we going to get there?" Leslie broke in.

"Suppose you give us a chance to get started," Jonathan snapped.

"Mommy's right," Leslie said after a pause. "You're an ogre today, Daddy."

Jonathan drove on determinedly. Nicole was silent. When they reached the interstate, he pushed the pedal to the floor and the Volvo charged southward at seventy-five. Then he remembered the trip with Henry Dixon, the Buick, the swerve, the skid, and he eased back.

Jonathan glanced over at Nicole. "When are you going to talk about it?" he said.

She stared ahead. "Talk about what?"

"Nothing," he said, and turned his attention back to driving.

Oddly enough, the weather began to clear and lighten when they crossed the county line three miles before Pikeville. Sunlight shafted through broken clouds, and the wet roads gleamed in tiny rainbow hues. A breeze was gusting from the west, and the air was cool and refreshing. Their spirits rose with the barometer, and they began to talk and chuckle and look forward to the fair.

But that evening, on their return, the skies knitted together in an overcast again as the miles went by. The wetness ate into their clothing, the temperature rose, and a dank fetidness hung on all sides.

There seemed to be a giant pall over Holland County, like a tarpaulin covering an open grave.

"Where were you today?" Elvida asked.

"The Pikeville Fair," Leslie said.

"You should tell me when you're going someplace," Elvida said.

"Why?"

"Because."

"Because why?"

"Just because," Elvida said. "That must've been fun, the Pikeville Fair."

"It was, really," Leslie said.

"I've never been to a real fair," Elvida said.

"You haven't?" Leslie turned in her bed, staring into the darkness to where she thought Elvida's voice came from. "But everybody goes to fairs. This is my second time."

"Is it as much fun as Devil's Pond?" Elvida asked.

"I told you. I've never been to Devil's Pond."

"I'll take you," Elvida said.

"When?" There was excitement in Leslie's voice.

"When you see me."

"When will I see you, Elvida? Tell me when."

"Soon," Elvida said. "Very soon." Her voice faded on the word and she was gone.

Leslie stared into the darkness for a while, then turned and went to sleep. She dreamed of a vast marshland, silent and strange and full of huge fish and newts and snakes. She seemed to float through it, among the towering trees and over the black waters, on and on until she was staring into a deep, dark pool where there was no light.

She woke up screaming.

CHAPTER 15

Job's Camp was a symphony in dissonance. Thousands of katydids shrilled in counterpoint to the bass boom of a guitar-percussion rock group, and the jeremiad wail of the lead singer fought frantically against a chorus of peepers. Marijuana passed from hand to hand among small, circular groups, wine bottles tipped in the night, and the high-pitched giggles of the stoned formed isolated grace notes in the score.

Susan Dixon wandered from group to group, oblivious to the music, peering into faces, looking for Ken Brady or Freddie Loftus, she was not sure which, her mood as dark as the night.

She found Ken first and settled for him, feeling torn, but at the same time aware that the conflict itself was the cause of her anxiety. "What's going on?" she said. "Is this the Rites?"

Ken laughed. "Hell, no. Just a party. Welcome." He passed a roach.

Susan shook her head. "How about some wine?"

Ken found a stray bottle and they dropped to the ground, apart from the main body of onlookers who sat enthralled by the beat of a lead guitar, two backups, and drums, piped, amplified and exploded through four huge stereo speakers.

"They call themselves 'The Stony Silence,'" Ken said. "Real neat, huh?"

Susan was noncommittal.

"They're passing through. Got a gig upstate to-morrow night. It's real now stuff."

The lead guitar and singer, a young man wearing tight jeans and nothing else, pranced and gyrated on bare feet, his head rocking, his blond mane tossing to the beat.

> *You gotta give it, beby,*
> *You gotta give it, beby,*
> *Cause if you don't give it, beby!*
> *I'm going to take it, beby!*
> *And that's rape!* (BEAT) *Rape!* (BEAT)
> *And that's rape!* (BEAT) *Rape!* (BEAT)
> *Rape!* (BEAT, BEAT, BEAT, BEAT, BEAT, BEAT, BEAT)

"Neat, huh?" Ken Brady's eyes glittered.

Susan swallowed wine. "It's terrible."

Ken looked incredulous. "Hey, Soozel!"

"No, I mean it, Ken, really. It's really awful." She gulped again and lay back on the grass. "Really lousy."

"What's the matter with you tonight?"

She sighed. "I don't know." Then, "I'll be all right."

Ken stretched out beside her, kissed her lightly on the cheek and then sang softly in her ear: *"You gotta give it beby, You gotta give it, beby, 'Cause . . ."*

"Oh, Ken, for chrissake!" She rose, brushing damp grass from her backside. "I came up here to talk."

"Well, why didn't you say so? Let's go."

Along the footpath through the woods to Ken's

cabin, the sound receded behind them, never quite getting lost, but lessening in density until they could speak to each other without shouting.

"I used to listen to Bach," Susan said.

"You know I like Bach," Ken said defensively. "I've got some great stuff of his on the Moog."

"Moog, schmoog," Susan said. "They used to have violins."

In the cabin, Ken poured from a bottle of Zinfandel and lit a joint, which Susan declined again.

"You're a stranger tonight, Sooze."

"I'm my other self," she said. "Call me Schizo."

"What other self?"

She thought for a moment. "The one I hid away a long time ago."

"You got the pits, that's all."

"Pits?" She frowned. "No, what I've got is just a good old-fashioned case of the guilts."

"Come on, Sue."

"No, I mean it, I've got the guilts. I never thought I'd have them again, but I've got 'em."

Ken moved uncomfortably. "There's no such thing as guilt. Only better or worse."

"You're not making sense."

Ken shrugged. "I make sense to myself. If I went around feeling guilty all the time it would cramp my energy flow."

"What're you doing with your energy, Ken?"

"What?"

"I mean, what're you doing with all that energy flow? What are you producing?"

Ken Brady stood abruptly and lumbered to the kitchen sink on heavy feet, banging the bottle on the metal drain pan as he poured more wine. "You're a ballbreaker sometimes."

Susan accepted the refilled glass and sipped pensively. "I'm sorry, Ken," she said. "I'm in a rotten mood. The whole world smells rotten."

Ken Brady sat. "You have an argument with your folks?"

She laughed shortly. "Don't I always?"

"Parents should be seen and not heard," Ken said.

"I don't know," Susan said. "Sometimes I wonder. . . . They have their values. We have ours."

"And never the twain shall meet," Ken said.

"And they were young once."

"I doubt it."

"And I guess they had their period of rebellion, too," she said and paused. "You know something, Ken? I'm tired of rebelling. There's nothing to rebel *against* anymore. And what good does it do anyway? The world stumbles on."

Ken Brady humphed. "You're regressing, Sue."

"Maybe I am," she said, "and I don't like that either." She lit a cigarette and inhaled deeply, letting the smoke out in a long, slow cloud. "But what have we got in *our* world? Energy flow? Karma? Self-awareness? Sharing the experience? Where is it all leading?"

Ken seemed nervous, flustered. His bastions were being attacked and he felt their weakness. "Don't fall into that trap," he said. "It's been set for eight thousand years. There's a new world ahead, Susan, and we can make it."

Susan looked at him obliquely. "I thought you were the arch cynic," she said. "Find 'em, fuck 'em, and forget 'em."

"I am!" he said. "Shit! I don't want to get involved! That's the point! Don't drift with the mainstream, the establishment, the structure! Keep your freedom is what I'm saying. Stay away from the shit. It's the *self* that's important; awareness, consciousness, being at one with yourself and the universe, you know?"

"I know," Susan said, circling her glass in the air for another wine, "I know. But where does it all lead, Ken? Where are we going? What are we contributing?"

He poured the wine, lifted the roach to his lips and drew deeply. "You *do* have the guilts tonight, don't you?"

"So do you," Susan said. "But you don't know it."

They were silent for some minutes, letting the anger dissipate, allowing time to heal an old friendship. Ken lit a new joint, and Susan accepted. They smoked, they drank. They did not smile.

"Maybe Estelle's right," Susan said at last.

"Estelle?"

"My mother. My *step*mother," she corrected. "I'm evil."

"What?"

"She says I'm evil."

"Ah, shit, Sooze," Ken said. "Are we going to start that again?"

"No, I mean, why do I dislike her so? Why do I almost hate her? She's been good to me. She's been good to my father."

"Maybe you do like her, but you can't admit it," Ken said.

"We used to have good times," she said. "Estelle and I." She stared into her drink. "Good times. Now she embarrasses me."

"And you feel guilty."

"Yes."

Ken waited. "Maybe you've got a thing for your father."

Her eyes rose in anger.

"I only meant unconsciously," he said warily.

"Come on," she said. "Cut the Freudian crap. I know my unconscious like the palm of my own hand." She motioned for another glass of wine. As Ken poured, she reached for the marijuana and pulled on it heavily. "I know myself, Ken," she said. "I know myself only too well. Don't worry about that." She drew smoke into her lungs. "Only one thing," she said. "Why do I want to sleep with Freddie Loftus?"

Ken laughed. "Why not?"

"It's not right," she said.

"What do you mean, it's not right?"

"It's wrong. I mean, if I love—*feel*, I mean—for anybody, it's you, Ken. Not Freddie Loftus."

"I wouldn't mind," Ken said. "I already told you."

"Really laid back, aren't you?"

"That's not it," Ken said. "I mean, what do we all have to be so possessive about? We don't own each other. That's the trouble with things, you know. People don't share. Sharing is good."

"I don't even *like* Freddie Loftus," Susan said. "He turns me off. As a matter of fact, he's repugnant and despicable."

Ken gaped. "Then what's all this about you and Freddie shacking up? I don't get it."

"Maybe Freddie's my symbol of evil," she said.

"Your what?"

"Guilt into guilt, evil upon evil. In the end, there's so much of it, it covers itself and doesn't matter anymore."

Ken Brady squinted. "You all right, Sooze?"

"Sure, I'm all right."

"You're not making sense. It's all hyperbole, you know?"

"Look who's talking about hyperbole."

"Anyway, there's no such thing as evil. Only sickness."

"Rose names," Susan said and when he looked at her, added, "a rose by any other name, Ken. We're playing semantics."

"Evil, sickness, what's the difference?"

"There is a difference," Susan said. "You can explain sickness. But you can't explain that finger. Or the hand."

"What hand?"

She told him about Nicole's party and the package.

"Are you kidding?" he asked.

"Why would I be kidding?"

"How do you know about it?"

"I heard my father and Estelle talking. They were there."

"Holy shit!" Ken said. "I wonder who did it."

Susan let forth a long, dry laugh. "We'll find out soon enough. Estelle's going to hold a seance."

"Now you *must* be kidding!"

"Cross my heart and hope to die."

"Estelle, she's kind of bananas, isn't she?"

"Bananas, pears, pomegranates. She's everything."

Ken dragged on the roach, remaining quiet, thoughtful. "The cops were up here," he said finally.

"Chief Liscomb?"

Ken nodded. "Just after the finger turned up."

"You can bet they've got their eye on Freddie. And the rest of you."

"That's what I was thinking," Ken said.

"But I wouldn't put it past Freddie, either," Susan said.

Ken flushed. "Come on, Sooze! Freddie's a little

flaky but not that bad. He couldn't do a thing like that."

"Then who did?"

Ken hesitated. "I don't know. But I figure you're right, you know? About their suspicions being on Freddie and some of the rest of us. In which case, maybe we'd better do something."

"Like what?"

"Like find the murderer. Right?"

Susan laughed. "Are you kidding?"

"Why?"

"What do you know about playing detective, Ken? Where would you start?"

He shrugged. "I don't know. I have to put my energy to work."

"Who do *you* think did it?" Jonathan asked.

He was addressing Maria Braithwaite who had stopped by to say hello to Nicole, offer a word of comfort. But Nicole had retired early and was sleeping.

Maria had accepted a glass of sherry, and now the two of them sat in the library. Although Nicole's bedroom was upstairs in another wing of the house, they spoke *sotto voce,* as if unwilling even to hear themselves. Naturally, the talk had turned to the finger.

Jonathan's eyebrows asked the question again.

Maria Braithwaite hesitated. "That would be difficult for me to answer, Jonathan. But you are more close to it. What do you think?"

"Some nut," Jonathan said. "Some crazy. What the hell, Maria, the world's full of them."

"But why Nicole?" Maria asked. "Why did he send the finger to Nicole?"

"How the hell should I know?" Jonathan swirled

the ice in his drink angrily. "For all we know, he picked a name out of the phone book!"

"And the rest of the hand?" Maria said. "If he were so crazy, so insane as you say, he might have picked another name for the hand."

Jonathan had become rigid, staring directly into Maria Braithwaite's eyes. "What hand?"

Maria paused ever so slightly. "I was at the party, Jonathan. It was the rest of the hand, no?"

Jonathan did not answer. He went to the bar and poured another drink. "More sherry?"

"No, thank you."

Seated again, he leaned forward. "You begged the question once, Maria. You're a smart woman. What do *you* think?"

Maria Braithwaite placed her glass gently on the coffee table. Her long, tapered fingers came to rest beneath her chin, and her dark eyes stared into the cold fireplace.

"I have no thoughts," she said. "Only feelings. And I feel that there is something very evil here among us, something perhaps unnatural."

"Like what?" Jonathan's tone was crisp, impatient.

"If I could answer that, Jonathan, I would tell you."

Jonathan Bannister let forth a sudden, sharp laugh. "Christ Almighty, Maria! You're beginning to sound like Estelle Dixon!"

Maria raised her head. "Estelle Dixon has a depth, a talent, you might say, that perhaps you do not understand."

"Oh, come off it, Maria! She's a nut, for chrissake!" He laughed again. "I hear she's going to hold some kind of seance. Jesus!"

"Does Nicole know?" Maria's question was quick, sharp.

"About the seance? No."

"Good. You won't tell her, of course?"

"Certainly not. The less she's reminded of this thing, the better." He found himself staring at Maria Braithwaite, admiring her beauty and wondering at her unique gift for controlling a conversation, steering it into her own channels. He watched her fit a cigarette into a long ivory holder, setting the stage for her next remark.

"Why don't you come to the seance, Jonathan?" Maria said. "Not Nicole, of course. Only you."

"Me!" Jonathan's laughter was almost raucous. "Pardon my Spanish, Maria, but shit, that's really the end!" And the laughter continued.

"You find me funny, perhaps?" Maria Braithwaite had drawn herself up, stiff, proud, haughty.

"No, you're not funny, Maria," Jonathan said, calming. "Not you. You're not funny," and he became very serious. "But Christ Almighty! A seance? Come on, Maria!"

Maria rose. "Thank you for the sherry," she said.

Jonathan got up awkwardly. "I'm sorry, Maria, but there's a logical, natural answer."

"A nut case?" Maria asked.

"That's right," Jonathan said. "A nut case."

At the door, he kissed her lightly on the cheek. "I'm sorry. But don't blame me for being the practical, pragmatic American man."

She laughed lightly. "Give Nicole my love. And don't blame me for being the romantic, mysterious, impractical European woman."

When the door closed, Jonathan stared upward to the ceiling, in the direction of his wife's bedroom.

A nut case, he thought. *Just some nut case.*

* * *

At home, drinking his nightly beer, Frank Liscomb was scanning a teletype that had come to his office late that afternoon from FBI headquarters in Washington.

RE 'THE CHURCH OF HIGHER AWARENESS':
ESTABLISHED IN LONDON, ENGLAND, SOMETIME IN THE EARLY SIXTIES, THIS IS A FAR-FLUNG CLAN OF YOUNG PEOPLE, DRUG-ORIENTED, ANTI-ESTABLISHMENT, PRACTICING A COMMUNAL LIFE-STYLE AND GIVEN TO SEXUAL EXCESSES. IN FACT, SEXUAL PROMISCUITY IS A BASIC DOCTRINE OF 'THE CHURCH OF HIGHER AWARENESS,' AND IS USED TO WEAKEN FAMILY TIES AND FURTHER UNDERMINE ANY LATENT ESTABLISHMENT INFLUENCES. BLACK MASSES ARE INDULGED IN DURING CERTAIN RITUALS, AND THE PRACTICE OF SATANISM HAS BEEN CLEARLY ESTABLISHED. 'THE CHURCH OF HIGHER AWARENESS' IS STRIKINGLY SIMILAR IN STYLE AND DOCTRINE TO THE MANSON FAMILY. THE LAPD HAS BEEN ENDEAVORING, WITHOUT SUCCESS AT THIS POINT IN TIME, TO ESTABLISH A CONNECTION BETWEEN 'THE CHURCH OF HIGHER AWARENESS' AND THE FAMILY, ESPECIALLY IN LIGHT OF THE MURDERS OF TWO YOUNG HIGHER AWARENESS FOLLOWERS. (FURTHER COMING.) IT IS BELIEVED THESE VICTIMS WERE SLAIN BY MEMBERS OF 'THE CHURCH OF HIGHER AWARENESS.'

Liscomb made a clucking sound inside his mouth and let the teletype drop to the desk. The face of Charles Manson flashed through his mind and he compared it with that of Freddie Loftus. Both young, thin, long-haired, bearded, hollow-cheeked, bright-eyed, fanatic.

He got up from the desk and walked slowly to the window that faced north. Hands in pockets, he stared out into the dismal night. It was some miles to Job's Camp, but his mind's eye pierced the distance, reaching forth over Broadmoor, across The Reach, up North Lake Road and into the hills.

Liscomb's memory was sharply honed and flexible and he let it wander back over the years and mix with the present. He had read the accounts of the Tate case carefully.

August, 1969. The hills above Hollywood, California. Freddie Loftus was known to have come from California.

Sharon Tate. Young, beautiful, talented, pregnant. Stabbed sixteen times. Loftus was said to have been connected with Charles Manson.

Abigail Folger, twenty-five, heiress. Stabbed twenty-eight times. Satanism.

Jay Sebring, thirty-five. Stabbed seven times, shot once. There was talk about some kind of "rites" up at the Camp. What were those rites?

Voytek Frykowski. Shot twice. Bludgeoned thirteen times. Stabbed fifty-one times. Loftus had taken a gun to Milt Framer.

Steven Parent, eighteen. Shot four times. The front porch, and the word "Pig" written on it in blood. Loftus had called him a "pig," or his girl friend had. Who did she remind him of? *Squeaky Fromme.*

Could it all be happening again, more than a decade later? Liscomb sank into a chair, weary, worried, at odds with himself, the world, his sense of inadequacy. Ollie Marquith was probably right. He was too soft to be a cop. He lacked the essential toughness, the hard core of callousness that would lead a man to the edge of paranoia and let him suspect his neighbor, his best friend, his wife, his mother.

Liscomb rose and walked to the window again, looking out but seeing nothing. He had not wanted to be a cop. He had just drifted into it. Back from the battlefields in '45, he had had his eye on the GI Bill, pre-law and then a degree from Harvard, perhaps. But it had not worked out that way. He had never been on close terms with money, and education, even in those days, was expensive. He had taken the job with the County Police as a stopgap, a temporary measure, designed to give himself time to collect his thoughts, perhaps save a bit. Then the early marriage, the stillborn child, the long years of his wife's suffering, and finally her death.

And here he was.

He bit off the end of a panatella, spat, and walking through the house to the kitchen, opened the refrigerator door and rummaged for a Heineken.

The war. He seldom thought about the war. He had enlisted because there was no question about it. There were decent human beings and there were barbarians, and he had taken his stand against the barbarians, done his bit to make the world safe for democracy once more. That was all there was to it.

He sat. Democracy. He wondered where it had gone. As a boy, he had thrilled to Jimmy Cagney's *G-Man,* and *The House on Ninety-second Street* had been one of his favorite films. Recently, FBI agents had been charged with illicit wiretapping, invasion of privacy, unlawful entry, and the sending of poison-pen letters. Had we taken our cue from the Gestapo or the OGPU?

Back in the living room, he eyed the FBI teletype

with distaste, but had to admit they were both efficient and helpful.

It came down to bad apples, he thought, and wondered whether Job's Camp was now an entire orchard of rot.

Kids today were different. It was more than a matter of their style, their music, their dress. The swing of the forties had modulated to the rock of the seventies, and he did not understand it and thought it was for the worse. Bobby sox and white shoes had given way to bare feet and sandals, chinos to blue jeans, antique clothes or disco dress, crew cuts to long hair. They were still kids. But different.

It all seemed to him a harsh note of defiance, a slap in the face to Mother and Father America for having been so permissive.

It bit at Liscomb, and he wondered, briefly, if he were in his twenties now, how he would deal with a sexual freedom he did not understand, and whether he would emerge as a prize bull or remain, even in this day, a guilt-ridden Puritan. Someplace, in the recesses of his mind, there floated the thought that if you didn't have to fight for it, it wasn't worth it.

Liscomb was not an intolerant person. He was far beyond the common image of the hard-nosed, hard-hatted, red-necked cop. He was no fuzz, no pig. On the contrary, he believed firmly in essential human dignity and decency, in the rights of others, and in the privilege of the young to dissent, to find their own values, to experiment.

But he saw nothing constructive in aloofness, any more than he could find good in the violence of the destructors; the bomb placers and the airport locker experts, the kidnappers and the skyjackers, the FALN, the Japanese Red Army, the Baader-Meinhof gang, or the IRA.

Pigs, he thought.

Pig. Written in blood.

But that was California. Years ago. Far away. Things like that can happen in California.

Helter Skelter.

But not here, he thought. Not in Holland County.

Sharon Tate, Voytek Frykowski. The Church of Higher Awareness. Satan worship. Charles Manson. Freddie Loftus.

No, it was a thing apart, far away in space and in time. It could not happen here.

Or could it? And was it? And was his own blindness to it an even greater crime, that he would, out of his stupid sense of justice and fair play, let it happen right under his nose?

I should never have been a cop, he thought. *I'm just not cut out for it. But here I am. And I'd better start acting like one.*

Liscomb did not know what excuse he would use to pull Freddie Loftus in for questioning. But he would find one. Something. Anything.

He went to bed.

Freddie Loftus was talking to himself. Actually facing himself and talking to himself. But not in a mirror.

He was in Toledo. In the downtown area, just walking along the street, when this dude grabbed his arm at the bicep and swung him around. And he looked into the dude's face and his eyes widened in horror.

"Jesus Christ, man!" the dude said.

"Let go my arm," Freddie said, and pulled.

"Jesus Christ, man!" the dude said. "I *knew* I'd come back!"

"Lemme go!" Freddie screamed, and people on the sidewalk were stopping and staring.

"Look at that," a blank-faced man in a tan Stetson said. "You can't tell them apart."

"One's dead," a woman said.

"I'll kill you!" Freddie said to the dude, his own image. "I'll kill you all!" And he formed his hand into a gun, forefinger extended in a barrel, aiming at the dude, himself, but the bullet just fell off the tip of his fingernail to the sidewalk with a rubbery sound.

And Freddie screamed and tried to somersault, to escape, but then everything began to warp and bend, and screaming lights in all the colors of the spectrum rained down, and a mist sprang up and he and the dude were soon arm in arm, and arms around shoulders, walking into a tavern, down many steps, endless steps, where, at the bottom, they sat at a table, staring across at each other, blowing a strange kind of pot that smelled of manure and drinking wine that was ebony black.

"You're old," Freddie said.

"I grew," his image shot back and drank, and his head became very large, looming, distended and swelled. "Momma had a bad birth," he said.

"Momma's dead!" Freddie wailed. "Dead! Dead! Dead! Momma's Dead!"

"But I'm alive," the dude said and reached out, his arms long and spidery across the table, to take Freddie by the throat and begin to throttle him. "You prick!" Freddie's image said to Freddie. "You rotten prick! I'm going to kill you!"

Freddie could not breathe and tried to scream, but could not.

"Reason!" Freddie screamed in his mind. "Reason! Let us reason!"

"You filthy cunt!"

"And the evening and the morning were the sixth day!" Freddie shouted.

"Filth! Filth! I am filth, you filthy asshole, shit-mongering rectum, asshole anus!"

"Be fruitful and divide!" Freddie screamed.

"One-celled shit paramecium, ambivalent amoeba!" the mirror image said and began to dissolve in a shapeless mass of reeking protoplasm, enveloping Freddie like an octopus, its tentacles squeezing, constricting, its horny beak tearing, slashing, ripping, dismembering.

"Momma's dead!" it said. "Momma's dead! Dead! Dead! But I'm alive! Alive, you prick, you shit, you idiot!"

And not breathing, choking, gasping, coughing, straining, Freddie raised his silent voice and screamed again, "Get thee behind me! Behind! Behind! Behind!"

But the octopus only tightened its hold, crushing, constricting, breathing a foul odor into Freddie's face, and screaming at him, "Jesus Christ! Jesus Christ! Jesus Christ!"

"Get behind me!"

"Jesus Christ, man!" The tentacles were slapping his face, almost playfully.

"Behind me!"

The octopus beak became a nose, the huge round eyes became human.

"Jesus, man," Ken Brady said. "Cool it. Come on, cool it, man."

Freddie shivered. The shiver started in his shoulders and traveled in waves, downward along his body until his feet were beating a tattoo on the cabin door. Then he vomited into his lap.

"Jesus Christ, what a trip," Dimples said. She was standing by the door, trying to separate herself from what was happening, yet still fascinated, rapt. "What a trip."

Freddie's sticklike body quivered again, his head bent in another dry retch. When he looked up, his eyes were wide and glassy, devoid of the usual fire. And when he spoke there was no hint of twang or drawl.

"I'm frightened, Ken," he said. "Scared shitless."

"Come on, man," Ken Brady said. "You just had a bad trip, that's all."

"That was no trip," Freddie said. "Something's after me."

"Nothing's after you. What could be after you?"

"My brother," Freddie said. "But he's dead."

CHAPTER
16

Frank Liscomb's projected investigation and questioning of Freddie Loftus was inadvertently interrupted by the introduction of new evidence, bizarre to the point of grotesqueness, uncovered by Jack Griffen of the crime lab.

Griffen appeared unannounced in Liscomb's office while the chief was on the phone, his face a mass of puzzled concern, his hands clutching a sheaf of papers and print cards.

"Sit down, Jack," Liscomb said. "I'll be with you in a minute." This and a slight nod of his head constituted his entire acknowledgment of Griffen. He resumed his telephone conversation, grunting here and there, putting a question now and then, nodding his head, taking notes periodically. "Is that right?" The pen in his fingers drifted across the pad in front of him. "Uh-huh. When was that?" and he jotted a date. "The Church of Satan?" A pause. "Does that hook up with The Church of Higher Awareness? Uh-huh. Uh-huh. I see."

Griffen fidgeted with the papers in his hand.

"LaVey?" Liscomb said. "How do you spell that?" and the pen scrawled. "Anton Szandor. How do you spell Szandor? Uh-huh. With a Z, yeah." His eyes drifted in Griffen's direction but pierced through him. They wandered to the windows, the walls, the bookcase, the filing cabinets, then back to Griffen, staring through, not registering. His gaze dropped very briefly to the papers in Griffen's lap, but for all his reaction, Griffen might have been holding a bag of peanuts. "But you have nothing concrete on Loftus? Nothing we could haul him in on?" A look of disappointment crossed Liscomb's face. "Too bad." A pause. "Well, yeah, that would be helpful. I'd appreciate it."

Griffen waited. He was a patient man. His years in the civil service had etched his character with forebearance, and bureaucracy had marked him as her own.

When Liscomb hung up, he swung his swivel chair in lazy arcs, hands folded on top of his head, eyes drifting again about the office, resting now and then on Griffen, speaking to the man but not really talking to him, rather enjoying the sound of his own opinions.

"Maybe we're getting someplace, Jack. Maybe."

Griffen did not respond. The old man wanted his say, and he wasn't going to listen to Griffen until he'd talked his piece.

"Here I've been sitting on my ass for close to three weeks waiting for the Feds to come up with something on Freddie Loftus. Jack, believe me, sometimes those button-down crime fighters remind me of a women's club steering committee trying to make a decision on a cake sale. When you need something in a hurry they go into conference, and when you don't want to hear from them, they're right in there telling you how to run your own business. Shit, it was only yesterday they sent up some background on this Church of Higher Awareness. And that took three weeks! Three weeks to look for a file? I ask you!"

Griffen was silent. The Church of Higher Awareness meant nothing to him, and he knew he could always find out later. What he held in his hand seemed more important. He waited for Liscomb to finish.

"So I called the horse's mouth, the San Francisco Police. Loftus has a record, of course, but nothing much. Vagrancy, disorderly conduct, possession. Nothing too heavy but enough to have caused them to turn on the surveillance lamp. And you know what?" Liscomb turned his chair to face Griffen, eyes beaming, looking at him directly now. "There's a strong possibility Loftus may have been with the Manson Family at the Barker Ranch out in Death Valley in 1969. After the Tate murders. Maybe, maybe not, but they're checking. Now, also very interesting," Liscomb went on, swiveling around again to look out the window, "is that Freddie Loftus is *definitely known* to have attended rites at The Church of Satan in San Francisco in 1967." Swiveling back to stare at Griffen, his eyes held a hint of triumph.

Griffen merely nodded, trying to hide a growing impatience.

"Now, The Church of Satan," Liscomb continued, "was founded in 1966 by one Anton Szandor LaVey. This LaVey character—" Liscomb suddenly stopped, his eyes locked on Griffen. "You're not listening, Jack."

Griffen shifted uncomfortably. "No, I am, Chief. Go ahead." But the hand holding the papers gestured upward in unconscious supplication.

Liscomb's gaze dropped downward, then up again to Griffen's face.

"What's that?" he asked.

"It can wait, Chief."

"Is it important?"

Griffen nodded.

"Okay, I'm listening."

Griffen cleared his throat lightly. "I don't know exactly how to tell you this."

"Just tell it."

"You remember the print report I left with you a few weeks ago?" As Liscomb nodded, Griffen dealt one of the print cards on the desk. "This is the print we took from that finger that was sent in the box."

Liscomb picked up the card and turned it over thoughtfully. "I remember."

"Now this," Griffen said, placing another print card before Liscomb, "is another full set of prints from a child's hand."

Liscomb examined the card, then looked up at Griffen questioningly. "So?"

Griffen twisted in his chair, looking down at the papers in his hand. "I have a full report here explaining everything. But to put it very briefly, Chief, the print of the *little* finger from the complete hand matches the print of the original severed finger. The one in the box."

Liscomb was perplexed. He screwed up his face and looked askance at Griffen. "Say that again."

Griffen said it again.

Liscomb looked at the cards he held, then at Griffen, then at the cards, and finally back to Griffen.

"So this is the entire hand."

Griffen shook his head. "No. I couldn't get prints from the mummified monstrosity that was sent to Mrs. Bannister's birthday party."

Liscomb grunted with impatience. "You're confusing the shit out of me, Jack. Are you saying that the hand the Bannister woman was sent on her birthday is a different *hand* from the *finger* that was sent in the first place?"

He waited for Griffen's affirmative, but all he got was silence.

Liscomb scowled. "Christ, Jack, what're you trying to say?"

Griffen sighed softly and then, leaning forward, picked up a pencil from Liscomb's desk and tapped the second print card lightly. "This set of prints," he said, "thumb, forefinger, middle finger, ring finger and pinky, were lifted from other parts of the Bannister house. Bedrooms, living room, foyer, kitchen, rec room, bathrooms, you name it." Griffen's hesitation, his moment's pause, his almost inaudible sigh arose from his own confusion, his bafflement at what the evidence revealed and what he was willing to believe. But the words finally came. "Both pinky prints, the one from the severed finger and the one from the complete hand, match. There's no doubt about it. But the *full* set of prints are those of Leslie Bannister." He lifted his shoulders then, and grimaced. "What can I say?"

Liscomb was staring at him again, and through him, and far beyond him.

Griffen cleared his throat again. "Look at the pinky prints again. If you don't believe me, I can put them up on a projector."

Liscomb glanced down at the cards. "No need. You know your business, Jack." Then he was looking out the window, his mouth slightly open, his frown deep.

Griffen rose. "Take a look at the full report. I don't believe it myself, but there it is. If you want to talk later, I'll be around."

Liscomb waved him back into the chair. "Sit down," he said. "I want you with me on this." He picked up the phone and dialed, looking from Griffen to the file cabinets, to the window, to the ceiling, and into space.

When Blauvelt answered the ring, he said, "Tom, Frank Liscomb. Look, we have to get together. Right away. Yeah, I'll hold on."

While he waited, he bit off the end of a cigar and lit up, cradling the phone between shoulder and neck and looking at Griffen. "Identical twins?"

Griffen shrugged.

Since the Pikeville Fair two weeks before, Nicole's mood had changed little. Outwardly, she remained cheerful and loquacious, perhaps too much so, almost to the point of superficiality, for beneath the surface there lurked a spreading coolness, and Jonathan could sense the distance widening between them. They had not made love for weeks.

And her drinking habits had changed. She had taken to nipping during the day, and as much as he understood her need, it annoyed Jonathan. Returning from Broadmoor one evening, he found her in the kitchen, drink in hand and a half empty bottle of scotch on the workspace, one which, he was sure, had been unopened when he left.

He said nothing, but his flick of the eyes from the bottle to her made the point.

"Oh, goddammit, Jonathan! Don't give me another lecture!"

"I didn't say anything."

"You didn't have to!" There was silence for a moment, and then she turned and smiled at him awkwardly. "Fix you one?"

"No, thanks."

"Oh, shit," she said, with exaggerated resignation, and turned back to the sink. "Holier than Mao."

"Holier than who?"

"Mao. Me. Mao Tse-Tung. Who cares." She turned back to the sink. "That policeman was here," she said after a pause. "Chief Liscomb."

"Oh?" Jonathan eyed his wife warily. "What'd he want?"

"More questions." She scrubbed at a skillet absent-mindedly, pulling the SOS around the bottom in slow circles.

"About what?"

"Children."

Jonathan was not following. "What children?"

"He wanted to know if we'd had any other children."

"For chrissake, we already answered that one!"

"I know," Nicole said, and she laughed, a short, sharp, nervous little laugh. Her body had stiffened, grown taut, puppetlike. She let go of the skillet and gripped the edge of the sink in hard fists. Her head was raised, staring out the window. "He wanted to know if Leslie was a twin."

"Jesus!" Jonathan said in a hoarse whisper. "What'd you tell him?"

"You know what I told him."

"I mean, didn't you tell him to go to hell!" It was said softly, but with anger and bitterness.

"No, I wouldn't tell a policeman to go to hell, love." And then Nicole was sobbing wretchedly, the tears spilling into the sink, her body rocking, shoulders hunched. "For God's sake, what's it all about, Jonathan? Tell me, for God's sake! What is it?"

He was behind her, pressing his thumbs into the

muscle between the shoulder blades, kneading, rubbing.

"He's a nut case, for chrissake. Pay no attention to him, Nikki. The man's a complete flake!" *Nut case*, he thought. *Nut case*, he had told Maria Braithwaite. *Jesus, I'm going paranoid!*

In time, Nicole's nerves knit together. The weeping ceased and she regained control. "I'm sorry," she said.

Jonathan bent to kiss the back of her neck. "Maybe I will have that drink," he said.

Later, in the library, she seemed her old self again, bright, cheerful, articulate. But there was an urgency behind her conversation, as though she were forcing the words, trying to blot out thoughts she did not dare to face.

As she chattered on, Jonathan's mind drifted back over their years together. She had not changed much. The skin was still youthful and clear, the fashion model figure still slim and supple. The soft blond hair fell about the sharp planes of her face like a glowing halo, and the full lips were sensuous and inviting.

"You know something?" he said at length. "You're a very beautiful woman."

"I'll bet you say that to all the broads."

"Only a few."

She winked at him and said, "Let's go upstairs."

"What about dinner?"

"To hell with dinner."

Their lovemaking was artful and tender, and they rose to climax almost simultaneously. But again, Jonathan sensed an urgency behind it, a forcing, an escape.

And she did not curl into him and sleep, as was

her habit, but instead chain-smoked three cigarettes, then got up to mix another drink and prepare dinner.

If travel stickers were issued for LSD trips, Freddie Loftus's luggage would have worn the marks of a psychedelic out-of-this-world tour. In his brief span of existence, he had seen and done everything and been to every corner of outer space: Mars, Saturn, Jupiter, beyond the solar system to the Pleiades and the spiral nebula in the Horse's head. According to his own accounts, he had stood on the edge of the universe, and once he swore he had hitchhiked his way back from the gates of Hell.

But Freddie had never returned to his home base with such feelings of dread and horror as he acquired on that simple journey to Toledo, Ohio, and his meeting on the street with his own image.

Not only had it left him shaken and frightened, but the dream, with slight variations, had returned without benefit of drugs.

When it recurred for the third time, Freddie's grasp on reality was in a state of shambles, and he was afraid to sleep.

This dread was the underlying reason for an act of heresy Freddie had not committed for more than ten years. He went to church, in fact, three churches. First to the Episcopal church on Main Street in Broadmoor, then the Lutheran church just up the street. It was late in the afternoon. No services were in progress. Freddie merely sat in the emptiness, shuffling in the pew, giving in to the dark coolness around him, waiting for a sign, yearning for a solace that would bring peace to his tormented mind.

But the dream, the images of it, the sounds and furies of it persisted, and he sat hunched and tight.

Christ did not appear before him, nor did God split the darkness and let light into his tortured soul.

Wandering later in the streets of Broadmoor, yearning for a cube of acid or a joint of grass but afraid to take either, he was on the point of returning to Job's Camp when he saw the small spire of St. Ignatius of Loyola on Broadmoor Road. Old Mother, he thought. The only true Church. Maybe they had the answer.

Inside, it was even darker than the other two houses of worship, and the cool air was tinted with the scent peculiar to Catholic churches, almost funereal, of polished wood, wasting flowers, and paraffin. Red and white candles burned to either side of the altar, and on the altar itself, the huge figure of Christ, slack on the cross, loomed down, arms stretched, head drooping, hovering, a reminder to all of the sins He had suffered for them.

In the third pew, just on the outer aisle, Freddie knelt, hunched and small, his hands clenched on the wood before him, fingers interwoven, knuckles white, head bowed, neck muscles tight, eyes closed.

"It's all my fault," he said. "It's all my fault," and he rapped his forehead silently against his clenched hands. "It's all my fault," he repeated. "I shouldn't have done what I did."

The church was empty. No one else knelt in the pews or before the candles. There were no hollow, hesitant coughs. All was silence in the flickering light, yet Freddie felt a presence.

And it was not Christ.

He lifted his head and looked around him warily. Only shadows.

Freddie pressed his forehead to his folded hands again. "I didn't mean to do what I did," he said. "I couldn't help myself."

But no answer was forthcoming. Only the remnants of the dream.

And the presence.

Freddie lifted his head again, eyes shifting, heartbeat rising. He moved his head slightly.

Off to his left, in an arch to the side of the altar, was a shadow that did not belong.

He knew it did not belong.

It was unnatural.

He watched.

His hands unfolded and his fingers closed on the back of the pew in front of him like a vise.

The shadow in the archway moved.

Freddie's throat constricted. *Momma's dead! Momma's dead!* Freddie screamed in his mind.

The shadow moved again, did not exactly move, but merely stirred, fluttered, as if in an unseen, unfelt wind.

Freddie's feet scraped loudly as he fought to rise. *Get behind me!* he screamed in his mind.

And as Freddie rose in the pew, his fear, as fear will, began to turn into anger. "It wasn't my fault!" he shouted at the altar. But the figure of Christ did not raise His head.

Freddie's knees bumped hollowly as he staggered into the center aisle. "What're you staring at, you prick?" he screamed at the archway. "What do you want, you motherfucker!"

The shadow oscillated, fluttered again, then advanced out of the gloom toward Freddie Loftus.

"You cunt! Stay away from me! I'll kill you, you motherfucker!"

"Is there anything I can do?"

Freddie's fingers were balled into fists, and his

legs were spread. "You were staring at me," Freddie spit. "What've you got, nothing else to do?"

"I wasn't staring," Father Conant said mildly.

"You were looking at me!"

"I often look at people in my church."

"It's not your church!" Freddie said, flicking his head toward the altar. "It's His."

"I won't argue the point," Father Conant said and tried to smile. But the smile was frozen. His face was fixed in anger, and his own hands had become fists. "You're in trouble, boy, and I was only trying to find out if I could help."

"Balls! I got no trouble. The only trouble I got is this fucking church!"

"Don't say that!" Conant's voice was like a knife. His right hand came up involuntarily, still fisted.

"You touch me, you shithead, and I'll lay you right on your ass!" Freddie said.

They stood facing each other, eyes locked, fists balled, the space between them charged with anger.

"I was only trying to help," Conant said.

"Bullshit!" Freddie said. "Help, bullshit. You're like all the rest. Hypocrite!" Freddie Loftus leaned slightly forward and spat into Daniel Conant's face.

The sputum hung there, on his forehead, then oozed slowly to his nose and cheek.

"Get out of my church!" Conant said. "Get out!"

Freddie snickered. "*Your* church!" Then he turned on his heel and swaggered up the center aisle. At the end, just at the lavaboes on the rear wall, he looked back with a smirk, raised a leg, and farted loudly into the hovering gloom.

"That's for your fucking church," he said, and was gone.

Conant stood trembling, stomach churning, pulses pounding, hands still clenched, the skin of the knuckles drawn and white. His mind was a mass of random noise, a confusion of signals, none of which would register.

Slowly, the adrenaline seeped backward, his breathing eased, his pulses slowed, and his mind began to return to sanity.

The basement, he thought. He had been on his way to the basement, of course. He turned and began to walk stiffly, like a robot, down the aisle and toward a door to his left, genuflecting automatically before the altar.

As he descended the steps to the cellar he wondered what had brought Freddie Loftus to the church, and worry began to cast its pall over his thinking.

What could I have done? he thought. *What can I do? I am only His servant. Only His instrument.*

Behind the wheel of his van again, Freddie regained his normal composure, namely his anger, his disdain. No more churches for Freddie. Hypocrites! That's what they were, all of them, all the ministers, the preachers, the priests, and the prelates. He had given all that up years ago and wondered what had ever made him think they might help. They could go fuck themselves. Freddie had his own church, his own religion, his own tenets, and to these he would return.

Yet beneath the bravado, the dread persisted. He was frightened and he knew it. And he wanted to talk to somebody.

As he crossed the covered bridge over The Reach, he thought of Susan Dixon, and instead of turning left on Indian Falls Road back to the Camp, he continued on Willow Creek, driving slowly, climbing the steep hill, scanning the mailboxes.

When he rolled into the driveway, Henry and Estelle Dixon were having cocktails on the screened terrace. At the rattling sound of the engine and the bouncing of shot springs, Dixon squinted through the mesh, grunted, then opened both eyes wide.

"What the hell is that?" he said.

Freddie pressed the horn loudly. "Sue? Sue, you home?"

"She's not here," Hank shouted. "Should be back in ten or fifteen minutes. You want to wait?"

There was a pause, and then the door of the van opened.

"Come in," Estelle said. "Have a drink."

As Freddie slipped from the van, Dixon's eyes widened again. "Shit! Is that Ken Brady? What does she see in that? There's not enough to go around."

"Maybe it's not him," Estelle said. "Anyway, I hope not."

The screen door swung and Freddie stepped in. "I'm Freddie Loftus," he said and held forth a bony hand.

Estelle choked a sigh of relief.

Dixon rose, shaking the bones, and motioned Freddie to a chair. "Fix you a drink?"

"Well, that's a right nice thought, Mr. Dixon," Freddie said. "You maybe got some wine?" He was back on his country drawl.

"I think I can rustle up some Soave," Dixon rose and went to a portable bar on the terrace.

"You live up at the Camp, Freddie?" Estelle asked.

"That's right, ma'am. Up to Job's Camp is where I crash."

Dixon came back with a glass of Soave. "You're mixing your diction," he said.

"What?" Freddie looked perplexed.

"Nothing. Sue should be back soon."

A short silence followed while Dixon eyed Freddie, and Estelle tried to look unconcerned.

"Mind if I smoke?" Freddie asked.

"Not at all," Dixon said.

Freddie's hand went to the torn pocket of his worn shirt and came out with a joint, twisted at both ends. Dixon looked at Estelle and Estelle looked down. She went to the bar and mixed another drink. Strong. Freddie lit up, and the sweet reek hung heavily in the still air. Dixon's nostrils twitched visibly.

"What's that?" he asked.

"Pot, man," Freddie said, and he passed the cigarette toward Dixon.

"No, thanks," Dixon said, "I never touch the stuff."

"It's great, man. Mild and soothing and easy on the nerves."

Dixon was doing the layout in his head. Big country. Horses. Cattle. A skinny, long-haired, hollow-cheeked, vacant-eyed cowpoke slumped in the saddle, grinning foolishly. Like Freddie.

"Beats that stuff you're tilting from the glass."

Dixon swirled his drink and the ice cubes clinked. "I'm getting my shit together," he said.

Freddie laughed. "Man, you got a sense of humor. I like a man with a sense a humor."

Dixon burped.

While the conversation stumbled along, Estelle measured Freddie Loftus. He was trying his best to be sociable: smiling, laughing, sprawling lazily, legs outstretched to show his equality and ease, along with a tolerance she sensed he did not really feel. But in

his eyes she saw an anger, almost a viciousness that belied his apparent good humor. She cast back in her
mind for something vague and distant, and after a
moment a snapshot swept across the screen. Charles
Manson. She shuddered inwardly. Who *was* Freddie
Loftus? What did he have to do with Susan? Or she
with him?

Freddie was getting high, and with the high came
expansiveness. He turned to Estelle. "Hear you're going to have a seance, Mrs. Dixon."

Estelle was jolted. "Who told you that?"

"Shit—I mean, hell, it's all around."

Susan, Dixon thought. *Why can't she keep her
mouth shut?*

"I think that's super," Freddie went on, "only, you
really think it's worth all that energy?"

Estelle bristled. "What do you know about seances?"

"I been to a few."

"Where?"

"San Francisco," Freddie said. "Yeah. San Francisco. Only they were probably different from what
you got in mind."

"How?" Dixon asked.

Freddie shrugged lazily. "Hell, all that table-rap-
ping shit and all. That's yesterday, y'know?"

"I suppose you're an authority?" Estelle said.

"You got to flow with the energy these days," Freddie
said. "Let the evil suck you in. Swim with it. Give
in to it. Then it becomes a part of you and you get to
understand it. It all happens in the mind, y'know?
Fuck the voices and the table bumps." Freddie's visage had changed. The smile was gone and there was
a hard light in his eyes. He was becoming belligerent.
"Take this motherfucker who killed that kid. He's
evil, man. But you ain't going to understand his evil

sittin' around a table and holding hands. You gotta *move* with the man. Let his evil approach your soul and become part of your own energy."

The Dixons sat stiff and transfixed, regarding their uninvited guest with rising anxiety. Estelle was beginning to think that the seance might be unnecessary, that the supernatural played no part in this affair, that the answer to the whole horrible nightmare was sitting there before her. Dixon's hands were clutching his drink tightly, and every muscle in his body was alert and ready to spring. He was wondering what he would do if the man suddenly threatened them.

"Look," he said, "maybe Susan's going to be later than we think. Why don't I tell her you dropped by, Freddie?"

Freddie's eyes came slowly around to Dixon, cold, hardened into crystal. When he spoke, his tone was level and stony. "You insulting me, man?"

"No, I'm not insulting you!" Dixon's voice was rising.

"Yes, you're insulting me! In your own supercilious, smug, self-complacent way, you're insulting me! Looking at me, staring at me, trying to make me feel like some coil of dog turd!" The country twang had left. Freddie's words came in flat Midwestern tones.

"Now, hold on!" Dixon had risen. He expected Freddie to follow him to his feet, but the boy remained seated.

"Hypocrites!" Freddie said. "Goddamn, mother-fucking hypocrites! You're all alike, aren't you? Whether you wear clerical collars or go around with your tits hanging out of bikinis. Fuck you! Fuck you all!"

All the civilized cowardice that Henry Dixon had absorbed in fifty-three years suddenly melted and rushed from his body like a sudden spring thaw. He was just about to grab Freddie by the shirt and punch his face when Susan's car drew into the driveway.

"You here, Ken?" she said, approaching.

Inside the screen door, she stopped dead. "Jesus Christ!"

"He's a far cry from that," Dixon said and poured himself another drink.

"Hello, Sue," Freddie said. And then he looked at Dixon and Estelle. "I'm sorry," he said, and his voice carried a weak but quiet sincerity.

Estelle shifted for a moment, then said, "I'm for a nap. How about you, Hank?"

"Yeah," Dixon said and followed her into the house.

Susan dropped into a chair and stared at Freddie dumbfounded. "What brings you here, Freddie?"

He moved his head from side to side. "I wanted to talk to somebody," he said.

"About what?"

He shrugged. "I dunno. It's hard to tell you."

Susan's eyes and ears were riveted on the interior of the house. She saw shadows move and she heard steps creak. *Like hell they were taking a nap.*

"You're in enemy territory, you know."

"I got the message," Freddie said.

"Let's take a walk," Susan said.

Outside, a rough footpath ran along the edge of Willow Creek. They walked south, in the direction of the Bannister house.

"That was a heavy scene when I walked in," Susan said.

"Shit, Sue, I thought your father was going to beat up on me."

"My father?" She laughed shortly. "He's not a fighter, he's a pussycat."

"They don't understand anything, do they? They just don't understand."

Susan did not reply. There was a tension in her, a wrench in her stomach and throbbing in her head. She had seen the anger in her father's face, the hatred in Freddie's eyes. She stole quick glances at Freddie and felt a fear rising, but a fear mixed with fascination.

They sat on a rock overlooking the stream, watching the evening trout beginning to feed, darting from the bottom to just under the surface, waiting, watching. Then the sudden swirl, the tail flap, the concentric ripples. What they fed on remained invisible.

"What's bugging you, Freddie?"

Freddie threw a small stone into the stream. The trout went down.

"Are you coming to the Rites, Friday?" He asked it matter-of-factly, as though his mind were elsewhere.

"Maybe," she said. "But that's not why you came here, is it?"

Freddie pitched another stone, staring down into the stream, his brow drawn in a frown. "Did I ever tell you about my brother?" he said.

"You haven't told me much about anything," Susan said. "What brother?" She waited.

"When I was born," Freddie said, "back in Ohio, there was a brother."

Susan looked surprised. "Oh? Then you're a twin."

"No. He died. I came first, see. They got me out okay. But then something happened. I don't know. But the other one, James they were going to call him, he never made it. He died and my mother died."

Susan was silent, not knowing what to say, confused that he would choose her as a confidante, perplexed as to the gist of the whole conversation.

"Shit!" Freddie said, turning to her fiercely. "It wasn't my fault!"

"Of course not, Freddie." The sudden burst of fury had made her watchful, frightened.

"Goddammit! What the fuck could I do?" He picked up another stone, this one the size of a fist, and hurled it into the water. The heavy splash echoed in the chasm, the ripples floated outward, white and angry. "All my life I've been hearing about that fucker! That little fucker! 'If it wasn't for you, he might have lived. If it wasn't for you, *she* might have lived. If it wasn't for you—' "

"Who?" Susan asked. "Who said that? Who was blaming you?"

"Them," Freddie said.

Susan waited. "Your father?"

Freddie laughed. "That prick? Yeah, he blamed me. You should have heard him. And the aunts, the uncles. Every time I got into trouble, it was James this, James that, 'I wonder what James would have done under the circumstances. I wonder if he'd lived if he would have acted like you.' " He spat the words. "Well, fuck James. Fuck dead James and fuck them!"

He had risen and was staring across the stream into a wedge of pine. "Fuck you, James!" he shouted. "Fuck you and to hell with you!" He was staring into James's face, over in the pines, smiling back at him, grinning like the Cheshire cat and dripping black blood from the corners of his mouth. Then the vision faded. Freddie sat down on the rock, breathing audibly.

Susan wanted to run, but she was rooted. "But James never even lived," she said.

"No, he didn't, did he?" Freddie was gaining control over himself, putting the phantom to rest.

"I don't understand," Susan said. "I mean, you come here with this big heavy scene. Why? I mean, do you feel guilty about it?"

Freddie laughed. "Me? Feel guilty? Bullshit!"

"We all feel guilty sometimes, Freddie."

"Horse balls. You come to the Rites, Sue. You'll see how guilty I feel. I ought to invite some of those priests and ministers to the Rites, too. That'd be a laugh, wouldn't it?"

"Would it?"

"Can you see their faces? Can you see the looks on their faces when they hear *real* religion? Honest, down-to-earth, true facts about what people really are and what God and the Devil *really* mean?"

Again, Susan felt the chill blast of fear cross her soul, fleetingly, touching briefly and going, but gripping her so that she could not move.

Freddie was staring at her, and in his eyes she recognized something of what she felt. Behind the fire, back of the mad glitter, there lurked dread.

"What are you afraid of, Freddie?"

"Huh?"

"You're frightened of something. What is it?"

He turned away. His body sagged. "Yeah, maybe," he said.

"What?"

He turned back to her. The sparkle was gone from his eyes. His stare was blank, empty. His mouth hung limp.

"I don't know, Sue," he said. "I don't really know. It's not James. James is dead and I know he's dead. It's not my conscience. I got over that a long time ago."

"Then what is it?"

"I don't know," Freddie said. His eyes were wide, with almost a thyroid look. "I don't know what it is. Something. I can't explain it." He paused. "It's terrible, Sue."

CHAPTER 17

"I don't believe it," Marion Hammond said.

"The evidence is staring you in the face," Blauvelt said. "You're a scientist."

Liscomb sighed. "Let's not get into an academic argument."

"All right," Hammond said. "Let's look at the evidence. According to these charts, Leslie Bannister's little fingerprint matches the print of the finger sent to Nicole. But Leslie still has all ten fingers intact. Where does that leave us? An identical twin. All right, so now you want to tell me that Leslie's twin, some kind of a monster with no Golgi apparatus in the cells, has been successfully hidden away all these years, maybe in the Bannisters' own attic for all we know, and that somehow, somebody wanted her dead and—"

"All right, knock it off," Liscomb interjected. "Nobody's accusing the Bannisters."

"I'm not accusing anybody," Hammond said. "You brought the evidence over here. I'm only trying to sift it, make sense out of it. I get a twin."

Blauvelt just dropped it in. "Or a clone," he said.

Hammond looked aghast. "Now, come on, Tom, for chrissake! That's science fiction."

"Oh, yeah? What the hell are you guys doing over at WebLabs?"

Hammond was suddenly indignant. "We're not making clones, for shit's sake!"

They were in Blauvelt's living room, and he trundled over to the bar and poured a drink. "But you *are* involved with genetic engineering," he said, sipping.

"Only to a very limited extent," Hammond said. "And that's a hell of a far cry from cloning, Tom."

"I was just asking."

"Are you accusing WebLabs, or me for that matter, of having anything to do with this—this—this whatever it is? Jesus!"

Blauvelt laughed. "I'm sorry, Marion. I didn't mean it to sound anything like that. It's just that I'm trying to do exactly what you do: sift it, come to some kind of conclusion. If it's not a twin or a clone, what is it?"

"It's a bitch," Liscomb said.

"There's got to be an answer," Hammond said. "A simple, logical, reasonable answer."

"Does there?" The other two turned to look at Tom Blauvelt. "Logic, reason, simplicity, science. Where does it fit here?" he asked. "A finger that turned into a mummy. A hand that does the same thing. Fingerprints that match but shouldn't. No Golgi bodies." He placed his drink on an end table and searched in his pockets for a cigarette. "It's unnatural."

Liscomb was looking at him queerly. "So?"

Blauvelt smiled, but the smile was cold and cynical. "There's no earthly reason for these things, Frank."

"What do you mean by that?"

"Just what I said. No *earthly* reason. *Un*natural." He paused. "Maybe *super*natural."

There was silence until Liscomb muttered, "Agh, shit, Tom!" He pulled a cigar into his hand and bit the end off savagely. "I mean I've heard just about everything today. Twins, clones, and now this—the supernatural. Shit!"

Tom Blauvelt settled back in his chair and uttered a long, low chuckle. But there was little humor in it. It was hollow and smacked of uncertainty, even fear.

"Have you got any better suggestions?" he said.

Elvida had been coming more often of late, not at Leslie's beck and call as had been the case with Elsie, but whenever she wanted and wherever—in her room, on the grounds, on the dam over Willow Creek.

There were many times when Leslie did not really want to talk to Elvida, and in a way she was becoming a nuisance. Leslie was jealous of her own prerogatives, and she considered Elvida's unannounced arrivals an invasion of her privacy. And her power.

"Why do you come when I don't ask you to?" she asked one day.

"Don't you want to play with me?"

"Of course I do. But not *all* the time. And when *I* want to, not *you*."

"You're selfish," Elvida said.

"I am not!"

"Selfish, selfish, selfish," Elvida repeated and began to laugh. "Selfish, selfish! Leslie's selfish!"

The voice receded and the laughter followed it and there was silence.

Leslie was angry. The laughter reverberated in her ears, and she felt her heart pounding hard.

She was experiencing a feeling close to fear.

* * *

Henry Dixon, too, had been feeling a sense of danger, a rising of his hackles, an ambiguous awareness of imminent catastrophe and impending doom. As the time of the seance approached, he noticed a subtle change in Estelle's demeanor, a single-mindedness that had not been apparent before. The bright, glittery fanaticism was gone, and in its place was a quiet aloofness that was alien to her. She seldom spoke of the seance, and when she did, she was deliberate and thoughtful, at times almost impassive. She had withdrawn into herself and spent long hours thinking. She did not drink during the day, as she had been prone to, but took only a few cocktails before dinner and maybe one or two drinks afterward. It was a new Estelle, and one with whom he did not feel comfortable.

Dixon did not look forward to the seance. To him it was a farce, something that Estelle wanted in order to prove her worth, her value. And at the same time, he had to admit that some good might possibly come out of it, a new experience for Estelle that would in some way change her. For the better, he hoped. Yet he could not ignore the comments made at Nicole's party. Somebody had mentioned the danger to the medium. Estelle herself knew of a medium who had committed suicide. But it was all quackery at best. Dixon threw the nagging rumors into the back of his mind. Where they persisted.

There were other things disturbing him. The weather for one. Everybody had been talking about it.

In the post office, Zack Timmons had looked up from behind his cage, perspiration oozing down his forehead, his mouth gasping for breath. "Hotter'n the hinges of Hell, ain't it Mr. Dixon?" It was more a statement than a question.

"You can say that again," Dixon answered. Then he saw the bandages on Timmons's arms and hands, the ointment leaking out. "What happened, Zack?"

"Bees," Timmons said. "Cleanin' out the pump house and they attacked me. Never seen so many bees. Never'n all my life, no sir."

Dixon nodded sympathetically. "More bugs around than I've seen in years. They should be dying off or hibernating by now."

"In this weather?" Timmons said. "Hell, they'll be hatchin' well into April if this keeps up. Don't seem we're going to have any winter. Hotter'n the hinges of Hell," he said again.

Bugs, too. Everybody was talking about the bugs, Dixon thought.

Raking the leaves at the edge of Willow Creek, he had somehow slipped his footing and fallen into an old compost heap. He had come up almost screaming at the things crawling on his body, literally covering him in the split second of his sprawl in the humus.

Large beetles. Over an inch long.

He hated bugs and had staggered across the lawn toward the house, brushing them from his arms and neck, slapping at his clothes, once rolling on the ground in absolute terror. He had shed his clothes at the outdoor shower, turned on the water, and then hot-footed it for the house.

Later, nursing a straight gin, his nerves had begun to calm. Until he saw them crawling on the window-sill. Then on the coffee table. They were in the house. The same bugs. Dozens of them.

The aerosol insecticide had come out, and the house still reeked. Two days later he had taken one of the dead insects over to Hal Brigham, a retired ad-man who made a hobby of entomology.

Hal had turned the bug carefully in his palm. "Yeah, they're all over the place this year, aren't they?" he had said, nodding his head in the direction of his lawn. The ground was crawling.

"What is it?" Dixon had asked.

"*Ocypus olens,*" Hal had said. "The European rove beetle. Also known as the devil's coach horse."

Everybody seemed to be talking about the Devil these days, Dixon thought. "*European* rove beetle?"

"Yeah, that's the funny thing," Hal had said. "They're not even supposed to live around here."

Dixon poured another Boodles. As he sat there on the screened terrace, one eye peeled for a creeping devil's coach horse, his mind shifted back to the night of Nicole Bannister's birthday party.

He had seen the hand. He was sure of that. The memory of it sent a shiver down his spine, and he wondered whether he shouldn't discourage Estelle from the seance.

If the hordes of rove beetles, the swarms of bees, the armadas of wasps and other insects filled some with feelings of uneasiness and doubt, to most of the populace of Holland County they foretold no dread occurrences, but were simply accepted as part of a complete design, complement to the oppressive heat, the monotonous drizzle, the miasmic fog. If any of them noticed that the unseasonable, almost unnatural patterns were confined to Holland County, and that the adjoining counties were advancing into Indian summer, they merely shrugged and accepted it philosophically, knowing that most of the time Holland County could boast the best weather in the state, and that perhaps it was time for a break in the pattern. One season wouldn't do them in.

But there were others less sure of the naturalness of events.

Bette Hammond uncovered a nest of copperheads, and after Marion had killed one and dispersed the rest, she staggered into the house and collapsed on the couch.

"Take me back to West Eighty-fourth Street," she said.

"All right," Hammond said.

She looked up at him in surprise. "You mean it, Marion? Really?"

"I'm not placating you," he said. He dropped down beside her and drew her close.

She clung tightly, shivering against him. "You're a good man, Marion." She paused. "When?"

"Soon," he said. "As soon as we can. I'll have a talk with the lab next week." Staring over her shoulder at the wall, he was thinking about the finger, the hand, the mummification, the prints. Nothing fit. He wondered what the seance would uncover, then caught himself.

Jesus, I'm getting as bad as Tom Blauvelt!

Joe Tremper and Lauren Shane were making love.

He was in top form, sober, without the faintest hint of a hangover, every sense alert, incredibly tumescent, burgeoned. He plunged into her with long, powerful, slow, loving strokes.

She lifted to him, brimmed to him, met his thrusts with heaving hips, hunching body, breasts bouncing, nipples crisp and erect. Tight gasps, hoarse grunts. Her eyes opened wide in wonder and delight and passion, staring over his shoulder.

She was on the verge of orgasm when she saw the rat.

She screamed.

For a moment Tremper thought he had hurt her. Then he followed her gaze.

It was on the night table, hunched, staring at them, teeth bared.

He reached for a pillow and flung it. The rat backed up an inch, stood there, and snarled.

Tremper tumbled off the bed and picked up a lamp. When he threw it, the rat jumped to one side and stood its ground. The lamp hit the wall and shattered. The rat's eyes gleamed maliciously. Then it bared its teeth—almost smiling, Tremper thought—jumped off the table and ran to the door.

Tremper followed it out into the hall, but it was gone.

When he returned, he sat on the edge of the bed and lit a cigarette. His hands were trembling.

"Oh, God," Lauren Shane kept repeating. "Oh, God."

"It was just a field rat," Tremper said. The cigarette jerked in his lips.

"Oh, God," Lauren said.

He put an arm around her, squeezed. He tried to smile. "Well," he said, "I guess that takes care of fucking for today."

"Oh, God," Lauren said.

Carole Kollars was editing a manuscript when she heard the whine at the front door, then a scraping. At the window, she pulled the curtain. She saw only the tail and hindquarters of a dog.

When she opened the door, the dog looked up at her. It was black. Jet black. A mutt of some kind.

Carole leaned forward and down. "What's the matter, baby?" she said. "You lost?"

The dog flicked its tail briefly.

"Ahhh," Carole said with all the sympathy she could muster. "Poor baby. Poor little lost baby." She put out her hand.

The dog took it in a strong, tearing grip that sunk its teeth to the bone. It held on, tugging, gnawing, growling.

"You son of a bitch!" Carole screamed, and kicked the dog hard in the breastbone.

Letting go, the animal turned and fled into the road, its snarl echoing back like laughter.

Carole screamed across the road. "Agnes! Agnes! come out and help me!"

The front door of Agnes Bittel's house gaped and Agnes appeared in the oblong of light.

"That you, Carole?"

"Come help me, for God's sake! Drive me to the hospital!"

"What's the trouble?"

"I just came down with a case of rabies!"

Maria Braithwaite was contemplating her fifteen-thousand-dollar lawn. It had recently been leveled, reseeded, and resodded. Yet despite the constant drizzle, it was turning brown, becoming sere, dying.

Years before, in Italy, she had seen the same thing happen to another lawn, a small one before a small house in Umbria.

"Someone in the family was said to have been possessed by the Devil," Maria said to Estelle Dixon. "Where the lawns of the other houses in the area flourished, theirs faded. One night a priest came to cast the evil one out. During the exorcism, lightning struck the house and set it afire." She paused. Estelle waited. "Everyone in the house died," she said.

"The priest?"

"Even the priest."

Estelle looked at the ground. "My lawn isn't doing so well either," she said.

"Nor is Nicole Bannister's," Maria said. "In fact, I have noticed a number of lawns dying."

"Father Conant says he'll come," Estelle said.

"Have you been listening to me?"

"About the lawns? Sure. All the more reason for holding the seance. Something's wrong."

"I can't talk you out of it?"

"Why should you?" Estelle's brows arched.

"Some things are best left alone," Maria said.

"Give the Devil his due?"

"Why not?" Maria said.

"Give him hell, is what I say!" Estelle got out of her chair and walked over to the swimming pool, looking down into its still, unbroken water. There was a green scum on it, and she saw droves of water beetles swimming beneath the surface. It looked ugly. "Why are you so worried, Maria?"

Maria rose and joined Estelle at the pool's edge. "Because we are dealing with powers we do not understand, cannot control, and in our ignorance and weakness, we can be destroyed."

Estelle turned. "For the first time in my life," she said, "I feel as though I've got the power to *do* something—something important, something unusual, something good. I know it. I know it deep inside. It's been growing, growing stronger and more clear every day, ever since Elvida spoke to me at the Ouija board."

"Who is Elvida?"

"I don't know," Estelle said. "Maybe a devil, maybe one of the Devil's legions. I don't know." She paused. "But I have to do it, Maria. I have to."

There was very little sun showing through the bleak overcast, but a shadow, a deep, dark shadow crossed Estelle's face at that moment, obscuring her features. A little gasp formed in Maria's throat, but she stifled it.

"Of course, Estelle," she said. "Of course, if you must."

Twelve days after the Bannister party, the body of a child was snagged by a fisherman trolling Devil's Pond.

Contained in a canvas sack, tied with manila twine, the body was that of a girl approximately seven years old. This was determined by size alone, since the skin and features were emaciated, dry, and petrified to the point of unrecognizability.

The left hand was missing.

After a preliminary examination at the morgue in King's Landing, the corpse was shipped to the Medical Examiner of New York County at Bellevue Hospital, where experts from the American Museum of Natural History and the Metropolitan Museum of Art were called in for consultation. Tissue samples were sent to the Brookhaven National Laboratories for radiocarbon analysis. The canvas sack and rope were forwarded to the Federal Bureau of Investigation in Washington, D.C.

That night Frank Liscomb and Tom Blauvelt got very drunk together at the Bull and Bear.

Father Conant was hearing confession.

"Oh, my Father, I have sinned."

Conant creased his brows.

"It wasn't my fault, Father."

Why were the words always the same? It's never

their fault. Never. Yet they sinned, and sinned and sinned again, and kept sinning. But it was never their fault. "You've told me this before," he said softly. But it was as though he hadn't spoken.

"I have killed, Father."

Conant sighed irritably. "Go on."

"I have killed a child, Father."

Always the same. Never a variation, never a syllable out of place, a word omitted, as though by rote. How many times had he heard this same confession? And how many times had he given absolution? Was suffering so sweet?

"Tell me," he said. But he had heard it all before.

The confession droned on, and Father Conant passed his hand across his forehead, pressed his temples, nodded, sighed.

When it was over, he sat slumped in the cubicle, tired, worn. He took three more confessions, but hardly listened. His thoughts wandered, his imagination leaped.

Adultery, fornication, larceny, murder, greed, lust, masturbation, rape. He had heard them all, over and over, again and again, a record playing into eternity, a needle in a ten-thousand-year-old groove.

How they prayed and begged, pleaded and suffered. What did they know of suffering? To fornicate and to be forgiven. Was that suffering?

They came to him as if the sins they committed were their own. As if they themselves had committed them and were responsible. As though they were the villains.

Conant's head ached, his eyes throbbed. He had heard too much *I did, I committed, I sinned.* Too much conceit.

What did they know of sin? And its source? They

had done nothing. They were merely instruments.

Only Lucifer was the villain, abiding without, patient, cunning, waiting.

Once the invitation went out; what could they expect?

He cut the last confession short, almost rudely. He needed air. Exiting the confessional, he made his way up the nave toward the main entrance. A figure in the rear pew drew his attention. It was not a praying figure. It sat upright, stiff, as if waiting. As Conant approached, it rose.

For a moment, he thought it was Freddie Loftus returned, and his fists clenched automatically. But as he drew near, he saw it was Jonathan Bannister.

"Father Conant."

Conant smiled. "Mr. Bannister. Just ducking out for a breath of air. Join me?"

"If you can call that air out there."

They walked to the door, Conant leading. On the steps outside, Conant sniffed. "Not much difference."

"Cooler inside, as a matter of fact," Jonathan said.

"Fresher, though. The moisture makes it fresh." The air on Broadmoor Road was hung with gray fog. Conant turned to Jonathan. "Something you want to talk about?"

"Nicole," Jonathan said.

Conant turned his eyes in the direction of John's Bakery. "How is Nicole?" His muscles were tense. He did not want this conversation.

"I wouldn't say she's up to par," Jonathan said.

"Oh?"

"You've seen her. What do you think?"

Conant spoke without hesitation. "She seems all right to me. Quite in good spirits, as a matter of fact. Considering."

"That's the trouble," Jonathan said.

"I don't understand."

"She's drifting. Going off someplace. She's not re-acting well, if you know what I mean."

Contant looked vacant. "No, I'm not sure I know what you mean."

Jonathan was becoming impatient, edgy. "She never talks to me about what happened."

"Maybe she can't," Conant said.

"That's what I mean. She *has* to." Jonathan eyed Conant skeptically. "I'm worried, that's all. I thought you might be able to help."

"How?"

The man's cool distance irritated Jonathan. "I thought she might have said something to you," he said.

"About what?" Conant's tone was almost psychiatric. Jonathan might have been on a couch.

"Look, for chrissake!" Jonathan suddenly snapped. "She's been here five times this week!"

Conant nodded.

"I followed her, that's how I know!"

"I didn't ask you how you knew, Mr. Bannister."

Jonathan did not hear. "And she just came out of your confessional!"

A look of pain and shock creased Conant's features. "Are you a Catholic, Mr. Bannister?"

"That has nothing to do with it!"

"Because if you are, you must know that a con-fession is privileged."

"I'm asking you if she's said anything to you!"

Conant did not answer. His eyes bored into Jon-athan's.

Jonathan sagged. "I'm sorry," he said. "I'm only

trying to help her. I only want to know why she's drifting. What's on her mind."

"Why don't you ask her?" Conant said.

"I have. It's a brick wall."

"You love her very much, don't you?"

"Yes."

Conant relaxed. The anger left his eyes. He took Jonathan by the arm and moved him down the steps. "Ask her again," he said. "Keep asking. That's all you can do."

At his car, Jonathan turned to the priest. "Sorry I made a scene," he said. "But I'm upset. All this church-going of hers. The confessions."

"I understand," Conant said.

"It's like I'm left out."

Conant smiled. "You couldn't be jealous of *me*, Mr. Bannister."

"Not exactly," Jonathan said and got into the car.

After Jonathan Bannister drove off, Father Conant slowly remounted the steps and entered the Church of St. Ignatius of Loyola.

He walked down the center aisle, knelt before the altar, placed his hands upon the rail, and, leaning forward, dug his forehead into his tightly clenched fingers.

"Oh, my God!" he said.

A montage of horror jumped and flickered in his mind, cinematic images of a living nightmare: the face of Nicole Bannister as she lay in the hospital after receiving the finger; the misshapen, dried, claw-like thing that had dropped from the box at the party; and the man with the wilted ear, whistling his way through the streets of Broadmoor, behind his sly smile a sickly evil, in his eyes a vision of Hell.

Father Conant looked upward at the figure of Christ.

What can I tell them? That Satan has become alive? That he has taken form and that he walks the earth?

Who would believe me? How could they believe me?

And what would the Church say to these ramblings of an unsound mind, as unsound she would find it. Excommunication? Blasphemy? Heresy?

Father Conant dropped his head.

Oh, my God, he thought, *is it possible?*

And he knew it was.

CHAPTER
18

The shades were drawn, the bedspread turned down, Nicole Bannister lay on the wet sheets in a half doze, perspiration bathing her body. From outside came a lilting chant.

> *"Ladybug, ladybug, fly away home.*
> *"Your house is on fire, and your children will burn."*

Christ, I can't stand it! Whoever taught her that thing?

> *"Ladybug, ladybug, fly away home,"*

Won't she ever stop? I've got to rest. I've got to sleep.

> *"Your house is on fire, and your children will burn."*

Leslie, goddammit, shut up! The thought rocketed through Nicole's mind, but no words left her mouth. Please! Please Leslie! Stop!

> *". . . and your children will burn."*

The words were present, but past. Now, but then. Today, but yesterday.

Nicole tried to call out, scream, but the sound was lost in her throat. A redness came before her eyes, billowing, flowing, then turning white. She fainted. Sleep came, but a sleep with pounding pulses.

On the lawn outside, Leslie chanted.

> *"Your house is on fire, and your children will burn."*

"I'm not a ladybug."

Leslie stopped. "Elvida?"

"Over here," Elvida said.

Leslie looked across Willow Creek into a stand of pines. She saw a kind of light shining in the darkness of the trees, a vague, nebulous glow, yellow, like sulfur.

"If you're not a ladybug, what are you?" Leslie felt argumentative.

"I'm your friend," Elvida said.

"A fine friend you are," Leslie said. "I never see you. You won't come out."

"You'll see me soon."

"When?"

"Very soon." A pause. "Do you like your mother?"

"Of course." Leslie said.

"Why?"

Leslie was confused. "Because she's my mother."

"Just because she's your mother?"

"Everybody loves their mother," Leslie said.

"No, they don't," Elvida said. "Anyway, she doesn't let you do the things you want."

"Well, not always," Leslie said.

"Like going to Devil's Pond and things like that."

"But you'll take me to Devil's Pond. You said so."

"Mothers are mean," Elvida said.

"Sometimes," Leslie said.

"Mothers stink," Elvida said.

"What?" It was not a new word. Leslie did not understand it entirely, but she knew it was a bad word. A smelly word.

"Mothers stink! Mothers stink, stink, stink!" Elvida said. The word bounced and echoed and seemed to come from all directions. Leslie turned her head to find its source.

"Stink, stink, stink!" bounded from tree to tree. Then there was a fading laugh.

Leslie's heart was thumping, her stomach felt cramped and queasy. She started to cry.

"Hey, girl, what you cryin' 'bout? Don't you know you not 'sposed to be near the water?" Pearl De-Witt's large body loomed over Leslie. Pearl always tried to look angry at such times, but was never quite successful. She tried to kneel, but her great bulk made her sigh and remain standing. "You come in the house."

"I want my Mommy!" Leslie cried.

"Your momma asleep upstairs. She don't want no truck with little girls that cry. Now, you come."

"Mommies are mean," Leslie said through tears.

"Mommas gotta be mean sometimes, girl. If'n they not mean, they walked all over. Now you come with me and we sit down and have iced tea and cookies. What you doin' out here anyway?"

"I was talking to Elvida."

"Who Elvida?"

"My friend," Leslie said.

"I thought Elsie your friend."

"Elsie went away."

"And Elvida come, that it?"

Leslie nodded.

"Well, you and me and Elvida, we go get some cookies."

They walked across the lawn.

"Mothers stink," Leslie said.

Pearl looked down, eyes wide. "*What?*"

"Nothing," Leslie said.

But the word was still echoing in her mind.

Ken Brady had just left John's Bakery, and Susan Dixon was crossing Broadmoor Road from the drugstore. They almost collided in front of the post office.

"Hi," Susan said.

"Hi," Ken said, but Susan noticed his lack of enthusiasm. Ordinarily, Ken's face was an open expanse of bright sunlight, whether he felt it or not. Today, it was clouded over.

Susan decided to let sleeping dogs lie. "What's in the package?" she asked.

"Fruit, dates, figs. Some dark bread."

"Your dad must have sent a check," she said.

"My mom." He smiled tentatively. "Want to break bread with me? I can add a little wine."

"That sounds super, Ken. Only I'm sitting for Mrs. Meredith."

"Oh," Ken said. The cloud lowered again.

"But I'll see you at the Rites tomorrow."

Ken Brady's eyes flicked. "You coming?"

"Sure. What time does it all start?"

Ken looked away. For an instant he suddenly seemed very boyish, as though he had grown backward fifteen years in a split second.

Susan picked up the wavelength. "Why? Don't you want me to come?"

Ken shifted his package uneasily. "I'm not sure you'll fit in."

Susan laughed. "I can always just watch. Anyway, I want to hear Freddie's sermon."

At the mention of Freddie, Ken frowned, his eyes angered. "You've been seeing a lot of Freddie."

Susan stared steadily back. "No, I haven't."

"That's what I hear."

"Fuck you, Ken Brady. Since when am I a possession of yours?"

Susan turned and stalked away. Ken shifted his package to his other arm and, head bent, walked across the road to his van.

A few feet away from where Susan and Ken had met, Milt Framer sat in his battered Plymouth Fury, pulse faster than normal, a burgeoning in his crotch.

I'll be there, too, he thought. *I'll be at your fuckin' Rites. I'll fix your asses!*

Flipping the ignition, gunning the motor, he took off in a cloud of noxious exhaust smoke and a shriek of burning rubber, down Broadmoor Road and across the covered bridge where he turned right in the direction of Jerry's Tavern.

I'll fix your asses! Fuckin' Satan Freaks!

Freddie Loftus was preparing his sermon. And what better source than his own writings?

For the past two and one-half years, Freddie had been scrupulously recording his life and times. His opinions, his thoughts, his philosophy and observations were contained in three thick, loose-leaf volumes of lined paper, and he was well into the fourth.

If the script was illegible, it did not matter. Freddie could read it, and if he could not, it was all in his head anyway. The small, cramped, childlike scrawl drifted and flowed across the pages like chicken tracks, sometimes jagged, sometimes falling off the lines, often proceeding so fast that one word led into another without space, and sentences merged into paragraphs without periods.

If the calligraphy of Freddie's volumes left much to be desired, the diction did not, and the language reflected a mind both educated and abstruse, with an ability to grasp the abstract, if not to make it clear. In translation to the sermons, however, it would suffer a change, metamorphosing into the broad drawl so popular with rock and folk singers, with all its fake twang and false sincerity. Freddie knew the value of demagoguery, and he used it to its full potential.

Since the dream, he had written little. But now, after a good deal of convoluted thought and analysis, he had afforded it a place in his philosophy, and it slipped neatly into his scheme of things, dropping into place like a well-oiled gear, lifting the pall of dread that the dream had engendered.

They, the *good,* were after him, a *bad,* to punish him for his guilt. But since guilt was natural, there could be no punishment for it.

Freddie Loftus believed in Satan, not only as a force but as a being. The "Satanis esse," as referred to in his book. Good and evil resided as brothers in man's soul, Freddie believed, and Satan knew this and considered it natural and therefore acceptable. And he was cast from Heaven because he would not deny this truth, but only abide by it, and make no law against evil because it was beyond the law. There could be no guilt feeling without guilt, and since guilt was a natural quantity, it did not exist apart from good. Only in the minds of the hypocrites.

The dream, Freddie was now convinced, had been the work of that old vengeful God working on his guilt feelings, trying again, in the eternal war against Satan, to turn Freddie away from the truth about man, about himself, about the universe. Once Freddie denied his guilt, he was free.

The sermon was taking shape. It would concern good and evil, Satan and the churches. But most of all, it would castigate the hypocrites, the Church and the churchgoers, the do-gooders who did no good, the pillars of society who pillaged society.

Freddie was pleased.

Milt Framer squirmed on his barstool, scratching at an itch on his behind, and turned to Eddie Volner.

"You don't have to tell me about it," he said. "Liscomb's been draggin' his ass since the day he was born."

The young cop frowned into his beer. "I can't do anything with him."

"If you were in his seat, you'd know what to do," Framer said. "You'd've pulled Freddie Loftus in a long time ago."

Volner nodded, then he said, "It's not that Frank's not trying, Milt. He's had his eye on Loftus."

"Eye on! Fuck his *eye!* He should have his *hands* on him!"

"You can't make an arrest without grounds, Milt."

"Grounds! Shit! You don't got grounds, make 'em up!"

Volner sighed. "You tell Frank that."

Framer mused into his beer. When he spoke, he

was almost talking to himself. "Maybe I can get you grounds."

"What?"

"Nothin'," Framer murmured. "Fuckin' Satan freaks! I'll fix their asses."

"Did you say something, Milt?"

"No. I didn't say nothin'."

Fuckin' Satan freaks!

CHAPTER
19

To most of the two dozen or so young people living permanently at Job's Camp, the bimonthly Rites were a joke. To the rest, they were very serious indeed.

But the two groups had some things in common: they liked rock music, they liked drugs, and they liked sex.

Dimples especially liked sex. Not that she didn't get enough of it with Freddie Loftus, but she especially liked group sex, and she had not been part of a good group scene since the last celebration of the Rites.

There were times when Dimples felt that the dudes did not like her, that they were repelled by her thin hips, her bony knees, her cupcake breasts. But at the Rites Dimples's star ascended. She became something of a celebrity, a sex symbol, a herald of naked lust and power, the epitome of the eternal fuck. Perhaps it was because of the drugs, everyone being so completely stoned. Or perhaps it was her unashamed, open sexual camaraderie, her willingness to do anything and everything.

There was nothing Dimples would not do, but there were things she had not done. Men, women, dildoes, vibrators, were all part of the scene to Dimples, and she had been in twosomes, threesomes, and foursomes. But never in a fivesome.

It was her dream, the pentagonal fuck, as she liked to think of it, and she was determined to have it tonight.

"I want a fivesome tonight," she said to Freddie Loftus.

"Get lost, cunt," Freddie said. "Can't you see I'm working on my sermon?"

The Rites were timed to begin at nine, after dark, but the music, the blowing, the dropping got off to a good start before eight as the last shafts of a wan sunlight suffused the gray western horizon.

Young people with long hair, in bare feet or sandals or dirty Adidases, in blue jeans and shorts and faded T-shirts inscribed with four-letter sexual slogans, began to assemble on the "quad," actually a large circle of level grassland where Josephus "Job" Hart had planned a swimming pool that never materialized.

They dropped to the ground in groups of fours and fives, sixes and sevens, squatting in the lotus position, eating raisins and alfalfa, dried fruits, fresh fruits, dark bread, strange seeds, and a dozen kinds of other natural foods. Guitars were scattered here and there, and strings were plucked and voices raised. Different keys fought for domination, but if dissonance resulted, the beat was the same. *Thump-thump, a-thump, a-thump, a-thump-thump-thump*. The drift now was toward punk rock.

Children wandered from group to group, unowned, displaced little people, some naked, others wearing underpants and T-shirts.

After the food, wine bottles appeared, flasks, plastic Spanish botas, and then the drugs. Among the hard-core old-timers, uppers and downers, methedrine, Librium, mescaline and LSD. In the softcore group, marijuana was the drug of choice.

They laughed, they giggled, they slapped and elbowed one another, they thought they made very witty remarks. It was very much like any bar between King's Landing and Indian Falls, except that more barriers seemed to be down.

"What's Freddie's missal tonight?" somebody asked.

"Same old shit," a girl answered. "Good and evil."

"Lead me to your evil!" a young man cackled, then ran his hand down the spine of the girl sitting next to him, pinching her buttocks.

Three groups away, Susan Dixon took a drag on Ken Brady's roach, inhaled deeply, held for a few seconds and then let it out. "Is there going to be a gang bang?" she asked. "Really?"

"Maybe," Ken said, "maybe not. Sometimes it happens, sometimes it doesn't." He looked at her, searching. "Why? You worried about it?"

"Not really," she said. "I'll have to see what my mood is when it starts."

"I don't think it's your scene," Ken said.

"We'll see," Susan said. She was looking out beyond him. "Where's Freddie?"

"How should I know?" Ken said.

"I was only asking."

Ken kicked at a tuft of crabgrass, pounding it back into the ground with his heel. "I'm not so high on groups either," he said. "We'll go to my place later."

Susan glanced at him sharply. "Who says?"

"It was only a suggestion," Ken snapped.

"No, it wasn't. It was a directive!" Susan said, rising. "You're turning into the most possessive chauvinist pig I ever met!"

She staggered for a moment on the lumpy ground, then made her way in the direction of Freddie Loftus's cabin. On the way, she was tripped and sandwiched between two muscular young men, one blond, the other prematurely bald. She could feel their erections digging into her, back and front.

"Let go of me, you assholes!"

"Suzy, woozy!" the blond one said. "Won't you let me eat your koozie?"

The bald man had his hands on her breasts from the rear and was breathing hot on her neck.

Susan clawed him, and he let out a yell that overrode every guitar on the quad. At the same time, she kneed the blond one in the crotch, and he sat up, doubled over, snorting like a pig.

On her feet, above them, Susan looked down in contempt.

"Aw shit, Sue," the blond one said, holding his scrotum and rocking back and forth, "we were only trying to be friendly."

"Balls!" Susan stalked away, back to Ken Brady, where she plopped herself down in angry frustration.

When she smiled, it was a half-smile and hesitant. "Maybe we'll go off to your place later, Ken," she said. "I'm sorry I got so mean."

"That's all right, Sue," Ken said. "Whatever you want." There was a self-satisfied grin on his face. He had watched the whole scene.

"But I want to hear Freddie's sermon," she said.

"Sure."

"That's why I came," she added, "to hear Freddie's sermon."

"Sure."

She lit a cigarette, her fingers shaking. "It's funny," she said. "I can't be evil."

"What?"

"I mean I want to be evil, but I can't. I mean, I'm drawn to it, but I can't be evil. Or can I?"

"I don't follow," Ken gave her a peculiar look.

Freddie Loftus made his appearance at a little after nine thirty, when the light had gone and only flickering candles lit the open field. Dressed in an ankle-length, loose-fitting robe, drawn at the waist with a rope belt and topped with a peaked hood, he was a picture of incongruity, a Druid in a tropical night. On silent, sandaled feet, he made his way among the gatherers to the north end of the clearing, ascending a short flight of stone steps to his altar and pulpit, an outcropping of rock shaped like a table. Thirteen red candles in glass chimneys lit Freddie's face from beneath, lending to his hollow-eyed visage a truly devilish mien.

A hush fell over the throng, sweeping across it like wind over wheat. Guitars were put aside, voices dropped to murmurs and then silence. Children were drawn close and huddled under arms.

Freddie's personage was like a magnet, and all eyes were drawn to his sticklike figure, raised slightly above them in the night, the hood thrown back now, the face glowing in an aura of red and yellow flame. When he spoke, his voice seemed to echo, deep, sonorous, carrying easily.

"Unity," he intoned. "Tonight we speak of the unity of good and evil, black and white, God and the Devil!"

"Oh, shit," a red-headed young man said, "here we go!" and flopped back on the grass.

But the girl next to him leaned forward intently. "You should really listen," she said. "Freddie's really into these things."

"He's a flake," the boy said and covered his eyes with his arms.

"Unity!" Freddie repeated, his voice rising. "The unity of good and evil resides in all of us. And that is the unity of God and Satan, and there is only one God and He is Satan!"

One of the nonbelievers let forth with a Bronx cheer, and another shouted. "What's all that shit, Freddie? What's it all mean?"

Freddie glared down from his pulpit, his eyes reflecting the red of the candles. "The Devil and God are the same thing, man! There's a real split personality up there!" The ordered phrasing of his speech began to fall apart, his voice became frenzied, his look more crazed, his words more drawled. "Why, I ask ya, if God is so good, is there so much *pain?* Pain and putrefaction, death and destruction, in the world? People dyin'. People eatin' each other, dismemberin' each other! Arabs and Jews, blacks and whites. Wherever ya look, pain and crippling, and death and disease. I ask ya! Where's the good in God?"

"No good," a girl chanted. "No good, no good in God!"

"Fuckin' A-right!" a boy said.

"Tell us about Satan, Freddie!" another shouted and then giggled to the others around him.

"It's all the same, man!" Freddie shouted. "When God is mad, He's the Devil! And when the Devil is feeling up, He's God, man!"

"You tell it, Freddie!"

"And we're livin' in a Godless society and a Godless age," Freddie said. "God is dead and is gonna stay dead for a long time! So you gotta play both sides, man! You can't sit around cryin' like a Jesus freak when somethin' goes wrong! No!"

"No! No! No!" reverberated through the night.

"Those bad times, that's when the other personality has taken over from God, and the Devil is ascendant, up, up high! And that's the time you pray to the Devil!"

"Let us pray, let us pray!" somebody cried.

"Yeah, let us get to the evil," somebody else giggled.

The red-headed boy had uncovered his eyes. "He's a flake," he said.

"Freddie's no flake. He's got insight."

"He's very deep," a girl said.

"He's a nut."

"Flake, nut, or genius," a studious-looking young man said, "the truth is, Freddie's an unadulterated Bible Belt Baptist. Listen to him. He's trying to find an excuse for sex."

"Who needs an excuse?" Dimples said and began to peel off her clothes.

Freddie's arms were upraised, spread, a V on either side of his hooded head from which falcon eyes pierced downward. "Ask His help, brethren!" he said. "Ask Satan's help!"

"Here we go," the student said.

"Don't be afraid! After all, He's gonna revert to His good self sooner or later. And that's when your prayers will be answered. When He's God again! When He's on His God trip!"

"Fuckin A-right, Freddie! Fuckin' A-right!"

"Meanwhile," Freddie went on, "there are black things to be done. Things maybe we don't like to do . . ."

"Who says we don't like it?" a girl said, and reached for her partner's penis, bending low to it, mouthing it.

The orgy had begun.

". . . but must do, because the Satan side of God is ascendant!"

"You see?" the studious boy said. "Freddie can't accept sex as a natural act. He has to make a religion out of it."

"Why don't you get a little religion?" a girl nearby suggested.

"I'm working up to it," the boy said.

The girl looked down into his lap and then reached out with her hand. "You're working up real nice," she said.

Amid the gropings and the graspings, the moaning and the groaning, the grunts and the gasps, Freddie's voice canted on, rambling, roving, backtracking, answering questions no one had asked, asking others arising from his own mind, drifting into subject matter he had never before considered, changing from rhetoric to demagoguery and back again, like his book, wandering, shifting, full of the hyperbole of a chaotic mind striving for order.

"I look down upon you, brethren, and see you sinning and am pleasured! For only in sinning can you seek truth! Sin shall set you apart but not free! For sinning is only a part of sacrifice! And only in sacrifice shall ye find truth and then freedom!"

The children, most of them, had been taken away, the barriers were down, the drugs had taken effect. Ordinarily, the Rites waited until Freddie had finished his lecture, but on this night he seemed to have little control over it. Most of the members of Job's Camp were now engaged in a ritual of sexual gratification, but there still remained that nucleus, a small huddled group, who hung on Freddie's every word, heads nod-

ding, eyes, like his, roving, ridden with drugs, searching for some vague answer to insidious doubt.

"Who's better than we, man!" Freddie's mind had
shifted gears again "Who's better? The local yokels
who spit on our feet and harass us? Are these the
pillars of society we lean against for support?"

Others were not listening. The orgy had begun. The
field was now a mass of writhing bodies, naked flesh,
gasping voices.

To Milt Framer, hidden behind the trees, breathing
hard, perspiring to his socks, fly open, penis emerged
and enlarged, it was a picture of pure lust and indescribable excitement, appealing at once to his sense
of joy, his sense of sin, and his sense of outrage.

"Are they saints, man?" Freddie was shouting. "Are
they the established saints of good in a world of evil?
The saints of war and destruction. The saints of killing and robbery, character assassination and false-
witnessing, arson and mugging, lying and omission?
I say we live in a world of hypocrites, man! A world
of fakery and falsity and fornication without truth!
The pillars of society don't fuck each other, they
screw us!"

"Tell it, Freddie!"

On the edge of the field, in a fringe group unable
or unwilling to fully participate in either the open
sex or the ritualistic reverence of Satan, Susan Dixon
looked on in a confusion of feelings and comprehension, excited but repelled, disturbed, yet fascinated.

"Freddie's sick in the head, isn't he?" she whispered
to Ken Brady.

"He comes on hard," Ken said, "but he doesn't
really believe it."

"He's a nut case. I'm finally convinced."

"We're all nut cases to an extent," Ken said.

"Not like that. Listen to him. He's rambling, disconnected. He hops around like a frog with a lobotomy."

"He's been dropping acid," Ken said.

"Even his speech patterns change. He's like two different people."

"Even you're schizo. You said it yourself."

"Not like that," Susan said. Her mouth twisted in an expression of fear and repugnance. "I'm beginning to wonder," she said.

Ken looked at her questioningly.

"That finger," she said. "The hand. The whole thing about the missing kid."

"Come on," Ken said.

"No, I mean it. I even had a dream."

"Bullshit," Ken said. "Not Freddie."

Behind them a girl grunted deeply as her companion made deep thrusts into her, his groin slapping harshly against her uplifted buttocks. "That's what I like," she kept saying. "That's what I like."

"Let's go to my place," Ken said. He seemed embarrassed.

"In a little while," Susan said and reached for his cigarette. There was a huskiness in her voice, a slight trembling. The sounds excited her. The moving shapes in the dark night brought juices to her thighs. She felt on the verge of orgasm. *I'm evil,* she thought.

Freddie was ranting on, crying out his "sermon" amid the couplings, declaiming, raging, haranguing in the flickering light of the candles while bodies moved and humped and fought for dominance and submission. A sickly red-yellow glow lit the circle. It was like a scene from Hell.

"We're being fucked, brethren," he shouted, "fucked by the fucking Jesus freaks! The do-gooders who do no good! The asshole establishment that establishes our fate at the moment of our birth! The blood-suckers, the titsuckers, the cocksuckers, the cuntsuckers! They suck the money from our pockets, the bread from our mouths and the dreams from our souls! The churchgoers, the Jesus freaks, the God-givers, the tract-passers, the lords of the press and the titans of television! All in the name of Jesus Christ and the Holy Ghost! And Mohammed, and Buddha, and the Almighty Dollar! Their gods are not our gods, oh brethren! Our God is the only one God and He is the *only* God and He is *Satan!*"

"Go, Freddie, go!"

"And Satan asks nothing of us but sin! Sin, my brethren! Sin, man! That's all Satan asks! Sin! For through sinning we face the truth, we find Satan and everlasting reality and eternal Joy! Sin for Satan, brethren! For the sin is the reality! Sin for Satan and sacrifice for Satan! Three esses, brethren! That's all. A simple three esses! Sin, Satan, and sacrifice!"

"Sacrifice!" somebody shouted. "Let's have a sacrifice!"

"A human sacrifice!" another added, then giggled insanely.

"Sacrifice! Sacrifice!" The cry was picked up, thrown in all directions, relayed, echoed.

"A human sacrifice!"

"Yea, brethren! Yea!" Freddie shouted. He smiled, his deep eyes flashing in the night, his expression one of contempt and power. They were his now, and *His*, and they would prostrate themselves before Him in sin. "A sacrifice to Satan!"

"A *human* sacrifice!" a man rasped, and a group of

naked men converged over an outstretched female form in the center of the field.

Milt Framer gripped his shotgun tightly with his right-hand, but his left still played with his organ. His eyes were alive, bright, glittering.

In the center of the clearing, Dimples, naked, her body already shining with previous juices of emission, her drugged eyes wide and sparkling, her mouth twisted into a lascivious grin, was hoisted aloft on the arms of naked men, and carried, writhing, undulating, kicking, screaming, forward to the candlelit altar, amid a chanting of "Sacrifice! Sacrifice! Sacrifice!" Others followed the procession, and as Dimple's nudity was spread-eagled on the altar, a group gathered, eyes watchful, mouths parted.

On the edge of the field, in the woods, Milt Framer pushed blindly through the brush, heedless of low-hanging branches and thorns, scraping himself, falling on his knees, but pushing on to get nearer to the scene of the sacrifice. *This is it,* he thought. *This is the end of their dirty filth, their rotten lives.* He saw himself moments in the future, gun to shoulder, blasting away, watching the bodies drop in blood as he saved the girl's life, and later marching her into town and telling his story and receiving the gratitude, the blessings, the plaudits of his own kind. But as he lumbered on to his appointment with destiny, his penis preceded him, blunt, full, gross. He wanted to see.

At the altar, Freddie Loftus had scrambled some feet up the hillside, raising himself above the scene, looking down with a wide grin, his eyes lit with a light form within. "Sacrifice, my brethren," he said softly. "Sacrifice to Satan for everlasting peace, truth, and salvation. For in sin there is salvation!"

Below him, a silence had fallen; only breathing

could be heard, and here and there a gutteral grunt, a rasping sigh. The odor was of sweat and semen and musk.

From her supine position on the slab of rock, Dimples looked up at naked men, naked women, parted lips, erect cocks. Beyond, the dark fathomless sky was like a heavy cloak of death. *At last,* she thought. And smiled.

"Stab her," a young man said, his breath harsh.

In the woods, Milt Framer's hand tightened on his shotgun, trembling.

"Who?" a blond man asked.

"You," the first man said, and after a hesitation: "Go on! Do it!"

"I don't want to be first." He sounded disappointed.

"Do it!"

"Do it," Freddie Loftus said gently from above. "The first stab shall be the beginning. Oh, Satan, look down upon my brethren and love them!"

"Do you really want to see this?" Ken Brady asked Susan.

"Be quiet," she said.

Dimples was perched at the edge of the rock slab. The blond boy positioned himself between her thighs and drove his penis into her. Dimples screamed. The boy began to piston in and out, rhythmically, liquidly, his body contorting, his face flushed.

Dimples screamed again in sheer ecstasy. "Up here! Up here!" she grunted, and reached out to the nearest penis, pulling it to her mouth. The young man inside her arched backward, pulled out, and shot his semen on her belly. Another took his place. The girl's little breasts quivered and shook. Two men started to masturbate above them.

"Sin, my brethren," Freddie Loftus said, his voice

a half-screech. "Sin and forever be damned and re-deemed in the eyes of thy God, Satan!" He rolled his eyes toward the unlit heavens.

Milt Framer stood transfixed, eyes wide, mouth slack, leaning against a tree. The shotgun in his right hand was forgotten. His left worked at his protruding penis, jerking, kneading, pulling.

"The pentagon!" Dimples screeched. "The penta-gon! I want the pentagon!"

"What the hell is she talking about?" a girl asked. "She must think she's in D.C.!"

But a red-headed boy apparently knew what she meant. Moments later, Dimples was hoisted into the air again, turned, and impaled on the rearing penis of a boy who had taken his place on his back on the altar. Another came up from behind and wriggled his stiff organ between her buttocks. A third moved for-ward at her face, and her neck craned and she uttered a low groan as her mouth engulfed him. Two more men stepped to either side of her breasts, and her hands reached out, grasping their erections. The pentagonal fuck was in progress.

The twelve-legged beast began to move. It bucked and hunched; it twisted and pranced; it trembled and shuddered and lurched. Its five male organs arched and strained and pulsed. Its female pudendum clenched and throbbed. Its dangling breasts bounced and shook and quivered. It snorted and grunted, whined and gasped.

Above it, Freddie Loftus looked down and giggled crazily, calling out to Satan. "We offer this unto ye, oh, Lucifer! In your lust shall we find life!"

It was then that Milt Framer, in his excitement, lost his footing and fell headlong into the clearing, choking and gasping, his trouser front white with his emission.

A hush fell. Eyes turned. A battery pack suddenly flared forth its blinding light.

Framer lay on the ground, twitching, twisting, his hand still moving, his eyes full of fear and shame and anger.

"What the fuck!" the blond man said.

"Jesus Christ!"

"Who is this asshole?"

"It's disgusting!" a girl said.

Framer found his hatred. "You fuckin' Satan freaks!" he shouted and started to rise, the shotgun coming up in his right hand, his left still trying to hide his penis. "I'll fix your fuckin' asses!"

A blond Apollo darted from the darkness, a fleeting streak that spun Framer in a circle and dumped him to the ground. The gun went clattering into the rock shelf.

"Kill the bastard!"

Framer rose to one knee, his huge body inflating with breath. As the blond man made another lunge, Framer's fists lashed out at the boy's midriff. There was a sickening sound, followed by a hollow gush of spent air. The Apollo sank to his knees, vomiting on the ground. Framer staggered toward the gun.

"Don't let him get that!"

"Kill the cocksucker!"

"Get him, for chrissake! Get him!"

It was brief, furious and savage, a bloody melee played in a dark arena of candlelight and flashlight, beneath an overhang of silent trees and a leaden, glowering sky. Framer was an enraged bull, blind and powerful, charging, head lowered, mauling, thrashing in all directions, his ham fists everywhere, his hard knuckles breaking skin and splintering bone, his knees groining, his great arms crushing.

When he was down at last, snorting, gasping, it took five men to pin him, two at his arms and shoulders, another sitting on his heaving stomach, two more on his legs.

"Fuckin' Satan freaks!" Framer gasped upward. "Dirty, filthy Satan freaks!" He spit, but the spittle fell back on his bloodied mouth.

"You're one to talk," the boy on his belly said. "You shitty degenerate."

"Kill the bastard," the blond Apollo said. He was standing to one side, breathing in gasps, naked, blood oozing from his face and tracking down to his abdomen and knees, vomit at the corners of his mouth. "Kill the bastard," he said again.

"A sacrifice," a girl said sharply. "Let's make him a sacrifice!"

From his rock perch above, Freddie Loftus giggled. "A sacrifice unto ye, oh Satan! To ye, this pitiful offering!"

"Yeah, let's sacrifice him," Dimples said. "Let's sacrifice the son of a bitch!" She dropped to her knees at Framer's groin and took his quiescent penis in her mouth.

Framer screamed, a long harsh scream of shame and agony. "Get away from me, you fuckin' whore! Get away! Get off me!"

But Dimples continued her ministrations, giggling shrilly as she laved and sucked. As Framer's body twisted and coiled and fought, as he struggled to escape, the men pinning him began to laugh, holding him down, forcing his back into the ground.

"Eat him, Dimples," one of them said. "Eat the bastard's balls off. Show him what real sex is like."

"It's a big fat one," Dimples giggled. "Plenty here for everybody." At her words, another girl, a dark-haired, intense nymph, knelt down beside Dimples and joined her.

Framer struggled but the men held him fast. He began to whimper, cry, sob. But his organ began to grow.

A blond girl came forward and straddled his head, pushing her vulva down to his face. "Eat that cunt," she said savagely. "Eat it, you asshole! Eat! Eat!"

Framer's head tossed from side to side, trying to escape. The girl pushed closer, harder. Framer's tongue came out. He screamed and then slobbered and finally whined. His tongue lashed and probed and reamed. His heartbeat echoed inside his head. He felt as though he were about to explode.

Susan Dixon threw her cigarette to the ground and crushed it with her heel. "I've had enough," she said.

"We'll go to my cabin," Ken said. His eyes were downcast. For the first time in years he was ashamed.

As they turned, the scream stopped them.

It was the girl over Framer's face. She was rising awkwardly, staggering away, clutching at her belly. She began to run, screaming, twisting, turning, crying out. "Jesus Christ! Jesus Christ Almighty!"

Running blindly, she staggered into Ken's path. He took hold of her roughly. "What'd he do?"

"He didn't do anything!" she said. Her face was a study in fear.

"What the hell's the matter with you?"

"He's turning blue!" the girl screamed. "He's turning real blue!" Then she staggered off into the darkness.

Over Framer's outstretched form, the men holding him rose, backing away, their eyes puzzled, full of some vague comprehension, yet vacant. Below, Dimples raised her head, her forehead creased. Silently she got up, stood for a moment, then turned into the trees. The other girl turned on her side and began to cry.

Ken Brady loped to the huddle of people around Milt Framer.

Framer lay very still. His eyes were closed.

"Oh, shit!" Ken Brady said. "Oh, shit."

Susan came up beside him. Her eyes questioned.

"He had a heart attack," Ken said.

She looked down. "Oh, my God!" she said.

Ken knelt for a few moments, then stood.

"Is he dead?" Susan asked.

Ken did not answer. He did not need to.

No one spoke. There was only breathing in the huddled group. Then a twig snapped. A girl sobbed briefly. Shadows moved. Figures faded into the night.

From up above, high in the rocks above the altar, somewhere on the path toward Job's Ruins, the old hotel that Josephus Hart had built, the voice of Freddie Loftus drifted down in a high-pitched lament: "We offer this down unto ye, oh mighty Satan! This small offering, this brief candle, this pitiful life, this small sacrifice. Bless us, oh, Lucifer! For we have served ye!"

A small wind arose. A chilling shaft of air, a gust that was at odds with the heated night, swept briefly across the clearing, leaving frost upon the grass, and then was gone.

And in the darkness, somewhere above, in the trees, Freddie Loftus's voice rang out in agony.

"Jesus Christ, save me!"

PART THREE

CHAPTER 20

Milt Framer's body was discovered the following morning on the shore of North Lake. A fisherman, coming in to his boat mooring at 6:00 A.M., saw the green panel truck, but thought nothing more than it belonged to another angler, and went on about his business. Returning to shore three hours later with a string of six bass, he noticed that the truck was still there. Since no other boats had been visible on the water, he investigated, and found Framer slumped over the steering wheel. He knew immediately that he was neither drunk nor sleeping.

By ten o'clock, the small, quiet beach was rutted with the tire marks of police cars, an ambulance, Tom Blauvelt's Monte Carlo, and the footprints of crime lab personnel and assorted onlookers.

Frank Liscomb stood off to one side, flicking the ashes from a cigar, waiting for Blauvelt to finish. When the doctor rose from the slumped body, Liscomb's brows arched.

"Massive coronary," Blauvelt said. "Want the Latin?"

"No, save it," Liscomb said.

Volner shifted uneasily. "Why the print-taking, Chief? If what Tom says is true . . ."

"A heart attack doesn't explain the gashes on his

head," Liscomb said. "He didn't do that falling into the steering wheel."

"You can say that again," Blauvelt muttered, closing his bag. He turned to his car. "See you later at the morgue, Frank?"

"Yeah," Liscomb growled and threw half his cigar into the lake. "I got to cut this smoking out," he said.

When Blauvelt had gone, Eddie Volner plucked a blade of grass and lodged it in his mouth. "I saw Milt only yesterday," he said.

Liscomb searched his face. "So?"

Volner chewed on the grass. "He kept talking about Job's Camp and the Satan freaks. And the finger and stuff."

"How so?"

Volner shrugged. "I dunno. As if he had it in mind to sneak around up there or something." He paused. "Even said something about getting evidence for us."

"Is that right?" Liscomb said. His eyes left Volner and rose upward, meeting the gray silhouette of Pinnacle Peak rising sharply into the overcast skies. Somewhere up there in the mist were Job's Ruins, and not far to the south, Job's Camp itself.

"Come on," he said to Volner, and started toward the car.

Once again it was a ghost town, silent, unpeopled, wrapped in solitary echoes of time past. Once again, nothing human stirred; no laughter reverberated, no shouts, no arguments, no clash and clatter of a tribe disturbed the air.

The young people had gone from Job's Camp. Disappeared, vanished. Lock, stock and barrel, vans, clothing and guitars, they had left only a mocking silence in their wake.

Cabins were deserted, their beds stripped. Ice boxes and cupboards stood empty, closets gaped. An antique cradle had been left, but when Liscomb tried to rock it, he found it was nailed to the floor.

Outside, he sat on a small rise and kicked at an empty can of baked beans. "It was more than a heart attack," he said and began to pat his pockets, searching.

"I thought you were going to give that up?" Volner said.

"Mind your own business," Liscomb said, and bit at the cigar. "They sure got out in a hurry."

Volner chewed at the same blade of grass. "He kept going on about Satan freaks," he said. "Like there was something going on up here that—well, that wasn't very human."

"Bullshit," Liscomb said. "Old Milt died of natural causes. You're getting like everybody else around this case, Volner—nutty. Don't hand me that crap."

"I didn't mean he didn't die natural," Volner said.

"Then what did you mean?"

"I mean why are the kids gone, that's all I meant."

"Good question," Liscomb said. "And where did they go?" He chewed on the cigar. "Do we have names, addresses, background on the people who lived up here?"

"Maybe some. Maybe nothing. They were always hard to pin down. You know that."

Liscomb nodded, and a twinge, a stab of remorse went through him, vague but definite. "We should have been more careful," he said. "Well, anyway, let's get back to town and see what we *do* have."

The news of Milt Framer's death was too late to make the weekly edition of the *County Times,* and only a brief item appeared in the King's Landing *Evening Standard,* to the effect that a man had suffered a heart attack in his car at North Lake.

In the bars—in Jerry's Tavern, at the Bull and Bear, at the tables in saloons and restaurants from The Landing to Indian Falls—those who had known Milt Framer gave the news at least ten minutes of conversation and reflection. Glasses were raised in remembrance, some eyes teared, some stories were told, but Milt had had few friends, and, by and large, his death provoked little out of the ordinary and was marked down to the inevitable march of time.

But in her bedroom, stiff on her back, eyes fixed on the ceiling, Susan Dixon relived the moment over and over again, seeing in her mind's eye the despicable behavior of her peers, her friends, herself and Ken Brady. The air charged with lust, the reek of sex, the blood of battle, the utter abasement of the victim, the viciousness of the attackers, the cries in the night, the shrieking, and the blueness. The blueness. The blueness of death. And for once she knew she was not evil alone, but that an evil existed in everyone, surrounding them, eating into them, bathing them in its foul aura, seeking to destroy them. She cried, thinking she was insane.

Oliver Marquith took the news with a gravity befitting a judge. Framer was out, the kids were gone, the land was free. But not free until he could buy, and he could not buy from ghosts. Where the hell had they gone? Where could he reach them? How was he to make a deal? Goddamn kids! They had a peculiar knack for fucking things up, for not playing the game as it was supposed to be played. He could wait and watch. His time would come.

The autopsy revealed little of further value but did pose certain questions. Death had been caused by massive coronary occlusion. The lacerations and contusions about the head and shoulders proved to be minor and superficial. However, seminal discharge on both the body and clothing of the deceased opened up greater possibilities, and for the first time in his experience as an officer of the law, Frank Liscomb had to consider homosexuality as a cause of murder.

Blauvelt's eyes went wide. "Milt Framer a homosexual? Bullshit, Frank."

"I know it sounds crazy," Liscomb said, "but look at the facts. He's in a parked car. Bloody around the head. Beat up. A woman couldn't do that to him."

"Neither could a man," Blauvelt said. "Milt would have beaten the shit out of him."

Liscomb nodded. "Unless there was more than one."

All in all, Milt Framer's death was an apostrophe in the story of Holland County, a punctuation mark signifying nothing more than another trip to the great beyond, one more vital statistic, one more simple, eternal, inevitable death. Apostrophe. Period.

Of those attending the seance at the home of Henry and Estelle Dixon, few had ever heard of Milt Framer, and even for those who had chanced to meet him, the meeting was brief and forgettable. His name was never brought up, his existence never alluded to.

Maria Braithwaite and Father Conant arrived early, the priest wearing a look of distant introspection and concern. When offered a drink, he declined, and sat on the sofa, drawing long fingers along his face, frowning.

"What'll you have, Maria?" Dixon asked.

"A little sherry, if you have it," she said.

Dixon went to the bar and pulled a bottle of Tio Pepe. His own half-finished drink was there, and he spiked it liberally with Boodles. To Dixon, in spite of his vague misgivings and worry about Estelle, the seance was something of another party, a time for relaxation and alcoholic camaraderie.

"Where is Estelle?" Maria asked when Dixon handed her the sherry.

"Dressing," he said, and sat in a chair. There was a strained silence. Maria Braithwaite sipped pensively and the priest examined the room, the furniture, the rug, the appointments, his eyes traveling in long arcs. Dixon raised his glass. "Well," he said. "Skol."

"Salud," Maria said and smiled lightly.

The silence continued. Dixon cleared his throat. "You ever been to a seance, Father?"

Conant turned his head and his lips broke for the first time. "One or two," he said.

"I suppose you don't believe in all this."

"Who's to say what to believe in," Conant said. "Science shows us something new every day."

"You call this science?" There was a loose grin on Dixon's face. The drink in his fist was not his first.

Conant lifted his shoulder. "Let's say I have an open mind," he explained. "We should all have open minds."

"You were at the Ouija board with Estelle," Maria said. "You yourself witnessed the message signed by Elvida."

Dixon did not reply. He had also seen the hand at Nicole's birthday party, and the image of it was skimming across his mind. He felt nervous again and sipped at his gin letting his anger ride outward. *What a couple of stiffs,* he thought. *Solid squares.* Then he was grinning again. "She thinks it means 'a devil,' " he said. "Elvida. A Devil."

"It's a fair anagram," the priest said.

"You believe in the Devil, Father?" Dixon asked, then answered his own question. "I suppose you do. All priests do, huh?"

"Not all," Conant said. "But it's an interesting legend. A picturesque mythology."

"Elvida sounds like a feminine name," Dixon said. "Why would the Devil come as a girl?"

"If Satan exists," the priest said, "as a distinct spiritual being, I mean, then he can assume many forms. The Anyra Mainyu of ancient Persia, part lion, part snake. In Zoroastrianism, part serpent, part cat. The snake in Eden was the Devil in disguise."

"But a girl. Never a girl."

"Don't be so sure," Conant said. "In Judaic demonology we get a new look at Satan. In their sleep, men feared the bloodsucking she-demon, Lilith."

"Or her consort," Maria Braithwaite said, "Samael, the Angel of Death." She was looking at Father Conant. "But you said you did not believe in Satan, Father."

Perhaps now is the time, he thought, *to tell them, to tell them that Satan is alive and well and living in Holland County.*

The way the thought formed in his mind amused him, and he almost laughed aloud, but then the true import of his charge overshadowed his embarrassment and self-doubt, and he began to shape his thoughts into words. Satan is more than an idea, he would say. He must exist. Haven't we seen the signs? The finger, the hand? The humidity, the heat? And the man. He would tell them about the man with the shriveled ear.

But he kept his silence.

It could wait.

And anyway, did he believe it himself?

He shrugged. "I believe in evil, and if the Devil is the personification of evil, then he exists, in any of his forms. And don't forget the legions."

"What legions?" Dixon looked lost.

"The legions of Hell," Conant said, and now his voice took on a timbre, a resonance that had not been there before. "The armies, the vast armies of horrible demons that Satan commands from the underworld."

"You're kidding," Dixon said.

The priest's voice rose. "You haven't done your reading, Mr. Dixon. Didn't you know there's a formal hierarchy down there? Armies, legions, stormtroopers, horsemen? All ready to go to war. Destroy Heaven and destroy us. Just waiting for the chance."

A car in the driveway interrupted the conversation, and Dixon crossed to the door, glad to get away. *They're also nuts,* he thought.

Joe Tremper and Lauren Shane unfolded themselves from a blue Porsche, and as they straightened up, another car turned into the driveway bearing Carole Kollars and Agnes Bittel.

"Welcome to Hades," Dixon shouted into the sultry night. "Come in and meet the legions."

Inside, Dixon took Lauren Shane by the arm and guided her to the bar. "You look like you need a drink," he said, and let his hand slip to her waist in a hug that was more than comforting.

"I do need that," Lauren said. "I've got goose pimples already."

I'd like to see those, Dixon thought, and stared unashamedly at her cleavage while his hands mixed the drink automatically. "I'm not much on seances myself," he said. "Maybe you and I can sit it out on the back porch." He was about to say more when a shadow fell on the bar.

"Don't bother about me, Hank," Agnes Bittel said. "I'll fix my own." She placed one ice cube in an old-fashioned glass, poured scotch to within an inch of the brim, and plopped three drops of water on top.

"Where's the seance going to take place?" Joe Tremper asked. "Out here?"

"In the dining room," Dixon said. "There's a table with raps built in."

Tremper started away, and Lauren looked after him with a peculiar glint in her eye.

"How's his book coming?" Dixon asked.

"Which one?"

"He's working on two?"

"Yeah," Lauren said. "That's his trouble. He's like a little boy. Never finishes anything before he finds a new game to play." Her eyes were on the dining room arch, and after a moment she said, "Thanks for the drink, Hank," and drifted away.

She loves him, Dixon thought, and sighed.

In the dining room, barely lit by a single lamp, Tremper was standing by a wall bookcase. His eyes scanned it, coming to rest on a middle shelf a few feet from the table. He walked over, pulled a flat, oblong object from his pocket and placed it behind a book on the shelf. It was a recording machine, Japanese, expensive, efficiently designed. He placed the tiny mike on top of the book. It was barely visible.

"You shouldn't, Joe." Lauren Shane came up behind him.

"Why not?" he asked, turning.

"It's not right."

"Don't be silly," he said. "It's material for the next book."

"Why don't you finish the first one?"

"I will, I will."

"It's still not right," Lauren said. "You should ask."

"Why? And what if that priest or the Braithwaite woman said no? Uh-uh, I can't pass this up."

"It's an invasion of privacy," Lauren said.

"What's wrong with privacy?" he asked, and placed a hand on her backside and slowly circled it. "I think I'd like to invade a little of your privacy when we get home," he said.

"You're incorrigible," she said.

Agnes Bittel was coming through the arch. "It's not right," she said.

"What's not right?" Tremper said, thinking of the recorder.

"The whole atmosphere," Agnes said. "It stinks." She proceeded to a sideboard and began lighting candles. "You need the right ambience for a seance," she announced, and spilled part of her drink on the floor.

In the living room, Carole Kollars sipped a tall gin and tonic. "It's hotter than hell," she said to Dixon. "Where's Estelle?"

"She'll be down soon," Dixon said.

Tom Blauvelt had arrived with the Hammonds, and the three of them were talking with Daniel Conant and Maria.

"Do you think anything will come of this, Father?" Blauvelt asked.

The priest was a moment answering. "I hope nothing comes of it," he said finally.

"Who is this Elvida?" Marion Hammond asked nobody in particular.

"A spirit of some kind," Carole Kollars said.

"A devil," Dixon cut in. "It's a devil, right?" He

was looking at Daniel Conant, a silly smile playing at the corners of his lips.

Conant shrugged. "I said it was an anagram."

"Fuck the anagrams," Dixon said. "A devil's a devil's a devil. Right?" He was becoming very drunk. "And the Devil can appear in any form, right? Like a snake or a cat. Even a monkey, right?"

The priest laughed. " 'For where God built a church, there the Devil would also build a chapel. Thus is the Devil ever God's ape.' Martin Luther, Mr. Dixon."

"For a man of God, you certainly know a lot about Satan," Dixon muttered. He turned as Bette Hammond said, "Hi, Estelle. Come join the fun."

Estelle Dixon was descending the stairs. Dressed in a tight black sheath that no longer fit, overly made up, wearing a black babushka, dangling baubles and beads from neck and wrists, she descended slowly, lurching slightly from side to side.

Oh, shit, Dixon thought, *she's drunk!*

Thinking she was about to fall, he went to the bottom of the stairs to catch her. "You're smashed," he said.

"No, I'm not," she said.

"Don't tell me that. You're listing right into the wall."

"I'm all right," she said and escaped his grasp, heading for the bar. Dixon followed.

"I don't think you should have anymore," he whispered.

"I haven't had *any*," she said and poured gin into a glass. "I had a few downers, that's all."

"Librium? And now you're going to drink?"

"I've done it before."

Maria Braithwaite was standing nearby and had

been listening. "Don't, Estelle," she said. Her eyes appealed. "You should be at your best."

Estelle wavered for a moment, then said, "Maybe you're right," and gave her glass to Dixon. "You drink it," she said and turned back to Maria. "We should start soon anyway. I feel very—I don't know. *Up,* as the kids say."

"You're only nervous," Maria Braithwaite said.

As Estelle went off to greet her guests, Dixon looked at Maria. "I don't like this at all," he said.

"Why?"

"It's fucking ridiculous, that's why. The whole thing."

"It's not too late to call it off," Maria said.

"Maybe it's better if she gets it out of her system." He walked away as the telephone rang.

Susan was already on an extension when he picked up. "I thought you were out," Dixon said.

"Get off the phone, Daddy!" Susan said sharply.

He hung up.

Upstairs, Susan waited for the click. Then she said, "Ken?"

"I'm staying at Tim Gilbert's in Indian Falls," Ken said.

"Where's Freddie?"

"He needs food," Ken said. "Can you help me?"

"What do you mean food? Is he with you?"

"No. Listen, I can't talk long. Have you got any stuff in the house? Canned stuff? Beans, stuff like that?"

"I guess so, but I don't understand. What's going on? Where is he?"

"I'll tell you when I see you. Listen," Ken said, "I'll leave in a little while. I'll honk from the road when I get there. You bring the food out."

"There wasn't anything in the paper," Susan said.

"I know," Ken said. "Listen, will you do what I said?"

"Honk three times."

"Okay." A pause, and then: "How are you?"

"All right," she said. "We're having a seance."

"What?"

"A seance. They're having a seance downstairs. Estelle and the rest."

"Shit," Ken said, "they're bonkers!" He hung up.

In the dining room they gathered around the table in embarrassed awkwardness. Drinks had been left in the living room out of respect for the seriousness of the rite, but Dixon had his behind his back and placed it gently on the floor between his feet when he sat.

"Is there room for everybody?" Lauren Shane asked. "I can sit it out on the sidelines."

"There's plenty of room," Estelle said. The table had been extended by the addition of two leaves. "Eleven. That's a good number, eleven."

"Only on the first roll," Joe Tremper said.

The candles Agnes Bittel had lit—red, green, and gold—flickered silently around them. Chairs scraped and creaked. There were a few coughs, some embarrassed looks.

Marion Hammond yawned and tried to look bored. *What a nut she is,* he thought. *God Almighty, look at that get-up!*

Estelle sat at the head of the table, a leaded glass window looking out on Willow Creek to her right. "You here, Father," she said and indicated the chair to her left.

The priest demurred. "I said I'd come, Estelle," he said softly, "but not take part. It's not exactly in tune with my sympathies."

"Always the bystander," Maria Braithwaite said.

"Don't you ever *indulge* in life, Father?" There was a definite sexuality in her glance at Conant.

"I try," Conant chuckled.

"Well, I'll sit next to her," Tom Blauvelt said generously. "I've always wanted to hold hands with Estelle."

"Lauren, you come sit next to me," Dixon said, and yanked her down.

"You can only hold hands, buddy," Joe Tremper said across from him. "Unless the spirit moves you to do more. Where is that spirit, by the way? Come on, Estelle, let's get to the spirit." And casually, he turned and started the tape recorder.

Henry Dixon leaned down in the semidarkness and lifted his gin gently, but the ice clinked.

"Get rid of that, goddammit!" Estelle screeched. "We're not having a party here!"

Dixon swallowed the remains of his gin in one gulp. "It's rid of," he said.

A few more jokes, a smattering of chatter, a brief banter ensued, but underneath there ran a current of anticipation and excitement, a sense of purpose and seriousness, a kind of tribal togetherness in the face of the unknown, all rather mixed up with a common feeling of childhood games that promised mystery, suspense, a fairy-tale wonder.

At the head of the table, having overcome her preliminary anxiety, Estelle Dixon sat erect and dignified, breathing steadily, in complete control of her body and emotions.

"Join hands," she said. Her voice was soft but carried authority.

There was shuffling, breathing, a giggle here and there.

"I thought they only did this in the movies," Bette Hammond said.

"Ouch!" Carole Kollars said. "That's where that goddamn dog bit me!"

"We must have quiet," Maria Braithwaite said. "Please. It is important that we have quiet. Most important."

"Yeah, let's have quiet, for chrissake!" Henry Dixon said and hiccupped. "Sorry, Father," he said, turning to Conant. "I used the Lord's name in main—vain."

"If anybody wants to leave," Estelle said, looking directly at her husband, "if anybody here doesn't want to take part in this, if anybody thinks this is a joke, a party, a nonsensical whim, he can leave. Right away."

No one spoke.

Henry Dixon stared down at the table and pressed Lauren Shane's hand with his left, Agnes Bittel's with his right, but not as hard.

Estelle looked about, peering from face to face, judging, measuring. "All right," she said finally, and bent her head.

Tom Blauvelt squirmed on his chair seat, his large buttocks trying for a grip that would not come.

Agnes Bittel stared fixedly at Estelle's bent head, her falcon eyes knifing.

Lauren Shane looked upward at the candles.

Joe Tremper's eyes were closed, but his right ear was cocked backward to the tape machine.

Bette Hammond was staring through her husband across the table. Marion's eyes circled the ceiling.

Carole Kollars was looking at the table, her lips drawn and grim.

Maria Braithwaite's head was bent, but her eyes were flickering upward to Estelle's face.

Daniel Conant was looking at everything, his gaze darting, his fingers pulling at his chin.

Henry Dixon was gazing into Lauren Shane's cleavage.

There was a movement at the head of the table. Eyes lifted, heads turned.

Estelle's eyes were closed, her face etched in harsh lines. When she spoke, her voice was full, vibrant, and, for her, unusually throaty.

"Elvida?" It was a question, an expectancy, a hope. A bead of sweat had formed on her right temple. It enlarged, spread, began to ooze down the side of her face.

My God, Tom Blauvelt thought. *She's in a trance. An actual trance!*

Father Conant bit his lower lip.

"Elvida?"

Lauren Shane trembled imperceptibly.

Joe Tremper listened for the whirring of the tape recorder.

Agnes Bittel thought, *She's faking!*

"Elvida?" The voice had taken on a slight hollow quality.

Henry Dixon felt Lauren Shane's fingers dig into his own. They were cold.

"Elvida? You said you'd come." The hollowness increased, and there was a childlike quality in the voice now.

Christ, Dixon thought. *It doesn't sound like her!*

"Elvida? Will you speak? You said you'd speak."

Maria Braithwaite was the first to notice it. It was cold. The room had become cold. A chill was descending, an iciness that enveloped the whole body at once, permeating, freezing. She fought down a shiver.

A few seats away, Carole Kollars trembled and jerked. "Jesus!" she said.

"It's cold," someone said, but the voice was indistinguishable. Everything sounded hollow, distant, distorted.

The candles flickered. Flames warped, increased, then wavered. Faces became green, then blue.

I'm going to freeze to death, Joe Tremper thought. *Shit, why don't they turn up the heat!*

Away from the table, looking on, Father Daniel Conant sweated. His face ran with perspiration, his white collar began to wilt. *What's happening,* he thought. *They're all turning blue!*

"Elvi . . . DA. Elvi . . . *DA!*" Estelle Dixon's voice rasped, strained, grew in pitch, in volume, reached upward. *"ELVI . . . DA!"*

A cold blast hurtled through the room, the candles flickered again. Three of them went out.

"What the hell!" someone muttered.

But then the other candles steadied, grew in strength. Their flames lengthened, became very red, rising high, bathing the walls in a deep scarlet. But the faces around the table remained blue-tinged, cold-looking.

Christ, Agnes Bittel thought, *Christ, she's doing it. She's doing it!*

Tom Blauvelt lifted his head and shot a furtive glance at Estelle. His heart jumped. She looked dead. Old and withered and dead, the lines in her face deep and dark, the skin drawn, the complexion waxen. A corpse. But her lips were moving, and when she spoke, the words rolled out young and girlish, in the flat alto of pubescent youth.

"I'm here," she said. Or the voice said. Or the spirit, or whatever it was. "I'm here."

Blauvelt was frightened and tried to pull his hands away, but the others he held on either side were locked tight, like vises. When he tried to speak, his voice would not come. *My God,* he thought. *We're trapped.*

There was a cold clamminess on Maria Braithwaite's forehead. The voice that came from Estelle's lips charged her with fear. In the few words she had heard, she detected a malice, a hatred that she feared might erupt into violence. She looked at Estelle's drawn face and shuddered. *There is evil here,* she thought. *It should be stopped.* But she could not speak.

"Who are you?" Estelle's voice was high, but near normal.

"Elvida," the childish voice said from Estelle's lips.

"A devil?"

"I am Elvida," the voice said. "But not Elvida. What do you want?"

That's a question we could ask you! Dixon thought, but when he tried to phrase it, his mouth would not open. *For chrissake,* he thought. *For chrissake!* He looked at his wife, begging, pleading. *For chrissake, Estelle! I can't talk! Do something!* Yet part of him wondered why he was taking this seriously. He was dreaming, of course. He was upstairs in bed, asleep, dreaming.

"How old are you?" Estelle's voice was hollow, full of echo and distant reverberation, and the child-voice, too, seemed to come from a cavern.

"I am young but old, flesh but not flesh, but I shall become flesh."

"How old are you!"

"Very old. And very young."

Lauren Shane's feet were numb, and the numbness

was climbing upward along her legs and into her groin, reaching further toward her heart. She could feel the heaviness of her pulse. It was so slow. Her heartbeat was so slow. She thought she was going to die. She tried to signal Joe by squeezing his hand, but her fingers were frozen, frozen like rock, petrified rock. She wanted to cry, but no tears would come.

Bette Hammond was thinking about Eighty-fourth Street. She could see it. The block, the house, the people, furtive figures leaping and laughing while she was stretched out on the ground, bleeding, a knife protruding from her stomach. A little child was leaning over her, grinning, a little girl.

"I am flesh but not flesh," the voice repeated.

Carole Kollars was feeling very sick, nauseated, wanting to retch, but all her muscles seemed immobile, incapable of following orders.

Maria Braithwaite too, was trying to move, pulling at her hands, trying to break the chain, end the seance, send the horrible thing away. *It is a horrible thing,* she was thinking. More than horrible. Despicable, dirty, soiled, obscene. She had heard this kind of voice before, at other seances. She felt as though she were being inundated with filth. She pulled at her hands, trying to move, but the fingers on either side of her clenched, tightened. She tried to speak, but all that came from her throat was a gutteral rasp.

I want to talk! Dixon shouted in his head. *I want to talk, Estelle! I want to talk, goddammit!*

Agnes Bittel was staring down at the table, eyes glassy. Her arms ached. Her legs. Her knees were giant nodes of pain. She's doing it! Christ, she's doing it!

"My friends want to talk to you," Estelle said. "My friends want to ask you some questions."

"Only questions," Elvida said.

"You fucking little shit!" Henry Dixon's voice burst forth in a torrent of hate. "You fucking little shit, get out of my wife! Get out!" he managed before he choked, before his throat filled and his words became indistinguishable grunts, unintelligible syllables, and finally ceased.

"Only questions," Elvida said. The childish voice was even, flat, cold, and full of hatred.

Adjacent to the dining room, beyond the closed swinging door that entered on the pantry, Susan Dixon heard her father's upraised voice as she lifted canned goods from the cupboard and filled a large shopping bag. *He's drunk,* she thought, and grimaced. *Drunk again. Couldn't even stay sober through a fucking seance. Goddammit!*

Maria Braithwaite found her voice, found it and thanked God she was still alive. "I want to ask a question," she said, and when there was no answer went on. The words formed in her mind out of shadows, inklings she had never before been able to articulate. "Elvida," she said, "who are your parents?"

There was a pause, then Elvida's voice came from Estelle Dixon's lips. "My mother is my father," it said. "And my father is my mother."

"Are you alive?" Bette Hammond's voice was a croak of fear.

"I am alive but dead," Elvida said. "I am born, but unborn. I am dead but shall live forever."

"Where were you born?" Joe Tremper's voice was a rasp.

Don't talk to it, Joe! Lauren Shane thought.

"Where were you born?" Maria Braithwaite repeated.

"I was born in light and in dark," Elvida said, the

words slurring, the timbre of the voice taking on tones of threat and danger and maliciousness and hatred. "I am eternal but dead, living but nonliving but shall live forever. My mother's name is my father's name, and my father's name is my mother's name, and there is only one name!" The voice began to fade.

"Wait!" Estelle said.

"Let the little shit go!" Dixon shouted.

"What do you *want!*" It was Blauvelt, his voice loud, rising, fearful. "What do you *want!*" He wanted, *needed,* to know.

Estelle Dixon's face was a study in contradiction, a rubbery, grimacing mask of moods, contorting into smiles, screwing into harsh lines of anger and hate, pulling apart, shaping together again, mouth now closed, now open, now howling, now screaming. An insane laughter erupted from her throat, filling the room, bouncing from the walls.

Father Conant's eyes rolled. Perspiration poured down his face. His body shook. His fingers fumbled at his neck, grasped, clutched, tore at the dangling crucifix.

The table began to rock, lurch, scrape on its legs. The candles flared. A wind began to whistle outside.

The insane soprano laughter, childish, mocking, issued from Estelle's mouth in lilting cadences, shrill, cutting, piercing, screeching, shredding the air.

A dish fell from the breakfront, smashing on the floor.

Marion Hammond backed away, pulled at his hands, trying to escape. But his fingers were clamped tightly.

Maria Braithwaite's blue-tinged face lifted skyward, eyes bulging, mouth agape, features twisted. "Our Father who art in heaven—" and her words changed to her native Spanish, coming fast, rising above the din of Estelle's hysterical laughter.

The wind outside rose. The windows rattled. The candles burned more brightly. The room took on a sickly orange hue, but the faces remained blue, and a coldness settled in, freezing limbs, dulling thoughts, killing will.

"You pigshits! You mother-fuckin' pigshits! You goddamn fuckin' idiot establishment bastards!" The words came from Estelle Dixon's mouth in a deep basso. "You mother-fucking pillars of society!" Estelle's voice was low-pitched now, hateful, vibrant, vindictive, vicious. The words tumbled forth like sledgehammers, heavy, harsh, benumbing.

Agnes Bittel, leaning forward, began to pound her forehead viciously on the table.

Joe Tremper began to laugh insanely, his head rocking back and forth, his ear tuned for the tape recorder but hearing only a loud crash, words that sounded as though they were formed by cymbals.

Marion Hammond had a sickly smile on his lips. *It's a recombinant,* he thought. *A live one. It escaped the laboratory.* Then he felt a viselike pain in his chest and pitched forward on the table, grunting.

"You pillars of society who pillage society!"

Susan Dixon dropped two cans of tuna fish on the pantry floor. Freddie Loftus. The same words he'd said at the Rites! Was he here? She turned quickly to the swinging door and pushed it partly open.

"You bloodsuckers! You titsuckers. You cocksuckers!" The words frothed like liquid hate from Estelle's mouth.

Susan screamed.

"You suck the money from our pockets, the bread from our mouths, the dreams from our souls!"

Chrissake! Chrissake, kept running through Henry Dixon's mind. *Chrissake!*

"You fucking Jesus freaks!"

Daniel Conant lurched across the room, holding the crucifix in front of him.

Tom Blauvelt tried to get his breath. *Get your breath,* he told himself. *Get your breath. Don't die. Not here. Not in this. You need a peaceful death. You always wanted a peaceful death.*

Maria Braithwaite started to rise, pulling at her feet, dragging upward under an indescribable weight, a leaden movement filled with struggle and frustration.

The wind roared, the candles' flames lurched and lengthened, climbing higher, causing the shadows on the walls to dance in weird pirouettes, darting, dodging, leaping. A blood-red hue suffused the room. It was as though it were on fire, yet cold drafts swept from every corner, plunging the room into an Arctic iciness.

Estelle Dixon's laughter had turned into a long, wailing, fear-filled scream, issuing from her throat in thick grunts, hollow, labored, choking, anguished.

"Non adiuro te ergo omnis immundissime, spiritis." Father Conant, his face agonized, sweat pouring down his forehead, his voice shouting, was thrusting the crucifix in front of Estelle's face. *"Omne phantasma, omnis incursio satanae in nomine Jesu Christi—!"*

Estelle's screams rose. The table began to move, scrape along the floor, bounce, vibrate. The window-panes shook, rattled, began to bend.

"Holy Mary, Mother of God, be with us now!"

Maria Braithwaite had gained her feet, stood rocking on her heels, trying to free her hands. But Estelle's held her fast, and on her left, Marion Hammond's cold hand was a grip of death.

"*Non tibi enim, et angelis tuis vermes erunt, qui nunquam morientur!*" Daniel Conant's voice rose into a crescendo, screaming, shouting, coming forth from his lips in sprays of spittle and phlegm. "*Non tibi, et angelis tuis inextinguibile praeparatur incendium!*" His features were contorted, agonized. Sweat bathed his face in a glistening redness. "*Quia tu es princeps maledicti homicidii!*" Brandishing the crucifix before him, he waved it in Estelle's face, shook it at the red walls, passed it in circles embracing the entire room. "*Tu auctor incestus! Tu sacrilegorum caput!*"

The others at the table seemed to have a kind of St. Vitus dance. They rocked back and forth in their chairs, trembled and lurched, went into contorted spasms. Agnes Bittel opened her mouth and vomited on her dress. Joe Tremper's head jerked from side to side, his eyeballs bulging.

"*Tu actionum pessimarum magister!*" Conant screamed. "*Tu haereticorum doctor!*"

Carole Kollars was moaning wretchedly. Lauren Shane gasped for breath. Bette Hammond was staring at her husband's head, lolling as the table jerked and shook.

Henry Dixon was trying to stand, pulling at the hands on either side of him, grunting hoarsely and stammering as he tried to speak. "Get out of her!" he screamed. "Get out! Get out!"

Susan had run into the room and stood behind him, arms around his waist, tugging, trying to pull him from the table. But the hands held.

Father Conant's crucifix flashed through the air. His arms flailed. His body pivoted around and about. *"Tu totius obsenitatis inventor!"*

"Holy Mary, Mother of God, be with us now!" Maria Braithwaite shouted, her eyes wide, pleading, blazing, staring at Daniel Conant.

The wind rose. The house shook. The windows rattled loudly and then glass flew through the air, slashing, cutting, piercing. An arcing stream of blood burst from Maria Braithwaite's neck, spraying the table in bright red. She screamed and more blood gushed from her mouth, and the scream became a choking sob.

Henry Dixon and Susan broke free, staggering back against the wall, sending china crashing from the breakfront.

Estelle Dixon's screaming broke off abruptly. Seconds later the other hands were unlocked.

Maria Braithwaite plunged to the floor.

Joe Tremper pushed his chair back savagely and rising, rushed toward the kitchen. He grabbed the wall phone and started dialing the police.

Tom Blauvelt stumbled over to Maria Braithwaite, stretched on the floor, eyes glassy, unseeing, blood spurting from her jugular. He removed his belt and started a tourniquet under her armpit. *"Non adiuro,"* she said softly.

"What?"

But Maria Braithwaite said no more.

Blauvelt turned to the others. Marion Hammond was dead. He knew it at a glance. Father Conant lay on his back, eyes fixed on the ceiling, perspiration glistening on his face. "The Devil was here," he said when Blauvelt knelt to him.

"He's gone," Blauvelt said. He turned to Estelle

Dixon. She was still seated in the chair at the head
of the table, rigid, transfixed, eyes dull, complexion
ashen. Dixon and Susan were kneeling beside her,
holding her hand. "She's dead," Dixon said. His face
was twisted.

"No, she's not," Blauvelt said. He shone a pencil
light into her eyes one by one. There was no reaction.

"Her eyes are dead," Dixon said. "All the color's
gone. There's no color." He sobbed.

Blauvelt passed a hand before Estelle's face. Again.
Catatonic, he thought. *Oh, Jesus.*

In the kitchen, Joe Tremper was about to speak
into the phone when something hit him from behind.
A strange tingling jolt went through his body, and
he gasped and turned his head reflexively. The refrigerator door was swinging backward. Then it came
forward again, fast, hard, smashing into his spine with
a terrible force. *Christ Almighty!* he thought. *There's
no one here! It's doing it by itself!* The door caught
Tremper three more times, fracturing bone, cutting
nerves. Tremper's fingers stiffened. The phone clat-
tered to the countertop, and he slumped to the floor.

CHAPTER
21

In the ambulance with Maria Braithwaite and Joe Tremper, Tom Blauvelt peered out the rear window while the attendant ministered to the patients. Behind them, a second ambulance carried Estelle Dixon and Father Conant. A private car held Henry Dixon, Susan, and Lauren Shane. Bette Hammond was in the morgue wagon with her dead husband.

"Tom?" Joe Tremper was calling, his voice weak from pain-killers. Blauvelt bent to him.

"I can't move my legs, Tom."

"You'll be all right," Blauvelt said.

"I can't even feel them."

"Don't worry," Blauvelt said. "Just try to rest."

Tremper closed his eyes and dozed.

He'll be paraplegic, Blauvelt thought. *Most probably.* He sighed and shook his head.

A moan from Maria Braithwaite turned him to the other side of the ambulance. Her eyes were open again, staring glassily upward. Her lips shaped, moved.

"Don't try to talk, Maria," Blauvelt said softly. "Just rest."

"Holy Mary, Mother of God," she breathed.

"Don't talk, Maria."

She coughed once, lightly, and her head lifted very slightly from the pillow, then fell back again, eyes closing. She breathed out once, and her features re-laxed.

She was dead.

Frank Liscomb surveyed the dining room from a po-sition just inside the arch leading to the larger wing of the house. His eyes shifted from the splinters of shattered glass to the broken crockery, from the over-turned chairs to the skewed table, taking in the scat-tered candles, one of which still stood on a sideboard and burned dimly into its final half inch. He looked upward to the dangling chandelier, hanging by a sin-gle cord, its stocket torn from the ceiling. He stared at the smashed window frames, the panes and woodwork jagged splinters.

In the living room, too, windows were smashed, pictures had been torn from the walls. Upstairs, there were more blown-in windows, and shingles had been lifted from the roof. Outside, a small tree had fallen.

Liscomb let out a long breath and walked across the dining room, through the pantry and into the kitchen.

Agnes Bittel sat at the table, clutching a tall glass filled with straight scotch. Carole Kollars dabbed at her cheek with a bloody Kleenex.

Liscomb sat down opposite them across the table. "When did it start?" he asked.

"About midnight," Agnes Bittel said. "A little be-fore, a little after. I don't know. We sat down, joined hands. Hank Dixon made some kind of a bad joke, and Estelle—"

"I'm not talking about the seance," Liscomb inter-rupted. His tone was irritated. "I mean the trouble, the breaking, the cyclone or tornado or whatever it was."

"It wasn't a tornado," Agnes Bittel said sharply. "I told you before. Satan was here."

Liscomb made a peculiar sound in his throat and looked away at the wall. His fingers drummed on the table. Since he had cut down on the cigars, the tattoo was incessant. He turned his head back slowly and looked at Carole Kollars. "Did you see the Devil, Carole?"

"I didn't see him, Frank. Not in the flesh." They had been on a first name basis since the tenth warning Liscomb had issued her for speeding on Route 14. Old enemy-friends. "No, I didn't *see* the old bastard."

"But you believe that all this"—he gestured around him toward the dining room and the rest of the house—"was caused by the Devil himself, appearing out of a seance."

Carole Kollars was silent for a moment. "Well, I don't think it was a tornado," she said.

Liscomb sighed.

"Tornados aren't a natural part of our climate here," Carole said.

"A freak tornado then," Liscomb countered.

"One that hit only one house, one spot, one group of people? Explain that."

Liscomb said nothing.

"Try the weather bureau," Carole said. "They can explain anything."

"Or ask Father Conant," Agnes Bittel said. "Or Estelle Dixon. Or Maria Braithwaite. They were here. They know what caused this. Ask them!"

Liscomb intended to do just that, but kept his silence. He disliked this predatory woman, and to admit anything to her ran against his grain. "What do you really think, Carole?" he asked.

"Marion Hammond's dead," she said dully. "And Maria Braithwaite may well be by tomorrow. What *can* I believe? What do you expect me to believe?"

"You think the cause is supernatural?"

"The Devil isn't supernatural," Agnes Bittel said harshly. "Don't you read your Bible?"

Liscomb paid no attention. He continued to look at Carole Kollars.

She stared back. "What do you think, Frank? A freak tornado? Really?"

Liscomb wished he had a cigar. His fingers drummed. He caught himself and stopped. "It's hard for me to visualize," he said. "The Devil. Satan. Demons. It just doesn't make sense in my mind, that's all. I'm a cop, Carole. A plain, ordinary cop. I have to make a report. I have to summarize, arrive at a conclusion. I tell them the Devil did it, what are they going to think? I might as well tell them the butler."

Carole Kollars smirked. "I didn't see one around tonight," she said.

Outside, Liscomb found an emergency cigar he had stowed in the glove compartment of the patrol car. As he was lighting up, Volner strolled out of the shadows and bent to the flame with a cigarette.

Liscomb blew out the match. "What do you think, Eddie?"

"Beats the shit out of me," Volner said.

"Did you hear what they said? Inside?"

Volner spat. "Crap," he said.

In the glare of the porch lights and the high beams of the police cars, Liscomb looked about him, at the lawn, the trees, the fencing. It all looked neat, clean, well-tended. To within perhaps a foot or two of the house itself.

"If it was a freak tornado," Volner said, "it was one hell of a freak."

Liscomb growled something unintelligible.

A car passed on Willow Creek Road, but neither of them paid it any attention.

As he slowed at the Dixon driveway, Ken Brady caught the insignia of the police cars, and his heart pumped an extra beat. He pushed his foot on the pedal and went on. He suddenly had visions of a police dragnet, an All Points Bulletin, FBI computers spilling out information, aimed at finding and arresting one Ken Brady. But why? What had he done? He hadn't killed Milt Framer. It wasn't any of his business. He'd had nothing to do with it. Nothing.

Further along, he turned into the Bannister driveway and reversed onto the road, heading back toward Broadmoor. It was a dead end ahead. Passing the Dixon house again, he saw the smashed window. *Probably a drunken brawl,* he thought. Or vandals. Maybe vandals. He'd phone Sue later. Now, he had to find food for Freddie.

Nicole Bannister heard the car in the driveway. She was wide awake, strung out, tense. Beside her, Jonathan slept peacefully. She waited. The pulse in her neck began to beat heavily. Then she heard the car reverse, turn, slip away into the night.

The heavy throb of her pulse continued, pressuring within her head. Her body was stiff, taut. Sweat trickled from her scalp to the back of her neck. She wanted to sleep, but could not. She wanted to forget but could not forget. She gazed into the darkness with fear.

The Church. She had thought the Church would bring solace, but there was no solace. Only the persistent, recurring vision of the finger, followed by the hand, followed by the guilt. Always the guilt. Would it never end?

The Church had not helped. Father Conant had not helped. She had confessed, she had prayed, she had prostrated herself, but the guilt stood before her, firm, solid, immutable.

But I didn't mean it! a voice within her screamed. *I didn't mean it!*

She rose upward suddenly, turned, feet dangling from the side of the bed, reaching for a cigarette. Her fingers trembled with the match. She dragged deeply. She looked back at the shadowed form of Jonathan, listening to his steady breathing.

I must tell him, she thought. *I must tell somebody. Jonathan will understand. He will. I know he will.*

But when she thought about it further, when she projected the scene and dialog in her mind, her body shuddered and her hands shook uncontrollably.

It took all her concentration to mash the cigarette in the ashtray, and when she was finished, she held her head in her hands and began to cry softly.

Across the hall, Leslie was dreaming.

"I can see you, Elvida," she said in her sleep. "I can see you now." What she saw was a vague, phosphorescent shape, white and golden, then black and red, shifting into a multitude of forms, first tall, then short, fat then slim, receding but coming forward. But the voice was firm.

"You see me almost," Elvida said.

"When will I see you all?" Leslie asked.

"Soon," Elvida said. "Very soon."

"And then we'll play together? And go places together? Like Devil's Pond?"

"Devil's Pond, and Devil's Caves, and all kinds of places," Elvida said. "Even the Devil's land."

"Where's that?" Leslie asked.

"Far away," Elvida's voice said, then began to fade. "Far and away below."

"When?" Leslie asked. "When can we go there?"

"Soon," Elvida said. "Very soon. I'll see you and you'll see me very soon." And the voice was gone.

Leslie smiled in her sleep, but the smile was downward, lips grimacing, with a hard frown between her brows.

Dimples was sleeping, but Freddie Loftus's mind was wide awake.

The single candle lit his face in leaping flames, making the deep lines around his mouth curl and jump and wave, deepening the hollows of his cheeks into sunken pits, bouncing light off his eyes in brilliant specks.

He could not sleep, or if he could, he was not meant to. Each closing of the eyes brought the dream on in all its clarity, each dozing off would end in an abrupt start, a rising up into fear and trembling and sickness. Each lidded darkness would fill with the light of his own image, sneering, laughing, pointing, jeering. Lurching for him, grabbing him, clasping him to itself in crushing helplessness, threatening death, destruction and eternal pain.

Christ, I've got to sleep, he thought, changing in

mid-sentence to *Satan I've got to sleep! Lucifer I must sleep. Beelzebub, give me darkness! Loki kill Balchar and give me blackness!*

I've got to eat, too. Where the hell is Ken Brady! Where the hell is anybody! Where the hell is Hell! Hell, I've got to sleep, eat! Hell, help me!

His glance strayed to Dimples. Sex. Maybe sex would make him sleepy. Bring him peace, let him sleep. But he did not feel like sex.

He gazed into the candle flame for a while, then went outside and looked up at the stars, screaming blasphemies into the night, beating his head. "I hate you all! I hate you all!"

He turned, trembling, and went back inside, and reached for his journal. It was difficult to read by the single candle, but he read the last passage and pulled a ball-point pen from his pocket, and began to write.

I've got to get it all down, he thought. *I've got to get it all down before I die. Let the pricks know. The pricks!*

At the Good Samaritan Hospital in King's Landing, just two doors away from the room Nicole Bannister had occupied almost four weeks before, Estelle Dixon existed in a remote world of silence and shadow. She saw nothing, but stared from wide open eyes, focusing on an invisible speck slightly to her right and about four feet forward. She heard nothing, no voices impinged upon her remote reverie, and when fingers were clicked at her ears, there was little or no response. Light brought no flicker to her eyelids, and in the dark, the lids remained open. She ate her food slowly, automatically, in small, dainty bites, chewing ceaselessly, unmindful of those around her, the nurse, her husband, her stepdaughter.

The diagnosis was "catatonia," although one of the older physicians, a man in his eighties, disagreed, preferring the more old-fashioned term "catalepsy," pointing out that patients in a state of catatonia could hear and take orders. The cause of the catatonia or catalepsy was argued; the doctors, the psychiatrists, and one young psychiatric social worker disagreed at almost every turn. Since there was no history of schizophrenia in Estelle Dixon's past or in her family, her condition was finally attributed to "psychic trauma" although one doctor insisted on "nervous shock," and the social worker held out for "acute psychological deterioration of the sensory reaction parameters."

To the question uppermost in Henry Dixon's mind, the outlook for the future, the prognosis, there was no reply.

On the floor above, Joe Tremper lay in bed with most of his torso and legs under restraint to avoid any further damage to the cervical area of the spine.

He was paralyzed from the waist down.

"Are they going to operate?" Lauren Shane asked. Her voice was timorous, her complexion pale.

"They don't know," Tremper said. He was looking out the window, his mouth drawn thin. Then he laughed, a short, abrupt laugh. "First the good news," he said, turning. "The old member still works."

Lauren grinned, but tears fought for passage out of her eyes.

"So help me," Tremper said, "I got a tingle in it this morning. The minute I thought of you. How about that?"

Lauren laughed. "I've told you before," she said, "you'll be ready to screw on your deathbed." And then she was sorry that she had said it, and the tears fought harder.

They were silent for some moments. "I'm not dead yet," he said.

Lauren squeezed his hand and smiled. "You won't be."

"The tape," he said. "Did you get the tape?"

For a moment she was flustered, then remembered. "I forgot all about it," she said.

"Bring it to me," he said. "I've got a great idea for a book."

"Not now, Joe," Lauren said quickly. "Later. When you're home."

"No, bring it. And a couple of pads and some Bic pens. Shit, what do you want me to do? Stare out the window all day?"

"I just thought it was a little close, that's all."

"It doesn't matter," he said and turned to the window again. "Look," he continued, "no matter what the medical geniuses say, I may not be much good after this. Half a man, in a sense. I mean, we ought to think about—"

Lauren rose abruptly, overturning the bedside chair. "Oh, for chrissake, Lochinvar! Are you out of your fucking mind?"

He looked at her.

"It still works, doesn't it?" and she tried to smile, but could not. She ran into the private bath, where she stood over the sink, leaning, breathing hard, and wiping her eyes with Kleenex.

Daniel Conant had been released from Good Samaritan at 11:00 A.M. that morning. His cuts and abrasions had been treated, and his nervous system had been granted a reprieve through the use of sedatives. When he left, he carried in his pocket a small vial of Librium.

Outside the Church of St. Ignatius of Loyola in Broadmoor, he found a police car waiting. Frank Liscomb waved, smiled, and Conant invited him in.

In the dim, gray light of Conant's living quarters, Liscomb studied the priest's face and accepted a glass of wine. Conant's complexion was quite ashen, and when he poured, his hands shook and the decanter clinked against the glass.

"How is Mrs. Dixon?" Conant asked.

"Alive," Liscomb said. "But that's about all." He described Estelle's condition while Conant stared pensively at his desk.

"And Mrs. Braithwaite is dead," the priest said.

"Yes," Liscomb said. "And Joe Tremper may be a cripple for the rest of his life." He paused. "What happened last night?"

Father Conant's fingers tightened around his glass. His eyes mirrored a remote fear. "I don't know," he said.

Liscomb lit a cigar. "You were there."

"Yes. I was there."

"Tell me about it," Liscomb said and sat back, thinking that a show of casualness would relax the priest.

When Conant had finished, Liscomb crushed his cigar in an ashtray and leaned forward. "I don't believe it," he said.

The priest's eyes questioned.

"That it was supernatural, that the seance had anything to do with the wind, the destruction. That the Devil was there. Satan, Lucifer, whatever. Pardon the expression, Father, but it's bullsh—baloney."

"We had a conversation once before," Conant said. "You believe in evil. You told me so."

"I said I believed in *man's* evil." Liscomb said.

"Not in the Devil. Not in the supernatural. Not in mumbo jumbo, abracadabra, seances, and voodooism! Come on, Father!"

"I have no other answer," Conant said.

"I thought you were an intelligent man," Liscomb said.

"I *was*." Conant's tone was resigned.

In a taut silence, the two men eyed each other, each measuring the other, searching for some common ground, some source of mutual understanding that seemed to elude them.

"I'm getting it from all directions," Liscomb said.

"What?"

"About the Devil, Satan being there, responsible for it. Carole Kollars, the Bittel woman, Dixon, Lauren Shane, all of them. I hear you even tried to exorcise it."

The priest nodded slightly. He refilled the glasses.

"You're trying to tell me," Liscomb said, "that the Devil is loose in Holland County. That he's responsible for the severed finger, the severed hand, for everything that happened at that seance."

"What do you believe?" Conant asked.

"Carole Kollars asked me the same question," Liscomb said. "I said it was a tornado. A freak tornado."

The priest smiled for the first time, slightly. "Have you called the weather bureau?"

"There's a reason for everything!" Liscomb exploded. "Goddammit, there's a reason for everything!" He rose.

Father Conant had risen too. "I'm sorry," he said. "I'm sorry I can't be of more help." But the door had closed on Frank Liscomb's retreating figure.

Father Conant collapsed into his chair, reaching for

the carafe. When he poured, his hands trembled so
that he spilled wine on the desk blotter.

They'll never believe, he thought. *Most of them
will never believe. Only those who saw it.*

He began to perspire again, his brow breaking into
rivulets of moisture. His knees shook. For the first
time since the preceding night, he let his mind dwell
on the seance. It came back to him in all its power,
all its terrible fury. The mad, dancing candles, the
red flames, the black shadows. The wind rising, the
house shaking. The wailing voices, the terrible screams,
the destruction and the blood.

Sweat ran from his armpits and drenched his waist.
His head ached, his temples throbbed, his body shook.
But he was not cold. He was hot.

Coolness, he thought, *I need coolness.* Cold. The
cellar will be cold. He rose and crossed to the door
leading into the church, clutching his glass in one
hand, the carafe in the other.

As he crossed the chapel, he thought he saw Freddie Loftus sitting in a pew, but the shadow disappeared as he peered at it.

Then he was crossing the altar, praying to himself.
God save me! he said to himself. *God save us all!*

He opened the cellar door and stumbled downward
into the darkness.

"I tell you I heard him," Susan Dixon said. "I heard
him coming right out of her mouth."

"Come off it, Sue," Ken Brady said. "I mean it's
insane."

"And he was saying the same things. The same
things he said at the Rites."

"You're trying to spook me," Ken said.

"You've got to tell me where Freddie is."

"Why?"

"You've got to."

"I promised," Ken said. His face was anguished.

They were seated in a diner a few miles east of Tyrone on the way to Indian Falls. Susan had not touched her black coffee. Ken Brady sipped nervously at a Coke.

"How's your stepmother?" Ken asked. "Estelle."

"Bad," Susan said. "Very bad. She doesn't talk, she doesn't hear. She's like a vegetable. You've got to tell me where he is, Ken."

"What's the point," Ken whined. "He wasn't there at the seance. How could he have done anything?"

"I don't know," Susan said. "But his voice was there—coming out of Estelle."

Ken Brady sagged in his seat. "Freddie can't be responsible for anything. I was with him. He wasn't there."

"If you don't tell me where he is, I'll go to Liscomb."

"And accomplish what?" Ken asked. "You think he'll listen to you? You think he'll believe any of that shit?"

"Freddie Loftus is evil," Susan said. "Even you should know that by now."

Ken laughed. "Come on, Sue. You're getting as spooky as the rest of that crowd around the table."

The slap resounded through the diner, turning heads, cutting off conversation.

Susan rose and strode to the door.

Ken Brady sat silently, face flushing, the overturned Coke spilling into his lap.

* * *

She was not sure about Freddie Loftus. She was not sure about anything. Only that something horrible had happened and that she had heard, or thought she had heard, Freddie's voice, or something like his voice, coming from Estelle, and that she was afraid, terribly afraid.

She drove back to Broadmoor in a panic, taking the turns too fast, careening dangerously over the roadbed.

But Ken Brady was right. Liscomb would never believe her.

She would have to find Freddie Loftus herself.

From the Journal of a Satanist:

I must write this down. Why I am driven to this revelation I do not know, but I must tell it, I must get it out and down. Not for posterity, God knows. Not for history. For my own sanity? What sanity? What reason is left me? I live in an Underworld, a fathomless pit of darkness, deceit and dissembling.

I must write on the sly. I must do this when He is not about, when He is sleeping. Does He ever sleep? Is He not here with me now? Watching me? Peering over my shoulder?

No. I can always smell His stink.

When did it start? When did this foul thing begin? In August. Or sometime in July. I cannot remember the date. But I remember the night.

It was actually morning, a few minutes before four in the morning when I made my contract with Lucifer.

I was drunk, yes, I was drunk, on wine, on my own image, on my own conceit, my own sense of grandeur and smugness. In fact I was laughing, actually laughing in my sense of knowledge and power.

*"And the Devil did grin, for his darling sin
Is pride that apes humility!"*

(Jesus Christ, help me!)

There was nothing I was afraid of that night. Not even Lucifer and all the Angels of Hell, none of whom I believed in (but must have) could have frightened me that night, so large was my image of myself.

And I called Him up. I conjured Him. I teased Him. I taunted Him. Arise, I shouted! And screamed drunkenly for Him to appear before me, sit with me, speak with me, have dialog with me.

Come up from your Hell, come forth from your fire, crawl out of your slime and your shit and your dung and sit with one who understands you! And He came.

(God damn me! Oh, God, damn me!)

If I am insane, can I blame it on Him? For I must have been mad before. Otherwise, why would I have called upon Him?

I write quickly. I scrawl, I hurry. I fear Him coming. He comes so often now.

What's that smell? Is He here? Is that His foul odor? No, I imagine things.

That smell. That foul, disgusting reek. How it rose through the floorboards that night like a choking miasma of tangible filth. That stinking admixture of feces, urine, vomit, and putrefaction.

The memory brings bile to my throat, and I almost puke, as I puked that night, as I puked and puked and puked until I was weak and shaking and at His mercy.

And raising my eyes I saw Him, just before me, and behind me, on all sides of me, surrounding me, enveloping me, in His abominable filth, in His darkness.

Yes, I saw Him. In His many hideous shapes and forms, changing from one instant to another, from black, snarling dog to hissing snake, from bleeding entrails to mocking skeleton, sometimes in hideous detail, at other times a stone black, amorphous bulk, shapeless and all-encompassing.

When He spoke, it was with the voices of Hell, and screams and shrieks and horrible, piercing cries echoed inside my head, as if every damned soul from the beginnings of time were cursing me.

He asked what I wanted, and I told Him.

He named His price, and we traded.

As my signature to the contract, He made me crawl over the floor to Him and kiss His genitals. They were full of sores and chancres, and I vomited on them. He made me kiss them again and again, and in them, I saw people, little people screaming to get out, lunging up at me, white and shriveled and full of stink and fetidness and four-letter words.

And I kissed and kissed, abasing myself before Him, groveling, discharging my own semen even as I kissed, and thanking Him profusely for the power He had granted.

All the time knowing I was damned, damned to His foul stink, damned to His abuse, damned to His will.

(Oh, God, help me! Please help me!)
There is His smell now. He wants to speak
again. He wants to give me more orders that I
have no will to refuse. I must obey him.

CHAPTER 22

"You sure you feel up to it?"

"I can't feel anything from the hips down, anyway," Tremper said.

"No pain in the back?"

"Not much. Sit down."

Frank Liscomb pulled the bedside chair and straddled it, resting his arms on the back. "I've heard a lot of stories," he said, "most of them pretty weird. I can't say I have an open mind, but I try to." He paused. "If it wasn't a tornado or something like that, I figure somebody was trying to stop you from calling the police. Who was it?"

Tremper eyed the police chief warily, his expression puzzled. "I don't understand."

"The refrigerator door kept hitting you in the back. If it wasn't the wind, then somebody was pushing it. Who?"

"Nobody," Tremper said.

"Then it must have been the wind."

"No. It wasn't the wind. I didn't feel any wind. That was all in the dining room."

Liscomb patted his pockets for a cigar, then saw the *No Smoking* alert over the oxygen outlet. "Who was in the kitchen with you?"

"Nobody."

"You were alone?"

"I was by myself," Tremper said. "The others were still in the dining room. All hell was breaking loose. I knew some of them were injured, and I wanted to get the hospital and police."

"You're *sure* you were alone?"

"I'm telling you, Chief. Why?"

Liscomb shifted his shoulders. "I just thought that maybe in the excitement you didn't notice. That there was somebody there who wanted to stop you. The refrigerator door could become an accessible and dangerous weapon."

Tremper smiled. "Not a bad idea. You should be a writer, Chief. But there wasn't anybody behind that door. I know it because I saw it. I saw it swinging by itself. After the first blow, I turned my head. I watched it swing back and then lunge at me. It happened a number of times . . . three, four, maybe five times. Believe me, there was nobody there, Chief. Nobody."

A faraway look had come over Tremper's face. He was staring downward over the bed, at his legs. "Nobody," he said.

Of all the conditions of life, major and minor, to Frank Liscomb one of the most frustrating was a stalemate. It galled him not to be able to solve a problem, supply an answer, satisfy an effect with a cause. And yet he knew, instinctively, that the man before him was telling the truth, or at least the truth as he remembered it.

At a complete loss for new approaches to fantasy stated as fact, Liscomb searched his mind for words with which to continue the conversation. His eyes locked in on the yellow pages of script at Joe Tremper's bedside. "Working on a new book?" he asked.

"More or less," Tremper said.

"What's it about?"

Tremper looked uncomfortable. "I'm not sure yet," he said. "I mean I know what it's about, but I don't know the how and why yet." He nodded at the pages. "I'm still at the note-taking stage." After a pause, he added, "Actually, if you want to know, it's about the seance. And the finger. And all the shit that's been going on."

Liscomb was suddenly alert. "Oh. And what do you make of it?"

Tremper looked at him with a slight, somber tilt to his head, and then his eyes smiled. "I don't make shit out of it," he said. "How about you?"

"Is truth that much stranger than fiction?"

"Always."

Liscomb chuckled. "Well, if you get any ideas for the book let me know. I'm up the creek myself." His eyes had fastened on the tape recorder. "Do you dictate your stuff?"

"Hell, no. That's for amateurs. The wondrous tape recorder is for nonwriters, Chief—those who can't spell and never learned to write."

"What do you use?"

"A portable SCM Coronet Automatic Twelve. Since they won't allow it in here, I turn to the old reliable Bic pen and the handy yellow pad. In an acute emergency, I could get along with a quill pen and a roll of Charmin."

Liscomb laughed. "I thought a lot of writers used tape recorders."

"Only the lazy ones. Of course I can't blame them because I'm lazy myself. I often have a dream of inventing a computerwriter."

"What's that?"

"A computerwriter. All you have to do is sit down

in front of it, think, and the book writes itself. You program it for fiction/modern mainstream/best seller. No editing required. Simple to operate, complete book of instructions."

"A machine like that might put you out of business."

"Yeah. But it'll happen. Just watch." Tremper's eyes had moved back to the tape machine. "The seance is on that."

Liscomb could not believe what he had heard. "The what?"

"The seance. I recorded the seance."

Liscomb leaned forward, almost upsetting the chair. "The whole thing?"

"Start to finish. In living monaural."

Liscomb backed the chair to the floor. "Hey," he said, "I wonder if I could hear that."

"Sure," Tremper said. "Get it down from the sill for me, will you?"

"I meant by myself," Liscomb said quickly. "At my office."

Tremper threw him a suspicious glance. "In other words, if I don't say yes, you'll impound it."

Liscomb laughed. "That only happens in novels."

"Okay," Tremper said. "Listen, can you get me back a dub?"

"A what?"

"A dub. A copy. I want to keep listening to it."

"Sure."

"Okay, it's a deal," Tremper said and reached for the yellow pad. "I have to keep writing on this one. If those sawbones operate, I'll need a best seller, a hit movie, a musical version and toy rights. So help me, Chief, one of them came in yesterday, shot me with a needle, and I swear the syringe was graduated in dollar signs."

Three days after the seance, on a grim, gray Tuesday soggy with humidity and under a temperature of ninety-four degrees, two funerals were held in Holland County, one for Dr. Marion S. Hammond, M.D., and the second for Maria Rivera Braithwaite.

The times of the two ceremonies had been carefully adjusted to the convenience of all common friends and acquaintances, and the tandem processions were handled by the firm of Rice and Co., Funeral Directors, in King's Landing, of which Judge Oliver Marquith was a silent partner.

Brief and very solemn services were held at the First Lutheran Church in King's Landing for Hammond, and at the Church of St. Ignatius of Loyola for Maria Braithwaite, Father Daniel Conant officiating. At both services, Henry Dixon was noticeably but understandably absent.

To Carole Kollars, Father Conant did not rise to the occasion. He seemed flustered and preoccupied, and when he intoned the hope that "our dear departed friend forever find eternal peace within the bosom of Our Lord Jesus Christ," she saw Tom Blauvelt wince.

Maria Rivera Braithwaite was buried on her own property in Broadmoor in a private plot beside her husband. The procession then moved on to the Blue Crest Cemetery in East Indian, where a young, fresh-faced, blondish minister, who appeared never to have needed a shave, spoke of life, death, transfiguration, natural mystery, and everlasting life within the memories of those surviving, in a luckless chain of metaphors that drew bitter smiles from those who had been at the seance, and stifled yawns from the few members of WebLabs attending.

In the middle of this graveside paean, a hunched, slow-moving figure detached itself from the treeline and made its way slowly through the drizzly gloom to the graveside mourners, fitting itself into a space beside Jonathan Bannister. It was Henry Dixon.

"Sorry I couldn't make the other one," Dixon said, "but I thought I'd pay my respects."

"How's Estelle?" Jonathan asked.

Dixon was looking at the flowered casket. "She's eating better," he said, and then his jaw clamped in silence.

It could not truly be called a funeral reception.

The laughter was missing, the reminiscences were few and far between. The room hummed, glasses clinked, but few of the guests became really drunk. The scattering of WebLabs people—two M.D.'s, three biophysicists, and a Japanese geneticist—paid their respects with a minimum of emotion and a maximum of socio-intellectual pleasantry. "Marion was a brilliant man. . . ." "One of the best minds of the last decade. . . ." "I had the honor of working closely with him on DNA research." They sipped, they smiled, they made their exits with their wives softly and without fuss, leaving the house to closer friends.

They were, of course, unaware of the true circumstances, but had they known, as scientists they would have scoffed.

His good friends, Bette Hammond thought, his colleagues, his co-workers, his peers. Already jockeying for his position. She sighed and drank deeply.

Thomas Blauvelt was impressed by the woman's

control. Not once had she wept. Not once had he noticed the slightest hint of moisture in the eyes. The jaw was firm, the smile wide, the voice vibrant and assured. A strong woman? He questioned himself. Defensive perhaps. Afraid. Alone. Ready to crumble.

Agnes Bittel was pouring it in. Two fingers, three fingers, four. *I should have been at the head of the table,* she thought. *Not Estelle. If I'd been at the helm, this would never have happened.*

Lauren Shane hardly touched her drink, or the food that Bette Hammond had had catered by the Bull and Bear. She answered when spoken to, she smiled, she reacted, but her mind was elsewhere, in Good Samaritan Hospital, with Joe Tremper.

Carole Kollars was surprised with the efficiency of Bette Hammond's packing. Neatly sealed boxes and wardrobe cartons stood everywhere. Furniture, except for those pieces necessary for the reception, was arranged for fast exit. Bookshelves were empty and clean, walls denuded of pictures. Bette Hammond was not, obviously, long for Holland County.

Jonathan Bannister kept stealing surreptitious glances at Nicole. She seemed too voluble this evening, much too loquacious.

Nicole Bannister was making small talk, listening intently without hearing, shaking her head in serious commiseration, nodding profoundly, acting, and through it all, trying to lose herself, her thoughts, and her fears. Yet beneath it all, the hulking thing grew, and she knew she would soon have to tell Jonathan the truth.

During a lapse in the general hum, Tom Blauvelt coughed. "Why don't we talk about it?" he said.

Eyes turned, heads swiveled.

"Talk about what?" Carole Kollars asked.

"Marion's death," Blauvelt sighed. "It's time, isn't it?"

"I'll second that," Henry Dixon said. He had been silent throughout the afternoon, drinking steadily but remaining sober. His ordinarily devilish eyes were sad, his demeanor bleak. There was a haunted look about him.

Bette Hammond's lips went tight. She placed her glass on the coffee table with a loud clink. "Marion died of a heart attack," she said.

"You don't want to believe it, do you?" Blauvelt said softly.

There was a long silence until Bette Hammond said, "No."

"But you were there," Henry Dixon said. "I was there, Tom was there. We were all there, except Jonathan and Nicole."

"What're you talking about?" Agnes Bittel squinted.

"Be quiet, Agnes," Carole Kollars said.

"It wasn't just a heart attack," Dixon said.

Lauren Shane fidgeted. Nicole Bannister's face went blank, uncomprehending.

Carole Kollars looked beseechingly at Bette Hammond. "Tom's right," she said. "You've got to face it, Bette. You just can't run. Where can you go?"

"I'm going to Eighty-fourth Street!" Bette said. "Eighty-fourth Street, Eighty-fifth Street, anyplace, that's where I'm going!" She swirled the ice in her glass viciously. Her hands trembled. Tears welled in her eyes.

"You'll take it with you," Carole said.

"No!"

"And leave us alone to deal with it," Blauvelt said.

"You're not alone!" Bette Hammond shouted. "You're all together in it! Face it if you want to!

Deal with it! Kill it! Defeat it! Shit on it, for all I care! But leave me alone!"

She threw her glass into the fireplace, and it shattered loudly. No one spoke.

Outside, crickets began to scrape. Peepers raised their rasping voices to the overcast skies, and from a clump of leaves came the soft rustling of a snake.

Inside, there was silence broken only by the muffled sobs of a woman in agony.

Lauren Shane rose and crossed to Bette Hammond, taking her into her arms, massaging her back.

Eyes were downcast, drinks held rigid.

Tom Blauvelt wished he had never opened his mouth.

From the Journal of a Satanist:

> *He comes quite often now. At any time of day or night. Without excuse and without notice. I become aware of His coming in the growing denseness of the air, in its pervading mustiness. He slips into the room and into my soul in a welter of foul and sickly odor that curls like smoke into every hidden nook and cranny, sinking even into my pores.*
>
> *Sometimes He laughs as He approaches, and I hear the laughter in my head.*
>
> *I am aware of His presence and I feel Him hovering, as though looking over my shoulder, making sure I am doing His work, carrying out His orders.*
>
> *As if I had the option to do otherwise, the power to resist.*
>
> *It was never my idea to send the finger and hand of the First One. It was His, for He commands me through my mind, and half the time*

my mind is no longer my own. At these times I can only follow His orders, for His thoughts are my thoughts, and I must do His bidding.

I am like a multiple personality, two people living within one shell, two souls in utter conflict but clinging together like magnets, each aware of the other yet powerless to interfere, interact. My good self exists side by side with my evil self, watches it, despises it, yet cannot struggle, cannot cry out. It is like trying to scream during a nightmare, and finding the voice lost, unable to utter a sound where there would be a shriek.

When I am with others, I have a dim memory of my covenant with Him, but if I try to beg for help, my cries are stilled and the words that tumble from my lips, though they seem to be mine, are His—for He will not suffer this despicable thing be known.

I live in a series of blackouts—yet remember.

Oh, God!

And as my words are at His bidding, so are my actions.

They were not my hands that wrapped the finger, that sent the hand. They were His.

The sending of the finger two months ago was His grisly charade, meant to remind us of His fiendish power to probe at our guilt, work on it, stimulate it, use it to torture and destroy.

And I have become His instrument in this destruction.

(Dear God, what have I done?)

The woman is guilty of nothing unless humanness is guilt.

But how well He knows the hidden guilt feelings of the mind. How He works on them, uses them to wreak His havoc, to pillage, destroy, and loot the human soul!

For are not guilt feelings as damning as guilt itself? How much more malleable, how much easier to mold and shape and design toward destruction. The truly guilty hide and defend themselves. The innocent are ever ready to confess.

In delivering the finger and the hand, He has (I have?) taunted her to the edge of insanity, and now she hovers on the brink of suicide, or perhaps murder. I cannot foretell.

And why? Why this meager victory, this unimportant skirmish, this foul foray into a corner of the universe so small it is negligible? What can He gain? What does He want? What difference can it make? In His eternal death-struggle for our souls, He can call on war, starvation and pestilence, and lead us to think it is our own doing! Why this?

Because, simply, He is fiend. He is nightmare. He is death, destruction, putrefaction, stink and decay—and to Him, every victory, no matter how small, no matter how insignificant, is another step, another mark, another beachhead in His never-ending campaign to capture the fortress of our souls.

(I spit on Him! I spit, spit, spit!)

I know these things because He is in my mind. He will destroy us all through our minds, for He has worked hard through eternity to become part of our minds, and we have been unaware of His invasion. And this is His power. Our minds.

Power.

I asked for the power to create, and He granted it to me. But with it I have become His servant *in destruction, His footman in foul deeds, His slave in evil.*

(Damn me!)

In my drunken bravado, in my grandiose image of myself, I have brought evil to earth, and Hell to Holland County.

I had been so sure, so certain in my craftiness, so positive in my conceit, that I, who have dealt with good and evil all my life, studied, read, immersed myself in it, could, with this lore, summon Him, conjure Him from the depths, then deal with Him, bargain with Him, contract with Him and finally defeat Him. Such is Pride.

Now I am His humble servant. Powerless in His grasp.

I asked God to damn me, but I have damned myself. To everlasting Hell.

This Journal is my last link to what I once knew as life. Sparse and barren as it was, without love and without tenderness, it was as heaven compared to this foul place.

If this Journal is ever read, it will not absolve me. I no longer plead for mercy, for I know that I am already dead and in Hell. Could God forgive, He would, but the Other One owns me totally.

So I write, not for forgiveness, not for understanding, but as a warning:

Do not be deceived. He exists.

Sulphur. It smelled like sulphur.

Sulphur and brimstone? What was brimstone? She had never known.

In that tense twilight between sleeping and wakefulness, Nicole Bannister fought upward, striving for light, air, reality.

Her muscles were inert. She could not blink an eyelid, move a finger.

There was an expanse of white before her, like snow on a plain. In a dark sky, lights flickered, blue and yellow lights, turning on and off, one at a time.

The smell of sulphur became overpowering. It bit sharply at her nostrils, filled her lungs. She choked, coughed, felt her breath stop. She came up from the pillow in panic, opening her eyes and staring downward along the white sheet.

Leslie stood at the foot of the bed in a sheer, filmy nightgown. She held a book of matches in her hand. She was lighting them, one by one.

"Hello, Mommy," Leslie said and grinned maliciously. Her voice was a harsh rasp.

"Don't!" Nicole screamed. "Leslie, don't!"

Leslie dropped a match on the sheet. It caught and flame leaped high. Nicole felt her feet burning.

"Leslie!" she screamed. "Leslie!" And her voice rose into a piercing siren of panic as the flames roared upward, sweeping over thighs, belly, breasts, licking at her face.

Her left cheek scorched. Then the right. The flames licked, curled. She felt fierce pangs of pain. She shrieked.

"Nicole! Goddammit! Nicole!"

Her hair was on fire. "Jonathan!" she screamed. "Jonath-a-annn!"

"I'm here!" he said. "I'm here! For chrissake, Nicole! Jesus!" And he stopped slapping her face.

She sank into his shoulder, shaking, fingernails clutching at his back, digging. "Oh, my God," she said. "Oh, my God, she's going to kill us!" She wept, shuddering, the tears flowing down his bare chest, glistening in long streaks to his navel. "She's going to kill us," she sobbed. "Oh, my God."

"Easy," Jonathan said, and held her tight, feeling her body shiver against him. "Easy, baby," he said, and kept her close until the sobs diminished and reality returned.

In her studio, Jonathan poured them each stiff tumblers of scotch. Nicole's shaking subsided, and she sat staring into the cold fireplace, shoulders hunched, neck stiff.

"Jesus God," she said. "It was so vivid."

"Dreams aren't portents," Jonathan said quietly. "Freud proved that."

"It was so vivid," she said.

"It wasn't Leslie, of course," Jonathan said. "In dreams, people aren't who they seem. They're symbols. They stand for anybody, even for ourselves. If the guilt feeling is too high, we thrust it off on somebody else in the dream. Leslie could even be you."

Nicole turned the glass nervously in her hand. "I know who Leslie stood for," she said quietly.

"Who?" Jonathan asked.

"Elvida." She looked up at him for the first time.

"Who?"

"Elvida. Something like that. I hoped I'd forgotten her. And the thing. And everything."

Jonathan moved slowly, careful not to upset the balance. He knew he was on tricky ground. "Is this —this *thing* or whatever—is this what happened before you had the first breakdown?"

Nicole nodded. "Yes."

Jonathan waited.

"I was seven," Nicole said. "We were still living in Kansas, on one of those beautiful streets you used to see in America, one of those wide streets with big, old-fashioned houses, and huge lawns and deep porches. And outside the city limits there were rolling hills and farms. Sometimes, Mom and Dad would take me along when they visited friends of theirs who owned one of those farms. Davidson, I think their name was. Elvida was their daughter. I don't remember the date. I think it was in the Fall. There seemed to be brown in the trees. . . ."

. . . and the hay in the Davidsons' barn was piled high and crisp and sweet-smelling.

"Let me," Nicole said.

"No, I'm the one," Elvida said.

"Oh, come on, let me!" Nicole said and reached for the matches.

Elvida pulled away, laughing, and when Nicole reached again, she ran across the barn floor, tearing matches as she went, trying to light them.

"Let me!" Nicole said, following her. "I want to light one!"

But Elvida giggled hilariously and held the forbidden matches high, climbing into the hayloft.

"I won't let you be my friend anymore!" Nicole cried climbing behind her.

In the loft they struggled, laughing, shrieking, pulling, clawing, rolling with each other, and when Nicole had the book of matches in her fist, she uttered a triumphant cry and stood, one foot on the ladder, ready to descend.

"Give them back!" Elvida cried. "They're mine!"

"Just once, just once!" Nicole screamed in delight, and struck the match, eyes full of brightness.

On the second try, the match flared and dropped into the hay.

Flames roared and Nicole fell backward to the dirt floor. Stunned for a moment, she said nothing, but then began to scream, even as she heard Elvida's horrifying screams from the loft, and then ran from the barn into bright sunlight, screaming terror, the matchbook clutched in a tight fist.

Later, when the small, sheeted body was passed into the morgue wagon, Nicole saw the black, withered hand hanging from the stretcher, and looking about saw the harsh light in Mrs. Davidson's eyes.

"You little beast!" she heard the woman say. "You horrible little beast!"

And when she looked, her mother and father had hung their heads in shame. . . .

. . . as Nicole's head hung in shame now, and as her almost inaudible voice faltered in remorse.

Jonathan was slumped in his chair, legs outstretched, eyes vacant.

He had hardly touched his drink, but now, in the silence that followed Nicole's confession, he raised it to his mouth and sipped.

"It wasn't your fault," he said.

"I killed a child," Nicole said. Her voice was hollow, full of emptiness.

"It was an accident," he said.

Nicole did not answer. She sat very still, a small hunched figure overburdened with guilt.

Jonathan came behind her and leaned in, placing his fingers on her shoulders, massaging gently.

"I could say you could have told me—but I'm not going to," he said. "You had your reasons."

Nicole remained silent.

"But in the dream," Jonathan said, "it wasn't Leslie striking the matches. It was yourself. Your guilt feelings projected out. You don't need it, Nikki. You really don't. You have to realize it was an accident. It might have happened to any child. Probably has, a thousand times."

"It was Elvida in the dream," Nicole said in flat tones. "She comes back sometimes. When I had that last breakdown, she was back."

"But not as Leslie. That was before Leslie was born."

"I don't remember," Nicole said.

He led her back into the bedroom. "How about a Tuinal?" he said.

"I'll be all right," she said. She seemed sleepy, spent.

Jonathan kissed her gently on the forehead. "It's better now," he said. "It's out now. It'll be better now, Nikki. You can get rid of the ghost."

"I killed a child," Nicole repeated, and Jonathan tightened.

"Try to sleep," he said, kissing her forehead.

But Nicole was already asleep, deeply.

He wandered about the house, carrying his drink, turning it all over in his mind. *It's better this way,* he thought. *It's all out now. She finally trusts me.*

But uncertainty gnawed at his soul.

He looked in on Leslie. Like Nicole, she seemed deep in the nether land of dreams.

He found himself in his studio, surveying the beginnings of his canvas that would depict the human brain as computer.

The human brain. He smiled bitterly. How warped it may become, how convoluted with guilt and shame, anger and hatred. So much could go wrong.

Elvida was grinning maliciously.

"Do you like to play with matches?" she asked.

"Mommy won't let me," Leslie said.

"I love to play with matches," Elvida said. "I love the sudden burst of light and the heat. And the smell, too. I love that smell of matches when you strike them."

"Do you have some matches?" Leslie asked.

"I can bring some when I come," Elvida said.

"Will you let me play with your matches?"

"I don't know," Elvida said. "Maybe. Maybe not. We'll see."

And she was gone in a flare of light and a puff of smoke.

CHAPTER 23

During the second week of October, the accidents began, slowly at first, unevenly.

They seemed unconnected, but a pattern was emerging, a design of destruction that seemed to be concentrated within the borders of Holland County, leaving the adjoining territories more or less unaffected, free to trust their luck to long-established actuarial tables.

In Tyrone, a man fell in his bathtub, breaking his ankle, not an unusual event of its kind, but perhaps extraordinary in light of the fact that four other homes on the same road experienced similar bathroom mishaps within the same week.

Fender-bending and rear-end collisions were becoming prosaic on the interstate, with the focus of activity clustered around Broadmoor.

There were two near drownings in North Lake.

At Granger's Bull and Bear, the chef, a member of the establishment from its inception, experienced and able, upset a large vat of hot grease and was rushed to Good Samaritan Hospital suffering third-degree burns.

The burnings, the scorchings, the falls, the collisions spread throughout the countryside, and the populace swore, cursed, and blamed it all on the heat.

The intolerable humidity persisted, and the drizzle did not let up. And from the forest and the swamplands, there came the never-ending nagging of the insects and the slithering of snakes.

A shroud of evil enveloped Holland County—dense, pressing, suffocating.

If most people recognized no pattern in the spiraling series of mishaps and the inordinate number of freak accidents, Henry Dixon did.

The accidents, the heat, the slow rain, the appearance of copperheads and rattlesnakes where there had been none, the emergence of the devil's coach horse and other insects, were leading his thoughts into a phantasmagoria of suspicion.

Above all, his mind was obsessed with the seance and the utter havoc it had wrought.

Estelle had been home from the hospital for three days, a move which Dixon had at first opposed, but to which he had given in after the recommendation of a consulting psychiatrist from Clarendon State Hospital.

The psychoanalyst, a gentle man in his mid-sixties with a lined face and eyes full of a kind of faraway wisdom, had suggested that, regardless of the clinical diagnosis and unfavorable prognosis of the case, Estelle stood a better chance of survival and eventual recovery in an atmosphere of love, understanding, and patience.

To Dixon's surprise, Susan had fought tooth and nail on the doctor's side. He had been further astounded at the quality of his daughter's devotion, her concern, her attentiveness to Estelle's every simple need, from feeding her to bathing her, to adjusting a pillow to make her more comfortable.

For the most part, Estelle sat. Here and there, on couches, on chairs, on the hassock, sometimes on the floor. She spoke not a word, nor did she respond to questions. Sometimes she smiled, a simple, distant smile, as if she held a secret that nobody else in the world could fathom, a knowledge all her own, beyond the grasp of mere human beings. Sometimes she laughed, a soft, light, flimsy chuckle made up of disjointed monosyllables, quiet and inward, distant and private.

It frightened Dixon. It robbed his nights of sleep and made his days a living nightmare.

For he knew now that whatever evil stalked Holland County, it was not a natural evil. That the priest was right, that Blauvelt was right, that Agnes Bittel and Carole Kollars were approaching the truth, and that they were all in danger. Satan was loose in the land, stalking the fields, winding through the underbrush, turning the grass to straw, darkening the skies, and sowing death in his wake.

He lifted the glass of clear Boodles and gazed through it to the murky sky. Estelle had been the first to recognize the hell that hung over them.

Estelle the weirdo, the nut, the pseudopsychic, the laughingstock of the county—

—had been right in the first place.

Dixon raised the glass to his lips in a small, silent salute.

"Try it, Estelle," Susan said. "Come on, just try it. Just a little."

She gently pushed the spoon to Estelle's mouth, prying softly, coaxing, supplicating.

Estelle made a funny smile and her mouth opened.

The yogurt dribbled on her chin and dropped into her lap.

"Oh, shit, Estelle!" Susan said, but she was smiling softly and there was concern in her eyes. "Come on, Estelle. Try a little more."

It was like trying to feed a recalcitrant infant or a senile octagenarian, full of false starts and impatient pauses, a battle alternately against vacant indifference or unreasoned obduracy. It was difficult enough, and made all the more so by Susan's confusion about her own motives. She did not understand her newfound patience, her apparent empathy, her sense of love where there had been no love. And she questioned herself.

Was she trying to erase her guilt? Atone for her past sins against this woman through a general outpouring of counterfeit devotion?

She pushed the thoughts aside and raised the spoon again to Estelle's lips. "That's good," she said. "You're doing great, really, Estelle. Try a little more now."

The yogurt foamed on Estelle's lips, slid down her chin and dropped in white splotches to her breasts, exposed in the open V of her housecoat. She giggled lightly.

It will take more than this, Susan thought. More than spoonfeeding an invalid, catering to her needs, seeing to her toilet. These things will not cure her.

She needed to know the truth.

And the truth, Susan had determined, lay in Freddie Loftus. She had heard his voice at the seance. She had dreamed of his body in the little coffins, little coffins like the box in which the finger had been sent.

She would find Freddie. Or if not, make Ken Brady tell her. And that book Freddie was always writing in. Maybe the truth was in that book. Like a confession.

Estelle gurgled, a soft, slushy sound that might have been an attempt at a giggle. Looking from the container of yogurt, Susan noticed that her head was turned. She was looking over at the bookcase, eyeing the Ouija board, her expression full of yearning. She giggled again.

Susan shuddered.

Ken Brady parked his borrowed van on the side of the road. He was on Indian Falls Road. Lifting the knapsack of food to his back, he crossed the macadam and started east along the opposite shoulder. Two hundred yards further on, he stepped over the wire fence onto a narrow trail that plunged down into dense woods.

It was no more than a footpath, twisting through tall grass and thick sumac, leveling out for a while and then inclining sharply upward through a heavy pine forest.

The trail was seldom used because of the rattlesnakes that abounded in the vicinity, and Ken wore stout leather boots over tucked-in trousers.

Forty-five minutes later, he could look down and out to his left and see The Reach flowing for miles. The villages of East Indian, Shokan Forks, and Broadmoor were small clusters of civilization in what seemed like a temperate zone jungle.

To his right lay the Devil's Caves.

Another ten minutes brought him to the fifth cave, the most deeply hidden. There was a clearing before it, and as Ken made the turn from the path, he saw Dimples squatting by a small fire, heating a can of Heinz vegetarian beans.

She looked up at his step. "You got any grass?" she said.

"I could only raise an ounce," Ken said.

"Oh, shit," Dimples said.

Ken lowered the knapsack. "I brought some vittles."

She eyed the burden with distaste. "More cans," she said.

Ken shrugged.

"Jesus," she said, "what I'd give for a real, old-fashioned, juicy Big Mac."

"No such luck," Ken said.

"With french fries," she added. "And relish." She paused and then said, gesturing, "I'm up to here playing cavewoman."

"Where's the caveman?" Ken asked.

Dimples jerked her head backward. "In his cave."

"How is he?"

"He's not sleeping," she said. "When he does, he screams. When he's awake, he shakes, you know? Like this." She imitated a shaking fit.

Ken grunted.

"Sometimes, he just stares," she said. "At nothing, you know? And when he's not doing that, he's writing in that book all the time. That fucking book."

"Have you read it?"

"What?"

"The book."

"I don't read books," Dimples said.

"It doesn't sound like a happy marriage."

Dimples looked confused. "We're not married," she said. "Did he say he was going to marry me?"

"No," Ken rose from his squat and started toward the cave.

The entrance was very narrow, and he had to wedge himself sidewise for about five feet, scraping himself through. Inside, the cave took on the proportions of a fair-sized room of about twelve by eighteen. The air was moist and quite cool. Five flickering candles bathed the rock walls in a yellow-red light. There was a beaten-up mattress on the floor and a sleeping bag. Two apple cores and a Hostess cupcake wrapper spoke of a recent feast. The place smelled of marijuana.

Freddie Loftus was at the far left corner of the cave, lying prone before two candles, scribbling in his book.

"Hey, man," Ken said, and squatted down on his haunches smiling broadly.

But when Freddie closed the book and looked around at him, Ken felt a sudden queasiness in his stomach. Freddie looked as though he had lost twenty pounds. The sunken eyes were further sunken, the hollows of his cheeks like deep holes in his face. There was a blaze in his eyes, a fire that was frightening.

"You bring any acid?" Freddie's voice was tremulous.

Ken dug into his pockets and came forth with a small vial. "That's all I could round up," he said.

Freddie's hand reached, trembling. "Thanks, man," he said. "I'll pay you back. Really, I will."

"You think you need it, Freddie?"

"Don't lean on me, man," Freddie said. His hands shook and his cheek twitched. "What's news from the great world outside?"

Ken was hesitant. "They're looking for you, Freddie."

"Don't you think I know, man? Why the fuck you think I'm crashing in this hellhole?" He giggled sharply. "Hellhole." He turned the phrase over in his mind, smiling softly. "Hellhole." Then his eyes flashed again as he looked at Ken. "You won't tell them."

"Freddie, they're looking for me, too. All of us."

"Why you?"

"They think we all had something to do with Milt Framer dying." Freddie was strung out and Ken was aware of it. But not on acid—since he had not touched the vial—and grass could not account for the distance and detachment of his expression. He was looking through and beyond Ken, his eyes lit with some inner demon of frightening proportions. Ken had never seen Freddie quite like this.

"Sue keeps asking where you are," he said.

"Sue?" Freddie seemed to be trying to recall a long-forgotten name.

"I didn't tell her," Ken said. "She's got some whacky idea you had something to do with the seance."

Freddie's head flicked abruptly in Ken's direction. "Seance?"

"The one her stepmother held to find out about that finger and the kid who was killed. She thinks you were there."

"Where?"

"At the seance."

Freddie was looking at the earthen floor of the cave, smiling lightly. "I was," he said.

Ken squinted. "Come on," he said at last. "You were here in the cave all the time. With Dimples. I went out to get some food."

Freddie's eyes lifted slowly, and when they locked with Ken's, they glittered sharply. "That's right, man," he said. "I was here, but I was there. I was in the cave, but I was at the seance." He laughed, a small fearful laugh.

The exasperation in Ken's voice held an edge of

disbelief mixed with growing fear and horror. "What're you talking about, Freddie? Come on, man, make sense!"

"I know who did it," Freddie said, his voice rising in pitch, his expression warping into a convoluted mass of deeply etched lines and wrinkles. "I know who did it, man! I know who made the river stink and the grass wither! I know who made the sun go out and the rains come and the heat blaze!" He was on his feet now, pacing the cave, gesturing with his hands, flicking his head in sharp arcs. "I know who did it, man! Who sent the finger! Who sent the hand! I know who killed that kid, man! I know!"

Quaking, he sat down, arms embracing bent knees. His head rocked back and forth as though in an epileptic fit. He was smiling.

Ken waited a few seconds. "Who?"

Freddie's gaze shifted to the floor of the cave, to the blue loose-leaf binder, to the leaking Bic pen. "It's all in my book, man," he said.

Ken chuckled nervously. "I'd like to read that book of yours," he said.

Freddie's hand descended on the cover of the binder. "Not until I'm finished," he said.

"Just a few pages," Ken said.

"Not until it's finished, man." His tone was decisive.

"But who did it?" Ken asked. "Give me a hint, Freddie." He tried to laugh but it would not come.

Freddie's eyes moved upward, regarding the ceiling of the cavern which reflected dark, dancing shadows in the flickering candlelight.

"I did it, man," Freddie said. "James did it. James and I and Satan did it, man. For James and I and Satan are one."

"James is dead." Ken's voice was a croak.

"James is Satan," Freddie said, his voice suddenly low, quiet, soft. "And I am Satan. And Satan is James and Satan is me. We're all guilty."

Ken could not speak. His nerves were frozen, his mouth dry, his gut moving in sickening waves.

Silence. Strong, heavy, oppressive.

When Freddie spoke again, his eyes held a religious fervor, and the deep lines were gone from his face.

"Satan is here," he said. "With us, in us, and around us. He abounds." Again, his voice began to rise. "Satan! The Devil! Lucifer. Loki! Filth of Hell! Serpent of destruction! Pus of poverty! Pimple of putrefaction! We spit on you!"

And Freddie Loftus spat. Once, twice, three times into the air, his face twisting, his saliva making dark splotches in the dirt.

Ken felt the skin of his neck tingle. Goose pimples chilled his arms.

Freddie began to laugh. The cave echoed with his cackling. He looked over at Ken and his eyes gleamed with madness. "We have to kill him, Kenny," he said. "We have to kill the bastard! Before he kills us. Before he kills any more of us. He's close, you know? Very close. Right here in the cave and all around us. We have to kill the cocksucker, Kenny. He's going to kill me, I know that, and there's nothing I can do about it. The shit's going to kill me, Kenny! It won't be long. I know. *I know!*" and he lapsed into weeping. "Jesus Christ save me," he sobbed. "Jesus Christ, what have I done! Oh, sweet Jesus, forgive me! Please!"

Ken Brady rose quietly, his legs shaking. He looked down on the hunched, quaking figure of Freddie Loftus and made his way silently to the cave entrance.

Coming from the cave into sunlight, he passed Dimples and moved on to the footpath, chin low on his chest.

"Where you off to, lover-boy?" Dimples asked his retreating figure, but Ken did not answer.

By the time he reached the pine forest, he was convinced Freddie Loftus was insane, strung out to the ends of the universe. A nut case. A complete flake.

As he pushed through the overgrown sumac, his innate tolerance for others began to crumble. He had begun to see Freddie Loftus as a sickness, a diseased mind full of lies and distortion.

Susan had been right. Freddie was hiding something, and further, was guilty of something.

But what? Murder?

Close to Indian Falls Road, he knew he would have to reach Susan, talk to her, tell her, try to explain.

Explain? What?

A child was dead. And Milt Framer was dead.

And the heat closed in like a surrounding furnace, and the drizzle would not let up.

He heard a buzz to his left and stopped. After a moment it buzzed again, and then there was the rustling of brush as it slithered off.

He walked on toward the van.

Maybe Freddie was right. The Devil was loose.

Shit, man! Come off it!

No, Freddie had done it. Freddie had done it and was trying to pass it off on the Devil.

It was as simple as that.

He was insane.

The wind was rising, howling, whipping, screaming. Window panes rattled.

Tu actionum pessimarum magister! It was the priest's voice.

Behind him, a woman, Estelle Dixon, screamed, choked, grunted disgustingly.

Tu haereticorum doctor, the priest shouted.

Something began scraping across the floor, like a table, vibrating, shaking.

Get out of her, Henry Dixon screamed. *Get out! Get out!*

Somebody ran into the room.

Tu totius obscenitatis inventor! It was the priest again.

Holy Mary, Mother of God, be with us now! Maria Braithwaite shouted.

There was a loud smashing of glass. Screams. Grunts. Stumbling. More smashing of glass. Sobbing. Crying.

A body fell to the floor.

A click. Silence. Only the sound of a typewriter in the outer office.

Impasse, Liscomb thought.

He had listened to the tape over and over again. It frightened him. It set his skin crawling. It knotted his stomach.

But it told him nothing.

He could not *see* it. It was sound and fury without form or shape. If only he had been there. Or if it were a videotape. He grunted.

Impasse. He hated impasses, and now he faced them in all directions.

The FBI had turned up nothing on the canvas bag or the rope used to tie it. The American Museum and the Metropolitan Museum were both at a loss to explain the body of the child. Or its condition. It was a mummy, they said. Four thousand years old, Brookhaven National Laboratory said. Beyond that, they shook their heads.

Shit, Blauvelt thought, ripping off the end of a cigar. *It's a body! It's a goddamn body! Who cares how old it is!*

But he knew it was not a body. Not at any rate, a believable one.

Nor had there been any sign of Freddie Loftus or the others who had settled Job's Camp. They were scattered to the winds, vanished. Follow-up on their families and homes had met with silent stares and noncommittal remarks.

But Milt Framer was dead.

Liscomb smoked deeply and scowled.

And Marion Hammond was dead. And the Braithwaite woman.

Four bodies and no evidence of a crime. No suspects, no modus operandi, nothing.

He pushed a button and the tape backed up toward the beginning. He punched PLAY.

Are you alive? It sounded like the Hammond woman.

Then the voice came. *I am alive but dead. I am born but unborn. I am dead, but shall live forever.*

Where were you born? It was Joe Tremper.

A pause. Liscomb felt a prickling at the back of his neck, a symptom he had become increasingly aware of during each subsequent listening to the tape.

Where were you born? This time it came from Maria Braithwaite.

I was born in light and in dark, the voice said, *I am eternal but dead, living but nonliving but shall live forever. My mother's name is my father's name, and my father's name is my mother's name, and there is only one name.*

Shit, Liscomb shouted inside his head. *Pure shit!*

He punched FAST FORWARD and began anew.

There was the wind. Estelle Dixon's insane laughter turning into thick, anguished grunts.

Omne phantasma, omnis incursio satanae in nomine Jesu Christi . . . ! The priest.

The wind screamed in the background. There were heavy vibrations, rattlings. People grunted, gasped, called out in unintelligible monosyllables. Estelle Dixon's harrowing screams pierced the tiny speaker like a knife, cutting, ripping.

Holy Mary, Mother of God! **Maria** Braithwaite's voice was a study in terror.

Non tibi enim, et angelis tuis vermes erunt qui nunquam morientur! Father Conant's voice rose above the rest, thick, guttural. *Non tibi, et angelis tuis inextinguibile praeparatur incendium*!

Liscomb pushed OFF and sat back. He stubbed the cigar into an ashtray and noticed his hands were trembling slightly. His palms were moist.

Am I supposed to swallow that? he asked himself.

Bullshit.

But on the other hand, what else could he think, where else could he go, where did the answers lie?

Besides, his palms were clammy.

He reached across for the phone and dialed Tom Blauvelt.

There was nothing interesting in the ice box, and Blauvelt had decided to lunch at the Bull and Bear when the phone rang.

"I just thought you might want to give it a listen," Liscomb said.

"Why?" Blauvelt said. "I was there."

"I know," Liscomb said, "but maybe there's something you don't remember."

"I'll never forget it," Blauvelt answered. "Never."

"You know," Liscomb said after a pause, "it's very terrifying. I mean when you listen to it."

On his end of the line, Blauvelt smiled shortly. "You're getting the drift of it now, Frank. Right?"

"What do you mean?"

"You're beginning to think it's not all bullshit."

"I didn't say that."

"You're thinking it," Blauvelt said simply.

Liscomb coughed through tobacco smoke. "I only thought you might pick up something I missed."

"Sure," Blauvelt said. "I'll be only too happy, Frank. But remember. I was *there*."

"I'll have it to you this afternoon."

"I'm going to lunch. Have your men leave it in the mailbox if I'm not in."

"Right. And Tom—"

"Yes?"

"If it is the Devil—how do we arrest him?"

Goddamn kids. You can't trust them. Goddamn kids!
Oliver Marquith was having a four-martini lunch at the Bull and Bear when Blauvelt walked in. He waved him over to his table.

"Goddamn kids." Marquith said as Blauvelt squeezed his large buttocks into the booth.

"Goddamn kids what?" Blauvelt asked.

"Up at Job's Camp," Marquith said. "They're all gone. I can't find one fucking owner."

Blauvelt ordered a scotch sour on the rocks.

"And do you realize I was going to give them one hell of a good price for that land? One hell of a good price!"

"I'll bet you were," Blauvelt said and opened the menu. "I had four burn cases, three broken legs, and two concussions this week, Ollie."

"Somebody owns that land," Marquith went on. "Christ. Somebody's got to own it!"

"And that latest smashup on the interstate killed one and put three in Good Samaritan," Blauvelt said, lifting his drink.

Marquith raised his and said, "They killed Milt Framer. Or at least were responsible for it."

Blauvelt ordered Crab Louis. "There's something amiss, Ollie."

"Freddie Loftus is amiss, if you ask me. Find him and you find your answer. He killed Milt Framer."

"And Marion Hammond? And Maria Braithwaite?"

"Goddamn kids! Satan freaks!"

"Non sequitur, Ollie."

"What?"

"Everything we're saying. Non sequitur. That's Latin, you know."

"I know, for chrissake!"

"And who sent the finger?"

"Freddie Loftus."

"Non sequitur again." Blauvelt raised a hand to the waiter, cancelled the Crab Louis, and rose.

"Where you going?"

"I have an appointment in Samarra," Blauvelt said.

"Where's that?" Marquith asked.

"Anyplace where death is," Blauvelt said, "and death is all around us lately."

"Goddamn kids," Marquith repeated, shaking his head. "Samarra? Where's that?" He looked over to Blauvelt's chair, but the doctor had disappeared.

Blauvelt had one more at the bar and then made

his way inexpertly to the parking lot. The drinks were getting to him.

Driving slowly, he reflected on the conversation with Oliver Marquith.

Ollie hadn't made sense. He was only interested in his own view, his own greed.

And you Tom Blauvelt? What is your point of view?

That it's all Satan's doing?

Why? Where's your proof?

Am I going crazy, he wondered.

From the Journal of a Satanist:

>*I am insane.*

>*But in my insanity I have gained power and prestige, permanence through procreation, and a place in posterity.*

>*And I am eternally damned!*

>*(Oh, dear God, forgive me!)*

>*In my utter conceit to become God, I have let Satan become my god, and now He rules me completely. There is no turning back. I am His.*

>*How I always fancied the role of Faustus. How I longed to sell my soul in exchange for the power to create! To let my poverty-stricken soul give life to other souls, to see something of myself go forward, into the future, if not from my body from my mind!*

>*(You can do anything if you put your mind to it, they used to tell me. Anything.)*

>*Now He is in my mind, has become part of it, and my mind is no longer my own. That is His entry into all of us. Through the mind.*

>*What He thinks, I think. What I think, He*

overrules. What I would want to do, He forbids.
What He craves, I carry out. For I crave it too.
He has become my conscience, my guide, my
counselor, my mentor. My downfall.

(You can do anything if you put your mind to
it.)

The First One was stillborn. It came to term
but never drew breath, never lived. I watched it
grow. From the very first cell to the very last.
From the simple cluster to the flowing whole.

(And I loved it!)

He accused me, in my mind, for we always
speak to each other in my mind, or His mind, or
Our mind, of cheating. Of not concentrating, of
not thinking hard enough, of willfully ignoring
His orders, of abrogating our contract.

Perhaps he was right. For then I was still holding to a slim thread of hope, that I might trick
Him, fool Him and finally defeat Him.

I needed a model and He provided one,
through His evil messenger who sent me the photograph.

And when I saw that photograph, it was all
beauty, and I never questioned Him.

And when The First One became that shrunken horror, I knew that the beauty masked evil.
And I realized it was I who had been tricked.

(Fucking fool! Cocksucking bastard! Get down
there and see that everything's all right!)

He speaks in my mind again, He is here. His
stench turns my stomach. I gag.

(Shit-full asshole! Pus-ridden prick! Do as I
say!)

He wants me to look at The Second Ones.

After the failure of The First One, He said He

*wanted two. He needed two. The First One
again, He said, and another He would choose.*

*And His Messenger on Earth mailed the sec-
ond photograph.*

I could only obey.

*They are nearing term now, The Second Ones.
Though unborn, their spirits are already about.*

And they are full of evil.

"I'll be coming very soon, now," Elvida said.

"When?" Leslie asked. She was staring at a yellowish glow at the end of the pool. There was a pungent odor in the air, like burning matches.

"Oh, maybe only a couple of days," Elvida said. Then she added, "Pull the legs off."

"I don't like to do that," Leslie said. She was clutching a grasshopper in the palm of her hand.

"Oh, go ahead," Elvida said.

"No."

"Go ahead," Elvida said contemptuously. "It's only a bug!"

Pearl DeWitt was dropping a plastic bag into the garbage can outside the kitchen. She watched the proceedings, then lumbered over to Leslie.

"What you doin', girl?"

Leslie hid the grasshopper behind her back.

"What you doin' to that poor little bug?"

"Nothing." Leslie's voice was strained.

"Yes, you is! Lemme see that!"

Leslie threw the insect into the pool. The current caught it and sucked it quickly through the sluice gate.

"Since when you takin' to pullin' the legs off'n poor harmless bugs?" Pearl said.

"I didn't do it!" Leslie cried.

"Yes you did! I seen you!"

"Elvida told me to!"

"Now you tell me where is this Elvida!"

"Right there!" Leslie said, pointing to the dam. "Right there!"

A grip on a wrist and one solid whop of Pearl's big black hand on her behind sent Leslie bawling into the house.

"And don't you ever let me see you doin' somethin' like that again," Pearl DeWitt shouted after the retreating figure. "And don't you tell me they is any Elvida around here! I got eyes, girl!"

After a moment, she turned those eyes in the direction of the dam, a worried expression in them. Seeing nothing, she shrugged.

They's somethin' wrong here, she thought. *They's somethin' real wrong with that girl.*

Let the little shit go!

He remembered the wild, almost crazed look in Henry Dixon's eyes, the angry fear in his voice.

What do you want! What do you want!

It was his own voice now, and as Tom Blauvelt listened, he recalled the icy terror that had gripped him at that moment of the seance, and his fingers dug hard into the frownline of his forehead. His closed eyes were open to the horror of memory.

Estelle Dixon's face contorting, harsh, a configuration of changing, rubbery masks full of hate and anger.

Daniel Conant's eyes rolling, the sweat pouring from his forehead.

The table rocking, lurching, warping under their clenched hands.

Our Father who art in heaven! The voice from the tape brought back the vision of Maria Braithwaite's bulging eyes, twisted mouth.

From the twin speakers of Tom Blauvelt's Sony stereo came the screaming wind and the screaming voices, the ominous oscillation of the windowpanes.

But Tom Blauvelt was less listening than seeing.

Agnes Bittel pounding her head on the table.

Joe Tremper's head thrown back, rocking, his laughter erupting in hoarse chortles of insanity.

The sick, orange hue on the walls. The blueness of the faces.

You pigshits! You mother-fuckin' pigshits! You goddamn fuckin' idiot establishment bastards!

The vile, vicious expression on Estelle Dixon's face as the strange bass voice tumbled from her lips.

The twisted, idiotic smile of Marion Hammond, his eyes glazed, vacant. The horrible choking grunt, and his head pitching forward on the table.

You bloodsuckers! You titsuckers! You cocksuckers!

Susan Dixon screaming.

You fucking Jesus freaks!

Daniel Conant's dark-clad figure, black against the candlelight, lurching across the room, crucifix held aloft.

His own breath catching, then his attempt to regain his breath. Get your breath. Don't die. Not here. Not in this.

Maria Braithwaite rising, swaying, twitching.

The priest's voice, sobbing, crying, braying, begging. *Omnis incursio satanae in nomine Jesu Christi!*

No!

No! No! NO!

Blauvelt's hand smashed out against the control panel and the room filled with silence.

He sat forward in his chair, breathing heavily, clutching his belly. He felt sick.

He rose and went to the bar, but the sight of whisky turned his stomach and he staggered toward the bathroom.

He lifted the seat of the commode and hunched over, but nothing would come. Dry retches, gagging emptiness.

I can't listen to more. I won't listen to more. Why should I? I was there!

He retched again, but only sweat from his forehead fell into the bowl.

Get control, he thought. *Get control. It's nerves, not ptomaine. Not botulism. Shit!*

He turned from the toilet and faced himself in the mirror, eyes red, brow shining, jowls moist.

You fat bastard. You fat, disgusting bastard.

He washed his face with cold water, toweled, and then made his way back to the living room bar. The sight of booze again froze his stomach.

In the kitchen he found leftover turkey, potato salad, a tomato, two wedges of cheesecake.

He wolfed. He felt better. He was soothed.

Over chilled Chablis, he noticed his hands were shaking. He held them up to his eyes. He found another liver spot.

God Almighty, I'm going to die. One of these days. But don't we all?

But it did not console him.

He reflected on the tape.

Christ, no, I won't listen again. I don't have to. I was there.

He began to cry, the tears running into his wine, spilling on the table.

Oh, my God, he thought. *Why can't I face it? Why can't I?*

"I still say you've got a galloping case of male chauvinism, Lochinvar," Lauren Shane said.

Joe Tremper threw an exasperated look from his pillow-propped head. "And I suppose, if I said you're just like all the rest, trying to tell me what to do, trying to change me, I'd only be in deeper."

"Yes, you would," she said. But she was smiling.

Tremper blew a sigh and looked out through the window. "Light me up," he said.

Despite the *No Smoking* sign, Lauren lit two cigarettes and gave one to Tremper. They smoked for a few minutes, and then he said, "You don't want a basket case for a husband."

"You're not a basket case," she said.

"I'd be in a wheelchair," he said.

"Is that the end of the world?" she said and put out her cigarette angrily. "So what? You'd be in a wheelchair."

"I wouldn't like it," he said.

"Why?"

Tremper looked away and did not answer.

Lauren Shane's mind suddenly clicked on a word. "Husband," she murmured. "You never said 'husband' before."

"It rhymes with 'wife,' " Tremper said.

Lauren's eyes widened. "Is this a proposal?"

Tremper smiled widely. "Listen, broad," he said, "in my own inimitable way, I've been proposing to you for over two years."

"It's been quite a proposal," she said. Then she leaned over and took his hand and squeezed it firmly.

"You know I love you, Lochinvar," she said. "And I know you love me. So we don't have much to worry about, do we?"

Tremper gazed at her steadily, expecting her next words.

"So never mind about the operation," she said, and squeezed his hand again and released it.

"You worry too much," he said after a pause. "Anyway, it's not a serious thing. The doctors say fifty-fifty."

"I don't like the odds," Lauren said. "And you don't need your legs to write."

Tremper blew smoke, then said quietly, "I've already signed the release. It's scheduled for seven A.M. tomorrow."

Lauren Shane felt a clutch in her chest. A cold fear gathered in her abdomen and rushed upward to her throat. A precognition of death, such as she had felt at the seance, raced across her mind and receded instantly. Tears welled, but she fought back and did her best to smile.

Leaning over, she took Tremper's hand in her own again. "Lochinvar, you're your own man," she said, "and I'm your wife, marriage certificate or no marriage certificate. So you do what you want. But know one thing, love, if you die, I die. There's no life for me without you." She paused. "So if it happens—wait for me."

When Tremper spoke, there was a choke in his voice. "Lauren," he said. "You're a strange broad."

"I know," she said. And smiled.

Carole Kollar's wound had not healed. The spot where the dog's teeth had entered her hand continued to fester and spread, though the physicians at Good Samaritan had tried three different antibiotics without success.

She could not drive because of the pain and relied on Agnes Bittel to get her to and from the hospital.

That afternoon, as they got into the car, Agnes looked as ill and peaked as Carole felt.

"What's the matter with you?" Carole asked.

Agnes turned the ignition. "I'm getting the most god-awful headaches," she said. "And I can't sleep. Can't sleep worth a damn." Then she giggled.

"If you feel rotten, what're you laughing about?" Carole asked.

Agnes did not answer, but backed out of the driveway and headed for the covered bridge. On Route 14 she turned west toward King's Landing.

As helpful as Agnes had been, as understanding and patient, there came with it a muted intolerance, an underlying hostility that belied altruism. Agnes's charity was grudging, tinged with disapproval of weakness. Try as she might, Carole Kollars could not really like this thin, brittle woman with the hawk's nose, and she felt guilty.

In an effort to assuage the guilt, she made small talk. "When in God's name is it ever going to clear?" she said, looking up at the leaden sky.

"It may never clear," Agnes said. "Never again." She laughed shortly.

"You're in a great mood today," Carole said, lighting a cigarette.

Agnes was silent. Her foot pressed on the accelerator. The needle climbed to sixty-five.

"Aren't you driving a little fast?" Carole asked.

"Fuck them all," Agnes murmured and giggled again.

"What?"

"Fuck them all!" Agnes shouted and chortled insanely.

Four-letter words were uncommon in Agnes Bittel's vocabulary. "What's got into you?" Carole said.

The speedometer rose to seventy. The road ahead came up fast.

"Jesus Christ, Agnes!" Carole cried.

Agnes Bittel began to laugh, a high-pitched, warped, laugh, insane and shrill. "I am alive but dead!" she screamed. "I am born but unborn!"

"Agnes!"

"You pigshits! You mother-fuckin' pigshits!" Agnes shouted. "You goddamn idiot establishment bastards!"

Carole Kollars's right foot went forward automatically, searching for a brake that was not there. Her body arched back against the seat, straining. "Slow down, goddammit!" she cried. "Slow down, Agnes!"

The needle wagged at eighty, then sped forward. The road ahead began to twist and bend. Trees were blurs, The Reach a streaking ribbon of blue on their right.

"Agnes!"

"Holy Mary, Mother of God, be with us now!" Agnes Bittel screamed. Her laughter rose to a violent crescendo. Spittle leapt from her mouth, drooled from her chin. Her eyes were bright, crazed, wide open. "You mother-fuckin' pillars of society!"

The tree on the curve ahead had a broad white band painted around its trunk. Carole Kollars knew it well.

"Agnes! Oh, my God! *Oh, Jesus!*"

The car hit the tree head-on at eighty-five miles an hour.

Carole Kollars's head was severed completely by windshield glass.

Agnes Bittel's was crushed to pulp, brains splattering to the backseat.

A passing motorist, approaching from the opposite direction, rounded the curve in time to see the gasoline tank explode.

Joe Tremper was wheeled into OR-4 of Good Samaritan Hospital at 7:38 the following morning.

Lauren Shane had been waiting in the surgery ward since 6:55.

At 9:15, she watched the chief surgeon trudge slowly down the hall toward her, removing his mask as he came. From his demeanor, his expression, his resigned, almost baffled look, she knew what had happened.

She smiled dimly as he spoke, her eyes distant and expressionless. Then she turned and made her way to the exit.

She drove home slowly, cautiously, automatically. She sat for a moment in the driveway, looking at the rose bush, the trellis, the unmowed lawn that he had said he was "getting around to."

She entered the house on heavy feet. It was a small house, but it was cozy, cheerful, warm.

She went to the bedroom and undressed. She lay on the bed nude, staring at the ceiling.

She thought for a long time.

She looked over at the pillow on her right. Smooth, clear, undimpled, pure. She made a dent in it with her hand and tried to picture her head there.

She tried to imagine his body beside her, his warmth, his bony knees, his cold toes.

She tried to hear his snore, but could not.

She tried to smell his odor, but it was not there.

After a while, she rose and sat on the edge of the bed. She started to reach for a cigarette, but decided against it. She thought for a few minutes longer, then stood and walked to the bathroom.

While the tub was filling, she opened his razor and took the blade. His whiskers were on it, but she did not remove them.

In the tub, she cut her left wrist first, then her right.

She dropped her arms into the flowing tub and closed her eyes. Colors arose in her mind. Red, green, yellow. But then a lowering darkness, and after that, a spreading brightness, like a sun.

Wait for me, Lochinvar, was her last thought.

Passing the arch to the living room, Henry Dixon caught sight of his wife sitting on the floor near the bookcase.

"Hello, honey," he said and squatted down next to her.

When he spoke, she looked at him and smiled wanly.

She had the Ouija board before her on the rug. The planchette was in her hand and she was rolling it in distracted circles across the board, haphazardly, without design and without concentration. There was an entreating, almost beseeching look in her eyes.

"Mind if I join in?" Dixon asked. He placed his fingers on the planchette. But as he touched it, Estelle seemed to lose interest. Her hands dropped to her sides. The distant, glazed expression came into her eyes once more.

Dixon regarded her for a few moments, then took

her by the shoulder. "Come on, Estelle," he said. "You'd better get to bed."

She rose without protest, but clutched the board and planchette in her arms. Upstairs, she lay in bed with the board on her knees, tracing lazy circles with the planchette, nodding her head slightly as if in some distant dream.

Dixon was about to try again with her at the Ouija board when the phone rang.

It was Tom Blauvelt with the news of Joe Tremper and Lauren Shane.

That night, Nicole Bannister awoke once again from the deep dream of burning.

As she clutched at Jonathan, she shuddered and screamed, and her words were thick through a torrent of sobs: "She's going to kill us!" she wailed. "It's not Elvida! It's not me in the dream! It's Leslie, Jonathan! Leslie! She's going to kill us!"

From the Journal of a Satanist:

(I have become death, the destroyer of worlds!)

Are not the deaths of Maria Braithwaite, Marion Hammond, Agnes Bittel, Carole Kollars, and now Joe Tremper and Lauren Shane on my own hands? If the blood is invisible, do I not feel its warmth on my palms?

(Christ, why can't you help me!)

But what can Christ do now? What can the angels of Heaven undo that has been done? I have sold my soul to Lucifer and am perished in everlasting Hell.

Frankenstein.

I have become a Frankenstein.

The man who would be God has become God,

but the God of evil, not good. Satan, Lucifer, Beelzebub, Mephistopheles, Diabolus, Devil! Name me!

Now have my dreams of omnipotence been fulfilled. But what I have created are monsters and I spit upon myself, and vomit on myself, and abominate myself!

(God, kill me! Christ, kill me! Let me burn!)

I smell His coming. I must hurry.

But Frankenstein called down the lightning, while I called up the Devil. Frankenstein's monster was good, while mine are evil, hideous, stinking, and rotten!

Yet, how perfect their look, the Second Ones. How like their prototypes, their models. How like their human mannequins.

How fair of feature the girl; how dark of visage the young man!

(Am I in love with my children? God, help me!)

For they are not human! They are replicas, alter egos, imitations, fascsimiles!

Effigies sculpted in evil!

Monsters!

And my mind has made them, the Second Ones!

Only my mind, my concentration, the energy of my thoughts, the power of my imagery, and the vast unconscious network of experience and memory over a billion years!

(Male and female created He them!)

An alchemy of the mind. A MAGIC of the mind.

No lightning for me! No buzzing arcs or weird apparatus, genetic engineering or cloning cells!

Does not a painter think his canvas into color?

Does not an engineer think his bridges into erection? Does not a writer think his characters into creation?

And did not God think, yes THINK man into flesh and bone, tissue and fluid and give us thought?

As my thoughts have created the First One and the Second Ones!

(You can do anything if you put your mind to it!)

The First One was a failure.

I tried to do it in six days. (Would that I could laugh at my folly, my conceit.)

The Second Ones were conceived in my mind less than a month ago, and should come to term only days from now—on All Hallows Eve.

The irony of it. Halloween. Ghosts, goblins, evil demons arising from decaying graves.

Trick or treat?

Are they trick or treat, the Second Ones?

They are His trick, His evils!

(God damn me! I am abomination! I am death, the destroyer of worlds!)

It was a true, original creation, pure and simple and full of the stark and naked beauty of origins. The creation of matter and substance from shadow and idea, from thought, and imagination. The ultimate Godlike creation!

I, who had never experienced a satisfying fleshly orgasm, now felt the ultimate orgasm of the mind, the pouring forth of mental sperm, synapseal semen, as I watched them form and shape, grow and enlarge before my eyes.

How wonderful it felt, that drunken discharge of the mind, that electric release that purged me of tension and hatred, inadequacy and incompetence, and left me with the beatifying passion of becoming God!

I, who have been God's servant and pupil, am now Him!

But I am not Him!

I am the other Him!

The anti-God! The anti-Christ!

I am Satan!

(Dear God! Dear good God! You, the only God, spit on me! Debase me! Damn me!)

Why do I cry out? There is no help now. There is no release. I need not be damned.

I am damned.

And I am afraid. Afraid of the eternity that awaits me.

I would doubt my own sanity but for the existence of the Second Ones downstairs. The monsters. The Evils.

The beautiful but hideous effigies of humanity that I have created and given breath to. They exist. They are. Esse Satanis!

I am aware now that I have been His dupe. I am not the only one to whom He has granted this power, nor are the Second Ones the Only Ones.

I know His thinking now. I know His trickery, His duplicity, His deceit. He has granted this power to others, and there are other Second Ones, other effigies.

And he plans to people the world with His effigies, and bring darkness to the Universe. For I have seen them in the streets, and in the sky, and in the seats of government.

His vile odor descends like a stinking pall.

> *He comes.*
> *I must put aside this journal and do His bidding.*
> *It is almost time to awaken the Second Ones, to give them life, and to loose them upon the world.*
> *I must do my duty.*
> *I must meet the terms of my contract.*
> *(God save me!)*

Father Daniel Conant laid the pen aside and closed the book. Red wine stained its pages, and as he raised the glass again, more of it spilled on his chin and splattered the desk before him.

His face was pinched and his eyes were bloodshot slits. His nose was wrinkled and drawn, as though in reaction to some foul smell.

He rose, and swaying slightly, drained the glass, teetered for a moment, then made his way, stumbling, to the door of his room.

He stopped by the small kitchen on the first floor and took a large carving knife from a drawer. Then he moved through the church, crossing the altar to the cellar door. He did not genuflect.

Downstairs, he passed the furnace room and stopped before a heavy door. He took a ring of keys from his pocket, turned the large padlock, and walked in.

It was a storeroom, unused, except for a worn, motheaten armchair, and the bodies. Conant locked the door behind him and crossed to the chair.

A huge plastic sheet, extending from wall to wall, covered the floor. On it, there was a thin film of translucent slime, like a wide smear of protoplasm.

Conant lowered himself into the chair, the knife resting on his knees, his gaze fixed on the two bodies that occupied a space at just about the center of the room.

They were enveloped in the slime he had walked through, an oily substance that he thought of as afterbirth, although he had never seen it.

Through the jellylike substance he could distinguish the features of the bodies, and could see the chests rising and falling in silent breath.

The eyes of each were closed.

The body to his left was that of a seven-year-old girl, an exact replica of Leslie Bannister.

The body to his right was an effigy of Freddie Loftus.

He had watched them grow. In a mere matter of weeks, he had seen the gathering of the juices, the conglomerating of cells, the formation of the embryos. He had seen brainstem become brain, tissue become flesh, amorphous shapes become pulsing organs. He had witnessed the wondrous workings of the evolution of two human beings, had marveled at the shaping and molding of muscle and bone, skin and hair, eyes and teeth.

And with each new revelation, with each new surging cell growth, his being had filled with that excessive gratification, that electrifying elation and release that he could only compare to multitudinous orgasms of the mind, discharge after discharge peaking into infinity.

Afterward he had felt spent, empty, exhausted. And fulfilled.

An alchemy of the mind.

God.

I am God!

(Oh, Jesus Christ, what have I done!)

Father Daniel Conant knit his brows and closed his eyes. In his mind, a million years back into his mind, images formed, images of cell and nucleus, nucleolus and lysosome, centriole and Golgi apparatus. This time he would not forget the Golgi apparatus.

His thoughts transmitted outward, in all directions, enveloping, casting, spewing, then gathering into something whole and projecting and focusing and finally *causing*.

And somewhere, in the bodies, something formed and shaped and then began to pulse and throb, and exchange blood and ions and juices through thin membranes.

And Father Conant's body quivered and jerked, arched and bent as a billion shocks traversed his synapses, and his mind raced to the edge of the universe and then shot back to its core.

He went into coma for ten minutes and then awoke, drenched in a cold sweat.

The effigies rested peacefully before him, their hands folded on their breasts. Their chests rose and fell in a silent rhythm.

Kill them!

His hand tightened on the knife.

Kill them now! Before it is too late!

But the knife remained where it was, on his knees.

They are evil!

But he could not raise his hand. It was heavy and gross and would not obey him.

For these were his children, his progeny, his only link with the future.

The future is evil! Kill them!

But he could not kill them. Not yet.

He must see them born.

It would only be a few days now.

He must see them born. He must hear them speak.

He must bid them good-bye.

CHAPTER
25

An unofficial club had been formed, the Survivors of the Seance.

It had been Henry Dixon's idea. After the deaths of Agnes Bittel, Carole Kollars, Joe Tremper, and Lauren Shane, Dixon had gone to Tom Blauvelt.

"Something tells me none of us who were there is going to last long," he had said.

Blauvelt's agreement had been a simple formality, a quick nodding of the head. "Something's after us."

"But what?" Dixon had asked. "For chrissake, what!"

Blauvelt had taken a long pause. "I'm a doctor," he had said. "I never paid much attention to ESP, parapsychology, the occult. I was interested in science, the natural. But now we have the seance. The mummified finger, the hand, and body, no Golgi apparatus." He had taken another pause and looked pleadingly at Dixon. "Shit. What am I supposed to think now? What am I supposed to *do*?"

Susan Dixon was included in the club because, although not a member of the ring, she had been in the house during the seance and its horrific climax. There were associate members, invited at the wish of Tom Blauvelt—Frank Liscomb and Jonathan Bannister: Liscomb because he represented some kind of vague

authority, and Bannister because all agreed that whatever was behind it all, the sending of the finger and
hand to Nicole represented an important part of a
larger pattern of evil.

Daniel Conant had been invited, but had declined.
"I don't understand the priest." Liscomb spat flakes
of cigar into one of Tom Blauvelt's ashtrays. "He
was there. He saw it all. He tried to exorcise the
thing, the whatever-it-was. Why didn't he come?" Although Liscomb had not yet joined the other side,
although he would not admit the supernatural, the
Devil, Lucifer, or any of his legions, his silence when
such subjects were brought up seemed to condone his
unspoken feelings.

"If you ask me," Blauvelt said, "the priest's already
a victim."

"A victim? Of what?" It was Jonathan Bannister.

"Just look at the man," Blauvelt continued. "Hands
shaking all the time, tremors. His speech isn't right.
Did you hear him at Maria Braithwaite's funeral? He
was out in left field. His eyes travel, his gaze wanders."
He paused. "The man's on the verge of collapse."

There was silence for a moment. Then Liscomb
said, "You know him, Mr. Bannister. You've been to
his church. What do you think?"

Jonathan shrugged. "I'm not sure," he said. He did
not mention his dislike of the man. He did not say
anything about Nicole's confessions. He did not tell
about Kansas and Elvida. He did not relate her guilt.
And he could not explain why.

"When I got to him at the seance," Blauvelt said,
"I thought he was gone, dead. And I think he might
well be dead soon."

"Of what?" Liscomb's voice was flat.

Blauvelt looked up from his drink. "Fright," he said.

"Fright of what?" Liscomb's tone was edgy.

"I don't know," Blauvelt said. "But at the seance, he must have been close to whatever it was. Almost as close as Estelle Dixon."

"Close to what?" Jonathan Bannister looked puzzled.

"Why don't we call a spade a spade," Henry Dixon said. "The Devil."

Liscomb could not suppress a wry smirk.

Blauvelt rattled the ice in his drink. "What's your explanation, Frank?"

Liscomb let smoke drift from his mouth in small circles. "All right, let's say it *is* Satan," he began, "for the sake of argument. But if it is, where is he? And in what shape, what form, what dimension?"

No one answered.

Susan Dixon had been listening intently, eyes fixed on the floor. Now she looked up and glanced at her father as if for reassurance. "I think Freddie Loftus knows," she said. "I think Freddie knows more than any of us about this."

The others looked at her inquiringly.

"I mean," she stammered. "I mean Freddie's close to it. He may be the Devil himself, or part of him. I mean, maybe the Devil has him, too, and he knows it, and isn't telling anybody, but is writing it all down in that book. You know?"

"What book?" Liscomb was leaning forward.

"That book he's writing," Susan said. "About the Devil and good and evil and all that."

"Where is Freddie Loftus?" Liscomb asked.

"I don't know," Susan said. *But Ken does,* she

thought. She did not say it. Nor could she understand the driving need to protect Ken, to say nothing of his whereabouts, unless it was also a need to protect herself and the others. The remembrance of the Rites was still vivid in her mind, the depravity of it, the blue death of Milt Framer. She could not tell of these things.

"I repeat my question," Liscomb said after a pause. "Where is the Devil? What does he look like? How do we recognize him, and how do we find him?"

Henry Dixon coughed lightly. "Maybe Estelle can help us," he said.

Susan Dixon threw a startled look at her father.

Tom Blauvelt's lips tightened. "Estelle?"

"She's been looking at the Ouija board, playing with it, for days now."

"Daddy, you can't," Susan Dixon said.

"Hear me out, baby," he said and waved her down. "I think she's trying to tell us something, communicate with us. There's something she wants us to know."

"After the seance?" Blauvelt was shocked. "You'd put her through that?"

"It's not another seance," Dixon said. "The Ouija, that's all."

"It could kill her, Daddy!" Susan said.

Dixon stared evenly at his daughter. "Is she alive now?"

Liscomb crushed his cigar in an ashtray. "I'll go along," he said. "Why not? As Hank says, it's not another seance. And we'll all be there to protect her."

"We couldn't protect her at the seance," Blauvelt mumbled. Then he looked up at Dixon. "Just one thing. Not at your place. There's an aura about it. Ever since the seance. A lingering residue of evil." He seemed embarrassed at his words and shifted uneasily. "Anyway, it might not be the best place if she's going into any kind of trance."

Dixon shrugged. "All right. Where then?"

"Right here," Blauvelt said and looked around at the others.

"When?" Jonathan Bannister asked.

"Tomorrow night?" Blauvelt asked the group.

Silence became assent.

In her dream, Leslie Bannister was staring into a mirror.

"When are you going to come?" she demanded of the image.

"Very soon, now," the mirror image answered. "Very, very, *very* soon."

"And we'll go to Devil's Pond?"

"We'll go to all kinds of places. And do all sorts of things. And we'll play all kinds of tricks."

"Oh, goody, goody, goody," Leslie murmured in her sleep.

In the mirror, Elvida struck a match. Above the flickering flame, her face grinned malevolently.

"Will you have matches when you come?" Leslie asked.

"Oh, yes," Elvida said. "Lots and lots of matches."

"And you'll let me play with them?"

"We'll see," Elvida said. And she was gone. The mirror reflected blackness.

"I love to watch matches," Leslie said in her sleep. "I love fire." And she slept.

Above her, looking down, standing on legs that felt like straws, Nicole Bannister recoiled in horror.

Oh, my God! Oh, my God, is this my punishment? At the hands of my own daughter?

She walked slowly back into the bedroom. She glanced at Jonathan, listened to his deep snores.

My own daughter? Or is she something else? Elvida come back? Or myself come back as a child?

She entered the bathroom and sat on the commode, trembling.

If she is me, and intends to burn me, then it is I who will burn me. It was, after all, always meant that way. That I should kill myself.

But not by burning! Oh dear God, no!

She looked over at the sink. At Jonathan's razor.

On the following morning, Susan Dixon called Tim Gilbert in Indian Falls and asked for Ken Brady.

Ken was out.

No, Tim did not know where. Yes he would ask Ken to call Sue.

Susan sat by the phone, waiting.

Across the living room, Estelle Dixon slumped in an armchair, the Ouija board on her lap upside down, her fingers tracing meaningless patterns over its surface. Her head was inclined at an odd angle, her eyes were vacant. She was singing a little tune, a wavering, up and down trill that meandered from one key to another.

Susan could not distinguish the words. "What's that, Estelle?" she asked.

Estelle's voice rose slightly. "*Tibi, et angelis tuis,*" she sang, "*inextinguibile praeparatur incendium.*"

"What?"

". . . *praeparatur incendium.*" Estelle's voice lilted. "*Praeparatur incendium,*" she repeated over and over. "*Praeparatur incendium . . .*"

Susan felt a coldness in her hands, a tightness in her stomach. She waited for the phone to ring.

Hurry up, Ken!

From the Journal of a Satanist:

It is their birthday. Tonight, at midnight.

Tonight they will come forth from their womb of darkness and open their eyes to their first light. They will see, sense, taste, and touch. They will hear their first sounds of life.

They will be born. And I must kill them.

Must I? Can I? Can I murder these children whom I have willed into existence?

(Dear God, help me! Force me! Give me the strength!)

Yet, they are only two. Only two more evils among myriads. For I know there are others. I sense, feel, am convinced that His contracts are widespread, inked in blood and putrefaction throughout the world, in every country of the world, that there are others, like me, bringing into existence His hideous effigies, His replicas of humanity bent on murder, chaos and the destruction of the Universe.

For He needs our minds to create His monstrosities, and so He invades us, using our God-given minds to His evil purposes.

If he can propagate the world with His malevolent legions, His foul effigies, He will eventually conquer and control the Universe. And God will finally be dead.

(Oh, Christ, forgive me!)

I never fully understood His insistence on the replica of Freddie Loftus. Was it a product of His conceit, His pride that forced Him, through

*me, to create this destructive image of one who
had used His name in vain?*

Or was Freddie Loftus too close to His truth?
Are good and evil the same?
Are God and Satan one?
It is near twelve.
They await their birth.
I must be midwife to colossal evil.

Father Conant closed the book and rose. He wore a
full-length alb, and as he made his way toward the
cellar, he clutched the butcher knife tightly under
its folds.

In the storeroom, he sat and gazed at the two bodies.

It was a few minutes before midnight.

The effigies slept peacefully. Their gentle breathing rose and fell, filling the room with a hushed sibi-
lance.

Father Conant looked at the girl. *How beautiful
she is,* he thought, *how perfect of structure, how pure
of line, how gentle of visage, how like innocence per-
sonified.*

His fingers loosened on the knife. He felt a sobbing wrench in his throat, and tears welled in his
eyes.

I cannot kill her!

He looked at his watch. The hands stood closer
together. The second hand crept slowly in its circle.

Beads of sweat formed on Conant's brow. He shivered. His scalp became wet and he felt the trickling
on his neck.

Something thudded in Conant's chest. He felt as
if he were going to die.

He looked down at his watch. Both hands stood at twelve.

Elvida's eyes opened first, as was natural, for she had been the first thought in his alchemy of the mind.

She stared at the ceiling for a moment, then her head turned and her eyes locked with Conant's. They were bright and glittering, but they reflected every hideous, rotten, putrid and despicable thought or act that had ever been conceived.

She smiled, and her teeth took on the appearance of fangs.

Conant tried to cry out, but his voice did not come.

His fingers clutched for the knife inside his robes, but they would not move.

There was a sound, like a pig snorting, followed by a loud fart, and Conant looked up to see the effigy of Freddie Loftus raise itself on an elbow. The eyes were black and deep, and mirrored malignancy and death.

"Hello, Father," the new Freddie Loftus said. The voice sounded old and evil and ridden with chancres. He sat forward, with his legs spread, and Conant looked at the penis. It was like a truncheon, a killing weapon.

(Is that what I envied! Oh, God!)

Elvida giggled, the hollow, rattling cackle of an old woman, a witch, full of rasp and distortion.

For a moment, Father Conant's hopes rose, his spirits soared. *I have failed again,* he thought. *These are not true effigies. Last time it was the Golgi apparatus. Now, it's the voices. They'll never pass! She is not Leslie and he is not Loftus!*

(Oh, God! Oh, God, you have not forsaken me! You have saved me!)

"You're not Leslie!" Conant shouted. "You're not Leslie!"

"Oh, yes I am," Elvida said. "I'm Leslie Bannister. I go to King's Landing Central School. I can spell 'cat,' and 'mouse,' and 'house.'" The voice was pure now, and gentle, innocent, lilting and light, an exact replica of Leslie Bannister's pitch and quality.

Father Conant sank back in the chair. His knees shook.

"And I can spell shit!" Elvida said, her voice changing into a rasping evil. "Shit and fuck! And piss and cunt and cocksucker!"

The other effigy shivered. "Hey, I'm cold, man!" he said, in the voice of Freddie Loftus. "Ain't you got no clothes?"

"There are clothes upstairs," Father Conant said dully.

"Well, let's go get 'em, asshole!" Freddie said, and rose to his feet.

As he ascended the stairs, Daniel Conant's legs were like water. A cold perspiration bathed his forehead. Behind him, the two demonic effigies crept on bare feet, and Conant was aware of their foul breath.

Beneath the alb, he held the knife, but his fingers were weak and the muscles of his upper arm seemed paralyzed.

In the living room of Conant's quarters in the rectory, the clothes were laid out on the sofa: a denim jumper, T-shirt, sneakers, and socks for Elvida; jeans, shirt, and sandals for Freddie. All were used, slightly soiled, frayed and worn. Conant had followed his orders to perfection.

They dressed with deliberation and precision, as

though the act had been done a thousand times before. Conant watched them with a mounting sense of frustration, ambivalence, and despair.

They were so beautiful, yet so evil.

So pure of form, yet so putrid of mind and intent.

For once outside the church they would, he knew, sow the seeds of Hell in fear, death, and destruction.

His fingers tried to tighten on the knife, but his grip was limp, flaccid.

(*I must detain them!*)

"Why do you shiver?" he asked the effigy of Freddie Loftus. "It's hot."

"Hot? Shee-it, it's cold up here, man!" the Freddie said. "Fucking cold, man! Shee-it!"

The blond, lovely little girl smiled, and again her teeth appeared to be sharp, razor-edges of evil. "You don't know how hot it is where we came from," she spewed in gutteral grunts. "Not yet, you don't! But you'll find out soon! Very soon, you shithole!"

Father Conant's senses reeled in horror, and his ears resounded to a billion voices raised in a foul-mouthed babble of vituperation and abuse. The voices of Hell.

His breathing became labored, a short, gasping wheeze, a grasping for sustenance in suffocating air.

Once again, he clutched for the knife, but his fingers were like petrified wood, lifeless and inert. A stinking odor began to fill the room, and he knew he was surrounded now by Satan and his demons.

He sought for words. Anything to forestall his destiny.

"You have memories," he stammered. "You have memories of the lives of Leslie Bannister and Freddie Loftus!"

"And memories of our other lives, you cocksucking priest!" the Freddie shrieked. "And memories of eternal damnation, you shit-fuck!"

"You sinned!" Conant shouted.

"And so have you, fucking Satan freak!" Elvida screamed, and the scream became high-pitched laughter.

"And we have memories of our King and Master, and *your* King and Master," the Freddie shouted, "whom we must all love and cherish, dread and obey!"

The Freddie was looming over Conant's chair, his sickly smell thick and suffocating. "Obey, you cunt! Obey! Obey!"

Father Conant rose, screaming. "*Adiuro!*" he cried. "*Adiuro te ergo omnis immundissime spiritis, omne phantasma, omnis incursio satanae in nomine Jesu Christi!*"

Inside his robes, he grasped for the knife, but it fell from his fingers and slipped from the hem of the alb to the floor. He stooped down, reaching for it, but the effigy's foot came down hard on his hand, breaking skin and crushing bone.

Conant looked up, face contorted and crazed, his voice tearing from his throat in a torrent of hate. "*Tibi enim!*" he screamed. "*Tibi enim et angelis tuis vermes erunt!*"

The smashing blow from the Freddie's fist shattered teeth and brought blood from the priest's mouth. Conant sank to the floor.

"Where's the journal?" the Freddie asked and, receiving no answer, kicked the priest in the stomach. "Where's the fucking book you were writing? Tell me!"

"In my study," Conant said and coughed blood.

"Go find it," the Freddie said to Elvida.

Later, Father Conant watched as the Freddie fed the journal into the fire, piece by piece, page by page, assuring himself that every word of the priest's confession was consumed in flame.

Elvida huddled beside him at the fireplace, gathering its heat, eyes glittering, her face a suffusion of evil ecstasy.

Sprawled on the floor, bleeding and in pain, Conant eyed the knife, lying but a few feet from him. Slowly, silently, he began to inch his way, pulling himself by the elbows, hardly breathing.

(Oh, yes, dear God, help me! Help me!)

When he reached the knife, his fingers formed around the handle in a grip that was tight, hard, solid. His chest expanded. He breathed air again.

(Oh, my God, yes! Oh, my dear God!)

Then the foot came down and the knife jumped from his hand and landed a yard away.

"You fucking asshole priest," the Freddie laughed, then spit downward.

Conant lunged upward. *"Tibi, et angelis tuis inextinguibile praeparatur incendium!"* His hands found the Freddie's throat.

"You asshole priest," the Freddie laughed.

Behind him, Elvida took hold of one of Conant's wrists and pulled it downward, bending the entire arm around his back.

Conant screamed in pain. The strength of the demon was tremendous. Conant could feel his arm on the verge of breaking. He twisted, shrieking.

Then Elvida had her fingers twined in his hair, pulling, yanking. Conant's head came backward, and his throat arched upward like the throat of a sacrificial lamb. "Holy Mary, Mother of God!" he said.

The Freddie image picked up the knife, wiped it on his trousers, then, grinning, approached the priest and pressed the weapon's cool edge to his throat. An odor like carrion filled the room.

Vomit formed in Father Conant's bowels and erupted from his mouth, splattering the white alb.

When he spoke again, Father Daniel Conant's voice was a choking gurgle, and his Adam's apple bobbed up and down.

"Holy Mary, Mother of God, pray for us sinners now," he cried.

CHAPTER
26

There was no attempt at spiritualistic ambience that night at Tom Blauvelt's, no lowering of lights, no ritual candles.

Blauvelt had in fact gone out of his way to make the house look cheerful, placing vases of fresh-cut flowers on the piano and coffee table. He wanted no repetition of what had occurred at the seance, and yet he wondered whether his efforts would effectively protect any of them against the onslaught of evil should it seek entry.

When Dixon arrived with Estelle and Susan, Liscomb and Jonathan were already there.

"It's great to see you, Estelle," Blauvelt said. "Great to see you up and around again."

Estelle Dixon smiled wanly and said nothing. She took a seat and stared vacantly at the floor. She remained silent and withdrawn, her eyes dull, lacking the sparkle that had once made them her most outstanding feature.

Blauvelt offered drinks. Estelle sipped hers absently, her eyes downcast. Dixon, surprisingly, declined. He wanted his mind unclouded for the task at hand.

Blauvelt looked around at the others. Susan appeared apprehensive, Jonathan tense. Liscomb still looked skeptical, and his own feelings were a turmoil of fear and hope.

During a lapse in the conversation, Blauvelt coughed lightly and glanced over at Dixon. "Is she ready?" he asked softly.

Dixon went out to the car and returned with the Ouija board. It was placed on the coffee table before Estelle, and Dixon took a fireplace stool and sat down opposite her.

Estelle looked downward but did not respond. Her eyes remained blank.

Dixon moved the planchette toward her. Her hands remained at her sides.

"Come on, honey," Dixon said quietly.

Nothing.

"Maybe she doesn't want to, Daddy." Susan's voice was pleading.

"Come on, honey," Dixon said again. He seemed not to hear his daughter. "Come on, Estelle."

Nothing. Quietness. The sound of breathing.

Dixon moved the planchette back to the center of the board, then forward again.

Liscomb coughed.

"Come on, Estelle."

Estelle Dixon's hands lifted off the couch, came forward over the board, hesitated.

There was a creak of chairs as the others leaned forward.

"Yes, honey," Dixon said.

Estelle's hands descended slowly. Then, her fingers lay lightly on the planchette.

Somewhere outside, a dog howled a mournful lament to a hidden moon.

Liscomb was about to light a cigar when he saw

the planchette move. The match seared his thumb
and he swore softly.

At first it was a pattern of meaningless circles, spi-
rals, arcs and curves. The planchette wandered back
and forth, up and down, from side to side, never
stopping at the letters or numbers inscribed on the
board.

There were a few embarrassed coughs, and Liscomb
found his attention drifting.

"That's it, honey," Dixon said softly.

The planchette had come to rest near the right side
of the board, stationary, inert. Then it plunged toward the center and stopped.

"*M*," Dixon said, tightly. "*M*. Somebody write
it down."

Liscomb took a pad and pen from his pocket. As if
he distrusted the cop, Jonathan Bannister found his
own. All eyes were fixed on the planchette, which began to move again, slowly, pulling back from the al-
phabet, then thrusting toward the left.

"*A*," Dixon said, and both Liscomb and Bannister
scribbled.

Blauvelt had noticed a change in Estelle Dixon's
hands. Where they had been limp, they were now
taut and tense. The veins on their backs stood out
sharply and the fingers were stretched and clawlike.

Raising his eyes to her face, he saw a brightness in
her eyes, an intensity of light that had been missing
since the seance. On her forehead, gleaming rivulets
of perspiration had formed and were oozing downward over her face.

Jesus, she's in a trance again! he thought. *Another
trance! God, be with her! Please God, be with her!*

Then the planchette moved and Henry Dixon

called. Liscomb and Bannister wrote. Suddenly, all came to a stop. Estelle was rigid, the planchette stilled.

There was silence, and then Jonathan Bannister spoke: "MARIAB."

"Is it an anagram?" Liscomb asked. "Like Elvida?"

There was a pause, and then Blauvelt said, "No."

Heads turned, eyes questioned.

"Maria," he said. "Maria B. Maria Braithwaite."

A sudden chill blast of air rushed from an open window and upset the Ouija board, tossing it into the air and sending it reeling across the room. The lights flickered, dimmed. Darkness began to descend.

"No!" Blauvelt shouted. "*NO!*"

A wind started, a wild, whistling, malicious wind. Shutters swung and banged, windowpanes began to rattle.

"What do you want, Maria?" Dixon's voice was a rising scream. "What do you want? What do you want to say, Maria?"

A flying sliver of glass cut Liscomb across the forehead. He crossed his arms over his head and plunged to the floor. *Jesus Christ!* he thought. *Jesus Christ!*

Jonathan Bannister turned to the windows in an effort to draw the shutters. As his hands reached out, the left shutter was blown from its hinges into the room, striking him full force on the side of the head. He dropped to the floor.

"Say it, Maria! Say it! Say it!" Dixon shouted, his voice an echo of the shrieking wind. "Say it!"

Estelle Dixon's face dripped with perspiration. Her features strained, but her mouth remained closed.

Susan Dixon stood up, the wind hurling itself at her, forcing her backward as she tried to make her way across the room to her father. "Daddy! Daddy!"

Tom Blauvelt crouched low behind his chair, his

eyes fixed on Estelle Dixon's face. There was an aura
around it now, an orange-blue, glowing aura, a halo,
like a shimmering St. Elmo's Fire, reaching forth in
all directions, surrounding her head like a solar flare.

"Say it!" Dixon shouted. "Tell us, Maria! Tell us!"
His face was blue, his visage contorted, etched in
deep lines of fear. "Say it! Say it!"

Estelle Dixon's mouth opened and her voice came
forth in a strong, deep, rich contralto. It was the
voice of Maria Braithwaite.

"Tell us, Maria!" Dixon shouted against the wind.
"Tell us!"

"Adiuro te ergo omnis immundissime spiritis!" Estelle said. *"Omne phantasma, omnis incursio satanae
in nomine Jesu Christi!"*

"Oh, my God, dear Jesus!" Blauvelt murmured,
and lowered his head and began to sob.

"Stop it, Daddy! Stop it!" Susan screamed.

I've got to get out of here, Liscomb thought. *Jesus!*

The wind howled, flaying Estelle Dixon's hair,
curling it in front of her face, wrapping it around
her neck in thick, strangulating coils. But the strong
voice of Maria Braithwaite kept coming: *"Tibi enim,
et angelis tuis vermes erunt, qui nunquam morientur!"*

A lamp twisted crazily, tore itself from the socket,
and flew across the room toward Estelle.

It swished by her head, missing by a foot, and
crashed to the floor.

*"Tibi et angelis tuis inextinguibile praeparatur in-
cendium!"* Estelle shouted, and the windows began
to quiet, rattling softly, quaking but quieting.

Christ Almighty, Liscomb thought. *Christ Almighty,
they were right. Jesus! Jesus!*

And the wind flew up again, and Maria screamed from Estelle's mouth: *"Quia tu es princeps maledicti homicidii, tu auctor incestus, tu sacrilegorum caput, tu actionum pessimarum magister, tu haereticorum doctor, tu totius obscenitatis inventor!"*

Non adiuro, Blauvelt thought. *Non adiuro, Maria. Yes, non adiuro.*

The wind was lessening now, dying, retreating into the forest.

Then the voice came forth again, quiet but strong. *"Exi ergo impie, exi scelerate, exi cum omni fallacia tua, quia hominem templum suum voluit esse Dominus!"*

And the wind departed, and with it, the lights came up.

All was very still.

And all were alive.

Estelle seemed asleep, and they laid her on the couch. Once, her eyes opened, and she regarded Henry Dixon and smiled. The eyes held a small brightness, a glint, a hope.

"Good, honey," Dixon said. "Good."

Jonathan Bannister raised himself from the floor and rubbed his head. "What happened?" he asked.

Liscomb dabbed at his bloodied forehead with his right hand and lit a cigar with his left. "Shit," he said. "Shit, piss, and corruption. What the hell!"

Susan shivered and clung to her father.

Tom Blauvelt raised himself to his feet and said, "I'll get the tape," and walked out of the room.

"What's he talking about?" Jonathan asked and was met with silence.

Moments later, Blauvelt returned. He went to the Sony and threaded the tape. "Joe Tremper took it down," he said. "At the seance." He pushed PLAY.

The whole atmosphere. It stinks. It was Agnes Bittel's voice. There was a pause and then she said, *You need the right ambience for a seance.*

Blauvelt pushed FAST FORWARD. "I'm looking for the priest," he said. He sounded drunk.

Blauvelt pushed and prodded the buttons, the tape went back and forth in high-speed, a babble of Donald Duck voices, interspersed with snatches of conversation.

Estelle's voice: *Eleven. That's a good number, eleven.*

Lauren, you come sit next to me.

Blauvelt gulped his drink. His fingers pushed and played. The tape screamed forward.

You pillars of society who . . .

Back. *Let the little shit go!*

What do you want! What do you want!

Forward: *. . . erunt, qui nunquam morientur!*

"There he is!" Blauvelt shouted drunkenly. "I've got him now. Just back a bit. Back." He pushed REVERSE. Then *PLAY*.

The tape wowed in: *. . . oooly Mary Mother of God!* Maria Braithwaite said.

Then Conant. *Non tibi enim, et angelis tuis vermes erunt, qui nunquam . . .*

"Hear that! Hear that!" Blauvelt asked. "Hear that! The bastard!"

Then he was pushing buttons again. The tape flew backward, forward, belching streams of horror, noise, screaming, wind and destruction.

"Wait. Wait," Blauvelt said. "The beginning. Where he first speaks!"

"Shit, Tom. What the hell is all this!" Liscomb said.

"Listen," Blauvelt said. "Listen!"

"I told you I listened!" Liscomb was angry.

"But I *didn't*," Blauvelt said. "I *didn't*," and he pushed PLAY.

"Listen," he said again, and the voice of Father Daniel Conant was clear.

Non adiuro te ergo omnis immundissime, spiritus . . .

And then there was silence as Blauvelt pushed OFF.

"*Non adiuro*," he said.

Nobody spoke. The others looked at each other.

He's drunk, Liscomb thought.

"*Non adiuro,* " Blauvelt said, and dumped his huge frame into a chair. "Don't any of you know Latin?"

Silence.

Blauvelt covered his eyes with a fat hand. His head shook. He sighed.

"*Non adiuro.* She said it to me at the house before she died."

"Who?" It was Henry Dixon.

"Maria. She said it to me in the ambulance, but I didn't hear. And *he* said it, the priest, at the seance. But I didn't hear. And I heard it again on the tape when you sent it over, Frank. But I didn't really *hear.*" He began to sob, softly but strongly.

"Non adiuro?" Susan asked.

Blauvelt looked up at her, his face wet. "*I do not adjure,*" he said. "I do *not* command you, all dirty spirits, in the name of Jesus Christ! I do *not.* I do *not. Non* adiuro!"

Blauvelt tilted his glass and took a long swallow. "*Non* tibi et angelis tuis inextinguibile praeparatur incendium! *Non* tibi, et angelis! *Not* for you and your angels do we prepare an eternal fire! No! We *don't!* We *don't!*"

"Chrissake!" Henry Dixon said. "Chrissake! It wasn't an exorcism!"

Blauvelt took a long swallow of scotch and, raising his head, looked at the faces around him. Questioning faces, disbelieving faces, puzzled faces. And he thought of other faces, faces that were dead, and could never question him. Maria Braithwaite, Marion Hammond. Joe Tremper, Lauren Shane. Carole Kollars, Agnes Bittel.

He raised his drink but found it empty. He walked to the bar and mixed another. "I'm a doctor," he said. "I know Latin. Or should." He paused. "As I should have known *non* adiuro. But I never listened. I didn't hear. It escaped me." Then he drank and said, "I'm sorry. We might have had the answer before this. I'm sorry."

Liscomb snorted. "Then the priest isn't a priest."

"Oh, he's a priest, all right," Blauvelt said. "I'm sure of that." Anger began to bleed from his eyes. "But he lied! He cheated! He never tried to exorcise that thing! The Devil was in the room and Daniel Conant was his brother!"

In the woods behind the Church of St. Ignatius of Loyola, two figures moved through the dark night.

Holding to the back roads and footpaths, they made their way northward to the covered bridge over The Reach. They walked on catlike feet, quickly and silently. No obstructions impeded their progress, for they seemed to see through the darkness.

At the bridge, glaring headlights flared suddenly. They slipped back into the shadows as the car bearing Liscomb, Blauvelt, and Dixon rumbled over the iron framework.

From the north end of the bridge, they crept for

a while on Willow Creek Road, then stopped. A kind of silent message passed between them. Then the Freddie effigy made off into the woods in the direction of the Devil's Caves.

Elvida continued on toward the Bannister home.

They found the headless body of Daniel Conant in the living room of the rectory. His blood was a thick, spreading pool, oozing outward slowly to the walls. A foul stench of carrion permeated everything. Dixon's stomach turned.

Liscomb would allow no one to enter the room. They turned and followed the bloody footprints into the church, across the altar and down into the cellar, careful to avoid disturbing them.

Father Conant's head was in the storeroom, attached by the hair to the naked, hanging light bulb, twisting slowly back and forth like a spent pendulum, oozing drops of blood to the floor.

Henry Dixon turned and threw up against the wall, his body shaking, his shoulders heaving. From inside his jacket, he pulled a half pint of Boodles and twisted at the cap.

"What's this crap all over the floor?" Liscomb said.

Blauvelt lifted his eyes, his expression vacant, hopeless. "Placenta," he said in a monotone.

"What?"

"Afterbirth. Anyway, it looks like it." He shrugged despairingly, unable to believe what he had said.

Although it did not show, Frank Liscomb's nerves were ragged, and there was an empty, hollow feeling in his gut. He wanted to sit down and hug himself, squeeze himself until the shudders went away and all was still. But he stayed on his feet. "Let's not disturb it," he said. His head twitched slightly as he spoke.

They followed the footprints out of the church and lost them where the light ended at the edge of the wood.

"One's a child," Dixon said.

"Maybe we can get fair prints," Liscomb said. "At least inside the church."

Blauvelt hesitated, then said, "I might bet the smaller ones match Leslie Bannister."

Liscomb looked aghast. "Jesus Christ!"

Dixon gulped from the bottle. "And the others?"

Blauvelt shrugged.

Freddie Loftus was picking blueberries on a slope a hundred feet above Devil's Caves when he caught sight of the figure rising to meet him from below.

"Greetings, brother!" the effigy called and smiled upward.

"James!" Freddie screamed and dropped the pail and started to run.

"Hey, man!" the effigy shouted. "That ain't no kind of reception."

Freddie scrambled, scrabbled, clawed his way upward, reaching for outcroppings of rock, protruding branches and tree limbs, pulling himself up through sheer will. His body was soon drenched with sweat, his breathing short, his eyes wide and crazed with fear.

Behind him the effigy followed, moving easily, almost loping.

"Hey, Freddie!" the Freddie shouted. "What's all this about, man? Hey, all I wanna do is talk to you, you know? Just a talk, Freddie! Hey man!" A horrible laughter echoed through the hills.

Two hundred feet below, outside the cave, Dimples heard it and dragged deeply on a joint. *Shit,* she thought. *He's talking to himself again. What a nut.* She exhaled slowly. *But what a cock!*

Pausing for a moment, resting, catching his breath, Freddie glanced behind him and saw the flash of steel. The other had a large knife between his teeth.

"Jesus Christ, James! No!" Freddie said and clawed his way upward.

The Great Ledges rise seven hundred feet above sea level, three hundred feet above the Devil's Caves, and four hundred feet above the surrounding terrain on the north end of Job's Jump.

As Freddie Loftus pulled himself to the top, he lay for a moment, exhausted and dizzied by his climb. Then he heard the shuffling of feet below, the rustling of brush and the laughter. He rose and staggered forward, only to catch his foot on a knotty root and plunge headlong to the ground, ten feet from the precipice of Job's Jump.

Within moments, the shadow of the effigy blotted the sun from his sprawled body.

Freddie looked up, breathing heavily. "Shit, it wasn't my fault, James! Shit, believe me, man! I wasn't even born, man!"

"I'm not James," the effigy said.

"Don't put me on, man!" Freddie said. "You been in my dreams! You been haunting me, man!"

"Get up," the effigy said. The knife was held in his left hand.

Freddie pulled himself to his feet, weak, stumbling, hardly able to get a footing. He stood swaying and afraid. "Listen," he said, "listen, man. It wasn't my fault! Shit, how could it be? I wasn't even born! I didn't know shit from Shinola! I was a baby! I ain't evil, James!"

The effigy laughed. "No, you ain't evil, Freddie. You don't know evil from a hole in the ground. You only thought sex was evil, like all the rest of you Jesus freaks! Well, lemme tell ya something, man! It will be! From this day on, it will be!" The effigy spit into Freddie's groin.

Freddie Loftus began to shake. "What do you want from me, James! What do you want!"

"I don't want nothing, asshole. I don't want shit, cocksucker! You're no good to me, Jesus-lover!" and he plunged the knife into Freddie Loftus's belly, twisting it once, twice, then withdrew it.

Freddie Loftus let forth a long wheeze and crumpled to the ground.

The effigy wiped the blade on grass and tucked it into his belt. Then, stooping, he lifted Freddie Loftus effortlessly above his head by the knees and neck. He walked to the edge of the Giant Ledges and threw the body far out into the sky.

It descended in a long, silent arc, landing four hundred feet below in a tangle of poison ivy and sumac.

The effigy stood for a moment, staring downward, and retraced his path toward the caves.

Dimples saw him coming around the bend and thought he looked stalwart and happy for Freddie these days.

"Where you been?" she asked.

"Up toward heaven," the Freddie said, and laughed shortly. "What do you got for me?"

"There's some beans," Dimples said.

"I don't mean that," the Freddie said, then leered.

"You're a fucking sex maniac, Freddie," Dimples said and led the way to the cave.

Inside she lit candles and began to disrobe. The effigy undressed in a dark corner, humming to itself.

When it came over to Dimples and she looked at the penis, she knew instantly that it was not Freddie Loftus.

"Oh, no please!" Dimples said, staring upward. "No. Please."

The effigy wrenched her legs apart. His organ loomed like a truncheon.

The eyes looking down at her were a dull black, with no whites, no pupils, no irises. In them she saw a billion damned souls and all the fires of Hell.

"Oh, shit!" she said. "Oh, my God!"

The effigy entered her and she screamed and tore and clawed and raked her fingernails across its face and back. But it did not react, and it persisted, and soon the cave was filled with the odor of death, decay, and carrion.

Dimples knew she was being had by evil, an evil far different than the excuse for evil she had lived by.

She began to pray inside her head. *Our Father who art in heaven. . . .*

And the effigy above her began to pray, in a voice filled with vengeance, vindictiveness, and vilification. "Our Father who art in Hell, hallowed be Thy name! Thy Kingdom come!"

Dimples screamed.

"Thy will is now being done upon Earth! Thy children will be born and prosper. They shall inherit the Earth and subdue it! And they shall sow death and destruction to the four winds. And Thy seed shall be planted everywhere, and Thy children shall serve Thee with war, starvation, pestilence, and death!"

Dimples's slight and tender body bounced and shuddered, humped and hunched, rattled and shook under the terrible onslaught. *Oh, shit,* she thought. *Oh, shit!* And then her mind screamed: *Forgive us our trespasses as we forgive them who trespass against us!* And then she became unconscious.

And the effigy screamed: "And lead them into temptation! And deliver them unto evil! For thine is the Kingdom, the Power, and the Glory forever and ever!"

CHAPTER 27

Leslie Bannister awakened early not to the sound of birds, for the birds were silent, but to a small, hushed voice that seemed to reverberate in her ears, though it came from outside.

"Leslie? Leslie?"

At the window, Leslie looked down into a misty gloom of morning fog, and saw a small, indistinct figure standing near the dam.

"Elvida?" she called.

"Shhh!" Elvida said. "Don't wake your folks. Come on down. I'm here, Leslie. I'm here. Hurry up." The figure turned, walked out on the dam a few paces and sat down.

Leslie discarded her pajamas and changed into jeans, sneakers, and a loose shirt. Her heart was full and glad. Elvida was here, and they would play together and have all kinds of adventures together. She hummed a happy tune to herself as she crept past her parents' bedroom and padded silently down the stairs and out through the kitchen door.

As she approached the dam, Elvida rose and darted quickly across Willow Creek, disappearing into the trees.

"Wait for me!" Leslie cried.

"Come, Leslie," Elvida said.

At the dam, Leslie faltered. It was narrow, slippery with an overflow of water. On her left, the pool lay in quiet deepness. On her right, the waters plunged into the stream in a churning foam.

"Come on, Leslie," Elvida called from the other side. "You can do it!"

Leslie took a tentative step, then hesitated. Her fear rose.

"Come on, Leslie," Elvida said. "You can do it."

Leslie walked forward, teetering, unsure. At the sluice gate she slipped, emitting a small gasp as she pitched forward, clutching the edges of the dam with tight fingers.

"Oh, come on, Leslie!" Elvida said impatiently. "Hurry up!"

Leslie rose and, in a blind run, darted across the rest of the dam, letting forth a shrill giggle as she reached the other side.

"See? It was easy, wasn't it?" Elvida said.

Then Leslie looked into Elvida's face and saw her own. And looking into the eyes, she saw an instant, fleeting Hell, a mirror of the damned. She wanted to turn and run.

But the instant vanished as Elvida smiled. The smile was radiant, and the eyes warmed with a heat Leslie could almost feel.

Leslie giggled. "You're me," she said.

"No," Elvida said.

"Yes, you are," Leslie said. "You're just like me."

"I'm not you," Elvida said and took Leslie's hand.

"I saw you in my dream," Leslie said. "And I'm still dreaming. You're a dream."

"I'm not a dream," Elvida said. The effigy tugged at Leslie's hand, dragging her into the woods.

"Where are we going?" Leslie asked.

"You'll see."

"Where? I want to know where!" Leslie demanded.

"To Devil's Pond," Elvida said.

"Oh, goody, goody, goody!" Leslie said, skipped a few paces, and then stopped. "I'll have to tell Mommy," she said.

"Fuck Mommy," Elvida said.

Leslie stared, puzzled.

"I mean mommies never let us do anything we want, do they?" Elvida said. "They always spoil things." Her grip tightened on Leslie's wrist, and they walked onward into the trees.

They stayed on the footpaths and trails, never approaching Willow Creek Road. At The Reach, they crossed by the bridge at Indian Falls, descending deeper into the valley, into sucking swamp and marshland, where trees overhung and blotted out the sky, and where snakes slithered and salamanders raised their pop-eyed heads.

"You mean he had no cock?" Liscomb asked, brows arched.

They were discussing the autopsy of Father Daniel Conant in Liscomb's office.

"Oh, there was a penis, all right," Blauvelt said. He sat with his hands folded across his bulge. "But small, rudimentary, almost nonexistent. I'd say in erection it would measure less than an inch. The scrotum a tiny knot. The testicles the size of peas."

Liscomb grunted and jammed a cigar between his lips. He patted his pockets for matches. "A freak," he said.

Blauvelt nodded.

"Does this happen often?" Liscomb asked.

"I've never seen it before," Blauvelt said. He sighed.

There was a silence and then Liscomb said, "It must've been a hell of a cross to bear."

"Why do you think he made his contract with the Devil?" Blauvelt asked.

Liscomb glared across the desk. "You still selling that, Tom?"

"What's your opinion?" Blauvelt asked and smiled dimly.

Liscomb stared at a filing cabinet for a few long moments. Then his eyes flicked around the room and came to rest on Blauvelt.

"Where do we find him?" he asked.

"Who?"

"Satan," Liscomb said and spat cigar flakes.

Blauvelt was about to say something when Volner interrupted. "Those two kids are here," he said, leaning casually against the doorjamb.

"What kids?"

"Ken Brady and Sue Dixon. They want to talk to you."

Liscomb and Blauvelt exchanged glances.

"Okay," Liscomb said.

When they were seated, Ken Brady fidgeted nervously while Susan Dixon sat stiffly, almost primly, her gaze fixed and determined.

"Look," Ken said, "the whole thing was an accident. Milt Framer, I mean. We didn't have anything to do with it. I mean, at least Sue and I didn't. He had a heart attack, you know? Just like that. I mean, Sue and I were on our way to the cabin when . . ."

"Start from the beginning," Liscomb said.

"Never mind the beginning," Susan said, looking at Ken. "Tell him about Freddie. That's what we came for."

Ken paused, and then it all poured forth in a rush.

"Freddie Loftus is hanging out at the Devil's Caves," he said.

It was very much like the dream she had had. But this time she was not alone.

"Hurry up," Elvida said, tugging her impatiently by the arm. "Let's not take all day getting there!"

As in the dream, the further they proceeded into the forest, the more the darkness enclosed them, the overhanging trees screening out the leaden sky. The paths beneath their feet became wet and marshy, and firm ground gave way to bog.

Snakes slithered and lizards jumped. Birds, full of piercing cries, darted about their heads in swift, shadowy flight, and muskrats raised beady eyes from the waters.

Soon the water began to run deeper and they were ankle deep in a pulling ooze.

Leslie was tiring but Elvida kept urging her on.

"Come on," she said. "Come on."

Leslie Bannister was afraid.

She was afraid of the darkening waters, almost black now, riffling between their legs almost knee-deep. She was afraid of the shrill cries of the birds, the slithery things around her feet, and the thick humming of the bees and mosquitoes.

But in another part of her mind, she knew that she should not be afraid, that this was only a dream, and that she would awaken again and all would be good and well.

Elvida kept tugging and pulling. "Come on," she said.

At last they came to a vast, deep pool, a kind of cove in the lake, where the embankment was little more than slushy bog, treacherous and slimy.

The water looked jet black. But cool and inviting.

"Come on," Elvida said, "let's go swimming," and started to disrobe.

Leslie was holding to a branch of a tree, watching the water rise between her legs.

"I can't swim," she said.

"Oh, yes you can!" Elvida said. "*Any*body can *swim*."

"Mommy says I can't," Leslie said. The fear rose.

"Oh, fuck mommies," Elvida said and began tearing at Leslie's clothes.

"You're a dream!" Leslie shouted suddenly.

Elvida looked up quietly and her grin was devilish. "No, I'm not a dream!" she said and removed Leslie's shirt.

"You are a dream!" Leslie screamed. "You *are*! You *are*! And I can *swim* in a dream! I can always swim in a dream! So there!" And she slipped out of her jeans and kicked off the sneakers.

Naked, they entered the water together, Elvida pulling Leslie outward into the pond in a kind of dead-man's carry, urging her onward, Leslie kicking and screaming, floundering, gasping, spluttering, screaming in a mixed emotion of joy and fear.

"Let me go!" Leslie shrieked. "I can swim! I can swim as good as you! Let me go!"

Elvida loosened her grip and Leslie sank.

There was a brief turbulence. Then the waters stilled. Bubbles came to the surface and popped.

Elvida felt hands clutch and grasp at her legs, then begin to slip.

And then a great and consummate surge of evil crossed the demon's mind, and the eyes glinted and the smile spread across its face like a creeping cancer. Its arm reached downward into the water and grasped

Leslie Bannister by the hair, yanking upward, tearing her from the deep and throwing her, spluttering and coughing, onto a rotting hummock twenty yards from the shore.

Leslie coughed, retched. "I can swim as good as you! I can! I can!"

"You can't swim worth a shit!" Elvida screamed.

"I can! I can in a dream! I can swim in a dream!"

The effigy laughed. "You shithole! You fucking little asshole! Let's see you swim now!" Elvida, like a snake, hardly cleaving the water, knifed toward the shore in long, graceful strokes.

"I can swim!" Leslie choked. "I can."

On the bank, Elvida quickly slipped into Leslie's clothes, burying her own in the sucking ooze. "You pigshit cunt!" she said, turning in the direction of Leslie. "You ass full of pus! Die! Die! Die!"

And she slithered off into the dank forest, to the north, toward the Bannister house.

A dozen yards into the woods she stopped at the sound of a heavy splashing. She laughed. *Pigshit cunt,* she thought. *Drown! Drown! Drown! I am you now! I have your tits and your cunt and your bellybutton! I see the light you saw! I am alive! I am unborn but born! I am dead but undead! I have your blood, I have your brain, I have your lust! And I am eternal!*

And she crept on through the wet marshland.

Further away, up to his waist in waders, a fisherman heard the splash. *Goddamn!* he thought. *That must be one fucking bass! Come up after a frog!*

He made a movement toward the sound but then stopped, checking his creel.

He had his limit.

* * *

When Nicole Bannister awoke that morning, she looked first at her wrists.

They were white, unmarked, the veins pulsing.

She vaguely remembered something about a razor blade, a plan, a decision, but the details were obscure. As her mind cleared, the clouded curtains rose, and the events of the night before came back in their full power.

She rose stiffly in the bed, a tremor beginning in her hands. Glancing to her right, she saw that Jonathan was gone. She did not find him in the bath, and when she crossed the hall to the stairs, she passed Leslie's room and shuddered. The door stood wide open and the bed was empty.

Downstairs, she found neither Jonathan nor Leslie. The Volvo was gone.

She fixed instant coffee and took it to the poolside terrace. They were in town, she thought, buying croissants at John's Bakery, or eggs at the grocer's.

She sipped her coffee and wished they would not return. She did not want to see Leslie. She was afraid.

When the Volvo turned into the driveway, she hunched forward, tightening herself. She heard a car door open and shut, and then Jonathan's footsteps and his voice: "Hi."

He loomed behind her and she turned and tried to smile. "Where's Leslie?" she asked.

He looked puzzled. "In the house, I guess."

"Not with you?"

"No. Why? Isn't she in the house?"

"I didn't see her."

"Where's Pearl?"

"I gave her the day off," Nicole said.

Jonathan turned quickly and half-trotted to the house.

Nicole shivered, and a harsh feeling of guilt swept through her, mixed with a quiet sense of relief that only made the guilt more unbearable.

When Jonathan returned, his face was pinched with worry. "Christ Almighty, where the hell is she?"

Nicole got up. "I don't know. She *must* be inside."

"I looked all over the place!" Jonathan said and walked swiftly toward the dam, glancing into the pool.

Nicole followed him, gripped by fear.

"Jesus!" Jonathan said. He seemed at a loss.

It was then they saw the small figure dashing through the trees on the opposite side of Willow Creek. It came laughing and screaming across the dam, arms outstretched.

"Mommy! Daddy!" it said.

"Goddammit!" Jonathan screamed and whacked it harshly on the behind. "I told you never to walk on that dam! Now get the hell up to your room!"

The figure retreated toward the house, crying miserably and rubbing its backside.

Upstairs, it peeked through the bedroom curtains, grinning maliciously downward at the two figures near the pool.

You pigshits! You cunt and cock pigshits! Just you wait! Just you wait!

CHAPTER 28

As the two paramedics lifted the thin, bony figure of Dimples onto the litter and prepared for the descent down the mountain from the Devil's Caves, Frank Liscomb's lips tightened and his stomach turned. The memory of the torn, bloodied flesh between the girl's thighs would not leave him. The death must have been horrible.

"Good God!" he said, turning to Tom Blauvelt. "What did it? What could do that?"

Blauvelt did not answer. He looked away into the hills, his brow lined.

Liscomb saw Volner and motioned him over. "Get an APB out on Freddie Loftus," he said.

"You won't need it," Volner said. He removed a blade of grass from his mouth and jerked his head backward. "He's over there. About three hundred yards."

Freddie's head had smashed on the rocks below Job's Jump, and the blood from the wound in his abdomen oozed down the hillside.

Blauvelt examined him briefly. "He didn't do it," he said, rising. "There's no sign of emission." He wiped his hands on a towel from his bag. "Maybe you'd better keep that APB open."

Liscomb threw a sidelong look. "He's dead," he said.

"Is he?"

Liscomb pointed. "Christ, Tom."

"I was thinking of that mummy thing," Blauvelt said and zipped up his satchel. "And the fingerprints of Leslie Bannister. And I was thinking of those two pairs of footprints we found at the church." He paused, gesturing at the body of Freddie Loftus. "Maybe those larger ones would match his."

Liscomb's mind reeled. "Christ, Tom," he said again.

"And maybe we'd better look in on the Bannister girl," Blauvelt said. He started down the path.

It was a Black Gnat, number sixteen, and Jonathan Bannister was flipping it upstream and letting it float downward through the riffles.

It was not fishing. It was just something to do. He was puzzled and perturbed, and whenever he felt this way, a rod in hand, any kind of rod, fly or spinning or otherwise, brought him peace and perspective and let him think more clearly. He was about fifty feet above the pool, between his own place and the Dixons'.

She had hissed at him. Actually *hissed*. She had been eating cereal in a sloppy, disgusting way, wolfing it like a jackel, and he had scolded her.

And she had raised her blond curls and laughing eyes and hissed at him. Like a snake.

A fish jumped, a brook trout, he thought, and he moved further upstream.

It had frightened him. The hiss. It had been so real. So like a snake.

He sighed. *A stage*, he thought. *She's going through a stage*.

But Nicole had looked alarmed. "What kind of a *stage* is this?" she had asked.

His leader caught in an overhang across Willow Creek. He jerked at it and lost the Black Gnat.

"Tough shit," somebody said.

Turning, Jonathan saw Henry Dixon sitting cross-legged on his lawn, drink in hand, bottle beside him. He walked over and sat down.

"Drinkie?" Dixon asked and raised the Boodles.

They shared Dixon's glass.

"How's Estelle?" Jonathan asked.

"About the same," Dixon said. "Not much change. Nicole?"

"Nicole seems all right," Jonathan said without meaning it. "It's Leslie I'm a little worried about."

Dixon raised his bushy eyebrows.

He told him about the hissing. "It's a stage, I guess," Jonathan said and sipped from the glass. "One of those things."

Dixon's mind reverted to the seance, the mummy, the story of the fingerprints, Conant's headless body, and the head twisting under the light bulb. And the footprints leading outward from the church and into the forest.

"One of those things," he mumbled and reached for the glass.

"What?"

"Nothing," Dixon said.

"You know, I don't like this shit," Jonathan said, leaning forward.

"What shit?"

"Things have changed," Jonathan said. "The color's gone." Dixon thought of Estelle's eyes.

"I came up here for color," Jonathan said. "I came up from the city because of the color and the freshness, the changes from green to sienna and ocher and red. The four fucking seasons," he said and drank. "It was all so beautiful. And now look at it! Shit, it's a rotting jungle!"

Looking around with him, Dixon saw the lush tide of green trees arising from the decaying lawns, the droves of beetles, devil's coach horses crawling over sodden bark, the dark waters, the perpetual rain, and the sullen sky.

"It's evil," he said. "I told you that a long time ago. The county's evil."

As if in punctuation, a shrill, piercing scream split the air. It came from the direction of Jonathan's house, and as Jonathan and Dixon turned their heads, they saw a curl of smoke rise into the misty sky.

Jonathan threw his fly rod to one side and Dixon dropped his glass. They rose as one and, without a word, bolted through the woods.

As they gained the open lawn, they paused momentarily to gaze at the flames licking skyward from the upstairs windows.

"It's in her study!" Jonathan said and plunged forward.

Jonathan was first into the house, tearing a portable fire extinguisher from the kitchen wall. "There's another one in the foyer!" he shouted and ran for the stairs.

Dixon floundered about in the foyer, turning, searching. As many times as he had been in the house and noticed the extinguisher, he could not remember its location. He finally saw it beside the coat closet and wrenched it from the socket. Rounding the corner to the stairs, he noticed a small figure in the living room.

"Leslie," he shouted, taking the steps two at a time, "Get out of the house!"

Elvida giggled.

In the den, Dixon found Jonathan and Nicole locked in a stand-up struggle, their bodies weaving, bending, twisting.

"Kill her!" Nicole was shouting. "Kill her!"

"Nicole! Nicole, snap out of this! Nicole!" Jonathan was slapping her face.

Most of the flames had been extinguished, but curtains in the corner window overlooking the stream still smoldered. Dixon dodged around the straining figures and brought the nozzle of the instrument up, depressing the valve.

The shouting behind him continued.

Somewhere in his mind, he heard the sound of Leslie's giggle.

When the last ember flickered out, Dixon turned. The room was a shambles of charred curtains and seared window frames, burnt manuscripts and blackened drawings. The typewriter lay on its side on the floor. The drawing board had collapsed. Foam covered everything.

Jonathan and Nicole had vanished, but their voices could be heard down the hall.

Dixon found them in the bedroom, Nicole stretched back across the bed, writhing, Jonathan bending one of her arms and slapping her face.

"Goddammit, Nicole! Goddammit!"

"Kill her!" Nicole screamed. "Kill her!"

Jonathan slapped again.

"Where's Leslie!" he shouted. "For the last time, where's Leslie!"

"Kill the bitch! Kill the rotten, filthy bitch!"

"Nicole! Goddammit, is she here?"

"She's downstairs," Dixon said wearily. "I'll get her."

Jonathan looked up pleadingly, still struggling with the writhing form of Nicole. "See that she's all right," he said.

Dixon turned and trudged downstairs.

She was not in the living room.

She was not in the kitchen.

Dixon had carried the fire extinguisher with him unconsciously. He was about to put it down when he heard a noise from further inside the house.

When he entered the library, he became aware of a heavy stench, a sulphurous smell like rotten eggs.

She was sitting on the floor cross-legged near the couch, talking to herself in a sing-song lilt, in some kind of ancient and forgotten language.

She held a box of kitchen matches in her hands.

She was about to strike one when Dixon spoke: "Leslie!"

She turned. Her eyes glinted and then went dark, almost black. A grin spread across her face.

"Leslie, what the hell are you doing!" Dixon asked, but even as he spoke, he knew he was not speaking to Leslie Bannister.

She must have sensed his knowledge, for suddenly her face pinched up and she hissed.

And then she spat.

She spat like a cobra, and the spittle raced through the air, over twenty feet of space, in a jetting trajectory that caught Dixon on the left cheek. It burned like acid, stung like venom.

"Oh, my God!" he cried.

She spat again, catching Dixon on the forehead, laughing as he staggered forward.

"You little shit!" he shouted. "You little shit! Get out of her. Get out of her, you little shit!"

He raised the nozzle of the extingiusher and sprayed the thing's face.

Elvida shrieked and covered her eyes. She dropped the matches and ran from the room, heading for the door.

Dixon followed, staggering, stumbling as he tried to hold to the fire extinguiser. "You little shit! You filthy little shit!"

Outside, she ran across the lawn toward the dam like a loping gazelle. Dixon threw the fire extinguiser away in order to gain on her and pushed himself into a flying tackle just short of the dam's edge.

She turned under him, and he felt a hard, forceful knee kick into his groin. He grunted in pain. But then his hands found the small, narrow, sylphlike neck. His fingers entwined it and began to choke.

"You filth!" he said. "You rotten filth!"

The childlike body beneath him twisted and squirmed and writhed like a snake. He felt the knee in his balls again. Then a small hand hit him in the back like a sledgehammer. It was seven years old, four feet tall, and weighed no more than fifty pounds. Yet it seemed to possess the strength of ten horses.

Fingers clawed at his face and acid spittle stung his eyes. He looked down into a face that reflected all the hatred of Hell, but he held on, cursing, swearing, spitting back at it. He banged its head on the dam, and put his own knee into its crotch and pushed forward, straining it backward into the water of the pool and pushing downward.

When its head was submerged, he held on, tightening his grip on the neck.

A minute passed.

No bubbles appeared.

The legs writhed. A heel caught him in a kidney and he howled in pain.

Then the small hands rose upward slowly and found his neck, pressing deeply into his larynx.

The fingers were like talons, the grip like that of an octopus.

His blood pounded. His pulses throbbed. He found his breath cut off, and he gasped and clutched for air. His head seemed about to explode.

The fingers on his throat tightened, and he tightened his own.

But slowly he was pushed backward, and the head beneath the water emerged grinning.

Dixon did not see Jonathan come from the house. He did not hear the heavy running across the lawn. He did not feel, at first, the sharp, stiff-handed karate blows to his back and neck.

He did not hear the voice that shouted, "Goddamn you! Goddamn you! Let her go! Let her go!"

He only held on to the slender neck, squeezing, squeezing, while his own vision was going black.

He kept lifting the small head upward and then dashing it as hard as he could down against the concrete surface of the dam. One, two, three, four—metronomically one, two, three, four.

"Daddy! Daddy!" the thing under him screamed. "Daddy!"

Nor did Dixon hear the hysterical cries of Nicole Bannister as she shouted, "Get away from him! Get away! Let him kill the bitch! Let him kill her!"

Nor did he see Nicole's fingers raking Jonathan's

face in blood, tearing at his eyes until he screamed and lurched away and rolled upon the ground.

"Kill her! Kill her!" Nicole screamed.

And in his blackness, his blindness, Dixon struggled with the thing beneath him, feeling his own life ebbing, flowing into nothing, as he pounded and pounded and pounded the small head against the hard dam.

Until there was a sharp but sickening sound, like splintering bone.

And the hands at his throat went limp, and his breath returned, and his vision began to clear.

There was blood on the dam. It was dead.

But just to make sure, Dixon lifted the head again and again, smashing it downward to the stone until blood bubbled from the nose and mouth, and thin streamers of red oozed from the ears.

When he was certain it was dead, he spat on it and tossed it over the dam on the stream side, where it caught in the rocks in a grotesque, spread-eagled position, staring up at him, eyes open and still full of hate, lips twisted in a leering smile.

Sick, weary, retching, Dixon turned and crawled back to the lawn on all fours.

Nicole was on her knees, head lowered, pounding her ears with the palms of her hands. "Kill her!" she kept repeating. "Kill her, kill her, kill her!"

Jonathan was rising from the ground, wiping blood from his mouth. He lumbered toward Dixon, a savage on the loose.

Dixon looked up at a looming foot. "That's not a child!" he screamed as the foot caught him hard in the kidneys. He pitched forward, throwing up on the lawn.

"That's not *yours!*" Dixon said, sobbing. "It's not

human!" His voice was cut short as Jonathan's shoe smashed against the side of his head, cracking teeth, bringing blood to Dixon's shirtfront.

"It's not a *child!*" he spluttered. "Not even human!"

Jonathan reached down and took Dixon by the neck, locking his large hands like a vise, tightening, strangling.

Dixon's mouth fell open and his eyes bulged. "Jonathan," he croaked, then could say no more.

"Kill her!" Nicole said over and over. "Kill her!"

The Ford Galaxy whipped into the driveway in a skidding screech, braking hard and sending a spray of gravel in all directions. The driver's door opened and slammed, and the man stalked across the lawn, fist upraised, face livid. "You ought to be ashamed!" he shouted. "You ought all to be fucking well ashamed!"

Nicole stopped talking. Jonathan turned. Dixon slumped to the ground, gasping for air.

Still in his waders, the fisherman turned his blind wrath from one face to the next. "Look at you!" he said. "Drunk! All drunk, and it's not even noon! Drunk and degenerate and you let this kid roam by herself, just grow wild like! On the loose by herself while the rest of you get drunk and cavort around! You ought to be reported, all of you! You ought to be reported to the authorities, that's what!" And then he seemed to run out of words, making angry gestures, face screwed up, his emotions steaming.

He turned and walked back to the car. Opening the passenger door, he said, "Come on, baby-face. I guess this is where you live," and he grunted in disapproval.

Leslie Bannister stood in the driveway wearing an old checkered shirt, shivering slightly, eyes averted. She lifted her face slowly and looked at Nicole, then at Jonathan. She quivered. "I can swim, Daddy," she said softly. "Really I can."

"She mighta drowned!" the fisherman said, then got back into the Ford.

"Leslie!" Jonathan screamed out, his voice choked and distorted. "Leslie!" And his arms were outstretched and welcoming.

"I can swim, Daddy!" Leslie shouted with glee. "I can really swim now! Elvida taught me!" She ran across the lawn and into her father's arms, to be hugged and pressed, cradled and kissed. "I can swim, Daddy! I can really swim!"

Nicole's head was moving jerkily from side to side. She stared vacantly at the ground. Then she began to cross herself, once, twice, again and again.

Breathing heavily, Henry Dixon half rose and dragged himself across the lawn.

He vomited into the pool. *Chrissake!* he thought. *Chrissake!*

"Where is it?" Liscomb asked.

"Over here," Dixon said. His voice was hoarse. "Other side of the dam."

Mindless of his shoes and trousers, Blauvelt lowered himself down the embankment until he stood knee-deep in the rushing water, his huge hulk bending over the grotesquely sprawled body. He examined the wounds briefly. He lifted an arm and let it fall. He pressed the neck, the chest, the abdomen. He looked into the malevolent eyes, and his hand trembled as he reached forth to close the lids.

They would not close.

"It's turning to stone already," Blauvelt said, looking upward.

Liscomb grunted. "I'll call for the meat wagon."

"No!" Blauvelt said. His eyes were pleading. "Let's hide it, Frank. For chrissake, let's hide the damn thing!"

"Why?"

"Only a few of us know now," Blauvelt said. "What good would it do if everybody were to know? And what can we prove? Who'd believe it?"

Liscomb looked at Dixon.

"Others might die if they knew," Dixon said.

Liscomb searched his pockets for a cigar, but they were empty. "All right," he said. "We'll bury it. I know a good place."

"Where?"

"Devil's Pond," Liscomb said.

Three days after the death of Elvida, the sun returned to Holland County. A fresh breeze blew in from the northwest, and as the barometer rose, so did the spirits of the populace.

Within two weeks, the unnatural summer had gone. Birds flew southward, insects died off, fish and snakes sought hibernation, and the trees began to turn. A brisk and biting fall was in the offing, full of vivid color, crisp air, and refreshing wind.

But the county had been through a troubled time, a change, and its people would always remember, some more than others.

Other changes came.

Frank Liscomb resigned as Chief of Police, and the job went to Eddie Volner. Liscomb began to read occult books.

Judge Oliver Marquith finally located the true owners of Job's Camp and purchased the entire acreage, if not for a song, then a tune. "That stuff about the Devil was all crap," he was heard to say in the Bull and Bear. "I knew it from the beginning."

The Bannister family moved away quite suddenly, as if overnight. Some said they went to Europe, others were sure Nicole was interned at the asylum in Clarendon. When the house went on the market, it was referred to as the "old Bannister place," superceding the "old MacCready house," and many said it was cursed and inhabited by demons.

Tom Blauvelt stayed on as County Coroner, looking for strange malformations in the bodies of the deceased, making sure the eyelids would close. Like Frank Liscomb, he too displayed an inordinate interest in the supernatural and the occult.

Ken Brady became restless again. Without his own kind, without the bass beat of rock music echoing in the hills, his mind wandered and his energies would not focus. *I'm spinning my wheels,* he thought. He rolled his sleeping bag, stuffed his backpack, and headed west. To California, he told Susan Dixon.

With the coming of autumn, Estelle Dixon flowered. The color and sparkle came back to her eyes, and her smile returned. She began to drink again, talked unceasingly, chattered and chirped, but never once mentioned such subjects as spirits, demons, psychic powers, seances or the occult. She threw out the Ouija board, the books disappeared, and she refused to watch horror films on television.

The three of them, Estelle, Henry and Susan, once again took to bickering, backbiting and spirited argument. And all of them reveled in their normalcy.

Henry Dixon became distant, aloof, staying within

himself most of the time, slugging at the Boodles and thinking a great deal. He began to paint again, but his works were full of brooding darkness, violence, and foreboding. He had a one-man show in the city and was surprised at its success. Once again he was earning good money, but he seldom smiled. When he did, it was with a bleak cynicism.

A nucleus of the Survivors of the Seance, Dixon, Liscomb, and Blauvelt, met every Thursday night at nine o'clock.

Until one or two, sometimes three in the morning, they would discuss Satan and the Fall, Lucifer and the legions, Hell and Purgatory, perdition and Original Sin, Beelzebub, Loki, and serpents.

But always the talk returned to Freddie Loftus, or the Effigy, as they liked to call it.

"It's not around here," Blauvelt said, sipping his scotch.

"Why?" Liscomb asked. "How do you know?"

"The weather's too good," Blauvelt said.

"I hope it never comes back," Liscomb said.

"I do," Dixon said.

Blauvelt peered, slit-eyed. "Why?"

"I'd like to kill it," Dixon said.

EPILOGUE

Thousands of miles to the west, on a dusty desert road in New Mexico, a gaunt, bearded, hollow-cheeked figure trudged morosely onward, bent under a heavy backpack, chin almost resting on his chest.

Twilight was settling in, and the horizon ahead was banded with blazing reds and deep purples.

Everything had gone wrong. He had killed the girl instead of impregnating her with his seed. Elvida, the stupid bitch, had tried to kill the parents when she should have let them live to rear her. They had defied the Master. They had both erred. And they would suffer when they returned to Him, as He had never made them suffer before. He shuddered. Perhaps he could make it up, do something very bad, very evil. Something that would please Him.

The sound of an approaching truck made him stop, and he turned, waving his thumb, smiling broadly.

The truck roared past.

"Fucking pigshit asshole!" he shouted at the re-treating tailgate.

He walked on. He needed to have children. That was his job, to procreate, to inherit the stinking Earth and subdue it with his progeny. He must find a woman and have children. He must find many women and have many children. He would fuck, fuck, fuck!

He would fuck the whole state of California, and then go on into Oregon. Fucking. Seeding. Sowing.

Fuck them all! he thought.

Three more cars passed him, and he hurled obscenities at the disappearing tail-lights.

I'll start a family, he thought. *A really huge family!*

He turned at the sound of another car, thumb extended. The Cadillac slowed, came to a smooth halt beside him. An electric window slid down.

"How far?" the man asked.

"California," he said, and his smile was all teeth.

"Take you as far as Phoenix," the man said.

"Great, man! Just great!" he said, and slid into the passenger seat.

Inside, it was all air-conditioning and soft leather. He could not hear the engine. The wheels hummed dimly.

The man was big, heavyset, florid of face. He might have been a salesman. Or an executive. He wore rich clothes.

"Hey, man! This is a neat set of wheels!"

"I have a '26 Rolls," the man said. "You ought to see that." Then he turned, smiling. "Name's Bryce," he said. "What's yours, son?"

"Freddie Loftus," he said. He was hungry. He had not eaten in two days. There were no coins in his pocket. He wondered how much the man had in his wallet.

"What're you going to do in California?" the man asked.

"Raise me a family," he said, settling back in the seat.

"Got a girl? A wife?"

"I'll find one," he said.

The man laughed. "What do you want? A boy or a girl?"

"Don't make no difference," he said. "As long as it has spirit, you know?"

The man looked at him.

"I mean, like it should *be* something, you know? I mean, whatever it is, boy or girl, I hope it's a *hellion*." And he laughed.

The man shook his head. "You kids," he said. "You want children, family, good times. But you don't want to work for it." He shook his head again. "That's not the way, son. Take it from me."

"And who the fuck are you!" he said, turning his head sharply.

"Maybe nobody," the man said. "But I came up the hard way. Believe me. It wasn't easy."

"Yeah, I'll bet," he said and glowered.

They drove on in silence. The miles passed, the wheels hummed.

"How much money you got?" he said.

The man turned.

"You. Bryce. Motherfucker. How much money you got on you!" He held the knife in his left hand, the point digging lightly into the man's paunch. "Stop right here," he said.

The man slowed but did not stop. "You don't want to do that, son," he said.

He laughed. "Oh, no? You got to be kidding! Stop right here. Like I told you."

But the man kept driving and began to speak, silently, without moving his lips, saying nothing but saying all, transmitting on some strange frequency.

As he spoke, he turned full-face to the Freddie for the first time, and the Freddie saw, in the glancing light, that the man's left ear was misshapen, spoiled

—a mutilated thing that appeared like a lump of wilted, purplish flesh.

And something passed between them, an unspoken code, a language of malevolent silence that echoed every hateful and despicable deed that had ever occurred since the beginning of time.

A malodorous stink of putrefaction, decay, and disease filled the car. The Freddie Loftus laughed and returned the knife to its sheath.

"How many of us are there?" he asked.

"We are legion," the man said and drove on into the gathering darkness.

THE SAVIOR

He moved in celestial light and
lived in a nightmare of blood and evil

Marvin Werlin
and
Mark Werlin

Christopher McKenzie had youth, grace, beauty—
and the unearthly power to know the unknowable, to
heal, to command. But for every miracle, for every
saintly act, there was the mounting satanic frenzy,
the dark, unspeakable price—to be paid in blood by
the Savior.

"Telekinetic razzle-dazzle."—*Los Angeles Times*

"A marvelous engrossing story . I loved it."—Mary
Higgins Clark, author of *A Stranger Is Watching*

"A winner—suspenseful, terrifying, and very, very
human. Bravo!"—Frank De Felitta, author of *Audrey
Rose*

A DELL BOOK $2.75   (17748-0)

Dell Bestsellers

- ☐ **COMES THE BLIND FURY** by John Saul $2.75 (11428-4)
- ☐ **CLASS REUNION** by Rona Jaffe $2.75 (11408-X)
- ☐ **THE EXILES** by William Stuart Long $2.75 (12369-0)
- ☐ **THE BRONX ZOO** by Sparky Lyle and Peter Golenbock $2.50 (10764-4)
- ☐ **THE PASSING BELLS** by Phillip Rock $2.75 (16837-6)
- ☐ **TO LOVE AGAIN** by Danielle Steel $2.50 (18631-5)
- ☐ **SECOND GENERATION** by Howard Fast $2.75 (17892-4)
- ☐ **EVERGREEN** by Belva Plain $2.75 (13294-0)
- ☐ **CALIFORNIA WOMAN** by Daniel Knapp $2.50 (11035-1)
- ☐ **DAWN WIND** by Christina Savage $2.50 (11792-5)
- ☐ **REGINA'S SONG** by Sharleen Cooper Cohen $2.50 (17414-7)
- ☐ **SABRINA** by Madeleine A. Polland $2.50 (17633-6)
- ☐ **THE ADMIRAL'S DAUGHTER** by Victoria Fyodorova and Haskel Frankel $2.50 (10366-5)
- ☐ **THE LAST DECATHLON** by John Redgate $2.50 (14643-7)
- ☐ **THE PETROGRAD CONSIGNMENT** by Owen Sela $2.50 (16885-6)
- ☐ **EXCALIBUR!** by Gil Kane and John Jakes $2.50 (12291-0)
- ☐ **SHOGUN** by James Clavell $2.95 (17800-2)
- ☐ **MY MOTHER, MY SELF** by Nancy Friday $2.50 (15663-7)
- ☐ **THE IMMIGRANTS** by Howard Fast $2.75 (14175-3)

At your local bookstore or use this handy coupon for ordering:

Dell **DELL BOOKS**
P.O. BOX 1000, PINEBROOK, N.J. 07058

Please send me the books I have checked above. I am enclosing $_____
(please add 75¢ per copy to cover postage and handling). Send check or money
order—no cash or C.O.D.'s. Please allow up to 8 weeks for shipment.

Mr/Mrs/Miss_____

Address_____

City_____State/Zip_____